NO. 1 CHESTERFIELD SQUARE

NO. 1 CHESTERFIELD SQUARE

Nick Jones

Book Guild Publishing
Sussex, England

First published in Great Britain in 2009 by
The Book Guild Ltd
Pavilion View
19 New Road
Brighton BN1 1UF

Typesetting in Garamond by
Keyboard Services, Luton, Bedfordshire

Printed and bound in Great Britain by
Athenaeum Press Ltd, Gateshead

A catalogue record for this book is available from
The British Library

ISBN 978 1 84624 308 0

For Chris, Emily, Ella and Edd, with my love.

(You see, I told you I was working!)

Prologue

1900

Sunrise over the sweeping hills of Lee Moor had always been Max's favourite time of day. He had grown to regard it as his own special time, and today felt just like all the others as he gazed across the undulating valley to the river below, beyond which stood the imposing outline of Mount Royal.

Lost in the beauty and growing warmth of this early summer's morning, he was startled by the distant chiming of the church clock. He looked back along the steep path he had climbed from the road, which snaked its way across the hills from the village, knowing that it was the quickest way back to Fern Cottage. Yet he hesitated, waiting for the shrill whistle of the mine to break the silence with its piercing tones, announcing to the world that another day's hard labour beckoned. A faint glow in the distance told him that it wouldn't be long, as the mine prepared to claim the men and women of Lee Moor, hurrying to begin another day of drudgery.

He glanced across his right shoulder, straining to see the last of the twinkling lights from the little group of cottages on the outskirts of the village. He couldn't really see them now, but he looked lingeringly in their direction as he set off for the big House and the bustle of Mrs Castle's kitchen. She would be up and doing by now, labouring over the hot range for the past hour as she and her small army of kitchen maids prepared upstairs breakfast. At least she'd had the luxury of a cup of tea in bed, thought Max, brought to her by Millie, the young kitchen maid. Max knew the Earl and Countess Gordon wouldn't countenance being kept waiting; breakfast was always 9 a.m. sharp. If he ran he might just be in time for leftovers from servants hall breakfast, as long as old Makepiece, the Gordons' steward, didn't catch him.

He followed the path back to the road, his feet sure and steady on the uneven ground. Climbing over the stile into the field next to the road, the crunching of his footsteps ceased as he started to run through the long grass. He passed through familiar rocks and the remains of

1

some old buildings, where he occasionally came to lie in the sun on his days off, careful where his feet landed in case he disturbed the adders that lived amongst the boulders in this part of Dartmoor. Often he'd heard tales of grisly adder bites befalling the careless. The woods were ahead of him now, stretching as far as Bickleigh to the west. Keeping the first clump of trees on his left, he hurried on, crossing a small stream and skirting a boggy area, heading for the granite cross. There it was, atop a pile of rocks built into a promontory that was once intended for a bridge across the valley. Pausing briefly to catch his breath, he turned to look at the ridge behind him before it became lost to view in the trees.

This marked the southern limit of the Mount Royal estate, an estate that stretched across countless acres of untenanted land towards Buckfastleigh and the river Dart away to the east, and further inland across more acres of the South Hams district to the north. It had been in the Gordon family for generations and formed the world that Max had known for all of his 15 years. The land assumed a benign peacefulness on a calm summer's day as this one promised to be. He had risen at dawn to witness it from his favourite spot, but he knew it could be a very different picture. When winter arrived with its long and harsh dominance of nature, the landscape would take on a desolate cruelty, bereft of life and beauty. The rain and snow could drive down mercilessly, exposing anyone foolhardy enough to be out to the full extent of their savageness. The wind howling across the valley attacked everything with a fierce intensity, wailing through the trees and warning of worse to come. Even the becks that criss-crossed the huge plateau of moorland ceased their playful tumbling and twinkling, frozen still in the icy air. Mists would descend suddenly, pervading the cold empty spaces with their thickness, demolishing the landscape in an endless blanket of dank greyness so that the land and sky merged into obscurity. There was little sign of humanity at this time of year and few, save the farmers desperate to preserve their meagre livelihoods, ventured out into the inhospitable reaches.

Max shivered involuntarily, banishing his dark thoughts of winter but knowing that they were closer to the reality of life in Lee Moor than this summer's day. It was time to move on. With one last glance behind him he set off, beginning his descent to the foothills that would lead him to Mount Royal. He had to reach the House before Mrs Castle cleared away in the kitchen whilst the parlour maids set the table for the family in the breakfast room, under the watchful eye of Makepiece. If he was late there would be nothing to eat until late evening when the Chambers, who he had come to regard as his own family, returned to Fern Cottage from their work on the estate.

By the time Max passed Jolly Lane Cottage, rumoured to be the last house to be built on the moor in a single day, back in midsummer 1836, his thoughts had turned to his one overwhelming obsession, single-mindedly devoted as he was to changing the grim circumstances in which he lived, dependent for his survival on the goodwill of Jack and Molly Chambers, head coachman and housekeeper to the Earl and Countess. Kind and as generous as their own meagre lives allowed, he didn't understand why his Ma and Pa, for that is how he thought of them, should work themselves half to death in the thankless pursuit of survival. Max had witnessed another kind of life since he had been old enough to roam around Mount Royal and, in his youthful naivety, he believed with a passion in bettering his lot. The old saying 'everyone and everything in its place' was not for him if he could help it, for he was innately perceptive for his years, quickly seeing the huge difference between life at Mount Royal and life in the village.

The Gordons lived in luxury, even opulence, to rival the splendours of old Queen Victoria in Buckingham Palace, as Molly Chambers was fond of saying, after a hard day's toil. 'She might 'ave three 'undred servants, God bless 'er, and the mistress nowt more 'n thirty, but she'll not be any better than them, 'tis a fact.' Cushioned from the harsh realities of the lives of the workers, whose endless and pitiless labours provided their world of comfort and privilege, families like the Gordons seemed unaware of any existence outside their own. Max had long realised that money meant security and freedom, as well as the ability to live life free of the incessant daily worry of how to put food on the table, or how the children were going to be kept warm and well. Even the shopkeepers in the village had some chance of a life free from the demands and whims of others. He had come to know from careful observation that money brought you power. The power to buy not only the basics of life, but also power over people and their lives. Used wisely, it made you safe, invincible to the evil of others, but used wrongly, it could corrupt and destroy. He had seen both sides of it. He knew from his own bitter experience that an accident of birth could place you on the wrong side of the tracks, that justice and fairness didn't exist on his side, where the poor grew weary helping the rich to grow richer.

Money was the answer, he had decided that, and he was determined to make lots of it. He understood already that it wasn't only the aristocracy who possessed it so it must be possible to acquire it other than by

3

inheritance. He knew that money didn't only come from owning large swathes of land and that he must be able to earn it from other means. Only when he had achieved that would he feel safe, and he refused to listen, whenever he dared to voice his belief, to the scornful words thrown at him by people prepared to accept their lot, willing to sacrifice their freedom and futures for those who already had more than enough, and who didn't deserve it.

Max always found himself thinking like this when he was on his way back from watching the sunrise in his favourite place. Perhaps it was because he was getting closer to the realities of life again as he approached the outskirts of the village; not that he would ever have agreed that his own private world was not *his* reality. He could not remember a time when he didn't feel like this. He might have been young, with little knowledge of life outside of the estate, but what he lacked in experience, he made up for in ambition and single-minded determination. He didn't know the meaning of defeat, even if it made him feel alone, battling against the hand he had been dealt, without a word of encouragement or support from anyone except his Ma and Pa. He had learned to be self-sufficient, acting on instinct to get him through the days when there seemed to be little hope for the future other than a miserable life down the mines in the service of the family.

His earliest memories centred on the Chambers at Fern Cottage. He must have been five or six when Molly used to sit him down next to the smouldering grate with a steaming mug of tea and slice of bread and dripping at the end of her long day up at the House to recount tales of village life. He remembered her attempts to teach him the rudiments of the alphabet and spellings with Albert in the background seeing to the fire, teasing the kindling into life before carefully placing the few lumps of coal they had, as if they were like gold-dust, between the logs that he had taken from the estate when the gamekeepers had their backs turned. 'One of these days they'll catch yer, Bert,' worried Molly, but she knew it would make no difference. Albert Chambers was a proud man, six feet four in his stockinged feet with powerful arms and shoulders developed from years of tending the horses and carriages for His Lordship. Too old to enlist to fight the Boers in Africa for Queen and Empire, he nonetheless could have finished a man with a blow from his massive fists. Max could vividly recall seeing him in his tailored livery that had cost three guineas at Doudneys of Old Bond Street, as Molly had once told him, leaving for the stables at the crack of dawn for another day's hard graft.

Banishing these recollections from his mind, for they represented the past and it was the future he was consumed by, he emerged from the woods at the bottom of the slope breathing deeply, his heart pounding. Ahead of him was Mount Royal. He felt all the old familiar venom rising again as he looked at the great stone walls that separated Home Park from the village street. How he despised what it represented. How he was determined to rise above it and gain his freedom.

PART ONE

DEVON

1900–1909

Chapter 1

Lord Gordon opened the door of the morning room and stood for a moment regarding the room, before slowly walking across the floor to the large windows overlooking Home Park. It was the room he liked the most, apart from his study, and the view still captivated him in the same way as it had when he was a little boy. He blinked as shafts of weak sunlight filtered through the windows, casting their magic on the cornflower-blue silk wallpaper. He thought back to his days as a young officer in the household cavalry as he gazed up at the portrait of himself resplendent in his dress uniform. Commissioned by his father, the eighth earl, to mark his graduation from the Royal Military Academy, the painting captured the strong features of the Gordon lineage, which were still evident in his proud face more than 40 years later.

'How are you feeling this morning, Hugo?' asked his wife, smiling as she got up to greet her husband.

Stooping slightly to brush the top of her head in his customary greeting, he decided not to worry her. 'A little better, my dear.' He turned away from the window and walked over to the white marble fireplace. The fire crackling brightly in the grate cheered him, and the chilled feeling that he had seemed unable to shake started to subside.

Looking at him standing there, directly beneath his picture, Constance could not help but notice the likeness with her father-in-law, and in that moment she felt the sense of continuity embodied by the figure in uniform. Generations of her husband's family had served in the Royal Horse Guards. The seventh earl had served under the Duke of Wellington when the regiment had been elevated to the status of household cavalry in 1813, and the fifth earl, Hugo's great-great grandfather, saw service when the Marquis of Granby, famous in regimental folklore, was in command during the Seven Years' War of 1756.

'Have you sent for the doctor yet?' asked Constance.

'No, my dear, later, later,' muttered Hugo, beginning to wish he'd stayed in his study. 'Where are the children? They were not at breakfast.'

'Hettie's changing to go riding and William is due back at tea time,' she replied, with a softness in her voice when she spoke her youngest child's name that she didn't entirely feel in equal measure for her son.

'Due back? Why? Where's he gone?' Hugo asked, irritation creeping into his tone. 'That boy wi...'

As he stood there, in front of the fire, an image of his son flashed into his head. Viscount William Bickleigh was the person on whom his hopes for the future of the Gordon name rested. They had had more trouble over the years with their son and heir than many of the other great noble households and it was high time he started to behave in a manner befitting his responsibilities. His father would have packed him off to India if he'd had his way but Constance had forbidden it, defying her father-in-law for perhaps the only time in her life.

'Now, Hugo,' she soothed, 'have you forgotten that he's gone to see Edwardes at the mine?'

'I wanted to see him before he left, damn him!' is all he could muster as he struggled to rid his mind of a mental picture of the strapping youth with that arrogant look on his boyish face, eyes blazing, standing before him all those years ago with his mother weeping behind him, wracked with anguish as if her world had collapsed around her.

With that he made to leave. 'I'll be in my study,' he said, smiling at his wife as he went to the door. Crossing the inner hallway with its polished marble floor and bronze busts of Frederick of Prussia and the Czar Alexander standing on gold and ebony plinths flanking the main staircase, his slow footsteps echoed around his ears. He entered his own private domain and sank gratefully into one of the leather winged chairs in front of his desk. He was exhausted and felt every one of his 65 years.

There was a knock on the door and Jackson entered the room, silently closing the door behind him. 'Yes, Jackson,' said Hugo, 'what is it?'

The butler came towards him, carrying a tray in his hands, 'Makepiece said Her Ladyship thought you might like this milord,' he replied, placing a decanter and glasses on the antique table beside his master. 'Brandy, milord.'

'Thank you, Jackson,' said Hugo, wincing as he sat up in his chair, averting his face so Jackson would not see the pain in his eyes. 'Has Lady Henrietta come down yet?'

'No, my Lord.'

'Ask her to come in when she does.'

'Yes, my Lord,' replied the butler as he turned and left the room.

Hugo sat quietly for a moment, holding his head in his hands as he waited for the pain to pass. Constance was right; the brandy was just what he needed. He had barely slept again. He eased himself up and poured himself a generous measure, the stopper clinking heavily as he replaced it in the fine, heavy straight-sided decanter that was part of the set that had been in his family since 1820. He waited for the pounding in his head to subside before he stood up and began pacing up and down the Spanish carpet, woven to the sixth earl's own design, taking careful measured steps as he did so.

The study had changed little since his father's day and it reminded him so much of the past. It was a room of unusual interest with its gilded frieze and ceiling in the style of Kent, furnished for its occupants' pleasure. Fine Regency rosewood tables were positioned alongside chesterfield sofas, upholstered in a deep red leather to match the two wing chairs, now mellowed with age. The polished oak floor framed the vibrant blues and slate greys of the carpet, the wood shining richly due to many thankless hours of back-breaking effort from Sarah and Maisie, the two under-housemaids. The day's newspapers and the Earl's favourite illustrated magazines were arranged neatly on an ebony library table next to the grey marble fireplace.

As he felt the familiar shivering start to consume his aching limbs and the dull pain in his head resume its grip on his thoughts, he took another long drink from the by now half-empty glass and determined not to let it overtake him. He had a meeting with his trustees at eleven o'clock and he would need a clear head as they would no doubt bring him more tales about William, which would only add to the distaste he felt for his son. He looked towards the great mahogany desk, which dominated the far end of the room, and contemplated the Constable hanging above it. The painting bought in 1822 captured his mood exactly. The combination of light and dark swirling clouds scudding across a leaden sky always reminded him of a stormy day up on Dartmoor and captured the turmoil of his jumbled thoughts.

Perhaps he should do as Constance suggested and call for the doctor. He knew that alcohol was not the answer to his troubles. The dulling effect of the brandy offered only temporary relief from the dark moods of despair, which seemed to envelope him with increasing regularity since he had cajoled William into taking a more active role in the family's affairs. He knew he had to allow his son the freedom to manage things if the future of the Gordon estates was to be safeguarded, and at least the trustees had stopped pressurising him about his lack of direction as far as that was concerned. But he had felt only anxiety and revulsion when they had started to come to him with reports of mistreatment of the miners at the pits, incidents apparently verging on cruelty, which could not go unchallenged.

He grimaced as he thought of the meeting to come. His fine chiselled features were etched with fatigue, his face pale and drawn. The blue-grey of his eyes was dimmed by hours spent awake at night wrestling with the demons that beset him as he tossed and turned in fitful sleep, only to stir feeling more tired than ever as the birds began their long dawn chorus. He was a tall man and his once jet-black hair now distinguished with streaks of silver, as his father's had been before him, was brushed straight back to reveal a strong, wide brow, strangely devoid of lines despite the advancing years.

He stopped his pacing as the door burst open and his daughter flew in, her face wreathed in smiles. 'Hello, Papa,' she said, 'Jackson said you wanted to see me.'

'Yes, darling, miss...'

'Whatever's the matter, Papa?' interrupted Hettie, all of a sudden noticing her father's strained look.

'Nothing that need worry you, darling,' replied Hugo, as he saw the look on his daughter's face, her luminous eyes betraying their anxiety. 'I was thinking about William, that's all.'

'Fool!' hissed Hettie, not quite under her breath, that brother of hers was always causing trouble as far as she was concerned.

Catching Hettie's barely audible exclamation, Hugo sank down on to one of the chesterfields by the tall windows on either side of the fireplace and motioned for her to do the same. 'The trustees are due this morning and I expect they will want to talk about your brother. There have been some more rumours of unrest at the quarries at Haytor, which must be dealt with. But I don't want your mother to be told, at least not until I know whether there is any truth in them,' he said wearily.

'There usually is where that brother of mine is concerned,' said Hettie, wishing that she could do something to help. Being born a lady was so unfair, she fumed to herself. Why couldn't she have been her father's heir, it would all have been so different, but she knew it was pointless to argue and she didn't want to upset her father further. But devoted as she was to him, she knew that she would have to tell her mother despite his instruction to the contrary.

The Gordon fortune was founded on trade as well as land, and included the arrival of some much needed cash from the eighth earl's second marriage to the Dowager Countess in 1855, which brought with her a dowry of £100,000. Tin mining had been in the family for over

200 years and Hugo's grandfather had started to quarry for granite commercially in the early nineteenth century, realising that years of excessive living beyond his and previous generations' means had proven disastrous for his bank balance. Dramatic action had been necessary to reverse the decline into penury. The advent of the Plymouth and Dartmoor railway in 1823 had enabled him to transport the granite from his Heckwood Quarry, west of Princetown, further afield on horsedrawn wagons running on iron rails. The granite from the Haytor quarries on the eastern side of the moor was taken on a granite tramway to the canal at Stover and then on to Teignmouth, where it was sold for the construction of many London buildings, including London Bridge in 1831, the one of which he was most proud. The boom time of the 1830s and 1840s had established quarrying as a major contributor to the family coffers, rivalling that of tin mining, which had been in the family for much longer. The Strelitz dowry in 1855 had allowed Hugo's father to keep abreast of the times as industrial development led to more efficient and productive ways of extracting the ore and granite from the ground.

Whole families relied on the mines and quarries for their livelihoods, and as the Gordon fortunes grew, so did their influence and control over life in large areas of Dartmoor. But everything depended on the land, and without it there would be no mining or quarrying. Hugo often found himself feeling eternally grateful that his forebears stretching as far back as the sixteenth century, had secured the basis of the family fortune by the fortuitous acquisition of land. Despite his time spent in the army, Hugo had continued the family's success by placing one man in charge of their commercial activities. In fact the man's son, Jim Edwardes, was the current manager of the village mine whom William was seeing that day. This had been an inspired decision, which had left him free to pursue his great military passion, which had in turn brought great honour to the Gordon name. His appointment as a Knight of the Garter, the oldest and highest British order of chivalry, dating back to 1348, was the crowning glory of his life. A copy of his Garter banner hung in the long gallery, the original being hung over his stall in St George's Chapel at Windsor Castle as custom demanded. It would be removed only upon his death.

Hettie was a sensitive and gentle person possessed with the ability to interpret a person's mood and know instinctively how to respond. But she was also a strong and determined character, cleverly concealing this side of her nature beneath a calm and beguiling exterior. A steely core

13

to her being surfaced only occasionally, when a situation demanded it, or when she felt a loved one to be threatened. She did not count William amongst her loved ones despite the fact that he was her only sibling. She could sense her father's distress and, like him, was fearful for the future when the time came for her brother to succeed to the title. But she was adamant that he would not bring shame or harm upon the family when he did so.

'I wish you'd let me help, Papa,' she implored, knowing that it was a fruitless request.

'Now, Hettie, you know I won't allow it. The trustees will take care of it,' Hugo replied, reaching for the heavy gold Albert chain that attached his Hunter timepiece to his waistcoat in the fashion of the time. It was a substantial piece, fitting comfortably into the palm of his hand. Opening the cover to look at the face, he exclaimed 'I must prepare myself for the meeting, it's already ten-thirty.' He rose from the sofa and crossed to his desk as he did so.

Hettie smiled up at him as she heard this familiar response to her offer. She followed him and kissed his cheek as she said, 'At least let me know what the trustees say, Papa. I'll look in after my ride.'

Chapter 2

'Potatoes, Max, me lad,' said Mrs Castle, thinking of the potato soup with oyster croutons she had to make for dinner that evening. 'And some carrots, nice ones mind, not like them yer pulled Sunday, ten oranges, three good ripe melons and a couple of lettuce, if yer please,' she called as she busied herself at the large black range in the middle of the kitchen. 'Get a move on, girl, we 'aven't got all day,' she shouted, as Rosie, the new kitchen maid appeared from the pantry door. 'An' mind yer don't get cinders in that drippin' tray!'

Max jumped up from his chair at the end of the scrubbed wooden table where he had been finishing the leftovers from servants' breakfast. He wiped his mouth on the frayed sleeve of his long green jacket that had belonged to his dad, well worn and threadbare at the elbows, and made for the door with a cheery 'Ta, Mrs Castle, won't be long!'

He spied Rosie hovering nervously over by the big oak dressers in which the below stairs china was neatly stacked on broad shelves behind gleaming glass doors. He winked conspiratorially at her. ''Er bark is worse than 'er bite yer know,' he whispered with a smile crinkling the edges of his wide, firm mouth. Rosie blushed a furious shade of red and scuttled over to where Millie was sorting through the large copper pans. It was true enough. Elizabeth Castle was a generous woman with ruddy cheeks and thick grey curls that always seemed to be fighting to dislodge her starched white cap, her apron strings straining behind her ample waist. 'Cuddly' was how Max had once heard the footmen describe her after one of their regular drinking sessions at the village inn. Her big, twinkling brown eyes betrayed her warmth and innate kindliness, so that her barked instructions and occasional acid comments were devoid of malice. She was like a mother hen protecting her chicks but Rosie, being new, had yet to realise this.

She gave the place its character, so consequently the kitchen at Mount Royal was a friendly place. The hustle and bustle of activity added to this feeling and Max loved it. It was warm and cosy on a cold winter's day when the fire glowed merrily in the grate, which meant that the little group of chairs by the hearth were always the first to be occupied whenever a snatched five minutes rest was allowed to ease aching joints. On bright, clear days, like today, it was light and cheerful, with sunlight bursting through the windows that looked out towards the kitchen garden. It caught the burnished copper pots and pans, casting its spell across the gleaming white tiles that covered the grey stone walls. These were intended to keep the room cool but the constant bubbling and steaming on the top of the range and the heat from the large brick-lined ovens beneath, made this impossible. Even the stone floor, worn smooth by the constant toing and froing of the kitchen maids' feet, took on a rosy hue where the sun caught the flags. He had always felt welcomed here by the below stairs staff, despite his hatred of all that Mount Royal represented to him, unless Makepiece was around. Then it was a different story, despite Mrs Castle's entreaties 'ter take no notice, lad'.

He opened the kitchen door and went out into the sunlight. He would have to go to the hothouses as well as the kitchen garden to collect the provisions. The entrance to the garden was closest, so he decided to go there first. As he set off down the path that led around from the back of the house, his mind dwelt on the new kitchen maid. She was a slip of a lass, barely 16 years old, he guessed, and obviously still finding her feet.

Her small round face and delicate features created an air of innocence that Max found sweet and oddly disquieting, inspiring a feeling in him that he was unfamiliar with. It was a nice kind of feeling that made him feel warm inside. He resolved to find out more about her and made a mental note to broach the subject with his Ma later. She would know, being responsible for all the indoors staff in the house, including Mrs Castle's girls.

The path wound through a small copse of walnut trees, past the rose lawn and wild garden before it reached the kitchen garden gate. The magnificence of the grounds had caught Max's attention from an early age and he loved the sheer variety to be found on the estate. The formal gardens to the east were laid out with a precision that required constant clipping and trimming to maintain the clean, straight framework of the low yew hedges, which were fashioned into a striking geometric pattern of squares and triangles. They were cut to a smooth flat top as only experienced gardeners can. The knee-high shrubs planted in the beds formed by the hedges were set around square stone centres that gave them a structure and discipline to great effect. Everything seemed to stand rigidly to attention and it often made Max feel like he should do the same, and he subconsciously stood up straighter whenever he passed through. Even the wide gravel pathways that bisected the beds were raked every morning as if to keep the pebbles in orderly rows. Here there were no curved lines and the whole effect was one of neatness and orderliness, which seemed to have a reliable permanence. The wild garden to the west of the house, on the other hand, looked almost as though it had given itself over entirely to nature, without any intrusion from the human hand. It had an atmosphere and character all of its own, with drifts of daffodils forming blazes of vibrant yellow, traversed by winding grass paths meandering through swathes of longer grass mixed with cowslips, primroses and periwinkles, amongst others, and leading finally to a pond surrounded by rocks. Here a small waterfall cascaded gently into the water, sending out ripples to disturb the otherwise mirror-like surface. This is where Max sometimes came to sit when he had only a short time off from his job at the village inn and his favourite spot in the hills was too far away, when the weather was warm enough and he wanted time and space alone to think about his future. The calmness and tranquillity that enveloped him there, by the banks of the pond, helped him concentrate as he searched for the key to his freedom.

The rose lawn, with its oak pergola in the centre, was probably Tomkins' pride and joy. He was head gardener to the Earl and Countess and had lived at Mount Royal man and boy. He knew the grounds like the back of his hand, from the grandeur and sweeping majesty of Home Park to the intimacy and beauty of the rose lawn. He used to tell Max as a small boy that planting flowers was like painting the landscape with living colour. This was a particularly eloquent phrase for a man of his background and it was possibly how Max first started to gain his appreciation for the beautiful and exquisite things of life, contrasting so vividly as they did with the harshness and brutality of daily life in Lee Moor, experienced by his friends and acquaintances in the village. Gracious borders were filled with a profusion of 'Jersey Beauty' roses and 'Blush Ramblers', entwined in a riotous display of cool blues and whites at one end, progressing through warm yellows and oranges to central fiery reds, their mingling scent making the air pungent with their fragrance. The result was a stunning array of colour that lasted all summer long and provided the formal rooms of the house with magnificent decorative arrangements whenever the Gordons entertained.

Pushing open the kitchen garden gate, Max entered the walled enclosure and closed it behind him, the hinges creaking as he did so. It had probably been there forever, he thought, judging by the look of the splintered wood and rusting latch. It fitted well with the ancient walls that were crumbling at many points along the top. Climbers had long since overgrown the weathered stonework, filling the cracks and crevices as they extended their reach over the tops and down the other sides. They formed a verdant green backcloth to the abundant fruits and vegetables growing in the rich dark soil. At this time in the morning it was a quiet place, but it would soon be invaded by the small army of gardeners who would spend the first hours of their long day tending the beds, painstakingly weeding and pruning to make sure there was always enough produce to supply the kitchen's prodigious needs. The Countess insisted upon the freshest home-grown ingredients for her table, believing that native fruits such as apples and pears, and others grown under glass, such as melons and grapes, were as good as any in the world. She was a stickler for quality and would permit only home-produced meat from cattle raised on aristocratic pastures to be used and she expected her cook's culinary skills to match the superb ingredients.

Mrs Castle was only too aware of how exacting the mistress could be and she had taken Max under her wing when he had first begged to be allowed to help her in the kitchen. Anxious to find some means to keep him out of sight of Makepiece, who seemed to have a feeling verging on hatred for the boy, she had struck upon the idea of teaching him how to gather the produce from the garden. She had imagined that he would soon tire of the novelty of the task and find other pursuits more exciting for little boys, but she had been surprised at how enthusiastically he had taken to it. Listening intently as he stood beside her, holding her hand as she bent over to point out a fully formed lettuce here, or a line of carrots ready for pulling there, she had carefully and patiently explained how to identify when a particular fruit or vegetable was ready for the table. He began to learn when one was at the point of putting on too much weight, which would mean that it would lose all taste and tenderness. His questions naturally progressed on to what each would be used for and how she would prepare it for whatever dish happened to be on the menu that day. Some days he fired these questions at her in rapid succession, with barely time to draw breath, so that she would cry, 'Whoa, whoa, lad, yer need ter slow down. Now then one at a time.' He was developing an interest in food, which only served to strengthen the affinity between them, and soon she felt able to let him go on his own, without her help. But then she had made a promise all those years ago.

He smiled to himself as he remembered her words and how he had trained himself to remember what she told him, repeating her words over and over again until they stayed in his memory. He rarely needed to be told the same thing twice and now, in the still of the early morning, he began to select the items on her list. As he crouched over the potato patch, scraping the earth from around the base of the plants to check where he should start digging, he sensed a movement behind him from the direction of the gate. He swivelled round quickly as he heard the familiar creaking of the hinges, surprised by an unaccustomed visitor to the garden at this hour of the day. In an instant his mind flashed back to a similar day several years earlier, which was still etched on his memory. He was twelve at the time and had been collecting some cabbages for Mrs Castle at about the same time of day when he was suddenly startled by the sound of footsteps gently crunching on the path behind him. Before he had a chance to turn round a hand had roughly grabbed his shoulder and pushed him forcefully to the ground. He had fallen awkwardly and cut his chin on the stony path. Towering menacingly over him when he looked up with the blood still dripping through his fingers was Lord William, with an expression of such malevolence on his face that it had terrified Max and given him nightmares for weeks afterwards. The most chilling part of the whole incident was that Lord William had then transfixed him with a stare for a moment or two before striding away without saying a word. He still bore the scar that had been left once the wound had healed. It would never completely disappear. Molly and Bert had quickly drawn a veil over the episode and it had not been mentioned again but Mrs Castle knew and had done her best to keep him out of Lord William's way ever since.

It was Rosie standing there, her face flushed prettily from exertion rather than embarrassment this time. 'Cook said yer'd forgotten these an' told me ter come after yer.'

She held out a grubby brown sack that he used for carrying the vegetables back to the house and a large straw basket that he would need for the hothouse fruits. Max stood up and smiled nervously at her. Without other people around, he was suddenly acutely conscious of her presence, as if seeing her properly for the first time. He remained where he was, stock still, not sure of what to say or do. He bit his lip and cleared his throat as he blurted out, 'It's Rosie in't it?'

Taking the proffered articles from her outstretched hands, he noticed a deeper flush rising on her neck and cheeks, which was not only from exertion this time. ''Tis that,' she stammered, although her gaze was firm and sure. ''Aven't bin in 'ere before. Don't it look big wiv all them plants an' fings,' she went on, as she looked around her. Her eyes darted left and right in wonderment. 'Blimey, there's enough ter feed the 'ole o' Bow 'ere.'

Max was struck by the girlish simplicity of her words and found the feeling of warmth that he had experienced earlier in the kitchen creep over him again. She turned to look straight at him now and his heart began to beat a little faster. Then to his horror he ran his hands through his dark hair, which was thick and unruly, wiping his palms on the front of his jacket. Cursing his clumsiness and angry with himself for feeling foolish, he started to explain the layout of the garden before stopping himself involuntarily.

'I'm Max by the way, pleased ter meet yer,' he said, offering his outstretched hand.

Rosie hesitated and then placed her hand in his. He smiled, tickled at her apparent shyness, starting to feel more confident now that the ice had been broken.

'Where yer from Rosie?' he asked, unfamiliar with her accent.

'East End o' London, Bow,' she answered, smiling back. As his gaze held hers, he was mesmerized by the startling blueness of her eyes. It was as if they filled the whole upper part of her face, piercing in their clarity, but they seemed to conceal a vulnerability just below their surface. Her mouth was small and pretty, as if fashioned by a sculptor's hand, and her high cheekbones, suffused now by only the palest blush as her awkwardness began to recede, gave her a gracefulness that made him catch his breath. Her long blonde hair shone with a rich golden hue, tumbling like gently rolling waves around her face. He was instantly reminded of the photograph of the young woman on the mantelpiece in Fern Cottage that Molly had treasured for as long as he could remember and which intrigued him to this day.

Releasing his gentle grip of her hand, her slender fingers, delicate but scarred from the injurious effects of her duties, slid through his as he bent down to pick up the sack. 'Me Mam warned me about talkin' ter strangers,' she teased, quickly concluding that the sparkle in his eyes meant that he could take a joke at his own expense.

She had noticed Max around the estate even though she had only arrived from London the previous week. He was certainly a figure it was hard to miss and she had already discovered that he was the subject of much discussion amongst the younger female servants in the house. In fact she had to admit to herself that she was secretly rather pleased when Mrs Castle had told her to run after him with the sack and basket that he had forgotten to take with him. He was not especially tall, standing about five feet eight inches in height, but he was powerfully built, which gave him a commanding presence when in the company of others. Rosie thought his build was like that of the boxers she had grown accustomed to seeing on a Saturday night at closing time in the dingy back alleys of the East End before her Mam had sent her down here. His upper body was dominated by broad shoulders and strong arms, which were accentuated by the trimness of his narrow waist. She could tell, despite his baggy, ill-fitting trousers, that his legs were long and well defined. There was not an ounce of spare flesh on him and he seemed to be well muscled, honed no doubt from the frequent manhandling of barrels up and down from the cellar at The Wheelwright Arms where she had heard he worked. His skin was lightly tanned, exhibiting none of the unhealthy pallor of the undernourished with which she was all too familiar in the slums of the East End. This gave him a vibrancy and vitality that was infectious. He was what her friends would describe as 'a bit o' all right' and she laughed to herself as she imagined what their reaction would be if they could see him now.

She would almost have been intimidated by the force of his physical appearance were it not for a certain gentleness of manner, which tempered any feelings she could have had like that. His strong face exhibited an intelligence and kindly charm that she found reassuring, and the sparkle that was never far from his deep brown eyes exuded cheerfulness and good humour. They seemed to twinkle like diamonds caught in a bright light. This was never more apparent than when he smiled and laughed, which he seemed to do often. It was a generous and sunny smile, which drew you in and warmed your heart. He was the sort of person that made you feel better when you were around him and Rosie detected a resilience and strength of character that gave him an appealing air of self-confidence.

'Only teasin',' she added, smiling back at him.

'Come on, give me a hand with these,' laughed Max, not wanting to admit that he had never heard of Bow.

'Oh, I can't,' hesitated Rosie, slightly crestfallen, 'cook said I weren't ter be long as we've got this dinner party ter night an' there's lots ter do.'

'Best get back then otherwise we'll both be fer it, an' I've got ter get off ter the Wheelwrights too,' he replied, trying to hide his disappointment. She turned around, her eyes flickering away from his in the direction of her feet and she hurried back to the gate, suddenly anxious to be gone. Max watched her go, staring after her with a thoughtful expression on his face before bending back down to resume his scraping of the earth around the base of the potato plants.

Chapter 3

The loud clatter of horses' hooves could clearly be heard in the small inner office at the mine as Jim Edwardes pored over his cluttered desk. Glancing sharply through the grimy window to his right, he muttered angrily to himself as he saw Lord William drive rapidly into the cobbled yard, 'That's all I need ter make me day.' His concentration was shattered as he stood up and put the production report he had been studying to one side. Marching past Agnes, his secretary and general factotum, he looked knowingly at her. 'Yer'd better put kettle on, smartish, before 'is Lordship demands it,' he said, giving her a crooked smile as he reached the door of the outer office, which led directly into the yard.

He was a smart man, always well turned out, and proud of his association with the Gordon family. His immaculate appearance was in vivid contrast to the muck and grime of the mine and this seemed to generate a quiet but solid respect amongst the workers, as if he was a symbol of reassurance and stability in their hard-pressed existence. He still vividly remembered the day he had been summoned to see Lord Hugo to mark the hand-over of responsibilities for the family's commercial activities upon his father's retirement. Lord Hugo had been fulsome in his praise for all that his father had contributed to the success of their mining and quarrying enterprises and generous in his confidence for the future under his own direction. That had meant so much to him, born and bred as he was in the South Hams area, and he had worked tirelessly since that day to justify the Earl's support for him. His visitor was a different matter altogether though, and he had found himself biting his tongue on innumerable occasions since Lord William had begun to assume greater control of the family's affairs.

Agnes brushed imaginary specks of dust from the front of her neatly ironed white blouse, as she always did when she was feeling nervous, and looked sympathetically at Jim as he went out to greet Lord William. She was a thin woman in her late middle years with wispy brown hair, cut short and held in place with a large tortoiseshell grip. Her face seemed set in a permanent expression of concentration, but her eyes were alive and warm behind the thin gold spectacles balanced in their customary position on the end of her nose. She had started work at the mine in old Mr Edwardes' day and had been passed down to his son rather like a treasured family heirloom. Jim knew he would be lost without her. Her desk was as ordered as his was cluttered and she kept the office running smoothly and efficiently. Her little touches of homeliness brightened the sparsely furnished rooms, but now she moved quickly to hide the flowers she had picked and carefully arranged that morning in the tall crystal vase that had been a present from the Countess to Jim's father. She knew Lord William disapproved of such things and he never failed to reprimand her for her efforts in the most unpleasant way. It was all so unfortunate, she sighed, and she longed for the old days when the Earl was in charge. He was a real gentleman, not like his son, who behaved with a meanness of spirit that made her feel distressingly helpless when it was directed at others.

Agnes knew most of what went on in the mine and her calm but friendly demeanour often meant that the workers came to her with their problems. She was a mother figure to many of them and they were her surrogate children, almost as if they were compensation for her childless state. Jim had found this particularly invaluable over the years. It was in this way that he had first heard rumours of more unrest amongst the underground workers, which was becoming manifestly obvious in the disappointing production figures he had just been reviewing. There were similar rumblings at Haytor and he was worried about productivity there too. 'No doubt that is the reason fer 'is visit,' Jim thought bleakly as he looked with concern at the panting horse, sweat streaming from its flanks as it stood restlessly in front of the trap that had been brought to an abrupt halt outside the entrance to the low wooden building. 'I'll 'ave somebody take care o' the 'orse milord,' said Jim carefully, as Lord William climbed down. 'He treats 'is horse like he treats the men,' thought Jim wearily, 'no wonder they're un'appy.'

'Leave it, man!' barked William harshly. 'Have my papers brought in from the trap,' he added, as he strode past without a backwards glance. Ducking his head to avoid the low doorway, he entered the office and nodded curtly at Agnes before making himself comfortable behind Jim's desk. His arrival had been noticed by the men working inside the engine house and within minutes word had spread throughout the mine. He looked distastefully at the mass of papers that littered the surface in front of him as Agnes placed a cup of piping hot tea by his side. The inner office was small and his commanding presence dominated the room; apart from Jim's desk and chair there was just a narrow wooden table pushed up against the wall, two straight-backed chairs that were uncomfortable if used for too long, and a narrow wooden shelf bowing alarmingly under the weight of the books and files packed tightly along its length.

Ignoring Agnes completely, William fixed Jim with a piercing stare. 'I'll get straight to the point,' he said, 'production is down again. How do you explain that?'

He was a big man and, in many ways, a product of his time like his father before him, but that was where the similarities ended. He behaved in the manner of someone who believed implicitly in the right of entitlement, but, unlike his father, he paid no heed whatsoever to the responsibilities of privilege. There was something corrupt about him, which led to frequent displays of egotism and calculated acts of cruelty. Elegantly dressed, his handsome features were coldly impassive beneath his dark, wavy hair, neatly brushed as usual, his suit unruffled despite the rigours of his drive, and the black leather of his boots shining brightly against the dull wooden floor. He had been preoccupied on the drive over from the House, weighing up the possible answers Jim might give to the questions he would ask. William always liked to be prepared and to feel one step ahead in any situation, and his mind had worked furiously, determined to deal with the problem in his own way, before his father had a chance to interfere. He had been unlucky again with the cards and if production continued to fall, and revenues with it, he would find it difficult to conceal just how much he owed to his creditors. He was secretly troubled, but arrogantly confident of his ability to handle matters. His thoughts had turned to Hettie as he had sped through the narrow village streets, oblivious to the glares of the villagers who jumped hurriedly out of his path as he urged the frantic horse on with gratuitous lashes of his whip. She was a thorn in his side and clearly his parents' favourite, but she was little more than a nuisance to be managed in his plans for the future. He was the only male heir and that was all that mattered. The family fortune and estates would come to him when his father died and then he would really be free to do things his way, instead of always feeling that his father was perpetually peering over his shoulder, holding him back and judging his actions. The insensitivity of his thoughts was entirely lost on him and he had laughed out loud in his excitement at the prospect of inheriting. He could hardly wait.

'Well, man, what do you have to say?' he demanded again, his voice taking on a dangerous calmness that seemed to echo around the room.

Jim stood his ground, the muscles in his face tightening as he searched for the words to reply. He was not frightened of William, but he was acutely conscious of the man's temper and hatred for anyone or anything that stood in his way. He clenched his fists, suppressing his natural desire to respond in kind. 'Production is down by three per cent milord, which is an improvement from the five per cent the week before. I'm sure it will be back up this week. The men . . .'

'You're not only a damn fool,' interrupted Lord William savagely, 'you're . . .'

'Things 'ave settled at Haytor, milord, they will do the same 'ere given the chance,' said Jim in a quiet and steady tone, looking him squarely in the eye. The subtlety of his last three words was completely lost on Lord William. Jim's interruption had stunned him and the ensuing momentary silence gave Jim the initiative, which he quickly seized. 'I think the men were upset by the reduction in their tea break, milord,' he continued evenly, 'but I believe it ter be resolved now.' He maintained his careful gaze, biting back more words that were on the tip of his tongue. There was so much he wanted to say and he felt beads of perspiration break out on his forehead as he saw the unmistakably incredulous expression on Lord William's face. It bordered on disbelief and it took all of his self-control to remain silent as Lord William launched into a ferocious tirade, upper lip curling with contempt as he berated Jim for his defence of the workforce.

'Have you any idea how much the lost production has cost me!' He did not wait for a response. 'And you tell me the men have a problem with the reduction in their tea break?' His tone was icy. 'Those were my orders and they will be obeyed!'

'But, mi . . .'

'You have allowed them to get away with this appallingly poor performance,' he went on, almost shouting, his eyes blazing with something very close to hatred as he took a step forwards. *'I hold you personally responsible!'*

The look on his face was enough to silence Jim, who stood there, tensing in readiness for the remainder of the onslaught.

'Let me make myself crystal clear.' His voice had grown ominously quiet now as he leant towards Jim. 'I will not tolerate another decline in output this week. You will remind the men that I am in charge and they will lose their tea break altogether if they do not pull their weight.'

Jim continued to stand in front of him, breathing deeply as he fought to restrain his natural inclination to answer back. He did not trust himself to reply.

26

'If you do not meet your target this week, you will join the troublemakers on the streets!' Lord William's mouth was twisted in a thin, mean line as he spat out his final words. 'And remember this, never interrupt me again.' Then, with a slow and deliberate movement of his right arm, he swept some of the papers from Jim's desk on to the floor. They landed at Jim's feet with a thud. 'Your office is a mess, man. Tidy it up!'

Agnes swallowed hard and willed her hands to stop shaking. Standing in the outer office she had heard every word of his vicious harangue. Her legs felt weak and she sank down in her chair and stared silently at the desk, unable to focus on the papers in front of her. The sinking sensation in the pit of her stomach made her feel sick; she was stunned, it had never been this bad before. Praying that it would end, she felt desperate for Jim and knew that he was right not to retaliate in kind. *Thank goodness* he had called a meeting of the entire workforce the day before to voice his concerns and to express his fears of what would happen if the figures did not improve this week. The men had seen Lord William's arrival and they would guess why he had come. She would have to let them know, surreptitiously of course; *they had to know.* They would not let Jim down. Retaliation was the cause of the situation in the first place, and who could blame them, the way Lord William handled them, pushing them around, bullying them, cracking the whip, reducing their tea break for no good reason. The men worked like slaves as it was. But it would do no good. It would only make matters worse, for them and for Jim... Yes, that's what she would do, she said to herself, talk to the men... Feeling slightly better, now that she had thought of something positive to do to help, she glanced towards Jim's office just as the door was flung wide open with an almighty crash.

Lord William strode past. '*Until Friday!*' he said menacingly as he marched out, throwing open the outer door into the courtyard with similar force. Climbing into his trap, he was quickly gone.

Jim stood motionless in his doorway and looked resignedly at Agnes. 'I guess we knew that were comin',' he said, aghast at what had happened. ''E really went fer it, that time, didn't 'e.'

Agnes felt her heart go out to him. 'It's not fair, Jim!' she cried vehemently. 'We can't let 'im get away with it. It's not right!'

'Fairness don't come in ter it with 'im,' replied Jim, fury still seething inside him, 'but 'e ain't goin' ter beat us!' Trying to calm down so he could think clearly, his face drawn and tense, he walked to the window and peered out. 'Gather the men together at the end of the shift would yer? I'd better tell 'em what we need ter do...' His mouth tightened as he thought of their reaction. He knew it would take careful handling, antagonising them now would spell disaster. 'I can't believe the bastard can show such poor judgement,' he said to himself. 'An' I blame the Earl fer giving 'im too much rein,' he thought bitterly.

Agnes touched his elbow gently and handed him a cup of tea as he half turned round to look at her. 'What would I do without yer?' he smiled, thanking God that he could rely on her.

She smiled back, relieved that she had been of some help and already planning how she would talk discreetly to the men.

Chapter 4

The heavy footsteps on the backstairs leading down from the inner hallway had an urgency to them, which normally only meant one thing. Mrs Castle looked up from her roasting pan as Makepiece stormed into the kitchen with a briskness that was so unlike his usual plodding gait. There was going to be trouble. She knew it so well.

'Where is that lazy wastrel, good for nothing bitch! I'll give 'er a good clip...' He stopped in his tracks and looked around him, his thin, mean mouth contorted in anger. Millie edged nearer to Mrs Castle and wiped her hands nervously on her newly starched white apron, leaving tracks of grease down both sides. Mrs Castle stiffened and eyed the household steward with contempt.

'Don't fret, lass,' she murmured to Millie, 'leave 'im ter me.' She moved around the corner of the range, slowly and carefully pulling the roasting pan to the side of the heat as she did so, in order not to spill any of the roast ptarmigan gravy in the process. No point spoiling upstairs luncheon on him, she thought grimly. ''Ow dare yer come in 'ere shoutin' the odds, yer nasty oaf!' she hissed. 'If I catch yer threatening that poor girl again, you'll 'ave me ter answer ter. I promise yer!' Her eyes flashed with anger and she was seized by a real hatred for the portly figure in front of her, her normally ruddy cheeks burning even brighter with the vehemence of her outburst.

Makepiece eyed her warily, his expression coldly hostile but determined. 'Lord William has just informed me that our kitchen maid has been neglecting her duties again and wishes me to deal with it,' he spat back, the ample rolls of flesh on his oversized neck quivering as he did so.

'Rosie is my kitchen maid an' not yers,' she glowered, 'an' what is 'is Lordship doin' concernin' 'imself with below stairs staff? Molly an' 'er Ladyship deal with the likes o' us.' She turned away in disgust. 'Lay one finger on that girl and I'll see that 'er Ladyship gets ter 'ear about it, that I will!'

Makepiece stared hard at her, breathing heavily. He fingered the top button of his winged collar and wiped the beads of perspiration trickling down his forehead with clenched fists. His large frame had long since gone to seed and he perspired easily. In his youth he had not been an unattractive man but years of excess had caused him to balloon to his present obese state. His grey and black striped trousers pulled alarmingly at the waist and his white shirt gaped over his corpulent chest. He constantly tugged at the buttons of his tailcoat in vain attempts to hide the paunch spilling over his waistband. His thinning grey hair was plastered flat across his forehead, which made his head seem bigger than it actually was. This highlighted the repellent appearance of his nose, which was mottled with bluish purple lines, and his narrow eyes were receding into the depths of his fleshy face. They were flat and devoid of intimacy, the colour of the granite hewn from the family quarries.

At that moment, just as a snarl of reply was forming on his lips, the drawing-room bell rang. Still bristling with rage, Mrs Castle managed to look at him again. 'That'll be Lord William. Just yer remember what I said!'

'Jackson will get that,' snapped Makepiece, in a glacial tone, before thinking better of it and dismissing the other servants with a curt nod as he turned back for the stairs.

Mrs Castle motioned to Millie and Sam, the first footman who had come into the kitchen to collect the silver cutlery for the dining-room table, to get on with their work. The uneasy silence that had descended was soon lost to the clattering of china, as Millie started to count out four each of the soup plates and fish plates before placing them in the waiters' lift to send upstairs, and the clinking of cutlery as Sam checked the silverware to make sure each knife and fork was spotless. Soup spoon, fish knife, fish fork, main course knife ... he intoned as he held each one up to the light. He knew the slightest mark would catch Jackson's eagle eye when the butler checked the table before sounding the dining-room gong to announce luncheon was served.

She was worried and struggled to concentrate on the fillets of sole on the board in front of her. Makepiece was a bully and a coward, she knew that, but she could not understand why he seemed to persist in mistreating Rosie so much. He had been this way with Max ever since he was a little boy and it was only the Countess's discreet favour that had stopped him from driving the lad away. Now he was old enough and strong enough to look after himself, but she knew Max still preferred to avoid the steward whenever he could, always trying to keep out of his way when popping in for leftovers every morning. Even the fact that Max was Molly and Bert's son didn't seem to make much difference to the man's behaviour, she thought bitterly, and now Rosie was receiving the brunt of his filthy temper.

It seemed to her that he enjoyed exercising such evil brutality. He had actually struck Rosie when she had accidentally dropped a glass after servants hall dinner the other day. She could have sworn that he had deliberately balanced it unevenly on the tray so that it would slide off when the lass had lifted it up to carry it through to the scullery. Tears sprang to her eyes as she thought about the poor girl's terrified expression when Makepiece had raised his hand to her in a display of temper that had caught everyone by surprise, shocking Millie into silence for the rest of the evening. 'It won't do, it won't do,' she muttered savagely to herself.

It had all started about two months ago, she recalled, as she ran her knife along the edge of the fillets to make sure she had removed all the tiny bones. Makepiece had caught Max and Rosie talking at the kitchen table. They had in fact been checking off the list of vegetables needed for that day. It was a long list because Lord and Lady Hersham were coming to lunch and old Lord Hersham liked his food, so the menu was fancier than usual. 'Consommé *printanier,* iced lobster soufflé and stuffed quail Mrs Castle,' Lady Constance had said, 'there's no one to touch your stuffed quail and I happen to know it's a favourite of Lord Hersham.' Rosie had been excited when they had discussed the menu by the fire afterwards and had beamed at her when she had been allowed to make up the kitchen garden list for Max the following day.

Mrs Castle smiled as she considered how well Rosie had settled in and how quickly she was learning, her anger and concern momentarily forgotten. 'A real interest in food, that one,' she mused out loud to no one in particular.

'Yer what, Mrs Castle?' said Millie, not catching the words over the sound of the bubbling pot she was stirring.

'Nothin' girl, an' mind yer don't let that sauce catch!' she retorted, but without irritation in her voice. There had been enough unpleasantness already for one day and it was not yet lunchtime.

The pair had not heard Makepiece come in from outside and he had hurled obscenities at them, advancing menacingly towards them. Rosie had looked over to Mrs Castle in fear but Max had squared up to him, a look of outright contempt on his face. He had clenched his fists and opened his mouth to respond before Rosie had said softly, 'Sorry, Mr Makepiece, I'll get on now. Didn't mean no 'arm.' She was brave that one, thought Mrs Castle, and strong too, beneath that quiet exterior.

Makepiece had not noticed the iciness of her piercing blue eyes and the intense paleness of her face as she got up from the table. He had been too busy holding Max in his rigid, arrogant stare, his face crimson with rage, swallowing hard as his breath came in shallow gasps from the depths of his heaving chest. She'll be surprising him before long if he's not careful, worried Mrs Castle to herself, and she knew Max could have killed him. It was only by sheer self-control that he had lowered his fists, picked up the list and walked out without saying a word.

Rosie came out of the scullery disturbing Mrs Castle from her thoughts. She had heard every word that had been said, standing quietly by the large iron sinks that would soon be full of the Royal Doulton bone china that was used when it was just the family dining alone. The Earl and Countess were personal friends of Sir Henry Doulton and he had made a dinner service with the family crest emblazoned on each item especially for them at his factory in Burslem. The broken glass was still fresh in her mind and every time she thought about it, she boiled with rage, her mouth set in a thin line, her slender hands tightly curled into balls. She knew he would have hit her again just now, if she had come out from the scullery where she had been hiding, hardly daring to breathe. He'll never do that to me again, she thought, as long as I live.

'I 'aven't bin neglectin' me duties, Mrs Castle, honest!' she cried. 'Honest I 'aven't!' The injustice of it all hit her like a thunderbolt, but she knew she could not say more. She bit her tongue, seething with frustration and anger. Just let them try, she thought coldly, then I'll show them.

Mrs Castle looked at her with a mixture of relief and puzzlement. Relief that Rosie had had the sense to remain out of sight in the scullery, but puzzlement at the accusation Makepiece had so nastily thrown at her. Why, she wondered, was Lord William even interested in a kitchen maid?

'Tell yer what, luv, after the dishes are done, get off early,' she said in a soothing voice.

'Oh, ta, Mrs Castle, if I've finished me work by then,' she replied, her tone flat and disinterested. Seeing the look of concern that descended on the cook's face, she flashed Mrs Castle a quick smile. 'Don't worry, I'll make sure I do,' she added quickly, not wanting to appear ungrateful or to worry her further. Mrs Castle was trying to be kind, she reasoned, and it was her afternoon off after all. She had promised to meet Max in the village, so the sooner she could escape, the better.

She hurried back into the scullery, feeling Millie's eyes boring into her back as she did so. Probably thinks I'm cook's pet. I'll have that to deal with too when I get back from the village, she sighed grimly. But she dismissed those thoughts from her mind, thinking of her afternoon ahead.

Lunch was a swift affair when the family were not entertaining, and little more than an hour later Rosie was busy at the sinks, struggling to keep pace with the steady stream of dirty china and cutlery appearing from the dining-room. She clasped the big handle of the tap in her small hands, needing both of them to turn it round. Warm water started to gush into the deep, uninviting trough in front of her, splashing the black sleeves of her uniform as it did. She added some soda, like she had been shown, and gingerly washed the first of the fine crystal goblets before gently placing them bowl side down on the wooden draining board. She was careful not to knock them on the sides of the sink, knowing that the slightest tap could chip or crack the delicate rim. She had seen Millie snap one of the fine sculpted stems of the Bohemian burgundy glasses when she had been too heavy-handed, and there had been ''ell ter pay' over that, as Millie had whispered anxiously at the time. It was not only that Jackson always counted them back into the glass cupboard in his pantry after each use, and so any damage could not be concealed, it was also that Rosie loved the appearance of the beautiful cut lead crystal and she treated them reverently out of a love and respect for their sparkle and magnificence.

As they were draining, she put some soft soap into the water and whisked it into a lather, her hands already starting to turn pink and raw from their immersion. She put the small silver into soak and proceeded to polish the glasses before they drained too much. If she allowed them to dry completely she would have to work twice as hard to remove the smeared watermarks, and the more she handled them, the more she increased the risk of breaking them. Holding each one up to the meagre light fighting its way through the bars on the small window in front of the sinks, she put them safely down on the wooden side, next to the door through to the larder. Sam, and Raymond, the second footman, would put them away later on.

She prepared the plates by scraping them, which helped to give her hands a short respite from the water, and then washed the silver. She grumbled at the amount of cutlery even a small family meal required, anxious to get finished before Makepiece came back down from upstairs. With five courses there were over thirty pieces to wash, rinse and then polish dry before packing away, so she did not have time to waste.

33

Humming softly to herself to keep her spirits up, she stretched to turn the old, stiff tap on again to add more hot water and soda in readiness for the plates, standing on tiptoes so that she did not saturate the front of her dress with the suds from the by now almost full sink. Suddenly she tensed, feeling her heart start to thump against her chest. She sensed someone behind her, gooseflesh racing along her arms as a shiver prickled her spine. She knew she was not alone. Please God, not Makepiece again, she prayed. Slowly turning around, Rosie frantically looked around for something to defend herself with, a cry for help forming in her throat.

'Cook sent me ter 'elp,' glowered Millie.

Rosie smiled across at her, desperately trying to stop her legs shaking with relief and aware the young kitchen maid's tone was full of resentment. 'Yer don't 'ave ter, I can manage. You've got yer own things ter do, Millie,' she replied carefully, waiting to see Millie's reaction.

'Cook said I 'ad ter,' she mumbled, clearly not wanting to make peace with Rosie just yet.

'Oh, Millie, I'll make it up ter yer, promise!' offered Rosie. 'There's just the plates and dishes to do now an' the silver ter polish. We'll soon 'ave it finished!'

The sound of water splashing on to the stone floor made her turn back round with a start. She had left the tap on in her confusion and it was now overflowing, bringing soap suds cascading over the lip of the sink with it.

'Quick!' said Millie, giggling now at the sight of the soapy water beginning to spread across the floor, 'or we'll be fer it!' dissolving into more helpless giggles as she dashed for the mops, which were kept in the cleaning cupboard at the far end of the scullery, all thoughts of injustice now forgotten. Rosie could not help herself, laughing too as she scrambled to reach the tap.

Chapter 5

William Gordon, the Viscount Bickleigh, put his spoon and fork down and pushed his plate away. 'Tell Mrs Castle that was too rich for me, Jackson,' he complained, his mouth still full as he spoke.

The butler glided over the deep rose and gold Aubusson carpet from his position in front of the gilt side table, which stood underneath a superb gilt-wood mirror. The two footmen stood to either side of the table waiting for the Countess's signal to clear the dessert plates.

'Really, William!' admonished Lady Constance. 'This Queen of Puddings is lovely and don't speak with your mouth full.'

Lord William glared across the table at his mother. 'I'm not a child any more, Mother,' he replied stiffly.

Jackson stopped in mid step and discreetly moved back to his position, motioning with his eyes for Sam and Raymond to remain where they were.

'Then stop behaving like one!' snapped Hettie, turning towards Jackson as she did so. 'That was perfectly delicious, Jackson, thank you.' She fixed her brother with a disdainful stare. She had watched him with distaste throughout the meal, wishing they had company to distract her. Her brother was 35 years old and she was ashamed of his manners. In fact she was ashamed of so many things about him. She had exchanged knowing glances with her father on several occasions since they had sat down and could imagine what he was thinking. At least her mother was there to keep the peace, she sighed.

Lady Constance nodded towards Jackson to clear the plates. 'We'll have coffee in here today, please Jackson. Mrs Castle has excelled herself, please let her know would you?' She had a gentle way of issuing instructions as if she was asking a question, in a pleasant tone that combined firmness with a hint of sympathetic benevolence.

'With pleasure, milady,' he smiled, slightly inclining his head as he did so. If only they were all like Her Ladyship, he thought wistfully to himself.

Lady Henrietta was demanding, but thoughtful and considerate, which inspired a grudging respect in the staff. Her long, glossy black hair had a lustrous shine that drew admiring eyes immediately to it. She wore it up as was the fashion of the times, giving her a patrician air that was accentuated by her fine bone structure, which she highlighted with the subtle application of rouge. This was the only make-up she used, believing that an over-reliance on cosmetics was a feminine frivolity she neither needed nor deserved. *Tatler* magazine, in their Easter edition the previous year, had perfectly captured her expressive hazel brown eyes, which had a softness to them, hinting at the sensitivity and gentleness she was always ready to display. She could not be described as classically beautiful, but her round face and pleasant, friendly features perfectly mirrored her energetic and engaging personality.

Her fiancé had been killed when the Boers besieged Ladysmith during the invasion of Cape Colony and it had devastated the family. James O'Mara had been a captain in the cycle corps of the Royal Dublin Fusiliers, under the leadership of Colonel George Knox who had commanded the cycling section of the artillery at Ladysmith. He had been killed when checking a railway line for demolition charges. The letter Hettie had received from his commanding officer contained the usual banal sentences, and when the Treaty of Vereeniging was signed in May 1902, annexing the Boer republics of Transvaal and the Orange Free State to the Empire, Hettie had cried bittersweet tears of pain, the memories flooding back in a torrent of grief. It seemed to her that her life was over before it had really begun and it was only her parents' calm and insistent support that saw her through the worst times. She could trace her interest and support for woman's suffrage back to the point when she had finally started to embrace life again. It had caused her to re-examine her future and she was excited by the recent founding of the Women's Social and Political Union by Mrs Emmeline Pankhurst. She had become friendly with Christabel and Sylvia, Emmeline's two daughters, and was looking forward to meeting them again when the family moved to London the following month for the Season. She knew that her parents did not approve but she was a headstrong young lady, determined to live life on her terms.

William scowled at his sister. He picked up the cream jug from the silver tray Raymond was proffering and clumsily poured a generous measure into the cup in front of him, so that it splashed messily onto the pristine white damask tablecloth. Lord Hugo stared with abhorrence at his troublesome son. 'That is quite enough from the pair of you!' he exploded, his voice echoing around the emptiness of the vast room. Hettie and William looked at him in startled surprise, unaccustomed to hearing their father rebuke them in front of the servants.

A chill silence descended in stark juxtaposition to the warmth and richness of the room.

'I wonder if Rosie, the kitchen maid, helped Mrs Castle with luncheon, darling?' mused Lady Constance to Hettie. 'She did tell me how well she was getting on when we were discussing the menus the other day. There's the big dinner for Mr Asquith on the twenty-first.'

'But that's in London, Mama,' replied Hettie, relieved by the change of subject so skilfully executed by her mother.

The London Season, with its exhausting merry-go-round of debutante balls, dinner parties, exhibitions, concerts and visits to the opera and theatre, no longer held any appeal for her, but she knew she would be expected to play her role.

'Yes darling, I was wondering if I should suggest Mrs Castle brings Rosie this year instead of Millie. Sarah will come as usual. What do you think?'

'I'd ask Mrs Castle and Makepiece if I were you, Mama,' replied Hettie.

'Perhaps I will,' answered Lady Constance, breathing a silent sigh of relief at the lightening of the atmosphere.

William's coffee cup clattered in its saucer as he put it down sharply, causing the others to glance at him with questioning expressions. Lord Hugo cleared his throat, throwing a swift look at his wife. 'What's the matter, William?' he asked with a penetrating look at his son, his voice hardening as he went on, 'did something startle you?'

'No, Papa, the coffee was just too hot, that's all,' he replied in a steady tone.

His manner did not deceive Lord Hugo. He had grown used to William's guile and cunning and he sensed his son was hiding something despite the artful nonchalance of his reply. But he did not wish to prolong the conversation, feeling that it was neither the time nor the place to do so. Draining the remains of his cup of coffee, which was lukewarm to the touch, Lord Hugo pushed his chair back and stood up to leave. 'Thank you, Jackson,' he nodded to the butler, 'I have some estate accounts to go through, my dear, and Sir Geoffrey is coming to see me at three o'clock,' he said to his wife as he made for the door.

William's ears pricked up at the mention of Sir Geoffrey's name. Why would the chairman of the trustees panel be coming to see his father? he asked himself, they normally only met every three months or so. He sat back, turning the words over in his mind, careful to ensure a bland expression settled on his handsome features. He would have to be more careful, he thought, and why would his mother be thinking about the new kitchen maid, let alone consider taking her to London with them? To his annoyance he found his palms had become damp and clammy and he wiped them surreptitiously on the legs of his trousers. Servants were like possessions, to be used and enjoyed until they no longer held any interest or purpose. He eyed his sister cautiously. She was clever and perceptive and their parents always seemed to take her side in their frequent spats.

'Are you going to London with Papa and Mama, Henrietta?' he asked.

'Of course I am! As I do every year and as you well know!' his sister exclaimed, impatient with his fatuous question. Hettie did not want to lose her temper again, but she was in danger of doing so. She struggled to control her mounting irritation as she poured herself a second cup of coffee. His question seemed innocent enough but her brother knew she disliked the whole charade of the Season.

'I just wondered whether you would be helping Mama with the entertaining,' he queried disingenuously.

Infuriated, but not willing to let him know by just how much, she fixed him with a stony gaze. 'Why, are you offering to help, William?'

'It depends on what happens at the quarries. I will be letting Edwardes know the dates next week,' he replied, silently cursing himself for falling into her trap. That was the last thing on his mind right now and he thought better of goading his sister any further. With that he stood up, unwilling to prolong their exchange in front of their mother. 'Thank you for lunch, Mama,' he smiled at Lady Constance, the phrase he had used since he was a little boy tripping easily off his tongue.

'That's all right, darling,' she said, as her mind was instantly cast back by his words to the image of her son as a small boy, smiling sweetly at her as he got down from the table.

He went straight to the long gallery and strode purposely across to the far wall, reaching for the nearest bell cord as he did so. It creaked loudly in the silence of the vast, empty room. He stood with his hands clasped behind his back, head bowed as he waited for Makepiece to appear. He was deep in thought as the door opened and the rotund figure of the steward appeared in the doorway, silhouetted against the dim light from the inner hallway. Makepiece advanced towards him, as smoothly as his lumbering gait would allow. He adjusted his tie as he eyed Lord William with a mixture of trepidation and obsequiousness that William found oddly amusing.

'Yes, my Lord?' he said in an ingratiating voice.

William kept his head lowered to hide the smirk playing on his lips. Makepiece had come to a stop about six feet in front of him and was hovering nervously. The man is getting fatter by the day, thought William, as he raised his head to look him straight in the eye. 'Tell me about the kitchen maid, Rosie. What are your plans for sending the staff to Chesterfield Square when His Lordship and Her Ladyship move up to town next month?'

Makepiece was taken aback. 'Begging yer pardon, milord?' he stammered, shifting from one leg to the other in his discomfort.

'The kitchen maid. Is she going to London with other servants or not, man!' snapped William, his irritation plainly obvious from his tone. His voice had risen sharply and he took a deep breath to calm himself down. It would not do to let anyone overhear his conversation.

Makepiece felt his throat go dry. 'I 'aven't discussed it yet with Mrs Chambers, milord,' he replied carefully, racing to regain his composure. The question had caught him by surprise and he sensed that he needed to tread warily.

William looked sharply at him, noting the expression on his face. My God, he's frightened of me, he thought. In that instant he decided to bite his tongue, his contempt for the unedifying figure in front of him complete. He would decide how he could use this sudden realisation to his advantage, but he needed to think calmly first. 'Very well, Makepiece, see to it that I am informed when you have done so,' he said, dismissing the steward with a curt nod.

Makepiece inclined his head in a gesture of obeisance and retreated from the room, cursing inwardly as he did so. Furious, but in command of himself, he failed to notice the figure on the stairs as he laboured across the shiny marble floor towards the door leading to the backstairs, almost hidden as it was by the plinth displaying the bust of Czar Alexander. Pushing the door open, he descended to the kitchen, ignoring the hostile look thrown at him by Mrs Castle who was still busy at the range. He went into his steward's room and slammed the door behind him. Millie, who was in the middle of clearing away the remains from upstairs luncheon, breathed a sigh of relief as he did so, praying that he remained there long enough for her to finish her duties so she could make herself scarce before Mrs Castle retired to her room for her afternoon rest. She felt safe when Mrs Castle was there to defend them against Makepiece's frequent tirades, and right now it seemed to her as if he might launch into another one at any moment.

The steward sat down heavily on the worn winged chair that had once belonged in Lady Henrietta's upstairs sitting-room to catch his breath. The room was spartan but comfortable, as befitted his status in the house. It was actually a small suite of rooms with a bedroom just big enough for an old mahogany single bed, a double wardrobe and a washstand with a faded brown rug covering most of the stone floor, a sitting-room with a table large enough to entertain the upper servants when necessary, and the worn wing chair, and a strong room for the secure storage of the family silver and gold plate. This room also contained a large heavy safe for the safe keeping of the family and guests' jewellery.

Makepiece sat there for a few moments as he went over the conversation with Lord William again in his mind. He was puzzled at the interest being shown in Rosie, which was certainly out of character. He knew the plight of the servants, especially the lower servants like Mrs Castle's kitchen maids, did not normally concern Lord William. In fact he doubted that he even knew who they all were, let alone remember their names. Yet there had been a number of occasions when Lord William had spoken to him about the girl and had even taken him to task over her apparent dereliction of duty. That had really riled him and he was not going to let a slip of a girl get him into trouble. He knew how nasty Lord William could be; he had seen it with his own eyes. Inexplicable situations like this bothered him and he had been in service with the family long enough to know the signs, especially when Lord William was involved.

He gave an involuntary shudder as an icy chill suddenly washed over him. Surely all that was in the past? he thought. It had caused such upset and he still trembled at the memory of Lady Constance struggling to come to terms with what had happened. No, not again! he thought, not again, as an unease descended in his mind that he could not shake. Perhaps he was wrong; he fervently hoped he was...

He stirred himself from the meanderings of his mind and decided to talk to Molly straightaway about the arrangements for the forthcoming move to Chesterfield Square, before he was challenged again. He would need to have the answers ready next time.

Chapter 6

'Sir Geoffrey Lee, my Lord,' announced Jackson.

Hugo looked up from the books in front of him. 'Geoffrey, so good to see you,' he said as he rose to greet the taciturn chairman of the estate trustees. 'Thank you, Jackson.'

'Would you like tea now, my Lord?' asked Jackson from the doorway of the study.

'Yes please, Jackson,' replied Lord Gordon as he looked enquiringly at Sir Geoffrey, who gave an almost imperceptible nod of his head in return. 'Do sit down, Geoffrey,' he said, indicating the nearest of the chesterfield sofas. He reached for the small leather case on his desk that was almost hidden by one of the books marked 'Home Farm Accounts' and sat down opposite his visitor. 'It's kind of you to come so soon,' he began as he opened the case and took out a letter.

'Not at all, Hugo,' replied Sir Geoffrey, 'it sounded urgent when we spoke.' He looked at Lord Hugo expectantly. 'I have to admit to being more than a little intrigued. It's not often that I am asked to see you in between our normal meetings.'

'Quite so,' said Hugo quietly, 'I'd like you to look at this please, if you would,' he added, passing the letter to Sir Geoffrey.

'What is it?' he asked, fishing in his top pocket for his spectacles. He began to read, peering at the closely spaced handwriting whilst he fumbled with his glasses. There was a silence as he rapidly scanned the page, his legal mind now fully engaged. 'Ah, I see.'

There was a knock at the door and Jackson and Sam came in, carrying the tea trays. 'Thank you, Jackson,' said Lord Hugo, 'put it down over there would you, we'll help ourselves today.'

'Very good, my Lord,' said the butler, concealing his surprise at being dismissed before serving it in the customary manner. 'Mrs Castle has made some cucumber sandwiches as well as the scones,' he added, as he placed the silver tray containing a selection of exquisitely cut triangles on one of the rosewood tables.

'Yes, thank you, Jackson.'

'My Lord,' said Jackson as he and the first footman made a discreet exit.

'Must be private then,' said Sam as he closed the door quietly behind them, 'don't want us earwiggin', I'd say.'

The butler silenced him with a glance. 'What have I told you about discussing the family's business, Samuel!' he remonstrated, although he had to admit the boy was right.

'As I was saying,' said Sir Geoffrey as Lord Hugo poured out the tea and offered him the tray of sandwiches, 'I understand why you asked to see me. It makes uncomfortable reading doesn't it?' He was a master of understatement. 'The boy will ruin himself in six months if this continues.'

'His mother and I had no idea. We know he plays cards regularly, most usually when he is in London, either at Chesterfield Square or the houses of his friends. I believe the Newbury boy is a regular too, but this...'

'Quite so, we shall have to make arrangements to pay his creditors immediately you know. If this were to get out there would be a scandal.'

'Yes, of course,' agreed Lord Hugo with a grimace, 'but it is the other...'

'I was just coming to that,' interrupted Sir Geoffrey soberly, 'this is much more serious I'm afraid. I've seen this sort of accusation before and it can be quite nasty if the other party chooses to make it so. The damage to the family name...'

'To hell with the family name!' exclaimed Lord Hugo. 'It's the deceit and dishonour I cannot abide!'

'Now you don't really mean that, Hugo, think of Lady Constance,' he chided.

Lord Hugo looked at him with a resigned expression on his face. 'Perhaps we should have packed him off to India after all,' he sighed.

Sir Geoffrey sat back in his chair and helped himself to another triangle from the tray. 'Lovely sandwiches, Hugo,' he commented with his mouth half full. 'Do we know this man, this ... Mr Danby?' he asked, looking down at the signature on the bottom of the letter.

Lord Hugo shook his head.

'Of course, there is always the possibility that it isn't true. We must not forget that. Cheating can be hard to prove unless it is caught red-handed. This might be nothing more than a crude attempt to extort money from your son.'

'I wish I could believe that, Geoffrey, but I suppose there is that possibility.'

'It should be perfectly possible to establish the veracity of this allegation with a few discreet enquiries. I could instruct Everson and Mayer,' he said, referring to the family solicitors, 'but I would prefer to conduct this myself, if you will permit me...?' His voice trailed off as he looked across to the opposite sofa with a slight smile. 'It's the lawyer in me, you know...'

'Of course, Geoffrey, that would be most kind,' replied Lord Hugo gratefully, 'and as to these debts?'

'They will be taken care of first thing in the morning. Now, as far as Lord William is concerned, I shall need to speak with him as soon as possible. I cannot decide how to approach this Mr Danby until I have done so. I hope we can issue a full rebuttal of his claims but we must be sure, Hugo ... Lord William must understand that I will need to know the truth...'

'Quite so, Geoffrey, I will talk to him and make that clear, as clear as I possibly can,' he promised quietly and firmly. He stood up and walked over to the window and gazed out at the manicured lawns beyond the terrace. 'I would prefer it if this could be kept from Her Ladyship for the time being,' he said, turning round to look at the man who had become a good friend to his family over the years, 'at least until we know more.'

Sir Geoffrey nodded his agreement. 'There is another matter concerning Lord William, which we should discuss,' he said, 'I was going to leave it until our next meeting but seeing as I'm here, Hugo...?' Lord Hugo looked blankly at him. 'It's really a matter for the trustees as a whole, but I would rather deal with it privately if we can. You will recall the annual annuity paid by the estate to the Rathbone family...'

'Of course,' replied Lord Hugo quickly, 'what of it? There is nothing wrong I trust?' He crossed back to the sofa and sat down heavily.

'No, no,' said Sir Geoffrey calmly, 'but the agreement stipulates that the payments must be reviewed annually on the anniversary date of their original commencement, and clause six allows us to cease all payments after the twenty-first anniversary is reached, which is in two months' time. Now I shall need to know how you wish me to proceed.' There was a brief silence as he paused to allow his words to register. 'We don't want to create any unnecessary fuss after all these years I imagine?'

'No, certainly not,' replied Lord Hugo quickly, frowning with distaste as he thought back to those dreadful events, 'I hadn't realised it was twenty-one years already.' He sighed heavily. 'I shall have to discuss this with my wife and let you know, Geoffrey, but I believe they must continue. It is, after all, the only decent thing to do.'

He shuddered at the prospect of reopening old wounds after the effect it had had on the family at the time, the memories of which were still raw in his mind. It was probably the blackest moment in their recent history, one that had threatened to bring shame on their reputation and illustrious past. All that he had worked for in his adult life and striven to enhance for future generations had seemed at risk, made vulnerable by the irresponsible and thoughtless actions of the very person who would one day inherit most of what he sought to preserve. He sighed again and recalled the saying of one of his oldest friends in whom he had confided at the time: 'One can choose one's friends but one cannot choose one's family.' How true that was, he said to himself, and here he was again, still sorting out the consequences of his son's misdeeds before they caused a scandal that would have them banished from Court.

'When will that son of mine grow up and start behaving in a proper manner befitting his station in life?' he asked bitterly.

Sir Geoffrey regarded him sympathetically. 'I know, Hugo, I know, but at least we've always managed to deal with the problems before they have got out of control. Scant consolation that may be but perhaps the boy will come into his own and, you know, giving him a greater role in managing estate affairs must be the right thing to do, it's just a matter of being patient ... you'll see.'

'He's a grown man for pity's sake!' protested Lord Hugo. 'But perhaps you're right,' he concluded rather helplessly before adding, 'We will continue the Rathbone annuity, I have decided, so I don't need to discuss it with Constance first. I can spare her that.' He knew that she would agree immediately with him anyway so there really was little sense in raking up the past, which would only distress her.

'Very well, Hugo, I will make the arrangements and inform the family accordingly. I will also remind them of the need for confidentiality and the penalty involved if this is breached.'

'Is that really necessary? Wouldn't a gentle touch be more appropriate? I should certainly prefer it.'

Sir Geoffrey smiled apologetically. 'It's better to be safe than sorry, Hugo. As I said earlier, it's the lawyer in me...'

'Very well, as you see fit,' he replied, 'and you'll let me know when you've made contact with this man Danby?' Sir Geoffrey nodded. 'Thank you. Now, Constance said she would look in when we've finished our business. I'll ring for her if there's nothing else, and we could do with some fresh tea I think.' He moved across to the bell to summon Jackson.

Chapter 7

Max pushed open the heavy double doors at the front of The Wheelwright Arms and stepped outside, peering up and down the village high street to see if Rosie was in sight. He screwed his eyes up at the distant figure just turning the bend by Turners, the little bakers shop, and his heart leapt in anticipation. He watched as the figure drew nearer before it turned right along Churchgate Street, which bordered the village green. It could not have been Rosie then, he sighed to himself, and he turned round to go back inside the pub, a look of disappointment registering on his face.

The sign above the doors clanked gently in the breeze, the sound catching his ears as he stepped back over the threshold. He glanced up at the picture of the solid red and black coach wheel that was heavily, but crudely, painted on the square black metal sign. The Wheelwright Arms was his place of work, a refuge really from the mines or a life of servitude on the estate. He loved it and the customers loved him. He considered it a stepping stone in his search for his future, although he did not yet have all those answers and he was grateful to old Jack Williams, the publican, for giving him the job as bar and cellar man.

The double doors swung shut behind him as he re-entered the main passageway that ran from the front to the back of the quaint thatched building, with its three-gabled roof presenting a solid and reassuring face to the high street. The corridor was fairly narrow with only a glimmer of natural light seeping through the opaque rectangular glass panels set into the front doors. The gas lights on the stained brown walls helped a little to dispel the dimness but the main impression created was not particularly welcoming. A permanent smell of old tobacco smoke and stale beer did nothing to improve the atmosphere. Max stepped through the opening about halfway down the passage on the left-hand side, which led into the main bar. This opening had once contained another glass-panelled door but Jack had grown tired of replacing innumerable broken panels caused by over-exuberant revellers and had eventually decided to remove it altogether.

The atmosphere was immediately brighter and more welcoming with light streaming in from the plate glass windows at the front. It would soon be filled with the chatter of busy voices.

'No luck, Max?' teased Daisy. 'P'raps she 'aint coming!' The barmaid's cheery face broke into a huge grin, and she chuckled as she saw the rueful expression on his handsome features. 'Don't yer fret, lad, she'll be 'ere soon,' she added, more in jest than sincerity.

Max gave her a quizzical look. Her auburn head was shaking with amusement.

'Nay, lad, there's plenty more where that'un came from,' she went on, enjoying her joke, 'Polly'll be in later, she fancies yer summat rotten!' Daisy concealed another huge grin that threatened to crease her face in two as Max was forced to smile back, his face reddening as her teasing struck home.

'Rosie will be 'ere. It's early yet!' he protested with as much dignity as he could muster. He looked at Daisy standing there, a startling sight in bright yellow cotton. He knew he could never be upset with her. At 25 she was only a few years older than he was, but she had assumed a motherly attitude far beyond her years from their very first meeting, as she did with all their regulars. Her auburn hair was permanently tousled atop a pretty face that was warm and inviting. She was rather on the large side and the dimples of her plump cheeks added a sparkle and gaiety to her features that was infectious. Her merry grey-green eyes positively danced in enjoyment and people always seemed to like speaking to her, even when she was at her most mischievous. Jack thought she was worth her weight in gold. That would add up to a sizeable fortune, Max had muttered one day, when Jack had said it out loud. The pairing of Daisy and Max behind the bar was a winning combination and Jack's profits had rarely been so good. He had married the widow of the licensee of The Ferrybridge Inn from Buckfastleigh the previous year and she had told him to hang on to the pair of them for all he was worth.

Max picked up his cloth and went back to polishing the glasses on the drainer behind the counter. The handful of men already drinking in the bar had heard every word and he studiously avoided their glances, staring unwaveringly at the pint pot in his hand. He knew them all well and he winced at the thought of the ribbing he would get later, especially from Jim and Bill, the two farm-hands sat huddled in the far corner. He surreptitiously looked in the decoratively etched mirrors that were hung along the wall behind the bar and heaved a silent sigh of relief as he saw them resume their pints and conversations. Two broad shelves of spirits stood in front of these mirrors, their reflections creating the impression of an extensive array of jumbled bottles, which was an interesting backcloth to the long bar counter itself. Max liked this effect, although both he and Daisy cursed loudly when every single bottle had to be taken down and dusted each week. The counter was of polished mahogany that stretched the entire width of the room, and at the end nearest the doorway stood a little box full of snuff that was for use by their regulars.

Despite its length, the bar still became packed with men clamouring to be served on a busy Saturday night, their loud demands for attention rising piercingly above the constant babble of background noise. Large kegs of beer and cider were arranged for convenience along the back wall, below the shelves, each standing ready to dispense their pale liquid as quickly as Max and Daisy could place a pint pot beneath them. On an exceptionally busy night it seemed as if the taps were never closed and beer would drip on to the ceramic tiles underneath the keg stands, before splashing on to their feet. Daisy said it was good for the skin.

The other room opening off the main passageway was the snug. It was not yet evening and given the earliness of the hour, it was still empty. This room was much smaller than the main bar and Max could faintly hear the quiet hiss of the gas lamps in the silence as he went in to check that everything was ready. Displayed above the door was a sign with the picture of a white lion rearing up on its hind legs emblazoned across it, with a bold golden mane and snarling teeth. This was a throw back to earlier times when the pub had been named The White Lion and Jack had thought it amusing to keep the original sign prominently displayed. A favourite saying had grown up amongst the regulars – 'I'm just poppin' next door ter The White Lion fer a swift one' – whenever they had reason to go into the snug. This had gone down in local folklore in much the same way as the tale about the ghost of a young girl haunting the cellar continued to be told. Max had never seen any such ghost but he participated in keeping the myth alive and had relished teasing Rosie with it on her first hesitant visit to see him there.

This bar was more comfortable than the other one, with small wooden round tables and chairs dotted around a slightly threadbare olive green rug in the centre of the smooth flagstone floor. A picture of Mount Royal dominated the wall behind the bar counter. This was the only thing about the room that Max disliked, preferring not to be reminded of the house and all that it meant to him each time he stood there to serve the next customer. A small upright piano stood in the corner nearest to the window, which often became the raucous centre of attention whenever anyone decided to give the rest of the pub a playful rendition of their favourite tune, egged on by the ever enthusiastic Daisy. The ceiling, once white, had taken on a dull brown hue, which was darker above the piano. Years of tobacco smoke drifting upwards from the incessant roll-ups and pipes clamped between the nicotine-stained teeth of the villagers had taken their toll. It was even worse in the main bar where only little patches of dirty white could now be seen, like clouds struggling to burst through a heavy sky.

'I'm just goin' ter check the yard, Daisy,' called Max as he opened the small door marked 'Keep Out' at the rear of the snug, 'ter make sure empty kegs are stacked right.'

'Right yer are, Max,' she called back, ''tis early yet, I can manage fer a bit, luv.'

There's nothing wrong with those kegs, she thought, so maybe he is worried she's not going to turn up! She felt a slight twinge of guilt about her earlier teasing as she glanced at the large round clock on the wall above the dartboard, where the Farrier twins were engaged in their customary desultory game. Any minute now and they'll be at each other's throats, she reckoned, as any game involving those two often resulted in them hurling accusations of cheating at each other. Sometimes it would even end with one throwing the remains from their glass over the other. A waste of good ale, Daisy always thought.

The light would soon start to fade, reckoned Max, looking up at the sky as he checked the empties that he had neatly stacked along the yard wall earlier in the day. Dray men will be here tomorrow, he said to himself, trying to keep his mind on the jobs he still had to finish before Jack would let him off for the rest of the evening. He had not yet sorted through the produce for the night's market dinners that had proven such a success since he had first suggested the idea to Mrs Williams. Jack had washed his hands of any involvement, saying it would never work, but Max was not deterred. His obvious determination and enthusiasm for the idea had won over her initial scepticism and they had started selling simple two-course meals including a cut of a meat joint, a variety of cheeses and a pint of ale for a shilling. It was a novel idea she had had to concede, but she had worried that people would not have the money to spare and so she had insisted that they only be offered one night a week to start with. True enough, demand had been slow at first, but gradually they found that they were selling sufficient to warrant a twice weekly menu. When word got round that it was

Max's idea, courtesy of Daisy, he soon became known as the village cook, much to Mrs Castle's pride when she had heard about it.

He leant against the wall, underneath the huge seventeenth-century steelyard arm protruding from the gable end of the pub. It had formerly been used for weighing farmers' carts and produce, such as hay and straw, before they went on to market. It could take up to four tons at a time and was reputedly accurate to within two ounces, or so Bert had told him when he had first got the job. But he was not interested in that now. He could not quell the nagging worry in the back of his mind.

Where was she? It was not like Rosie to be late. Had something happened? Maybe he had put her off? They had arranged to meet at the pub before going back to Fern Cottage for tea, for the first time since they had come to their understanding that they were walking out, as his Ma described it. Was that the problem? But why hadn't she said so if it was? Rosie already knew Molly from up at the House, so it couldn't be that, could it? She knew him well enough to tell him if she didn't want to go, didn't she? Questions tumbled into his mind like an avalanche that threatened to overwhelm him.

'Max, we need yer in 'ere!' yelled Jack from the snug door. Shaking himself free from his thoughts with a start, Max went back inside. 'Comin', Jack, sorry!' he said. 'Just bin checkin' the yard before we get busy.'

'Well we're busy now, lad, jump ter it!' he replied.

Just what he didn't need, swore Max to himself, he'd never get away early now.

Seeing the anxiety creasing his face, Daisy attempted to reassure him. She harboured lustful thoughts about him, secretly admiring the sight of his rippling biceps whenever she watched him manhandle the heavy kegs, imagining the muscles of his lithe legs, taut and pronounced beneath his baggy trousers as they strained to take the weight of each barrel. She definitely looked forward to delivery day. She dreamed about nestling her head against the contours of his broad chest and feeling his strong arms enveloping her as she snuggled against him. 'She'll turn up, Max, you'll see,' was all she could think to say but this time her tone was quiet and serious, all traces of her earlier teasing gone. His air of dejection struck at her heart and her throat tightened as she turned away to serve as the next man thrust an empty tankard across the bar in her direction.

Jack watched out of the corner of his eye as Max poured pint after pint to satisfy the thirsty crowd. After about 20 minutes of frantic activity he motioned for Max to get away, nodding his head in the direction of the door. Max smiled back at him gratefully and dropped what he was doing, making a beeline for the passageway.

''Ere, mate, what about me pint!' exclaimed the indignant man whose drink Max was about to serve.

'Now then, Charlie, stop yer fuss!' said Daisy quickly, adding before the man had chance to object, 'Yer usual was it, luv?' She smiled her appreciation at Jack for his thoughtfulness.

The last of the evening light was beginning to fade as Max hurried down the high street. He knew by now that something must have happened and he fervently hoped that it was just that she had got cold feet and not anything worse. By the time he reached the church where the high street bisected Long Lane, he had made up his mind to go home first in case she had gone straight to Fern Cottage instead of meeting him at The Wheelwrights. Deep down he knew that he had not mistaken their arrangements, but he was not sure what else to do. 'Please God let her be there,' he muttered, breaking into a run as he passed Clarke's General Store, before nearing the outskirts of the village and the little row of humble workmen's dwellings, at the far end of which, on the right, was Fern Cottage.

'Ma! Ma! Is Rosie 'ere?' he gasped as he burst through the front door, looking wildly around the little front parlour where Molly and Bert were sat waiting.

'Nay lad, she isn't,' replied Molly in surprise, startled by his sudden entrance. 'Whatever's the matter?'

Bert was on his feet now as Max stood there panting, his face a deep crimson red as his breath came in urgent shallow draughts. 'Calm down, lad! Calm down!' he ordered, placing a restraining hand on Max's shoulder, feeling him shaking as he did so.

'Rosie, 'ave yer seen 'er?' he demanded, his eyes darting around the neat little room. He was too consumed with worry to take in the small round table laid for tea with Molly's best white cloth that was carefully darned in two or three places. The faded blue of the Gordon family crest in the centre was just visible still if you looked closely, but Molly usually concealed it with her little china cake stand. 'She didn't come ter the pub like we said! I don't know where she is! Something must 'ave 'appened!' His words poured out in a torrent of concern.

Molly's eyes flew open in alarm. This was not like her son at all. 'Max, sit down!' she said firmly. 'Tell us what's 'appened, luv, quickly now!'

Max forced himself to do as he was told and hurriedly recounted what little there was to tell. 'So if she 'asn't bin round 'ere, we've got ter find 'er!' he finished fiercely. They listened with growing apprehension and Molly knew what she was about to say would upset him even more.

'Mrs Castle let 'er go early. Makepiece 'ad bin on the warpath again so she thought it 'ud be better if Rosie made 'erself scarce until things 'ad calmed down a bit,' she said with a steadiness she did not feel. 'I know that's right cos Elizabeth told me 'erself and she saw 'er go.'

'But that must 'ave bin hours ago!' exclaimed Bert, the tension mounting in his voice. 'Right, lad, 'ere's what ter do! You check yer usual haunts, any place yer might 'ave bin with 'er that she'll know. I'll knock up the lads at the stables and we'll check the grounds. Molly, get yerself next door an' see if Mrs Mears'll 'elp yer search the streets. Between 'ere and the pub first mind...' He hesitated. 'Yer don't think she could 'ave gone out on the moors do yer...?'

Refusing to contemplate that last terrible thought his father had left hanging in the air, Max shook his head vehemently. He had warned her over and again about getting lost on the moors after dark. Jumping up out of the chair, he bounded to the door, the handle slamming into the wall behind as he wrenched it open. 'Meet back 'ere in an hour!' he shouted over his shoulder. 'It'll be pitch black by then.'

He sped off towards the House.

Chapter 8

White-faced, Max stood absolutely still, not wanting to go any further. A look of fear trembled on his face as he peered through the darkness. The light had almost completely faded now but he could just see the outline of a figure lying spread-eagled in the long grass by the edge of the pond. 'No! no!' he whispered, 'no ... please no!' He felt his legs start to shake as he fought to control the panic rising in his throat. In the background he could hear the faint sounds of the stable lads calling out to each other in their search, as he slowly, but deliberately, advanced towards the prostrate figure.

He knew before he reached her. The long blonde hair was unmistakable. He bent over to touch her face, crying out her name softly over and over again. 'Rosie...? Rosie...?' The tears came as he knelt down beside her, unable to hold them back. 'What's 'appened ter yer?' he wanted to shout out but no sound came. His face crumpled and he put his hands up to his head. It seemed to Max that his world had stopped in that instant.

The distant voices had gone now and he was alone in the silence. He rubbed the backs of his hands furiously over his cheeks and blinked to banish the tears, but still they came, rolling unchecked down his face. 'I luv yer, Rosie,' he mumbled out loud, willing her to respond. He had never said it before and now it was too late. He touched her face once more and it was still warm. Gently, he stroked her hair and felt something warm and sticky on his fingers as they brushed the nape of her neck. It was too dark to see clearly but he knew it was blood.

Her life was trickling away as the crimson stain soaking deep into the collar of her Sunday best grew wider by the second. Anger mounted in his chest as he scooped her up in his arms, cradling her limp body close, pressing her gingerly against his chest as if to force his powerful strength and iron will into her lifeless form. He screamed at the blackness all around them, 'I knew it! I'll kill whoever did this! I swear I'll make them pay!' The shouts consumed only his mind, as they went unuttered.

He struggled to his feet feeling as if his legs would buckle beneath him. His hatred for the estate and his circumstances rose up again and he was shaken by its intensity as he stumbled in the direction of the village. These feelings, which were never far from the surface, threatened to swamp him, and they almost drove all thoughts of the fragile girl slumped in his arms from his mind. But he forced himself to think. He must get poor Rosie home, he thought, not able in his grief to focus on anything beyond that.

He made it back to Fern Cottage, half stumbling and half running, the tears still blurring his vision. The light from the gas lamps in the front parlour was blazing like a beacon as he pushed open the front door with his right shoulder. Mrs Mears was crouched by Molly's side talking in urgent whispers as he blinked in the strong light. There was no sign of Bert as Max laid Rosie gently on the settee, his arms aching like they never had before.

'By the pond ... found 'er ... like this ... bleedin'...' he managed to gasp desperately, his voice barely audible.

'I'll get the doctor!' cried Mrs Mears, springing to her feet as Max appeared.

'Out the way, lad!' barked Molly urgently. 'Let me see 'er,' she added as she brushed Max aside.

Leaning forwards, she peered carefully over the crumpled figure lying in front of her. Reaching for Rosie's wrist, she caught sight of the ugly wound on the back of her head and saw the livid red stain reaching to the waist of Rosie's neat little jacket.

'Hot water, quickly, the kettle'll be warm, and get me a cloth!' she ordered as she checked for any sign of life. Thinking she could detect the merest trace of a pulse, and praying she was right, she grabbed her best white cloth from the small table that she had so lovingly laid for tea earlier that afternoon, and placed it firmly against the patch of redness matting Rosie's beautiful golden hair, trying to staunch the blood still dripping from its core.

'She's alive, luv, but only just I'll be betting...' she said, turning towards her son. 'Where's that cloth? I need it now!'

Dazed as shock began to take hold, and still struggling to compose himself, Max handed her the cloth that always hung next to the range. His deep-brown eyes were dry now and the sobs that had wracked his body were subsiding, to be replaced with the occasional involuntary spasm as his body jerked in passive despair. He felt utterly helpless as Molly took over and he sank wearily into the chair, his gaze fixed unwaveringly on Rosie's deathly pale face.

At that moment the front door was flung open with a resounding crash and Bert appeared against the blackness outside, with the doctor just behind him. ''Ow bad is it, Mol?' he asked frantically. He turned an ashen grey colour as the doctor pushed past him and knelt down beside the settee.

'Leave us please,' he ordered, looking directly at Max and Bert as he fumbled with the catch of his black medical bag.

Max opened his mouth to protest but Molly silenced him with one look. Catching her husband's stricken face, she gestured with her eyes for him to take Max outside.

'Do as you're told, lad, there's nothin' more you can do fer the moment,' she said gently but firmly, 'Doctor Roley's 'ere now.'

Taking Max by the arm, Bert did as he was asked. They went next door with Mrs Mears and sat down in her little kitchen, which was laid out in a mirror image of their own. There were the few similar sticks of old, meagre furniture centred on a grubby, threadbare rug, with a battered but serviceable kettle hovering incessantly near boiling point on the top of the black leaded range, in which a smattering of mean, subdued flames could just be seen as the logs burned low.

'Tell us what 'appened, Max, if yer can,' said Bert in a tight voice as Mrs Mears made herself busy with the teapot.

Max sat there, motionless, as a rigid calmness now controlled him. He felt a jolt of absolute dismay in the pit of his stomach as he began to recall his actions since leaving the cottage. Tremulously at first, but then with increasing vigour, he recounted his first desperate search of the kitchen garden, thinking Rosie might have stopped there before setting off for the pub. He described how he had dashed through the hothouses when the garden had been empty, before thinking of the wild garden, and the place where he sometimes sat, down by the pond, when he needed peace and quiet to be on his own. His voice cracked when he reached the point of spotting Rosie's body in the gloom, and he fell silent for a moment, but he forced himself to continue, determined to get to the end.

'I shall never forget the feelin' of seein' 'er there,' he finished, his voice drained but resolute.

He looked at the two of them as Mrs Mears handed him a cup of tea. The cup rattled noisily in its chipped saucer as his hand shook badly, the sound disturbing the silence that had descended on the little room. Bert shuddered at the cold glint of determination he could see in Max's eyes. They had grown flat and dull during his account of what had happened but they suddenly came alive, blazing with hatred as he added, 'They will pay fer this, if it takes me fer ever.' It was a promise made in a tone that was so icily calm and so full of loathing that Bert shifted uncomfortably in his seat.

'Now, Max,' he cautioned, 'yer don't know what happened yet. Don't be 'asty, lad.' His blood ran cold as he saw the look on Max's face. He knew that his son had already decided the family were responsible but, as they sat there now, they could not be sure of that. 'Be careful, lad, jumpin' ter wrong conclusions...'

'*It was them!*' said Max with a finality that brooked no argument, 'damn them all to hell!'

Bert exchanged anxious glances with Mrs Mears who clapped a hand over her mouth in horror at what she had just heard. 'Calm down, lad!' he said for the second time that evening, but he knew he was wasting his breath. 'That's dangerous talk ... complete nonsense...!' His voice trailed off as Mrs Mears interrupted him.

'Drink yer tea, Max. There's plenty o' time fer that sort o' thing,' she said, wanting to change the subject.

His face, with its wide mouth set in a rigid and unyielding line beneath those vibrant dark eyes, dancing now with fire, filled her with dread. She had seen him grow up into the fine, strapping man who always had the time of day for anyone. She understood why Molly and Bert were so proud of him. She had gossiped with Molly about his attachment to Rosie, about how important she had become to him and how they had been relieved and excited to see that Rosie increasingly seemed to reciprocate those feelings. But she also knew implacable determination when she saw it and it frightened her. He possessed a strength that was almost shocking in its intensity and she was fearful of what it could one day do. The Gordon family, and all the rest like them, were all powerful. Their dominance of the lower classes was total and you crossed them at your peril. Max would be tossed aside without as much as a second thought. His spirit and will would be destroyed, snapped in two as surely as night follows day, ground into the mud like the remains of a cigarette under foot.

Max took a sip of the hot tea, feeling the warmth slowly course through him as he swallowed the sweet amber liquid. The first hints of dawn were starting to ease their way through the tiny panes of glass in the parlour windows, casting their gentle magic on the whitewashed walls. He was tired and starting to feel oddly ashamed of his tears. There would be no more, he vowed to himself, he had cried them all away and what mattered was Rosie. He knew now more than ever that he had to get away from this place and make something of himself. If he did not he would be consumed by *them*! All of a sudden he felt an overpowering need to be in his favourite spot high up in the hills, but he could not leave her. He had to know she would be all right, *if she would be all right*, and he felt the force of his bitterness at what *they* had done to her start to rise up again, pounding in his head with its evil ferocity. 'Stop it!' he shouted to himself. 'Think of Rosie!'

Bert watched him drink his tea, unaware of the thoughts going through his mind. He pushed himself up, out of the chair, and wearily made for the door. 'Better get meself ready for work, Max, it's time already,' he said. It wouldn't do to be late, although he wondered what reaction he would get from the household. They must have heard something of the night's disturbance, he worried. 'I'll go next door and see 'ow things are. You stop 'ere and finish yer tea,' he suggested, looking questioningly at Mrs Mears.

She nodded quickly in acquiescence. 'Why don't yer get yer 'ead down fer a bit, Max? Nothin' anyone can do until doctor says. There's an empty bed in the back room upstairs.'

'Thanks, Mrs Mears, but I'll be fine. I'm comin' with yer, Dad,' he said, jumping up to follow his father, despite the feeling of exhaustion that clawed at his aching limbs. 'I want ter know 'ow she is.'

Mrs Mears watched them go, the older man slightly stooped with weariness, the fatigue etched on his lined face, but with the steadfastness that Molly so admired, the younger one no less weary but with a youthful vigour and energy spurring him on, just as his father's once had. She was lucky to have them as neighbours, she thought, and she prayed for Rosie's safe recovery.

They pushed open the garden gate at the end of the low white picket fence separating the two cottages and walked up the narrow path to the front door with mounting trepidation. The lights were still burning and Max steeled himself to go in. He brushed aside the restraining hand Bert placed on his arm, paying no heed to his father's unspoken attempt to protect him from what they might find inside, and went in. Doctor Roley had his back to the door and was talking quietly to Molly, gesticulating carefully and precisely with his hands as he did so. Molly's face registered their entrance and the doctor spun round with a start. His face was inscrutable as he held Max's gaze in his for a second and then inclined his head towards the table, indicating that they should sit down.

Max did not move. ''Ow is she, doctor?' he asked quietly.

'Sit down, Max and let me explain,' he said, frowning at Max's stubbornness in ignoring his entreaty to sit down. 'She's suffered a nasty gash to the back of her head, which is not serious. She's lost a lot of blood and is very weak. I've cleaned it up and dressed it and given her a shot of morphine for the pain. I was just explaining to Molly how to apply the bandages. They'll need changing daily. It's the risk of infection we've got to worry about...'

'But will she be all right?' he interjected urgently, serious concern still clouding his face.

'Let Doctor Roley finish, Max!' said Molly, trying to remember what he had just been telling her about the dressings.

'She should be, Max,' he continued calmly, 'but as I was saying, we must make sure the wound stays clean and I can't be certain that there are no internal injuries yet.' Max's heart lurched in alarm. 'But she's young and fairly strong and with plenty of rest I'm pretty confident she'll pull through.'

'Where is she, can we see 'er, doc?' asked Bert.

'She's upstairs, in bed, where she must remain. I don't want her disturbed. You can pop your head round the door if you like, but she's sleeping now. She came round and was very confused. That's normal with a bad head wound and I gave her something to help her sleep. I'll be back before lunchtime but fetch me immediately if there's any change.' With that he snapped his bag shut and smiled sympathetically at them all.

''Ow could it 'ave 'appened?' Max asked him as he straightened up to leave.

'Now that's a question I can't answer, lad. Only Rosie can tell us that, if she can remember. But it'll be a while yet before we'll know and you mustn't worry her with your questions!' replied Doctor Roley.

'Now, Max, that's enough o' that,' said Bert briskly, 'we'll talk about it later, there's work ter be done first.'

Max was silent but Bert was not fooled and threw a knowing glance in his wife's direction as they watched him tiptoe carefully up the stairs.

Chapter 9

Max sat at Rosie's bedside, staring intently into space, oblivious to the familiar surroundings of his tiny bedroom. He paid no heed to them. Occasionally he gazed at her, sleeping quietly in his bed, but he mostly just stared at a spot on the wall above the black iron bedstead. He ached to be lying there beside her, but the sight of her heavily bandaged head would jolt him back to reality whenever he allowed his mind to deviate from its purpose. He saw the sunrise only dimly, seeing the dark shadows of the night growing gradually into the clear solid forms of well-known objects as if through a fine haze. A benign peacefulness enveloped the room in stark contrast to the horror of the night before, shutting all intruders out. He was lost in thought, concentrating like never before.

Max determined that from this moment on he would devote himself entirely to the future, *their future*, starting out as he meant to continue. The savage misfortune that had befallen them would become the catalyst to their success. He felt a renewed vigour to achieve his goal in life surge through him as he smiled grimly to himself. Only now it would include retribution for the perpetrators of this wicked act against them. He smiled again, and this time the smile was calculating and full of intent. He would show the Gordons, pay them back for the pain and suffering they had inflicted upon his darling Rosie; for all the years of slavery and servility they had inflicted upon his Ma and Pa and all the others like them. But one thing at a time, he reasoned. He had to free himself from the shackles of Lee Moor if he was to become rich. And he knew now that he would have to leave to achieve that. The realisation that his path to riches, and freedom, could not be achieved if he remained in the village had struck him like a thunderbolt the previous evening as he had sat with his father and Mrs Mears. His heart began to beat rapidly and he felt a tingling anticipation take hold as he thought of that now. He was both eager and apprehensive as he shifted excitedly in his chair.

He would do what he knew best. He had a natural flair for food and so he would work with that. He would make every second, every day, and every week count in his single-minded devotion to achieve his goal.

He would not let anything, or anybody, deflect him from his task. He did not know how long it would take, *but he would do it*, and he wanted, *no, needed*, Rosie to be a part of it. He sat back, elated at his clarity of vision; at last he had been able to answer many of the questions that had been swirling around in his head for what seemed like forever. He longed to begin.

He turned and glanced towards the landing as he heard his mother's soft footsteps creaking on the old wooden stairs, succumbing as he did so to a feeling of sadness at the thought of leaving his parents. For an instant a wave of guilt washed over him and he felt anxious for them, praying that they would understand and not see his departure as an act of disloyalty or abandonment on his part. He half rose as the door opened, pushing those thoughts to the back of his mind. They were for later; for when Rosie had recovered. Her recovery was what mattered now, for he also knew that he could not leave the girl he loved. Yes, he did love her, he was sure of that, and he willed her to get better so he could tell her, so that he could achieve so much for her.

'Shh,' he whispered gently, 'she's asleep,' as Molly silently entered the room.

She smiled tenderly at Max and bent over to check the heavy bandages that encased the passive figure stretched out on his bed. 'Doctor Roley said 'e would be back before dinner, Max, why don't yer get yer 'ead down fer a bit? She'll need us later but there's nothing we can do fer now. She looks peaceful enough.'

Knowing that Molly was right, but not wanting to accept it, he made to protest, but then checked himself. Standing up, he caught his reflection in the mirror that stood behind the white washstand in the corner of the room, and had to admit that he looked like he could sleep for a month. Abruptly, almost roughly, he jerked his head away, determined not to give in to this most basic of human frailties. He would have to be tougher than that to succeed in his quest, he told himself.

'I'm fine, Ma, honest. Yer right though about Rosie, there's nothin' I can do until she wakes up,' he sighed, 'I'll just 'ave a quick wash then I'll be off.'

'You're never going up there, surely ter goodness?' Molly replied, aghast at the thought he would go up to the House. 'Not today of all days!'

His eyes darting towards Rosie, Max put a commanding finger to his lips to stem Molly's outburst and, taking her gently by the arm, led her out on to the narrow landing. 'Ma, of course I am! Mrs Castle will be expectin' me.'

59

'But don't yer think it'ud be better if yer give it a miss, just fer a bit until Rosie is up an' about?' she said urgently. 'Mrs Castle'll understand, luv.'

Bert had told her about the vehemence of Max's belief that the family were responsible for Rosie's injuries, voiced with such utter conviction, and she was terrified of what he might do. She knew very well how he felt about the House and what it, and the family, represented to him. They had talked about it many times and his determination to make something of himself was one of the reasons why they were so proud of him. She understood his single-minded desire to break free from the subservience of their lives, but it would be disastrous for them all if the family became a target of his ambition. That was something quite different.

It was true that Makepiece behaved badly towards him, but that had always seemed to be so, ever since she had first brought him home as a baby. However, Her Ladyship, and Lord Hugo for that matter, had always behaved with a kind of aristocratic benevolence towards him and she frequently told him that, although she knew he did not believe her. She was desperate to avoid any conflict. If only she could tell her son why. Their future livelihoods depended on their continued employment and the goodwill of the family. But she underestimated her son if she thought he would deliberately do anything to jeopardise their situation.

'Don't yer fret, Ma,' said Max in a firm but kindly tone that invited no response. 'I'll be back as soon as I can. I'll ask Jack if I can get off early. Look after Rosie fer us.'

Leaving Fern Cottage a short while later, Max made his way briskly to Mount Royal. As he was walking around the side of the great house towards the kitchen, he noticed a horse and trap draw away from the front doors. It was unusual for there to be visitors at this early hour and he paused briefly to watch as it passed by, the sound of the horse's hooves clattering unmistakably on the gravel driveway. Above the small clouds of dust swirling around the wheels he could make out the solitary figure of Doctor Roley. One of them must be sick, doc's had a busy night, he thought to himself as he opened the kitchen door.

'Whatever are yer doing 'ere, Max?' cried Mrs Castle incredulously, in the middle of laying out strips of bacon in the heavy black cast-iron frying pan. 'Yer surely 'aven't left 'er, 'ave yer?'

'News travels fast, Mrs Castle!' said Max wryly. 'Ma's with 'er an' Doctor Roley's comin' back before dinner. She's sleepin' now. Isn't that the doc I've just seen leavin'? Who's sick?'

'Summoned 'e was. By 'er Ladyship I shouldn't wonder. No one o' them is sick as far as I know,' she said, jabbing her fingers skywards as she did so. ''Ow is that lass o' yers? There's been a right carry on 'ere, I can tell yer!' Fear and worry were evident in her voice.

Before she could say any more, Millie appeared from the scullery, her eyes red rimmed from crying. 'She'll be all right, won't she, Max?' she asked timidly. 'Makepiece says we'll just 'ave ter manage and it serves 'er right!' she blurted out between snivels.

Max's eyes hardened, instantly threatening and ugly. ''E said what!' he snarled, his chest heaving with fury at her words.

'Max, stop it!' cried Mrs Castle in alarm. 'She doesn't mean it!' she added, looking daggers at Millie, who stood there frozen to the spot.

They had clearly heard what had happened and Max was in no mood to stop; the reaction from the night before and the lack of sleep was making him light-headed. 'Serves 'er right?' he stormed scathingly, before beginning to laugh in an almost hysterical fashion. 'Is that all the bastard can say?' he demanded caustically, catching his breath as he sank down on to one of the chairs. 'That's mighty considerate of 'im,' he spat, his fists clenched and mouth contorted in rage. 'Well, well,' he said bitterly as Mrs Castle looked at Millie and jerked her head in the direction of the scullery, sending the kitchen maid scuttling back to the sinks.

'Listen ter me, Max,' she said slowly, sitting down beside him, meaning him to hear every word of what she was about to say. 'Yer don't want ter listen ter 'er, yer know 'ow she gets things all muddled. The important thing is ter make sure Rosie gets better. She will, won't she?' Max smiled thinly at her. 'Good! Thank 'eavens fer that. Now then, ignore t'others, particularly 'im,' she warned, meaning Makepiece. 'Yer Ma an' Pa don't want any trouble!' she added darkly. Before he could reply, not being quite sure of what she meant exactly, she caught the smell of burning. 'Me bacon!' she screeched, jumping up and rushing to the range. 'Get off ter the pub, lad, and look after that girl of yers!' she said without turning round. 'Be quick now!' she ordered, not wanting Makepiece to catch him there that day, 'an' let us know 'ow she goes on termorrow.'

Feeling utterly deflated and exhausted, Max did not argue. He rose from his chair and closed the door softly behind him as he went out, suddenly wanting to be back home, sitting by Rosie's side, talking to her, holding her hand, even if she could not hear him. But he banished those thoughts before they took hold. Instead, he steeled himself for the day ahead, preparing to fend off question after question as he was sure half of the village would have heard about Rosie. Gossip spread quickly in Lee Moor and he knew people were really only being kind, but even as Mrs Castle had been talking to him he had felt the urge for privacy, a strong sense that this was between the two of them, within their world, and everything and everybody else was outside that sphere. He reminded himself of his plan as he trudged on, and by the time the thatched gables of the pub came into view he had decided how to begin. 'Jack,' he called out as he went in through the yard gate, looking around him, 'Jack, can I ask yer somethin'?'

Hearing him calling out, Daisy came tearing out of the snug door and flung herself at him, her arms circling his neck before he had a chance to protest. 'We've been desperate, wonderin' what's 'appenin', Max!' she cried, not giving him a chance to reply. 'Where is she? Did yer find 'er? Why didn't she come? What 'ad 'appened?'

Her body quivered with a mixture of excitement and anxiety and Max felt overwhelmed by her closeness. Unravelling her arms from around his head, he stepped backwards, almost choking on the smell of her cheap scent as he patiently started to explain before suggesting they went inside. He wanted to find Jack. No point having to go through it twice, he thought resignedly to himself.

When the three of them were seated at the little table by the dartboard Max briefly explained what had happened, keeping his feelings to himself and trying not to appear too pleased when the arrival of the dray men's cart interrupted the flow of conversation. Daisy seemed almost disappointed when Max busied himself with the delivery for the next hour and kept throwing injured glances in his direction as he manhandled the kegs down to the cellar. When he had finished and everything was properly stored, and the empties were stacked neatly on the cart, the dray men stood at the bar for their customary pint on the house, keeping Daisy entertained with their banter. She revelled in their antics and Max smiled in relief, seizing the opportunity to talk to Jack on his own.

He carefully described the idea that had been forming in his mind. Jack listened intently, watching the expressions on Max's face as he outlined what he hoped to persuade Jack to accept. He could tell that Max was serious and determined, and as Max succinctly began to summarise the advantages to them both of his idea, Jack's mind was made up. He stretched out his arm and they shook hands on the arrangement. They smiled at each other, secure in the knowledge that neither would let the other down.

'Now home you go, Max. We're shipshape here. See you in the morning,' Jack said to his new partner, raising the palm of his hand as

Max opened his mouth to thank him. 'If your plan works we'll all be able to put our feet up!' he laughed, 'so one day won't hurt any.'

Max beamed at him and could not wait to tell Rosie. He shouted his goodbyes to Daisy with a cheery 'See yer termorrow, Dais,' as she continued the pretence of fighting off the two dray men, a flush of excitement enlivening her ample charms. She made no reply, but Max doubted that she had even heard him, focused entirely as she was on the attentions of her new companions. He walked quickly, his earlier tiredness replaced with an eager anticipation for the future. He felt confident of success, failure was not a word he had ever recognised, much less tolerated, and he was absolutely certain of his own ability and encouraged by Jack's faith in him.

Chapter 10

The horse and trap was waiting in front of the picket fence when he turned into the lane leading to their row of cottages. It was unmistakably the one he had seen leaving Mount Royal earlier that morning, not that Max had been in any doubt. The particular colouring of Megan, Doctor Roley's Welsh grey, was distinctive and there was not another one like her in the village. As he neared the garden gate the front door opened and Doctor Roley came out with Molly by his side. Max saw that his mother was smiling as the doctor was talking to her.

'Ah, Max, I'm just leaving,' said Doctor Roley as he climbed into his trap, 'your mother can tell you what I've said I'm sure. I must be on my way.' He turned and smiled at Molly who was untying Megan's reins from the fence. 'She's awake, which is a good thing, and groggy, but that is normal in the circumstances. I'll call round tonight. It's going to be a long haul,' he added, as he gave a gentle flick of the reins. 'Walk on, girl, walk on...'

Max stepped back to let her pass as Molly took his arm and led him indoors. 'She was askin' fer yer, Max,' she said, 'go on up and I'll bring yer a nice cup of tea.'

Max took the stairs two at a time as his heart leapt with joy. He was across the landing in two big strides and peering around the bedroom door almost before Molly had finished her sentence. His eyes swept the room in seconds and came to rest on Rosie who lay propped up on the pillows. Her eyelids were fluttering furiously as she imperceptibly turned to look in his direction, wincing with pain as she did so. Max was immediately struck by her paleness and, gazing tenderly at her, he swallowed hard and forced himself to smile broadly into her eyes. Her delicate face was wan and gaunt and, as he sank down beside her, he saw deep black circles under her eyes, which had lost their piercing clarity he so adored. He gently covered her hands with his as he bent over and kissed her cheek. The tell-tale signs of the horror she had experienced were etched on her beautiful face, but he did not allow his smile to falter.

''Ow are yer feeling, darling?' he whispered gently, and as she tried to answer, he touched her lips with his fingers. 'Doc says yer'll be fine. Just need plenty of rest, that's all,' he murmured and gently squeezed her hands in reassurance.

'What ... 'appened ... 'ead...' she managed to sigh, her mouth barely moving as she struggled with the bandages encasing her head.

'Nothin', luv ... don't yer worry,' he soothed. 'Yer just 'ad a bit of an accident, that's all,' he lied. He had to find out what had happened and he wanted so much to tell her about his agreement with Jack, but it would have to wait. A faint smile flickered on her ashen lips as she drifted back to sleep.

Max eased himself up from his kneeling position by the bed and sat down quietly in the chair that stood by the washstand in the corner of his room. 'I promise yer it'll be all right, Rosie,' he said, unsure whether she could hear him. 'I love yer, Rosie,' he went on, in a voice so full of emotion and relief that he did not recognise it as his own. Moving back to the bed, he carefully gathered her in his arms. 'Listen ter me, Rosie. We've so much ter do when yer better. Yer must get better quickly. Fight fer it. Now! Please! Fer our future!' He implored her with intensity, urging her on by his huge presence and strength of will.

She smiled faintly as her eyelids fluttered open again, slowly this time. 'I luv yer too, Max,' she said in a voice so low that it was almost inaudible. 'I will, luv, I will...'

He smiled again but this time his smile was broad and genuine. He lowered her ever so gently back to the pillows and sat down again in his chair. When Molly came up a little while later with his tea, she found him stretched out, his head tilted over the back of the chair and his chest rising rhythmically with each breath as he slept so deeply that he did not stir as she closed the door behind her, the cup of tea still in her hand.

The sound of a commotion downstairs woke him with a start and he pushed himself upright in the chair, rubbing his neck with his right hand as he looked around him. He blinked rapidly and looked over at Rosie. She was still asleep. He jumped up quickly, still rubbing the sleep from his eyes, and looked out of the window on to the lane below. A large four-wheeled barouche pulled by two chestnut geldings was stopped outside. The dark-green livery of the two coachmen sitting up on the front box seat was very familiar and he could see a crest painted in the middle of the carriage door. It was the Countess's carriage, he realised with a start, and he swore silently to himself as his mind began to race. He heard his mother's voice from the parlour as he tiptoed on to the landing, straining to hear what Molly was saying but unable to distinguish her words.

Slowly and deliberately, he descended the narrow stairs and stopped before he reached the bottom step. Lady Constance was standing in the middle of the floor as Molly hovered respectfully near her. She was a dominating figure in the small room, dressed in a grand afternoon gown of soft fluid silk in the palest eau-de-nil. The overall effect was extremely feminine and she carried an indisputable air of elegant luxury. Molly looked plain and down-at-heel beside her and Max felt his hackles rising as he noted the contrast between the two women, which could not have been more apparent.

Seeing him standing there, coolly observing the scene, Molly became flustered and her hands flew to her face in a gesture of confusion. 'Max, 'Er Ladyship has been asking after Rosie,' she said quickly, fixing him with a stare, 'in't that kind?'

Max regarded Lady Constance steadily. 'Yes, Ma,' he replied in a voice that was strong and cold. He gripped the banister rail firmly until his knuckles turned white.

''Er Ladyship is goin' ter pay all the medical bills,' continued Molly. 'We're ever so grateful, milady,' she said, turning towards Lady Constance as she did so and bobbing down in a half curtsey, 'aren't we, Max?'

Grateful! he screamed to himself, *grateful!* He stared impassively at the Countess and for an instant their eyes met. It was only fleeting but long enough for Lady Constance to comprehend: he hates me! She realised in amazement that his demeanour was not that of trepidation or fear but one of contempt and loathing. She nodded appraisingly at Max, suddenly aware that she had an enemy in the young man who had spent his whole life on or around the estate and who had been bound to them from birth. She did not understand it. 'Please keep us informed of the girl's progress, Mrs Chambers, and you must take the time you need to look after things here,' she said, drawing the encounter to a close.

'Thank you, milady!' said Molly, staring again at Max as he retreated quietly back upstairs without another glance.

He did not see his mother drop a second curtsey as Lady Constance swept her sable-trimmed stole around her shoulders and left. He waited until the sound of the horses pulling away from the cottage was receding into the distance before he came back downstairs.

'Ma, can I 'ave that tea now?' he asked. 'I want ter tell yer about my talk with Jack at The Wheelwrights this morning.'

Soon deep in conversation, neither Molly nor Max chose to refer to the visit they had just received, but both of them knew that a watershed had been reached, and crossed, in Max's plans for the future, and her heart swelled in a mixture of anxiety and pride for her son.

'Rosie,' he said softly, 'Rosie, can yer 'ear me?'

He had been sitting by her bedside since arriving home from work, only leaving the room when Doctor Roley arrived to check up on her, as he had been doing every afternoon for the last six months. The days since Lady Constance's arrival at Fern Cottage had passed in a blur of whirlwind activity for Max as he had immersed himself totally in his business, for that is what he now liked to call it. He still worked behind the bar at The Wheelwrights but restricted his duties to opening times only, and Jack had employed a young lad from the village to do all the behind the scenes preparation, much to Daisy's obvious delight when the strapping youth had turned up for work on his first morning. Max used the time that this created for him in the development of the catering side of the pub. He put all that he had learnt from Mrs Castle to effective use in the extension of the market dinners and the creation of his new midday specials, which were proving sufficiently popular to justify offering them four days per week. Word was getting around and they were beginning to win custom from the other hostelries in the area, which boosted profits handsomely. This was important to Max because he had struck a shrewd deal with Jack whereby they split the food profits equally between themselves.

When the little basement kitchen at the pub was not fully utilised in the production of the daily pub meals, Max had come up with the idea of using the facilities to bake and bottle other foodstuffs for sale to the Lee Moor general store. On these days he paid Jack rent and a small commission on what he sold, keeping the rest of these profits for himself. The meat and game pies, cakes, pastries, fancy pâtés, breads, jams, jellies and pickles, to name but a few from his range, were well received and he toiled flat out to produce enough to satisfy the early demand. Mr Clarke, who owned the shop, was a firm admirer of entrepreneurial enterprise and had promised to put in a good word for Max with the Area Retailers Association, of which he was branch president, when he saw that there was a market for the produce. In this way Max was beginning to receive enquiries for his goods from neighbouring towns and villages and he already had his sights set on Plymouth. He had decided that was where the real money was.

The years of helping Mrs Castle were paying off and he thanked his lucky stars for having had the foresight to keep all the recipes, menus and *aides-mémoires* that she had ever given him carefully filed away. They were proving invaluable now and formed the bedrock of his efforts. Her years of patient instruction in the growing and picking of the fresh vegetables and hothouse fruits helped him enormously in the sourcing of his raw ingredients; so much so that early attempts by one or two unscrupulous local fruit and vegetable merchants to sell him poor quality produce were quickly rebuffed, and word soon got around in that fraternity that Max was no fool. He had quickly found that he no longer had time for the kitchen garden run at Mount Royal and had at first worried about Mrs Castle's reaction when he summoned up the courage to explain his predicament to her. She had been delighted for him of course, and had handed him a whole sheath of new recipes and tips that she knew he would find useful. She was as pleased as Punch with her protégé and had refused point blank to accept his offer of free produce when he had tried to thank her for her help, telling him he needed all the money he could earn if he was to prosper in the long run. ''Ere today and gone the next,' she warned him, but that prospect preyed on his mind and he was ploughing every penny he earned back into the business to try and build a solid foundation.

'Yer never know what's round the corner,' Bert told him at the end of his first three months, when he had begun to hope that things might be working out. It was sound advice and he was never to forget it.

He worked day and night, seven days a week, spending every waking hour in the wholehearted pursuit of his ambition, searching out new customers and new sales and dragging Molly and Bert in to help whenever they could be persuaded to give up their precious days off. It was time they gave willingly. At the end of each long day he would collapse exhausted into bed to snatch a few hours of much needed sleep before starting all over again the next day.

And yet through it all he still found time for Rosie. 'Can yer 'ear me sweet'art?' he asked again, and this time Rosie stirred and smiled up at him.

She was making slow but steady progress, although she still found that she needed to rest in the afternoons after a morning of light work. She had not been back to Mount Royal since the accident and was secretly dreading that prospect, but she did not share those worries with Max, not wanting to burden him on top of all he had to do with the fledgling business.

'Rosie, wake up, luv, yer'll never guess what 'appened today!' he said, launching with enthusiasm into an account of his morning's efforts. He had been careful not to press her about what had happened, despite his deep-rooted desire to find out. His early, gentle attempts to coax the details from her had caused her visible distress. She just could not remember much about that evening, however hard she tried. Doctor Roley had explained that memory and anxiety problems were common symptoms of the type of head injury she had sustained and Max knew that he would have to be patient, even though he had a nagging suspicion that her anxiety was *because* of the accident rather than a symptom of it. Patient he was willing to be, if it meant that he would get to the bottom of why he had found Rosie collapsed and bleeding by the edge of the pond all those weeks ago, just before the family had left for the London Season.

Lady Constance had allowed Molly to remain at Mount Royal to care for Rosie, instead of accompanying them to Chesterfield Square as she would usually have done. With the family away in London she had been able to devote herself almost entirely to Rosie's recovery, and during this time together they had formed a close and loving bond. Molly had come to appreciate her courage and determination and her stoicism in the face of adversity. When the doctor had suggested Rosie undertake some light duties, Molly had thought for her to take care of some of the mending of the family's fine linens, arranging to have them sent over from Mount Royal so that she could remain at Fern Cottage, sitting quietly in the little parlour. Her skill with the intricate needlework that this demanded had both surprised and impressed Molly and she had encouraged Rosie to turn her hand to some simple dressmaking alterations and repairs for Lady Henrietta. The results had been just as good and the enjoyment that Rosie found in these tasks aided her rehabilitation.

She also realised she felt comfortable with the Chambers and considered herself blessed to have become a part of the family. When an anxious letter had arrived from Bow demanding her immediate return home after Lady Constance had sent word of the accident, Rosie had asked Molly to write and explain that she was remaining in Lee Moor and that she had never been happier in her life. It was true that she missed and loved her own family, but she knew that she loved Max too and her place was with him now.

Max had to grudgingly acknowledge, when pressed to do so, that the Countess had displayed great kindness towards Rosie. She had given Makepiece instructions that Rosie was to remain on full pay and had made him responsible for ensuring that Doctor Roley's fees were promptly paid. It was fortunate that neither Max nor Molly had witnessed the steward's reaction when told of her wishes, although Mrs Castle was present when Makepiece had expressed himself very plainly in the kitchen afterwards. It had led to another of their vicious spats, which was still simmering days later when Mrs Castle made her weekly visit to Fern Cottage with her basket of 'treats', as she described them, for Rosie. She had confided in Molly, who thought it wiser to keep the details to herself. They did, however, linger in the back of her mind and made her feel oddly disquieted whenever she allowed her mind to dwell on them.

'I've 'ad a great idea!' exclaimed Max, his eyes shining in anticipation as he came to the end of his morning's news: ''Ow about I take the day off termorrow and we go up ter the hills. It's Sunday, one day won't 'urt and it's luvley up there this time a'year. We could take a picnic, just the two o' us. What do yer say, Rosie? Are yer up ter it?' he asked with boyish excitement.

Rosie looked at his face, alive and full of eager charm. She sat up and stretched out her hands to him. 'Yes, Max, I'd like that very much,' she answered, smiling back at him, 'very much.'

Chapter 11

Max could not contain his joy as he pushed open the doors of The Wheelwright Arms and led Rosie into the snug. He was carrying a wicker picnic basket in his left hand as he guided Rosie to the only vacant table with his right. He had risen especially early that morning to prepare something special for them as he wanted the day to be a celebration. It was the first time Rosie had been out since her accident and she was looking and feeling much better; that he told her was worthy of the best celebration ever. The shrimps he had potted from the catch the day before were especially good and the bread was still warm. The day had dawned crisp and bright, and by the time they had left Fern Cottage, the autumn sunshine had begun to cast its warming spell on the distant hills.

They wanted to stop off at The Wheelwrights on their way as Rosie was insistent that they thank Jack and Daisy in person for the concern they had shown over the recent months, which had manifested itself in so many little ways. Rosie's misfortune had become common knowledge in the village and the village gossips had ensured that news of her progress was widely known. Their stroll along the high street was met with friendly smiles and nods and the occasional word of encouragement. The people of Lee Moor were very kind and supportive when one of their own was in trouble.

There was a throng of people around the piano laughing and clapping as Edward Clarke, the shopkeeper's son, belted out one of his well-known bawdy limericks, much to the delight of the watching revellers:

The comely young Duchess o' Dover
Loved ter roll with young men in the clover,
There was little to do, save rip a bodice or two,
And she managed that over an' over!

The words, sung with such gusto and enjoyment, brought a huge smile to Rosie's face and she giggled at the sight of Eddie's red flush of excitement and embarrassment as cries of 'more!', 'more!' reverberated

71

around the crowded bar. Eddie had seen them come in and he waved happily as he swept an upturned palm from one side of the room to the other, before bowing theatrically to his supporters.

'Give us another, Ed! ... There was an old man from Dartmouth ... That one! Do that one!' came a loud cry from the doorway as heads turned in that direction.

People from the main bar were looking in to see what all the fuss was about, wanting to join in the merriment. Max looked anxiously at Rosie, worried that the noise might be overwhelming, but she was beaming at the scene around her, laughing uproariously at Edward's antics as he continued to acknowledge the praise and good-natured abuse being hurled at him.

Bending down to whisper in her ear, his delight as obvious as hers, he caught sight of Daisy as she bobbed up from behind the bar counter. 'Let's just say thanks ter Dais an' then we'll be off shall we?' Rosie's grin as she glanced up at him, and the look in her dancing blue eyes, was agreement enough.

'Now then, boys! Now then! Remember it's the Lord's day,' cried Daisy in a half-hearted attempt to restore some propriety to the proceedings. To loud groans all round Daisy looked across at Max and mouthed 'Hello' above the din, as she too struggled to contain her laughter. Max mouthed 'Hello an' thank you' back, gesticulating towards the seated Rosie, as he abandoned his attempts to push his way through the mêlée.

Once outside, they breathed a collective sigh of relief as they were immediately struck by the peacefulness of the beautiful late September morning, after the tumult of the revelry inside the pub. Max and Rosie smiled happily at each other as they linked arms and set off for the hills overlooking the village, heading for the spot where Max had spent so much of his childhood. He was looking forward to spending the day alone with her, away from everything and everybody else. It had been six long months and they meant to make the most of their opportunity to spend some time alone together, just the two of them. The scar from the wound to her head had healed nicely but Rosie adjusted her bonnet with her free hand to make sure that it was properly concealed as a gust from the breeze rustled her long skirts, making them gently billow behind her. They walked on in companionable silence, lost in their own private thoughts.

Poor Max, thought Rosie, my Max... He's had a rotten time of it. He's so kind and generous and I'd have been lost without him, she mused, digging him playfully in the ribs with her elbow.

He turned his head towards her with a grin. 'What was that fer?' he asked in mock indignation.

'Fer being you,' she said gently and grinned back, looking up at him, her face glowing and vibrant as they held each other in their mutual steady gaze.

He stopped and deliberately placed the picnic basket down beside them. Then, slowly and with infinite tenderness, he kissed her, holding her face carefully in his large, strong hands, his long fingers delicately brushing her cheeks as he pressed his mouth to hers. She did not protest, responding willingly to the feel of his lips on hers as he enfolded her in his arms and held her. When Max slowly raised his head and looked at her as she opened her eyes, he thought he would drown in their dazzling purity as he held her close, feeling her body trembling next to his. His heart was beating faster as he softly released her from his embrace, bending down to pick up the picnic basket. They resumed their walk. Not a word passed between them; there was no need.

Soon they reached the foothills and they paused to catch their breath. 'Do yer want ter rest a bit, luv?' asked Max solicitously.

'I'm fine, ta!' replied Rosie impishly, feeling full of life for the first time in ages. 'Why, do you?' she said, with a mischievous smile. 'Come on, I'll race yer!' she cried, as she let go of his hand and ran off through the long grass, laughing back at him as she did so.

'Hey, that's not fair,' he shouted, holding tightly on to the basket as he set off after her. 'I've got this!' he roared, holding it up in the air for Rosie to see.

He was alongside her in a few easy strides and he grabbed at her waist to slow her down. She relented instantly, wrapping her arms around his shoulders as she held her face close to his so he could feel her breathing deeply as she regained her breath. This time it was her turn and she kissed his wide forehead, her moist smiling lips parting to reveal her pretty white teeth as she then tilted his head with her slender hands to kiss the tip of his nose. She brushed against the dark stubble on his chin as she did so, which sent a tremor tingling along the length of her spine. She giggled involuntarily at this unexpected sensation, causing Max to do the same. They collapsed into a heap of laughter on the grass, unable to contain their enjoyment of the moment and of each other.

'Oh, Rosie!' gasped Max, as she tore off her bonnet to let her golden tresses tumble around her shoulders, like a tumbling silken waterfall, 'I do love yer.'

His words sent a warm ripple of pure joy racing through her and she raised herself up on one elbow to gaze at him, her face hovering just above his. 'Do yer really, Max? Really love me I mean?'

'*Yes I do*, Rosie.' Suddenly a momentary feeling of panic struck him. 'Why, don't yer love me?' he asked in alarm.

She laughed again, softly this time. '*Oh yes* Max! *Yes I do!*'

Max breathed again and lay back on the grass with his eyes closed, savouring the sound of her words, spoken with such passion and conviction that he knew they were deeply meant. He sighed with contentment and opened his eyes to look at Rosie again. Her face was shining with a radiance he had not seen before and he reached out to stroke it, gently smoothing his fingers across her glorious cheekbones, fluttering them down over her neck and across her shoulders. They continued until they were lingering hesitantly over her breasts, tantalisingly unsure of themselves as a gentle blush started to creep across her iridescent face.

'Max,' she whispered softly, suddenly timid and a little frightened, but at the same time excited, 'no, we mustn't, it isn't right!'

A silence descended upon them, capturing them in its intensity and obliterating all else from their consciousness. They were at once reticent, and unsure, but yearning and excited. They lay there, perfectly still in the late morning sunshine, for what seemed like an age until slowly, and with great reluctance, they broke the spell that bound them, helping each other to their feet.

'Come on, luv,' said Max, as calmly as he could despite the pounding of his heart, 'let's go on shall we?' Taking her hand in his he said, 'It'll be lunchtime soon and we're not even at the granite cross yet,' unable to disguise the tremor in his voice.

They walked on, hand in hand, each lost in their own private reverie again. Occasionally they smiled at each other and squeezed each other's hand as if to seek reassurance that they were thinking similar thoughts. They passed Jolly Lane Cottage and gradually climbed on until they reached the granite cross, where they paused once more to catch their breath.

'Oh, Max, this is beautiful! It's so peaceful an' luvely,' said Rosie, looking around her in wonderment at the majesty of the scenery. It's so ... so ... luvely,' she finished lamely, unable to find the right words to describe how she felt, seeing it all close to for the first time.

Max nodded and held her near. 'It's my favourite spot in the whole world' he said softly. 'I used to come 'ere a lot when I was growin' up,' he went on, 'nearly there now, just a bit more to climb. Wait til yer see the view from the top! Ready, luv?'

Rosie nodded back, her eyes wide open as she continued to gaze around her. 'Yer so lucky to 'ave all this, not a bit like Bow,' she said, thinking suddenly of the narrow squalid backstreets of her neighbourhood.

'Yer've never told me about yer home Rosie, what's it like?' he asked.

'Shh,' she answered gently, placing a slender finger to her mouth, 'I'll tell yer when we eat. I'm starvin'!' She smiled tenderly at him, not wanting at that moment to be reminded of the deprivations and hardship of her childhood in the East End of London.

'Me too!' said Max. 'Come on then, another ten minutes at most,' he promised, gathering the picnic basket up once more.

True to his word shortly afterwards they reached the stile he had climbed over so many times before, and, perspiring slightly from the exertion of this final, steeper section of the climb, Max helped Rosie over it and on to the uneven path leading up to his favourite spot. As he did so, she hitched up her long cotton skirt and white petticoats with her left hand, holding on to his arm with her right, and he caught a glimpse of her slender, shapely calves and delicate ankles. Her smooth, pale skin shone like fine parchment and he longed to stroke it as he felt a warm stirring rise within him. She glanced down and saw him staring at her and she gave him a bashful look, feeling unexpectedly awkward at her shyness.

They scrambled up the steep path in no time and came to rest in the little hollow overlooking the valley and river beyond, which sparkled faintly in the distance as the autumn sunshine danced across its surface. Max unfolded the small carriage blanket that Molly had given him to tuck over the top of the basket and sat down, drawing Rosie down next to him. Taking off his short black jacket to reveal a broad expanse of white shirt, he spread that over the long grass too and together they unpacked the picnic feeling ravenous from their long walk.

'Ooh what are these?' cried Rosie, holding up two small bowls in front of her.

'Potted shrimps,' replied Max. 'An' there's some bread somewhere,' he said, searching around in the bottom of the basket. 'Ah, 'ere it is, it's still just warm if we're quick,' he explained as he unwrapped the small round loaf from the cloth that surrounded it. 'An' there's brawn an' cucumber sandwiches, chicken an' bacon pie, cheese an' apples an' sponge cake,' he added, opening the bottle of elderflower wine that he had wedged into the corner of the basket, pouring it into two small earthenware goblets. Handing one to Rosie, he raised his in the air and, with a mock flourish, proposed a toast, grinning broadly as he said, ''Ere's ter us!'

Not quite sure of what she should do, Rosie grinned back and held her glass level with his before taking a sip. 'Mmm,' she said as the unaccustomed liquid trickled down her throat, 'that's good in't it! Yer've pushed the boat out, 'aven't yer!' she exclaimed, as she cut them both a slice of the pie. 'No wonder yer customers come back fer more,' she said, as she bit into the succulent pieces of chicken and bacon, 'this is really luvely! Thank yer, Max, must 'ave taken ages, all this.'

Max could not help feeling pleased with himself and not a little relieved, for in spite of all the time they had spent together at Fern Cottage over the past several months, he felt that he knew her very well, and yet, at the same time, not well at all. And this was despite the strength of their commitment for each other. It was a feeling that left him oddly excited, eager to find out everything about her, to know her completely. They chatted happily for a while, in between mouthfuls of food, until they sat back, comfortably full and refreshed.

'I've never been ter London, what's it like?' asked Max.

'Big, noisy and smelly,' said Rosie promptly in reply, 'nothin' like 'ere. There's a couple o' parks out west, but not where I come from.'

'Is Bow nice?' said Max, interested to learn more about where Rosie lived.

'People are kind, most o' the time. It's a lively place, 'specially round the market. You got ter see it ter know it,' she answered, 'lots o' pubs, Max, yer'd be all right!'

He chuckled affectionately at her. 'Well, yer never know, luv!' he said, only half in jest, 'we might just do that one day. What do they sell at the market?' he asked, imagining it to be a world away from the Gordons and their life in Chesterfield Square.

Rosie caught his use of the word 'we' and looked sharply at him with a smile forming on her lips. She looked directly into his deep-brown eyes and sensed the seriousness of his words.

'Might *we* indeed!' she said in a soft but coquettish tone.

'Yes, *we* might!' grinned Max, suddenly nervous as he edged nearer to Rosie, his eyes betraying his longing for her. They were filled with a gentleness and intensity that he could not hide and Rosie rather timidly met his gaze as a feeling of apprehension and fear consumed her senses. He wrapped his arms around her and he felt her trembling under his touch, but she did not draw away. Carefully, and hesitantly at first, Max began to slide his hand across her shoulders and neck. Her skin was smooth and soft and she shuddered as his movements sent goose-pimples shivering down her back. He stroked strands of hair, like golden ribbons, from her face, being careful not to touch the back of her head, and she did not flinch as his fingers drew little patterns on her cheeks and neck.

'Yer beautiful, Rosie,' he said in a hoarse whisper, 'I've loved yer since that first day in the kitchen garden.'

'Oh, Max!' sighed Rosie, her eyes tightly shut, 'we musn't ... I've never...' as his hand brushed across her breast, sending her heart racing. She felt her face grow hot and her stomach tighten and she ached to succumb to the urgent sensation overwhelming her as she pressed her body hard against his. She could feel his chest rising and falling as his breathing quickened and felt his hands travel inquisitively over her, his touch light and insistent through her thin cotton clothing.

'Please, Rosie, I won't 'urt yer. We won't do anything yer don't want ter,' he whispered in her ear, sending more of the sensations flooding through her.

He paused and gazed at her in awe as she opened her eyes.

'Hold me, Max,' she said, wanting the security of his strong arms around her as her fear started to melt away.

She reached out and felt his whole body envelop her, imploring him silently to continue. Her hands shook as she fumbled with the button at the top of his shirt. Slowly he eased himself up and slipped out of it, the dark hairs on his broad chest glistening as his eyes never once left her face. His mouth sought hers and he kissed her again and again as he felt her respond with mounting intensity. Her hands caressed his back and caught on his thick leather belt as she sought his waist, feeling him struggling to contain his desire.

Max could bear it no longer and tugged gently at her thin cotton blouse, his movements clumsy as he trembled under her ardent caresses. Silently, he slipped out of the remainder of his clothes as she watched him, marvelling at his masculinity. Swiftly, she did the same and he gazed at her, mesmerized by her beauty and grace. Slowly they began to move together, awkwardly at first but quickly relaxing as he gently but exquisitely made love to her, their mutual inexperience dissolving as his adoration mounted expectantly. The sensations were unfamiliar but exciting, and she had never experienced such joy as she cried out, not wanting the ecstasy consuming her to subside. She felt as if her very being was laid open to him, although not a word was spoken.

Chapter 12

Rosie shivered slightly as a gentle breeze drifted across the hollow where they lay in a blissful daze, holding each other in sheer contentment. Max sat up and pulled the edge of the blanket higher, draping his jacket over her for good measure.

'I'm thirsty,' he announced, breaking the silence that surrounded them save for the gentle rustling of the trees. 'There's a bit o' drink left, luv, would yer like some?' he asked kindly, holding the bottle up to the light.

'Ooh, yes please,' replied Rosie, sitting up and scrambling into her underclothes and petticoat, 'an' I'm hungry again too!'

Max looked at her with a quizzical expression on his face, eyebrows raised, before bursting into laughter, unable to maintain his look of mock horror for longer than an instant. 'So am I!' he confessed, suddenly realising that he was too.

'Yer teasin' me, Max Chambers!'

He threw her a look of injured innocence as he rummaged in the basket for the remains of the picnic. 'There's a bit o' pie left, an' some cheese,' he announced, grinning broadly, 'oh, an' some cake, if yer like?' He cut a generous slice of pie and passed it to Rosie. Spying the cloth that he had wrapped the bread in out of the corner of his eye, he grabbed it and folded it over his left forearm, in the style of a waiter he had once seen in a magazine picture, and he jumped up. 'Would madam care fer some cheese?' he asked, just managing to keep a straight face.

Rosie collapsed into fits of laughter, tears streaming down her face. 'Max! Yer've nothin' on!' she cried in a scandalised voice. 'Someone might see!' She at once realised the ridiculousness of what she had just said. There was no one around for miles apart from the birds and the occasional insect buzzing through the long grass, and this realisation only made her laugh even more, until she was completely helpless and gasping for breath.

'It's not that funny!' he protested, trying to sound indignant. Max loved to see her like this after all that she had been through and felt no embarrassment at all at his nakedness, but nonetheless he bent down and slightly reluctantly pulled on his trousers. 'There, 'ow's that?' he asked, doing up the buckle of his wide brown leather belt.

'Well...' began Rosie as her giggles started to subside, 'yer've made me sides ache,' she complained, discovering that she really rather enjoyed the sight of Max's fine physique. 'I think I preferred it before ... yer could be one o' them gladiator figures I reckon.'

'Now who's teasin'!' laughed Max, sitting down beside her and putting his arm round her shoulders, blushing slightly. She nestled close to him. 'Tell me about yer family, Rosie?' he asked, changing the subject and feeling more serious for a moment. 'I'd really like ter know...'

Rosie saw the earnest expression on his face and regarded him softly as she took a little sip of elderflower wine, feeling the warming sensation spread deliciously through her. 'Me dad's name is Stan and he don't work much. Not 'is fault, he used ter, but he 'ad an accident an' lost two fingers an' the thumb of 'is right 'and. He worked at Smithfelds Market, cuttin' meat. Money's tight an' me mum an' dad can't look after us all. That's why I came 'ere.' She smiled at Max as she said that, before continuing. 'Me mum's Ivy an' she does what she can ter 'elp out, what with me brothers an' all.'

Max had been watching her closely as she spoke and detected an air of sadness about her as she mentioned her brothers. 'Are yer all right, luv?' he said anxiously, not wanting his interest in her family to upset her and spoil the day.

'Yes, I'm fine,' she replied, but Max saw her clench her fists as she said it. 'It's just me sister ... me an' me brothers 'ad a little sister but she died, took sick when she was four ... Grace, 'er name was, she'd 'ave been eight now,' she said, unable to hide the wistful tone in her voice as little tears of remembrance sprang to her eyes.

There was a momentary silence as Max searched for the right words but Rosie carried on, brushing the back of her hand across her cheeks, wanting him to know everything. 'I've got two older brothers, Richard, we call 'im Richie, an' Len. Richie's twenty-one an' 'elps dad's best mate on a barrer at the market an' Len, he's twenty an' good with 'is 'ands. He's learnin' ter be a carpenter. They both 'elp out with the 'ousekeepin' an' that. Then there's me little brother, Jimmy, 'e's gifted with 'is mind, mum says. 'E as a way with words an' writin' but 'e can only get ter school when me mum an' dad can spare the penny it costs. I send a bit 'ome fer 'im. It's a talent that musn't be wasted.' Her eyes were shining with pride as she finished and, as she turned to look at Max, he could plainly see how much she loved her family. 'That's it really. Yer don't 'ave any brothers or sisters then?' she asked him.

'It's just me an' me Ma an' Pa.' he replied simply. 'Lived 'ere all me life. On the estate,' a slight edge creeping into his voice as he said those last three words, 'but yer know all about that, luv, don't yer,' he added, consciously lightening his tone as he did so.

The momentary change in atmosphere, however, was enough to have them both pause for a second. 'Not much else ter tell. Me Ma an' Pa 'ave always worked fer the family.'

'But not you, Max, yer've never wanted that 'ave yer,' she said, squeezing his hand reassuringly, 'that's one o' the first things I noticed about yer. Yer different ter the others, like Sam an' Raymond. They're 'appy with their lot, or so they seem. But yer not, are yer?'

'No,' he said easily, 'I've never wanted ter spend me life workin' me guts out fer someone else, livin' the life me Ma an' Pa do, an' all fer a pittance. I want somethin' different, somethin' more than that.' His tone had grown fierce and his words came faster as he continued. 'The business is startin' ter work now, I think, and there's more in Plymouth, lots more I reckon!' He turned to look at her and Rosie could see the determination shining in his eyes. 'I've got fifty pounds tucked away already and that's just the start!'

She hesitated for a moment. 'I can't go back ter Mount Royal,' she said quietly, almost as if she was talking only to herself.

Max continued to gaze intently at her. 'What 'appened ter yer Rosie?' he asked softly, imploring her to remember something, anything, that might help explain how it was that he had found her lying unconscious by the banks of the pond. He had been so patient for these past several months, not daring to ask for fear of distressing her, but desperate to know. Rosie was silent for a moment, averting her eyes to look at the ground as if she was withdrawing into herself.

'I ... don't ... know,' she stammered. This time her words were so quiet that they were almost lost amongst the gentle background sounds of Mother Nature. 'I can't remember! I've tried ... I've really tried...' she whispered with a hint of panic as her voice trailed off.

Max took her hand and held it between his. 'Look at me, luv!' he urged, his tone kindly but insistent. 'Try again, please try...!'

Slowly raising her head to look at him, Rosie could see the anguish that tormented him, his eyes wide open, beseeching her to recall the slightest detail that might lead them to the answer. 'I remember cook sayin' I could go early. Makepiece 'ad been on the warpath again ... I was in the scullery...' A warning shot flashed through Max's mind as he heard that name. Her expression was taught and strained as she went on. 'I left the house...'

Tears sprang to her eyes and her hands began to shake. 'Hush, sweet'art, it doesn't matter...' soothed Max, worried that he had pushed her too far. The doctor had warned him about doing that.

'It's all right, darlin',' said Rosie bravely, her face fixed in concentration. Max let go of her hand and drew her to him in a comforting embrace.

'Did yer just slip ... or see somebody maybe...?' he asked gently, stroking strands of golden hair from her face as he listened intently to her every word.

'I don't ... think ... so...' she frowned, as she trawled the depths of her memory. 'Dogs ... barkin' ... not sure ... somethin' ... chasin'...' She slumped against him, feeling the tension that held him in its vice-like grip suddenly dissipate as she mumbled, 'It's all a blur. That's all I can remember!'

Max held her tight. They sat there together in the calmness of the grassy hollow, locked in an embrace that rendered words superfluous. Max tried to convince himself that he had heard enough to confirm his suspicion that it was more than just an awful accident. But, in truth, he knew he still could not be certain and he would not press Rosie any further. He consoled himself with the knowledge that as time went on she might recall a little more until, bit by bit, he could fit the remaining pieces of the jigsaw together.

Rosie shivered slightly. The afternoon sun had disappeared and a gentle coolness had taken its place. The mildness of the Indian summer would soon give way to the first light frosts and mists of autumn. The leaves had not yet started to fall but it would not be long before they formed their delicate carpet of blazing oranges, yellows and reds on the forest floor in one of nature's most spectacular displays.

'Come on, luv, shall we 'ead back?' asked Max, reluctant to break the spell that held them as he reached for his shirt that still lay crumpled where he had discarded it earlier. But Rosie did not move. 'What's the matter, luv?' he asked, suddenly cursing himself, thinking that he may have been too insistent with his questions. 'Was it somethin' I said?' he asked awkwardly, 'I didn't mean ter...'

Rosie contemplated her hands and seemed to be struggling to contain her emotions. Then, as if summoning up the courage, she blurted out, 'I can't go back ter the 'ouse!'

Max thought his heart would break as he looked at her but the dawning realisation that something inside her was going to prevent her from returning to Mount Royal came as almost a relief to him.

'But, Rosie, don't yer see, that's wonderful news!' he exclaimed, adopting the most cheerful tone he could muster, relief still flooding through him. 'Yer can 'elp me, I soon won't be able ter manage on me own. Yer can, can't yer?' He paused in his excitement and took her in his arms again. 'There's no need ter go back when the doc tells yer it's time, but that's not yet is it? Yer've a while before he declares yer fit, so there's plenty o' time ter decide what ter do.'

Rosie looked at him in surprise. She leant over and kissed him; it was a kiss full of passion, like before, but this time it was tempered with infinite tenderness and joy. They held each other for what seemed like an age, each secure in the knowledge that the afternoon had sealed their futures together; they had become lovers, partners, as well as just best friends and neither of them had ever felt happier.

They began to retrace their earlier steps, making the gradual descent that Max knew so well back to the village. They walked slowly, reluctant to bring their time alone together to a close, savouring the beauty of the landscape.

'We'll catch the sunset soon,' murmured Max, 'it'll likely be a good one.' He thought of the kaleidoscopic riot of oranges, purples and yellows that would soon explode in vivid strands across the evening sky, soaking into the edges of the clouds and topping the buildings with their jewel-like tones. 'I luv this time o' year, don't yer too?' he asked, smiling at Rosie as they held hands, pausing to look back at the ridge behind them, wanting to catch one last glimpse of their own private world, which now meant so much to Rosie too. 'It's almost like a new beginnin' I always think. The harvest is in an' yer can smell the change in the air as nature prepares fer winter.'

It was true enough, thought Rosie, beginning to understand what he meant and realising more and more how different life in the country was to the familiar surroundings of the city. 'It's not the same in London yer know,' she replied, ruefully, thinking of the chill fogs and damp squalor of autumn in the East End. 'Here it's different ... luvely,' she said, her face glowing with happiness as she looked around her, wishing the day could last for ever.

'Winters can be tough though in these parts. Indian summer, harsh winter, so the farmers say, and they're often right,' he said. 'Yer don't want ter be out up 'ere then, believe me,' he said with feeling. Then he laughed. 'I used ter go conkerin' round here when I was a lad!' he said, remembering the thrill of finding a conker before the squirrels.

'Conkerin'?'

'Don't tell me yer've never been conkerin'!' he exclaimed. 'Yer 'aven't lived until yer've been conkerin'!'

'Clearly not,' replied Rosie wryly, 'you'll 'ave ter educate me.'

'Consider it done,' he promised grandly. 'Yer speaking to the village conker champion of 1895 I'll 'ave yer know!'

'Oh my, an' I didn't realise. I do beg yer pardon!' she sighed, bobbing a little curtsey to him as she did so.

'Yer forgiven,' he said with exaggerated graciousness, 'on one condition mind.'

'An' what might that be?' she enquired, her fine golden eyebrows raised suspiciously.

He leant over and whispered in her ear. 'Max Chambers!' she cried in a playfully outraged tone: 'Yer incorrig ... incorregibal ...' She stuttered over the pronunciation of the word and not for the first time that day they were both overcome with fits of giggles.

Another five minutes' walk brought them to the outskirts of the village, with Mount Royal clearly in view ahead of them. They could see Home Farm in the near distance and Rosie gripped Max's hand more tightly as he started to point out the farm lads laboriously leading their respective pairs of horses yoked on to large heavy ploughs up and down the fields.

'Do yer know them lads work all year fer a measly eight pounds ten shillings! Not more than thirteen some o' them,' he hissed.

But Rosie was not listening. She was gripped by an inexplicable sense of foreboding that only receded when they were past, and the House was behind them. Max, detecting her change of mood, held her close and quickened their pace until he felt her relax again.

'We'll be all right, luv, just yer see,' he said quietly.

Chapter 13

'We're 'ere, lad,' said Tomkins, 'this is where yer get out.'

He brought the four horses yoked to the estate wagon to a smooth halt and turned round to look at Max. His large gnarled hands gently teased the reins as he waited for Max to jump down. He had a heavily lined face, which was tanned and weather-beaten from a life spent outdoors, loyally tending the grounds of the Mount Royal estate. He looked all of his 50 years of age. His manner was gruff and a little abrupt, but his grin was broad and genuine which belied the taciturn impression created by his dark, brooding eyes. There was, however, a softness in them which mirrored his nature and he was a popular figure with the lads on the estate, who found this comforting and reassuring. It was the softness in his eyes that had first put Max at ease when he was a small boy and a warm bond of friendship had grown up between them over the years.

Levering himself up from the pile of empty sacks in the corner of the wagon, Max stretched out his arms to ease his aching muscles, grimacing as he flexed his shoulder blades. They were stiff and sore from the effort of steadying himself in the back of the wagon on the journey to Plymouth and he was glad to have finally arrived. He looked around at the unfamiliar sights as he climbed down, excited to be there and keen to begin. He had only allowed himself one week to explore the town and he did not want to waste a single minute.

'Thanks fer the ride, Mr Tomkins,' he said, smiling up at the head gardener, 'hope yer pick up the fertiliser all right.'

'I'll be back same time next Thursday if yer want a lift home, lad, glad of the company,' he replied with a nod and a quick wave, pulling on the reins to guide the restless horses into the station yard, where he had orders to collect three tons of phosphate, enough to fill up the whole wagon.

Hitching the little brown bag higher on his aching right shoulder, which contained his overnight things and a few clean clothes carefully ironed and packed for him by Rosie, he waved back and looked down at the dusty marks on his clothes. With several vigorous strokes of his hand he removed the residual signs of his journey atop the old potato sacks and did his best to brush out the creases in his trousers. He needed to look the part if he was to succeed in his search for new opportunities, and Rosie had gone to a lot of trouble to improve the fit of the second-hand suit he had bought by means of a few clever alterations. It had cost him five shillings but he thought it money well spent and he was pleased with the end result. He considered it an investment in the future and he did not want it spoiled before he had even started.

The street outside Millbay railway terminus was busy and Max was unaccustomed to the bustle of so many people going about their business all at once. Suddenly he heard the insistent jingling of a loud bell, followed by a shout, behind him. 'Oi! Out of the way, mate!' Swivelling round with a start he realised the cry was meant for him as he saw a tram car bearing down in his direction. Stepping back hastily on to the pavement he watched it trundle past and he doffed his cap to the driver rather sheepishly. It was all very different to Lee Moor.

This trip had been in the back of his mind for a long time and he had begun to plan it in earnest after the afternoon he and Rosie had spent in the hills earlier that autumn. His catering and provisions trade continued to do well in the village and he was managing to put money away every month after meeting all his bills; so much so that Jack had jokingly suggested that they needed to renegotiate their business arrangements. It was said in jest but it reminded Max that his future was still reliant on the support of others, and that made him uncomfortable. He had gained a reputation for settling his accounts promptly on their due dates and suppliers now regularly contacted him in the hope of securing his business. He placed great store by this and was beginning to reap the benefits as they gradually came forward to offer him credit accounts, confident in the knowledge that he was good for the money. This had helped his finances enormously and he had begun to build up a small and growing surplus of cash, which enabled him to consider what opportunities might exist beyond Lee Moor and its immediate neighbourhoods.

He knew this was necessary because, despite his steady success, profits had levelled off and he needed to find new marketplaces, where he could reach new customers in larger numbers. He had confided in Rosie that he believed this was the only way he was going to continue to make progress in the pursuit of his dream ... their dream ... to amass riches. It had also become abundantly clear to him that he had to find his own premises if he was to achieve this, and that need was beginning to become urgent. The little steamy basement kitchen at the pub was really too small now for his needs. He had already ceased working behind the bar in order to devote all his energies to his own enterprise; he also wanted to try to break into the event trade, catering for parties and other special occasions and it was obvious to him that he couldn't do that from the basement of The Wheelwrights but he worried about there being enough scope for it to succeed in the village.

It was therefore particularly fortuitous timing that Tommy Sullivan had called in to see him the previous week. Max did a lot of business with Tommy, of 'Sullivan and Sons', purveyors of bread and fine provisions to the catering trade. It was a family concern and they had been in existence for more than ten years, during which time Tommy had established a network of regular customers throughout the South Hams area. He always enjoyed chatting to Max about his work and Max usually managed to pick up some useful snippets of information whenever Tommy paid him a visit. On this occasion they had been discussing Max's ideas for the event trade and Tommy had suggested that he consider Plymouth, where there were many wealthy and successful households. This had convinced Max that his earlier hunches about the area were right and that he should examine the possibilities for himself.

Looking around him again, Max rustled in the jacket pocket of his dark-grey suit for the piece of paper Tommy had given him, on which was written the name and address of lodgings. 'Just what yer need, Max, they're cheap but clean and tidy. Mention me name to Mrs Flanagan and she'll look after yer,' he had promised confidently. 'Used 'em meself many a time.'

'Number 2 Treville Street,' he read in the thin, spidery scrawl, studying the directions Tommy had given him. Pushing the crumpled piece of paper back into his pocket, he started walking, looking out for the street names he would recognise from the instructions. He was mesmerized by the sights and sounds of the town, most of which were new to him, and he felt the familiar stirring of adrenalin. There was too much going on around him for his senses to take it all in at once, so he decided to concentrate on finding his way to Treville Street. He continued on for nearly ten minutes until he reached the Assembly Rooms, a large and imposing building, which he thought must be as big as Mount Royal. He paused to get his bearings. At that moment a young man in a tattered black overcoat walked past, pushing a handcart piled high with fish. Max recognised them as mainly herring and mackerel, and he held out his hand to attract his attention.

''Scuse me, mate, I'm looking fer Treville Street,' he said boldly, looking directly at the man's face, which was partially concealed beneath a cap pulled down over his forehead.

Stopping, and putting the cart down with a thud, the youth straightened up and caught Max's gaze. Looking him up and down with an appraising stare, he replied, 'Yer not far, go down ter the end there,' indicating the direction with a sweep of his right hand, 'turn right in ter Gunter Lane and then second left in ter Southville Street. Treville Street is the first on the right after that.'

'Ta very much,' said Max gratefully.

'You 'ere on business then?' the youth asked, presuming from the sight of Max's smart grey suit that he must be a visiting businessman, 'yer not from round 'ere I take it?'

Smiling inwardly, and rather pleased that he had been mistaken for such, Max grinned. 'In a manner of speakin' I am. I'm lookin' fer new business premises as a matter o' fact.'

'What line o' work are yer in then?' came the next question, as the man seemed in no hurry to continue on his way.

The smell of the fresh fish had grown quite pungent by now and passers by were edging as far away from the barrow as possible, walking around the two of them on the far side of the pavement. 'Catering of sorts,' said Max, growing anxious now to bring the conversation with this total stranger to a close.

'Yer want ter try the Barbican then, mate, if yer know it. Plenty of places there I reckon.' He nodded and touched his cap as he bent over the thick wooden handles of his cart. He let out a loud grunt as he took the full weight of the mountain of fish across his shoulders before slowly trundling off.

'Thanks again, mate,' called Max to the retreating stranger, 'yer've been very kind!'

He set off again and in a few minutes he had reached the end of the street. Just as the man had said Gunter Lane was there, stretching out in front of him. The streets in this part of town were winding and narrow and paved with granite cobbles. They were bordered on both sides by tall buildings, wedged, cheek by jowl, some with white awnings stretching part of the way across the street in front of them. Max noticed one proudly displaying the words 'Webber and Sons, fancy leather goods', and he chuckled to himself as he wondered what a fancy leather good was. But he wanted to find Mrs Flanagan's house before he did anything else and so he did not stop to investigate. He was struck, though, by the wide variety of shops, houses and other buildings that were grouped together along the one street. It was certainly a lively area, he thought, as he hurried on, but not before he had taken note of the large number and diversity of people who were thronging the narrow walkways. Some of his fellow pedestrians were clearly engaged in their daily business, whilst others seemed to be simply strolling by. Good for passing trade he told himself as he turned into Southville Street.

His destination was about halfway down, on the right-hand side, just as the young man pushing the barrow had told him. Almost there, he said to himself, and he slowed to a saunter to enable him to take in the scene before him. On the corner of the junction with Treville Street stood a wide, glass-fronted building with large gilt lettering above the doors. Each letter stood out easily from the deep-red boarding behind them, which looked as if it had recently been repainted. 'Donovan's Dining Rooms', they proudly proclaimed. As he neared the entrance he could see the glass doors were constantly opening and closing with the busy comings and goings of the diners. Inside he could see there was an array of wooden tables, all of which were occupied by animated groups of people, mostly male, eating and drinking happily. He was tempted to go in but there was a small queue of people standing just inside the doors, waiting to sit down at the next empty table. Deciding he did not have the time now, he made a mental note to return later.

Treville Street was just like the others except that it seemed to be predominantly residential. Number 2 was a narrow, squat house at the Southville end, very near to the Donovan Dining Rooms. Stopping directly in front of the steps leading to the front door, he straightened his jacket and trousers, smoothed his hands over his hair and climbed confidently up them. The shiny brass knocker was in the centre of the dark-green door, and banging on it twice, he stepped back and waited. He did not notice the white lace curtain twitching in the downstairs front window, but very soon afterwards he heard the latch being turned from the inside and the door opened. A trim, upright woman with dark curly hair greying at the temples stood there, her hands on her hips and an enquiring expression on her rather angular face.

'Yes, can I help you?' she asked pleasantly, in an educated voice that Max had not been expecting.

'Is Mrs Flanagan available please?' he asked in his best manner. 'Tommy Sullivan sent me.'

'And you might be...?' she asked, displaying no flicker of recognition at hearing that name.

'Max Chambers, madam, I was hopin' you might have a room for a few nights?' said Max steadily, determined not to appear perturbed by her rather guarded manner. 'And is it Mrs Flanagan I'm speakin' to?' he added rather correctly.

'Yes it is, Mr Chambers,' she said, suddenly breaking into a wide grin, 'do come in. And how is Mr Sullivan? Such a nice man you know.'

Max smiled back and stepped into the dark hallway, deciding that she was no more educated than he was. 'Very well, thank yer,' he said, 'he suggested I try 'ere first, with 'im being a regular of yers.'

'How long will you be stoppin'? The room at the front is vacant if yer interested,' she asked. 'It's four shillings a week. That's fair for round these parts you know,' she stated slightly defensively.

Max just managed to stop himself from jumping in too quickly, sensing that he should not appear too keen, but feeling a little unsure whether or not her question and tone represented an invitation to barter. 'I'm in town until next Thursday. Does that include breakfast and use o' the bathroom?' he replied. 'I shall be out most o' the time on business,' he added, slightly importantly.

'Of course, Mr Chambers,' she answered stiffly, clasping her hands in front of her apron, so that Max thought for a moment he might have gone too far. 'Would you care to see the room?'

'Yes please, Mrs Flanagan,' said Max in a dignified tone, 'that would be very kind of you.'

'This way then,' she motioned, leading the way to the stairs at the back of the hallway. 'Through there is the front parlour, which I allow my guests to use in the evenings,' she said, indicating a room off to the right of the hall, at the bottom of the staircase. At the top of the stairs she announced, 'And this is the room,' pointing to the doorway at the other end of the short landing. Pushing open the door she stepped aside to let Max enter.

The bedroom was fairly small but perfectly adequate and Max accepted it on the spot, digging in his pocket for four shilling pieces as he said firmly, 'I'll take it!'

Chapter 14

It did not take Max many minutes to unpack the few belongings he had brought with him, and so, shortly after his introduction to Mrs Flanagan, he was ready to go back out to begin his search. He had almost reached the front door when Mrs Flanagan caught him in the hallway, rushing from the back kitchen as soon as she heard his footsteps on the stairs.

'Is everything satisfactory, Mr Chambers?' she enquired in her best landlady's voice, her neatly trimmed dark eyebrows raised in expectation of a suitably positive answer.

'Very satisfactory thank you, Mrs Flanagan,' replied Max, smiling inwardly as he saw the expression on her slightly pinched face.

'Going out so soon,' she said, managing to make the statement sound more like a question. Max had already realised that she was possessed of an inquisitive nature and he had no intention of yielding to her prying questions. He was used to dealing with people like Mrs Flanagan from his years of working behind the bar of The Wheelwrights, and so, with a firm but pleasant smile on his face, he fixed her with a steady gaze.

'Yes indeed, Mrs Flanagan, no time like the present is there,' he asserted in a manner that he hoped did not invite a response, edging nearer to the door as he did so.

'Can I help with directions anywhere...?' she asked cannily, determined not to be deterred.

He did actually need help to find the Barbican area, he conceded, which was where he planned to go first of all, as the young barrow man had suggested. He had seemed to be an honest and helpful individual and their brief encounter that morning had filled Max with hope and a resolute confidence for the task ahead.

He managed to obtain the necessary information in a manner that left Mrs Flanagan's curiosity suitably sated and, as he cheerfully walked back past Donovan's Dining Rooms, which seemed to be just as busy as before, he retraced his earlier route to the Assembly Rooms, from where he would pick up her directions. Leaving the familiar streets behind him, he found his new surroundings to be completely different but no less exhilarating. He was beginning to warm to this strange town, and his expectations of the opportunities he might find there were growing almost by the minute. It was much larger and busier than he had imagined and a lesser character could easily have been overawed by its sheer scale and complexity after the cosiness and tranquillity of Lee Moor, but Max was not in the least intimidated. He was excited and full of eager anticipation for the week ahead.

Plymouth had grown dramatically since his father was a boy, helped by the advent of the South Devon Railway, which had opened up the area tremendously, and what Max was seeing now was really an amalgam of the three separate towns of Plymouth, Devonport and Stonehouse, stretching across the peninsula between the estuaries of the Tamar and the Plym. When the weather was clear, as it was on this day, the blue edge of Dartmoor was distinctly visible to the north east.

As he strode purposefully on, he gazed in wonderment at the monumental buildings that had taken the place of the smaller, more homely terraces around Treville Street. They had a magnificence and majesty about them, which he found inspiring; he regarded them as statements of power and success which, to his mind, reflected the permanence and security of great wealth. In fact, as he was to consider later, all the things he was striving for and determined to obtain.

The wide streets were crowded on this cool but bright November day, packed with tradesmen and office workers rushing about their business and the fashionable gentry taking the morning air. The roads were busy too, with all manner of carriages jostling with tram cars and the occasional motor vehicle. Looking across the road from where he had paused momentarily to savour the atmosphere, he instantly noticed two uniformed men standing smartly on the opposite pavement, outside the imposing porticoed entrance of one of the grand edifices. It was their appearance that caught his eye; they looked remarkably similar to his father when he was dressed in his best coachman's livery. I wonder what that is? he said to himself, gazing at the impressive façade rising three storeys from the ground behind them. The two men were dwarfed by four huge columns supporting the rather ostentatious portico, which was reminiscent of Mount Royal, and for a moment Max felt a sinking feeling in the pit of his stomach. However, decisively taking a deep breath, he conquered the sensation that threatened to blacken his mood and, quickly looking to the left and right, he crossed over.

Big, bold letters proclaimed it to be 'The Royal Hotel' and, as he neared the entrance, Max could see the same name inscribed on the shiny brass nameplate prominently displayed at street level. 'Welcome to the Royal Hotel, sir,' said one of the uniformed men, discreetly bowing his head as he opened one of the tall glass doors before stepping aside to let Max enter. This was all accomplished in one single action, such that Max found himself inside before he fully realised what was happening. The splendour of the sight that greeted him almost took his breath away, and just for a moment he felt a little overawed. The lobby of the Royal Hotel was designed to impress on a grand scale. Splendid dark wood panelling adorned double height walls and a massive crystal chandelier was suspended from the centre of the glass cupola above. Marble fireplaces glowed on each wall and, in the centre of the floor stood an enormous ornate round table, upon which was placed the biggest flower display Max had ever seen.

He recovered his composure quickly and sat down on one of the many armchairs that were arranged in twos and threes on the polished marble floor. Feeling slightly uncomfortable, as if all eyes were upon him, Max picked up *The Times* newspaper that was one of several laid in neat rows on the rectangular wooden table in front of him. His eyes, however, were roving all around, and everywhere he looked there was something going on. An elderly, distinguished looking couple were talking to the hall porter who seemed to be explaining something to them. There was a small group of people at the front desk dealing with the frock-coated man behind it, his head nodding vigorously as he spoke animatedly to them. Liveried footmen were silently gliding to and fro, serving food and drinks in fine bone china to guests sitting comfortably in the other chairs. Occasionally a peal of laughter could be heard rising above the genteel background murmur of conversation. A bellboy struggled past with a heavy suitcase in each hand, followed by a young well-dressed lady with two small dogs on leads. There was an atmosphere of subdued vibrancy and the sense of prosperity was palpable. Max was fascinated.

'May I bring you something, sir?'

The voice at his left shoulder was unexpected and he was momentarily taken aback. Trying hard not to let it show, Max replied with the first thing that came into his head. 'Coffee please,' he said, in what he hoped was an insouciant tone. He anxiously checked his pocket for his money as the footman retreated with his order. He had not planned on this and did not want to squander his precious reserves on unnecessary frivolities. In no time at all a small silver tray appeared silently in front of him; on it was a pristine fine white and gold-rimmed bone china cup and saucer with a matching milk jug, sugar bowl and coffee pot. The coffee and sugar spoons were solid silver and he could see the hotel name discreetly inscribed on the end of each handle. Not a drop was spilled as the footman expertly poured the coffee before withdrawing with a gentle nod of the head, leaving the bill neatly folded in two beneath the sugar bowl.

Max was very impressed, almost spellbound, and as he took a mouthful of the hot, sweet liquid he knew he had found the answer. 'This is what I want!' he said quietly to himself, 'A hotel! Like this one!' He was mesmerized by the thought and he felt his heart begin to race. His hands shook with excitement so that his cup rattled on its saucer, making him quickly put it down on the table before the contents splashed over the trousers of his new suit. He had never felt more certain about anything, other than his love for Rosie, and in that instant he longed to be with her, to tell her how they were going to make their fortune. But that would have to wait he told himself, as he drained his cup and picked up the bill. Reaching into his pocket, he pulled out some coins and left them on the tray. He had so much to do before next Thursday and, buoyed up by his thoughts, he strode across the lobby to the front doors, smiling broadly at the doormen as he stepped out into the street. As he did so he turned round to look back at the imposing façade; *that was where his future lay.*

The Barbican was not far away according to Mrs Flanagan's directions and, as he walked on, his mind was racing ahead, a whirl of activity as he plotted and planned how to bring his tumultuous decision to fruition. To achieve it would take every ounce of his drive and resilience; his single-minded determination and stubborn tenacity, but, strangely enough and despite the odds stacked against him, he never doubted his ability to succeed. In fact he felt a strange calmness despite his frenzied thoughts, relieved that the final piece of the jigsaw had at last fallen into place. He was so engrossed in this new dimension to his plan that he barely noticed the change in the neighbourhood as he entered the oldest part of Plymouth.

The wide principal streets around the hotel and Assembly Rooms had become a maze of narrow winding lanes and alleyways lined with tall terraced houses and commercial premises, many with bay windows jutting out randomly across the street so that sunlight cast dark shadows on the cobbles below. Max sensed the difference in the atmosphere immediately; it was like that of a village within a town and after only one or two twists and turns he found himself on a broad cobbled quayside, alongside which were moored a number of small fishing trawlers. The quayside was a hive of activity despite many of the boats being still out at sea, and the loud call of seagulls circling overhead echoed around the harbour walls. At the far end of the quay Max could see two young boys selling onions that were hanging in strings from both ends of long wooden poles balanced across their shoulders. He could just hear the faint cries of 'Onions, onions, lovely onions' above the din of the seagulls as he stood there watching a trawler enter the harbour. The view out to sea was spectacular and as he looked on there was a sudden bustle of activity on the deck of the small boat as it prepared to berth alongside the others. A man who seemed to be the skipper was issuing a stream of orders to two men who were standing at either end of the boat, ropes in hand, and at the critical moment a third man and young boy leapt on to the stone quay to gather up the ropes as they were thrown ashore.

'Hello,' said a voice, 'yer took me advice then!'

Swivelling round in surprise, Max saw an outstretched hand thrust towards him. Instinctively taking it, he looked at the face smiling back at him and recognised the young barrow man who had helped him outside the Assembly Rooms earlier that morning.

'Me name's Billy, pleased ter meet yer,' he went on as Max smiled in return.

'I'm Max,' he said, 'pleased ter meet yer too, Billy. Fancy seein' you again! Thanks fer those directions. Found it no trouble.'

'So, 'ave yer seen summat yet?' asked Billy with genuine interest.

'No, not yet. I've only just got 'ere. Stopped off at the Royal Hotel on the way. What a place that is!' exclaimed Max. There was silence for a second as he mentioned the hotel's name and Max could see a look of instant surprise register on Billy's face, so obvious that the young man was unable to hide it. 'I was just passin' and didn't mean ter go in!' explained Max with a laugh. 'Not me usual type o' haunt!'

'Ooh ... fer a moment I thought yer were one o' the nobs! Yer gotta be rich ter go there,' replied Billy, with a look of relief on his boyish features.

One day, said a small voice in Max's head as Billy enthusiastically grabbed his arm. 'Come on, I'll show yer around if yer want. It'll be a while yet before *The Mermaid* is unloaded,' he said, gesturing towards the trawler that had just arrived, 'an' I'm not needed 'til then.'

With that, Max found himself led off into the maze of narrow streets by his new guide before he could protest. 'So yer work round 'ere do yer?' he asked Billy as they turned into a cobbled lane that was slightly wider than most of the others.

'Yep, I 'elp sell an' deliver the catch after the boats are unloaded. Been 'ere all me life. I work fer old man Masters. He's got four boats on the go so we're kept pretty busy.'

'What do yer catch?' asked Max.

'Mostly herring an' mackerel, sometimes flounder an' gurnard an' the smaller boat goes after the pilchards when they come close enough ter land,' explained Billy in an articulate manner that hinted at a depth of knowledge Max imagined to be unusual for a barrow boy.

Noticing a café further down the street, Max suddenly realised he was ravenous. It had already been a long day and he had not eaten since leaving Lee Moor shortly after seven that morning. 'Do yer fancy poppin' in 'ere, Billy? I'm starving!' he said, nodding towards the café.

'Me too! I've just got time if we're quick about it. Mind yer, it'll be a bit different ter Royal Hotel,' he joked.

'I'll just 'ave ter manage I suppose,' responded Max in such a dry tone that it had Billy wondering, just for a second, whether he was being serious. Catching each other's eye, they burst out laughing as Max led the way inside. They were soon seated with freshly grilled mackerel and a steaming hot mug of tea in front of them. Max was intrigued, trying to evaluate his extrovert, self-assured new friend as Billy sat there expertly running his knife along the backbone of the piping hot fish. With a few swift strokes he had extracted two clean fillets, leaving a neat mass of bone and skin on the side of the plate. Max was impressed. 'Yer've done this before then!' he commented with a grin.

'Only the once or twice! As I say, I've lived 'ere all me life,' said Billy, looking a little embarrassed at the compliment. 'So, what sort of catering do yer do, Max?' he asked, changing the subject.

Max found himself describing his business and his background in Lee Moor as if he had known the person sat across the table from him for years. He carefully told his willing listener all about his life at Fern Cottage and Molly and Bert's connections with Mount Royal and the Earl and Countess, although he left out the details of his antagonism towards the family and of his life with Rosie. As he spoke about his work at The Wheelwrights and how that had developed into the business he now enjoyed, Billy sat there quietly, engrossed in the story, looking at Max with growing interest. He came to the reasons for his trip to Plymouth as he drained his mug and sat back, thinking he had probably already said more than he had intended to. 'So that's about it, Billy, not much ter tell really,' he finished. 'Are yer still awake?'

Billy laughed loudly, his grey-green eyes twinkling in amusement. 'Very much so! In fact...'

'Hey! It's young Billy Masters,' a man from the doorway shouted out raucously, a broad smirk painted on his weather-beaten face. 'Skipper of *The Mermaid* is after yer, lad. Something about a load of fish!'

Reddening furiously, Billy jumped up, his earnest features looking crestfallen and embarrassed all at the same time. 'Got ter go, Max, sorry, come on down ter the quay when yer finished.' With that he hastily dropped a couple of pennies on to the table, which rolled on to the floor, and dashed out without a backwards glance. Max looked after him, a thoughtful frown creasing his forehead as he bent down to retrieve the coins. Running his hand through his dark hair, neatly trimmed by Rosie the previous evening, he sat back and wondered what he had been on the point of discovering about Billy Masters.

Adding his own pennies to the ones Billy had hurriedly left, Max got up and headed back to the quay. He had not expected the sight that greeted him; the harbour was now completely full of boats and those that could not moor directly alongside the quay were lashed together in rows two and three deep. They all looked to be remarkably similar, save for the occasional difference in the configuration of their rigging. The broad expanse of cobbles was teeming with people, all engaged in bringing the fruits of the trawlers' work ashore, where men in long white aprons and bowler hats were busy cleaning and gutting on a long line of makeshift tables. Heaps of turbot, sole, whiting, herring and mackerel, in fact all manner of fish, were piled high and gangs of barrow boys were stacking them in mounds on their barrows. The smell was overpowering and as Max stood there, trying to catch sight of Billy, he watched the bowler-hatted men conduct a type of Dutch auction. It seemed to Max's untrained eyes that pandemonium reigned but the steady stream of barrows departing after money had changed hands suggested otherwise.

'Over here, Max!' shouted Billy, waving his arms above his head from his position at the far end of the quay. Max saw him wave, but the sound of his cry was lost in the mêlée. Making his way over to him, Max passed a small group of boys smelt bashing with hand lines from a flight of stone steps leading down into the water beneath the local police station. There was almost a carnival atmosphere, despite the intensity of the activity.

'Sorry about dashing off like that,' apologised Billy sincerely, 'but yer can see why.' With a wide sweep of his hand he added, 'This don't wait for anyone. Tell yer what, this'll be goin' on fer another hour or more, how about we meet up on Saturday evening, if yer not doin' anything else?'

Max answered straight away. 'Yep, I'd like that. Whereabouts?'

'I'll come over your way, round Treville Street in'it?'

'Yer've got a good memory, Billy boy. How about Donovan's Dining Rooms?' said Max thinking of the only place he knew, other than Mrs Flanagan's front parlour, which he did not fancy at all. 'Six o'clock suit you?'

'It's a date, mate!' replied Billy, thrusting a fishy hand in Max's direction.

Chapter 15

Saturday dawned crisp and bright and Max rose early, determined to continue his exploration. He had spent the previous day trudging for miles throughout the area surrounding the Theatre Royal and the shops of Union Street, followed by the residential areas to the north of the town. He had then passed a solemn and gloomy Friday evening in Mrs Flanagan's front parlour. It was a small room dominated by several heavy pieces of dark mahogany furniture. The walls were lined with bottle-green wallpaper and a large aspidistra in an enormous round pot stood in the bay window, cutting out most of the natural light. The overall effect was rather depressing and it was hard not to feel overwhelmed by it. Max had at first been tempted to spend the evening elsewhere, but he knew he must limit his spending if his precious resources were to last the week. It was vital to hoard every available penny he had ruthlessly scrimped and saved to put towards his expansion plans. As he had sat there, writing down his findings and thoughts to share with Rosie, whilst they were still fresh in his mind, he had found himself worrying about what was happening back at home and how they were managing without him. These somewhat glum feelings still lingered the next morning, but after breakfasting on boiled eggs and toast, his spirits started to lift as he thought of the coming evening and Billy Masters. Gauging his moment to leave when the inquisitive Mrs Flanagan was busy in the kitchen, he quietly opened the front door and set out to explore the Hoe.

He walked briskly along, reflecting on his experiences of the last two days since arriving in Plymouth. It was a thriving town and it seemed to him that there were very good prospects for his supply business. He was confident of persuading the numerous shops and cafés he had seen to take his fancy consumables, which would enable him to widen his range and increase his sales. He was already thinking of creating a premium range with its own separate identity especially for the high-class shops along Union Street. This he reckoned would also improve his profit margins. The large mansions and villas in the main squares and terraces to the north represented potentially lucrative pickings for the launch of his events service, cooking for receptions, recitals and other gatherings; this he hoped would provide another boost to his earnings. The Barbican seemed to have a number of commercial properties for rent, although he had yet to establish their terms and there were also similar opportunities, although less plentiful, around Treville Street and Gunter Lane. He decided his first task on Monday morning, his first goal of the day, would be to investigate their suitability.

He realised too that there was a broad mix of people living in the town. He had noticed the strong presence of day-trippers and other visitors, and the townsfolk themselves seemed to go out and about in large numbers. It was so very different to Lee Moor. The local gentry and middle classes were exactly the sort of people who would buy his fancy foodstuffs, and it seemed to him that the workers engaged in the main manufacturing businesses, centred on the soap, cement and maritime industries, frequented the local pubs and hostelries on a regular basis. They would be the source of strong passing trade if he could establish an eating house here and, as he neared the seafront, he began to think particularly of the sailors from the naval base in Devonport who would be a strong source of business on their runs ashore. He would have to start with just one establishment, whilst keeping his business at the pub in Lee Moor going if he could, and then he would open his second, and then his third, and so on until he had amassed enough money to secure the ultimate prize, his own hotel.

He missed Rosie. It was the first time they had been apart for many months and every time he thought of her he found his mind starting to wander. This enforced, but necessary, separation made him realise just how much he missed her and needed to be with her. There was another five days yet before he would see her again and he groaned inwardly at the thought. But he consoled himself with the belief that it would be time well spent in the pursuit of their dream.

He caught the first smell of the sea as he reached the brow of a gentle hill, and in the middle distance he could see the masts of ships moored in the lee of an island close to the harbour itself. Ahead of him, although some way off, were rows of terraced houses beyond which lay the Millbay docks. Pausing to catch his breath, he stood comfortably at ease with his arms folded, looking at the scene below him. He watched as passengers alighted from a tram at the stop nearest to a long pier. They lingered before entering the pier itself to browse the carts and wagons set up by local traders at the entrance, each hoping to earn a few shillings with their bric-a-brac and novelties. A small pleasure fair was situated away to the left, its helter-skelter and merry-go-rounds lying idle on this November morning. At the far end of the promenade he could see the ramparts of the Citadel, built of sandstone and granite in the seventeenth century shortly after the town had withstood the long royalist sieges of the civil war. It was designed to guard the harbour itself, and just below it on the sloping grassy banks he could see sheep grazing and off-duty sailors strolling slowly in his direction, towards a tall obelisk that was surrounded by low chain-link fences.

He wondered what this pink granite column symbolised. 'In memory of Christian Victor, Prince of Schleswig-Holstein and grandson of Queen Victoria, who died in the Boer War…' he read as he went up to it. As he read the inscription Max thought of his father who had been determined to volunteer for war service, and of his mother's relief when he had been refused on account of his age. He was intent on making them proud of him and, standing there, with the light sea breeze ruffling his hair, he felt both humbled and proud to be part of the great British Empire, in a town that symbolised Britain's invincible maritime might. He was invigorated by these thoughts and by the success of his trip so far.

The sea was calm and there were one or two pleasure craft bobbing gently on the swell, weaving in and out of the path of the steamboat taking day-trippers out to the breakwater, situated about two miles south of the Citadel. It had been built to create shelter for the waters of the harbour and stretched for almost a mile across the central part of the sound. Max could see visitors taking the air along the slopes on the harbour side and others were waiting in a short line to re-embark the steamboat to return to the Hoe. He thought of making the crossing himself but that would have deflected him from his purpose, and he decided the time and expense could not be justified.

Looking at the scene around him, he was surprised to see it was fairly busy even though it was late autumn and he imagined it would become particularly crowded in the summer months. He could picture the small sea water bathing pools set into the rocks below him being packed with excited children splashing in and out as harassed nannies or indulgent parents looked on. Couples walked arm in arm along the promenade, the ladies smartly dressed and gently muffled against the cooling breeze; their husbands resplendent in frock coats and top hats. More off-duty sailors ambled along, gazing at the ships in the harbour and, here and there, individuals stopped to admire the view or to point out something of interest to their companions.

As he approached a large white bandstand he noticed a group of women huddled together in front of it, engaged in lively discussion. Suddenly, and without warning, they threw off their long outer coats, almost as one, to reveal vivid green, white and purple sashes emblazoned with the words 'Votes For Women'. Placards with the slogan 'To Fight, To Struggle, To Right The Wrong' daubed in white paint quickly appeared and, in one practised movement, they formed themselves into two parallel lines and started to march slowly along the promenade, towards Max. They created quite a stir with their strident cries of 'votes for women' and 'end this tyranny now', which they repeated over and over again. Very soon a crowd gathered to watch them in astonishment as Max stood there, transfixed. He heard some loud booing accompanied by ripostes of 'never!' but they were occasionally silenced by louder shouts of encouragement. A few passers-by turned away in disgust instead of joining the slowly growing throng, but Max stayed where he was, at the front of the heckling crowd, watching them intently as they paraded up and down the seafront.

He had never before seen such a public display of dissent and, as the determined band of protesters passed by for the second time, he looked at the faces of the women in the line nearest to him. *He could not believe it!* Staring straight ahead and marching in step with the others was Lady Henrietta Gordon! Max *didn't* believe it at first. He was incredulous, unable to take it in, his face registering his shock and surprise. What on earth was she thinking of? What would her father have to say? These thoughts ran through his mind as he pushed his way out of the crowd, intent on running on ahead towards the bandstand to catch them up before they turned around again. He just had to be sure he was not mistaken.

' 'Ere, watch out!'; 'Oi, what's your game!' Max was oblivious to the indignant shouts as he pushed his way back to the front of the crowd just before the marchers drew level with the bandstand steps. He reached the front row just in time. Leaning forward, he stared hard in her direction and then he knew he had been right. *It was her.* Just at that point the man behind Max pushed him sharply in the back, annoyed at his rudeness in elbowing his way past. It caught him slightly off balance, causing him to break ranks and stumble forwards. The commotion momentarily caught the protesters' attention and, in that instant, Max's gaze met hers.

Lady Henrietta stared coolly at Max, recognition flaring in her belligerently expressive hazel eyes. She was quickly past but the look had been enough. She had acknowledged him.

'Sorry, sorry,' he muttered apologetically to the crowd around him, as people were beginning to mutter.

The lady next to him tutted loudly, throwing him a disdainful look. Wanting to melt into the background as quickly as possible, he hurriedly eased his way back through the ranks of onlookers, many of whom were now jeering openly at the marchers. The mood was turning ugly and he sensed imminent trouble. As he reached the rear of the crowd he heard the shrill sound of whistles being fiercely blown and, looking up, he saw two policemen appear from around the right-hand side of the bandstand. They were running towards the women, waving their hands furiously. The crowd started to laugh and cheer as the protesters broke up in some confusion. A number of them defiantly stood their ground as the policemen drew nearer, including Lady Henrietta who linked arms with the ladies on either side of her.

Max stood and watched with amazement as one of the women started to run towards the obelisk, hotly pursued by one of the officers. She succeeded in chaining herself to one of the link fences surrounding it before he caught up with her. 'Votes for women,' she shouted loudly and repeatedly as he attempted to both handcuff her and release her from the fencing at the same time. His fellow constable meanwhile was gesticulating vigorously in a spirited altercation with the rest of the group who were still chanting raucously. Some of the crowd had by now melted away, leaving Max with a clear view of what was happening. The unmistakably high-pitched sound of more whistles reached his ears and he turned to see reinforcements running rapidly along the promenade from the Citadel. The protestors, sensing that they were about to be overwhelmed, hurriedly began to disperse in different directions.

The woman chained to the fence was the first to be arrested, but not before she had knocked her captor's helmet to the ground in a final show of defiance. Her protestations increased as she was led away in handcuffs, causing one or two of the remaining bystanders to clap enthusiastically. Max searched quickly for Lady Henrietta, spotting her running towards the bandstand with an officer in angry pursuit. He saw the policeman stumble and fall, which made her look round swiftly as the man rolled on the ground, clutching his ankle. She hesitated and, for a moment Max thought she was going to go to his aid. This was his opportunity and without thinking about the consequences of his actions he ran after her, intent on saving her from almost certain arrest.

'Lady 'Enrietta, quickly, this way!' he cried sharply as he linked his arm through hers and pulled her away.

102

Her bewilderment was obvious, and she looked at him with a thunderous expression. She opened her mouth to object but she was too out of breath to speak.

'This way, milady!' Max held her arm more tightly as he felt her try to break free. He spied a path leading down to the rock pools. 'Down 'ere, quick!' he ordered, glancing behind him as he did so.

'Let me go at once!' she gasped. 'How dare you. Let go at once!'

Her tone was imperious but Max paid no heed to her commands until they were safely below the promenade. 'Don't think they've followed us,' he said, nervously looking back along the path. He was panting too and concentrating now on the stone steps that led down to the edge of the bathing pools.

'Stop! Stop!' she hissed at him, 'I will trip over if you do not let go of my arm this instant!'

She pulled it roughly away from him so that she could lift up her long blue skirt with both hands to negotiate the uneven steps in front of them, which were steep and slippery in places. Max held back to allow her to go first and received a penetrating stare in return. They were on their own now, the crisis was passed, and he was suddenly conscious of her again as 'Lady Henrietta Gordon'. He felt his hackles rising as the old familiar feelings of antipathy started to overtake him. Don't thank me then, he thought petulantly as they reached the bottom of the steps.

He looked closely at her as she composed herself, adjusting her skirt and pulling the matching deep-blue jacket more closely around her shoulders with her right hand, whilst checking the clips that held her hair in place with her left. Her eyes were blazing rebelliously under the broad brim of her feathered hat and he was startled by the intensity of the expression on her face.

'I must thank you, Mr... I should call you Mr Chambers as you are now a man of independent means, are you not?' she said rather stiffly, although as Max later came to realise, without any trace of rancour.

It did not sound right to Max at all. 'It's Max, yer Ladyship, that'll be fine.'

'Very well then, Max,' replied Lady Henrietta, 'although you nearly pulled my arm from its socket.'

Max started to apologise before he could stop himself. 'Sorry, milady, but yer nearly...'

'Yes, I know,' she said rather contritely, but her eyes still betrayed her raging emotions. 'The Cause is worth the risk you see...'

But Max did not hear those last words; he was lost in his annoyance with himself. Why should he be apologising to *her*? Hadn't he just saved her from almost certain arrest?

'What were that all about? Votes fer women, I don't understand,' he said, looking her directly in the eye.

'It is a long story, Max,' she replied, 'and there is not the time now, but it is something I believe wholeheartedly in! We are fighting for the right to vote, to elect Members of Parliament. *To have a voice in the government of this country!*'

Her passion was obvious. Max could see that in her face and her tone was loud and determined. He found himself wanting to know more as his annoyance began to subside.

'I see,' he replied, although he didn't at all.

'And you, Max, what brings you to Plymouth?'

'That's a long story too, yer Ladyship. I'm looking fer premises ter expand me caterin' if yer must know.'

'Ah, I see. So, you *are* doing well then!' she said knowingly.

Max stared at her. Her words suggested that she had some familiarity with his affairs; what did she mean by that, he wondered? 'Can't grumble,' he mumbled cautiously and then fell silent. His guard was raised now and his instincts told him not to reveal any details of his business to her.

Lady Henrietta did not reply. Instead, she smiled graciously at him as she bent down to gather up her skirts again. 'I should be going, Max, do you think the coast will be clear now?'

'I expect so, milady, I'll go first ter make sure,' he said, taking control once again.

Chapter 16

Max smiled broadly as Billy pushed open one of the glass front doors of Donovan's Dining Rooms and walked in, his head swivelling from side to side as he looked around.

'Over here, Billy,' called Max, as he stood up from his table and raised his arm to attract Billy's attention. He greeted his new friend warmly. 'How are yer, busy day?'

Billy grinned back, pleased to see Max. 'I'm grand ta, what about you?'

'Same, mate, thanks. What'll yer 'ave ter drink?'

'Pint please, same as you,' replied Billy, nodding towards the half empty glass on the table as he eased his thin frame into the chair facing Max. 'Blimey, they don't give yer much room do they,' he said, as he surveyed the mass of tables packed closely together in the crowded room. 'Good job I'm not any bigger!'

It was true that there was little space between the round tables that were arranged to seat the maximum number of people possible. Those that were lined up along the outside walls were the most inaccessible, which meant that, in their struggle to reach them, the waitresses had to squeeze past other diners with plates of food and trays of drinks held aloft. Max had sat and watched them whilst he had been waiting for Billy to arrive, marvelling at their good humour as they squeezed through the narrowest of gaps, often dealing deftly with the wandering hands of less well-behaved customers. It struck him how important it was to have the right staff in an environment like this and how easy it would be for the wrong ones to wreak havoc with an establishment's reputation in a short space of time. He made a mental note to remind himself of that when his time came.

Seeing him squashed into the chair between the table and the wall behind, Max laughed sympathetically as he motioned for another pint to a passing waitress. 'Yer right! Sorry, it was the only one they 'ad left when I got 'ere. It's been busy ever since,' he said, trying to pull the table towards him.

'Always is I reckon. They must do a roaring trade 'ere. We sell a lot o' fish to 'em, I know that.' Just then the waitress appeared. 'Ah, here's me beer!' he exclaimed, smiling his thanks to the young girl. 'An' the service is good too.' Billy picked up his glass and took a long drink before placing it back down in front of him. 'So, how's yer day been?' he asked, eager to find out.

Max did not answer for a moment as he gazed reflectively across the table. Billy was thin and narrow-faced, with expressive and friendly features that were now looking quizzically in his direction. He was also wiry, exuding an air of self-assurance and reliability. His hair was short and very yellow, sticking up in tufts which accentuated the vivid green of his eyes. His skin was tanned and seemed to complement the colour of his hair. He was probably more than half-a-stone lighter than Max, but, nevertheless, his spare frame concealed unsuspected strength in his loose and lanky limbs.

'Interestin' ter say the least,' replied Max, thinking about his escapade with Lady Henrietta.

'Come on then, out with it!' urged Billy, intrigued by Max's response.

Max launched into an account of his experience on the Hoe, which had Billy hooting with laughter at his description of the policemen chasing the protesters. When he recounted how he had rescued Lady Henrietta he found himself being more forthcoming about the enmity he harboured towards the Gordon family and their way of life. He had been much more reticent when they were talking at the café two days previously, but there was something about Billy that made Max feel comfortable. It was as if he had known him for two years instead of two days.

Billy whistled softly as he signalled for two more beers. 'Whoa, that's some story, mate. Surely yer can't 'ate 'em all, can yer? After all, yer just rescued the daughter from arrest.'

Max nodded his head. 'I know and I don't know why I did that. It's odd, in't it? Spur o' the moment thing I suppose.'

He had been thinking about his act of goodwill ever since they had parted on cordial terms that afternoon. There was something about her manner that troubled him but he could not explain it. He would have been less perplexed had she been aloof, or even unpleasant, because he would have expected that but she had behaved with the utmost civility after her initial surprise. He had also been taken aback at her impassioned support for her Cause. He had not witnessed that side of her character before, or indeed been in such close proximity to her before; he was surprised to feel a sneaking admiration for her and he was not sure he was pleased with that discovery.

'I think I'd 'ave been 'appier if I 'ad of 'ated 'er. I wanted ter, but when she started talkin' I couldn't!' he admitted ruefully.

'Well, I think it was a noble thing yer did, Max, and I'm sure she's grateful ter yer. Now, what about yer business plans. Did yer 'ave any luck wi' them?'

Their drinks arrived before Max had chance to reply. 'Two beers, gentlemen. Can I get you any food with those?' The waitress smiled invitingly at them and they quickly scanned the menu that was propped up on the table.

'The steak an' ale pie with mash please,' said Billy. 'What about you, Max?'

'I'll 'ave the haddock an' chips please,' replied Max, fixing the young girl with a friendly grin. 'I 'ear the fish is very good.' He winked at Billy. 'It's busy in 'ere tonight, miss. Is it always like this?'

'Most o' the time, 'specially on a Saturday,' she said, rolling her eyes in mock despair. 'Better than being too quiet though. Time drags then.'

'And I bet the tips aren't so good!' wagered Billy with a chuckle.

'Fancy!' she exclaimed, winking exaggeratedly at him before hurrying off with their order.

'Hey, reckon she likes me, mate!' whispered Billy.

Max laughed, his eyes sparkling with amusement at his friend's boyish enthusiasm. 'The light's not good in 'ere, she couldn't 'ave seen yer properly,' he teased.

'You're just jealous she didn't fancy yer!' he retorted.

'Nah, I'm spoken for, mate,' said Max softly.

'Ho ho! Tell me more! Who is the unfortunate girl?' It was Billy's turn to joke now.

''Er name's Rosie an' she works at Mount Royal,' is all Max would say, lowering his eyes and becoming serious for a second.

Detecting Max's tone and not wanting to press him, Billy decided he should change the subject. 'So, come on then, what about yer plans?'

'Patience, patience... All in good time...' he protested, enjoying Billy's eagerness to find out. 'Tell me about yerself first. You were about ter tell me somethin' at the café the other day when yer were called away?'

'Ah, yes I was, wasn't I... But first things first. Let me explain about that man who interrupted us. He works for a rival fishing company, Reynolds and Clar, they've got six boats, two more than us. They've been trying ter...'

'Rival firm, Billy, two more than us...?' interrupted Max, raising his eyebrows. 'I knew there was more ter yer than meets the eye, Billy

Masters! Yer wouldn't be related to "old man Masters", as you described him, by any chance, would yer?'

'No flies on you is there, Max!' he declared, pretending to be surprised. Max chuckled in response. 'He's my father. Been in the business all 'is life, as I 'ave mine, an' 'is father before 'im. A family firm as yer might say. He's gettin' on a bit now and wants ter slow down. 'Is 'ealth 'as not been too good lately.'

'So why doesn't 'e hand it on ter yer? Don't yer want it?'

'Yer bet I do, but 'e can't afford ter give it all ter me, just like that. Reynolds 'ave been sniffin' around fer a while now, askin' to buy 'im out. But 'e doesn't want ter do that, wants ter keep it in the family if 'e can.'

'So what are yer goin' ter do?' asked Max, his brown eyes intense as he leaned forward.

Just then the waitress appeared with their food. 'Pie an' mash fer you, sir,' she said, handing the plate to Billy, 'and the fish fer you wasn't it?' she said, looking at Max. 'Can I bring yer anything else?' she asked helpfully.

'Some vinegar please, and two more pints,' replied Max, looking at Billy, who nodded his head vigorously.

'Right away, gentlemen,' she said, smiling again.

'As I was sayin', what are yer going ter do then?' asked Max, as they both tucked into the piping hot food in front of them. 'Hey, this is good, what's yers like?'

'Delicious!' mumbled Billy with his mouth full, before swallowing hard and taking a quick gulp of his beer as he gasped, 'Blimey, that was 'ot! Well, I'm not sure. We've got ter keep it in the family whatever it takes, or, at least, under our control. My grandpa 'anded it over with just one trawler an' a yawl an' me dad 'as built it up ter three trawlers with capacity fer a fourth. Maybe a trawl sloop would fit the bill. Business is good. We're sellin' all over now. We send hake ter Portsmouth weekly and we've just started takin' mackerel, herring and pilchards to the Channel Islands. The barrows take catch all over town, 'ere fer example, an' we've got carts deliverin' two an' three times a week ter surrounding parts, includin' Tavistock an' Launceston. It'll not be long before we get up country. London is our next stop.'

Billy's voice had grown animated as he described their enterprise in great detail and through it all Max could see the tell-tale gleam of excitement in his eyes. 'What's the difference between a trawler, a yawl and a trawl sloop then?' he asked, genuinely interested. 'I must confess I don't know anything about boats.'

'Size an' cost,' replied Billy succinctly. 'A trawler is normally forty ter fifty tons an' costs about five 'undred pounds new. That includes the net an' fittin's, which themselves cost upwards o' fifty pounds. A yawl is much smaller at eighteen to twenty tons an' a trawl sloop is in between at around thirty-five tons. But, an' 'ere's the point, it's cheaper than the bigger trawler but should produce as much profit as the larger boat. I reckon the future lies with the trawl sloops 'cause they only need a crew of a skipper, two men an' a boy, which is one less than the trawlers.'

Max was impressed with Billy's knowledge and experience given his relative youth. 'How old are yer, Billy?' he asked thoughtfully. 'Don't mean ter be rude, but yer seem to know a lot about the business already.'

'Nineteen,' he replied easily, 'but don't forget it's in me blood. I've grown up with it all me life. Anyway, yer a fine one to talk! Yer must be, what ... twenty-one ... twenty-two, somethin' like that?'

'Nearly right! Twenty-three, mate,' confirmed Max with a grin.

He had been listening so intently to Billy's explanations that he had not noticed the arrival of their beers, which had been placed discreetly on one side of the table whilst they had been engrossed in conversation. He took a long sip of his and looked across the table into the large square mirror hanging on the wall behind Billy. As he gazed at his reflection in the glass a mental image of himself flashed through his mind. He saw a picture of the successful businessman he wanted to become, and he knew that he was staring at an unexpected opportunity that might set him securely on the road to prosperity. Instinctively he felt he should seize it with both hands but his mind was awash with conflicting thoughts. Maybe he could solve the Masters' problem and make some money for himself at the same time, money that would be very helpful to the growth of his own business. He *was* trying to establish new sources of revenue, wasn't that why he had come to Plymouth in the first place? But could he afford it? Would Billy and his father be interested? He knew nothing about the fishing industry. But it could fit nicely alongside his provisions business, it was food after all. These concerns began to cast doubt and muddle his thinking, but the voice in his head was urging him to listen to his instincts; they had served him well so far.

'Max, yer food'll go cold... Penny fer 'em?' said Billy, giving Max an old-fashioned look. 'Come on, out with it.'

Max roused himself from his reverie. 'What would yer say if I was to buy into yer business? It might solve the problem fer yer dad...' he asked slowly, his eyes holding Billy's gaze.

There was a silence as Billy put down his knife and fork and wiped traces of pastry from his mouth with the back of his hand. He lowered his head and Max thought he had said the wrong thing. He began to curse himself violently. *Of all the stupid ideas, how could I...*

'Lemme tell yer about the new boat we're goin' ter buy,' said Billy quietly, the faintest of smiles hovering around the corners of his mouth as he looked back up.

For a moment Max hesitated, unsure of himself. Then Billy's face broke into the broadest of smiles. 'Yer don't mean ... yer like the idea...!' cried Max so loudly that heads turned to stare in their direction.

'Of course we'll 'ave ter talk to me dad, see what 'e thinks...'

Chapter 17

'Mr Chambers! Mr Chambers!' There was a loud and insistent knocking on the door. 'Mr Chambers, there is a visitor for you, a gentleman.' Max woke with a start as the sound of Mrs Flanagan's voice forced its way into his consciousness. 'Mr Chambers, are you there? There's a visitor downstairs!'

He sat up in bed and grimaced at the dull throbbing pain in the back of his head. 'Just a minute, Mrs Flanagan, I'll be right there,' he called, and winced as it got worse. He searched for his pocket watch but could not find it in the half light of the room. Pushing the bedclothes back, he swung his legs on to the floor and gasped as his feet touched the cold linoleum. 'Just coming, Mrs Flanagan. Who is it?' he spluttered in a croaky voice.

'He says his name is Masters.'

Max could detect the curiosity in her tone as he stumbled across to the chair in the corner of the room where he had left his trousers, even though the door was firmly closed. He smiled wanly to himself as he hurriedly pulled them on.

'Can you ask him to come up please, Mrs Flanagan,' he called, 'what time is it?'

'It's gone ten o'clock, Mr Chambers.' Her censorious tone was obvious. 'I don't allow visitors upstairs, Mr Chambers!' she bristled. 'I have shown him into the front parlour.'

'Thank you, Mrs Flanagan,' he replied as graciously as he could manage.

'He says yer expecting him. I'll let him know yer'll be right down shall I? Is there any message for him?'

'Yes please, Mrs Flanagan,' Max called again. 'No message thank yer.'

'Very well, Mr Chambers,' she said, unable to hide her disappointment. Max heard the sound of her footsteps retreating down the stairs.

He caught sight of himself in the washstand mirror and groaned as he pulled back the thin lace curtains, rubbing the sleep from his eyes as he did so. He poured some water from the heavy china jug that stood in front of the mirror into the matching bowl and splashed it on his face, shivering as its coldness hit him. Instantly it made him feel more alert. The recollection of the previous evening's celebration with Billy at Donovan's Dining Rooms came flooding back and he groaned again at the thought of how much they had drunk. He brushed his wet hands over his hair in an attempt to smooth it down as he looked around for his shirt. Billy Masters, his new business partner, he murmured happily to himself. That is, if Mr Masters senior approved of the idea ... he thought anxiously. They had arranged to meet this morning once Billy had discussed it with his father. He hoped Billy's early arrival meant that he had done so already and that it was good news. He reached into the brown bag containing his overnight things and pulled out a clean shirt. Slipping it on quickly, he hurried downstairs to rescue Billy from Mrs Flanagan, fastening the buckle of his belt as he went.

'Mornin,' Billy,' he said as he reached the parlour door. 'Blimey, yer look bad!'

'Me 'ead's about ter fall off,' whimpered Billy, sitting miserably in one of the armchairs.

The sound of Mrs Flanagan clearing her throat interrupted Max before he could reply. He peered round to see her standing behind the open door. He marvelled at the way she managed to sound both disapproving and curious at the same time.

'Yer'll have missed breakfast, Mr Chambers,' she said, with a hint of satisfaction in her voice. 'But I daresay I could put the kettle on, if yer think yer could manage a cup of tea?' she added drily.

'Thank yer, Mrs Flanagan, that would be very kind,' said Max, trying hard to keep a straight face.

'Mr Masters?'

'Yes please, Mrs Flanagan,' replied Billy meekly, winking surreptitiously at Max.

She bustled away and as soon as she was out of earshot, Max gave Billy an anxious look, unable to contain himself any longer. 'Did yer talk ter yer father then? What did 'e say?'

'Relax, partner, 'e wants ter meet yer.'

'*Partner!* Do yer mean 'e liked the idea then?' cried Max, the ache in his head suddenly forgotten. 'What did 'e say, did 'e talk about a price? When can we see 'im?'

Billy's face was wreathed in smiles as Max reeled off the questions, one after the other, unable to contain his excitement and obvious joy at the news. 'Slow down!' he protested, 'I'm not well...'

'Serves yer right. No sympathy, Billy boy!' He laughed delightedly.

'Yer a fine one ter talk. 'Ave yer looked in the mirror this mornin'?' retorted Billy indignantly, contemplating Max's pale face and tousled appearance.

'A good cup o' strong tea'll soon make yer better. We've got work ter do an' time's wastin'!' reassured Max. 'So when can we see yer dad?' There was so much to sort out, not least of which was agreeing the price and terms. Max wanted to see the trading figures before finally shaking hands on the deal and he was keen to get started as soon as possible.

'Midday 'e suggested. We've got a small ware'ouse near the quay, if we meet there yer can see the boats too.'

The rattle of china cups in the hallway heralded Mrs Flanagan's return with their tea. 'Here we are, gentlemen,' she announced tartly as she busied herself with the teapot. 'Someone's 'ad some good news by the look o' things,' she added, unable to resist the temptation as she took in their smiling faces.

'In a manner o' speakin', Mrs Flanagan,' replied Max politely. 'This is Mr Masters, my business partner.'

'Business partner, well...' she exclaimed.

'Thank yer fer the tea, Mrs Flanagan,' said Max quickly, before she had a chance to continue. 'Would there be any 'ot water fer a wash by any chance?' he asked, fixing her with a charming smile. 'We 'ave a meetin' ter go to an...'

'On a Sunday, Mr Chambers, it must be important...'

'It is, Mrs Flanagan. It is,' he said.

'Very well,' she sighed, 'but I wouldn't do it fer all my guests yer know.'

No, I don't suppose you would, thought Max, smiling at her again. As she left the room Billy could not help himself and laughed out loud, unable to stifle his amusement any longer. 'Shh!' whispered Max, 'she'll 'ear yer!'

'Sorry, Max, can't 'elp it!' Billy sniggered like a naughty schoolboy. 'I think she likes yer,' he managed to gasp between giggles.

'Oh no,' groaned Max, 'that's all I need. Wait 'ere, I'll be as quick as I can,' he added as he went out into the hallway. 'Is the water ready yet, Mrs Flanagan?'

He washed and shaved as quickly as he could, all the while thinking about the meeting ahead. He wondered what Billy's father would be like. He prayed they would get on, just as he and Billy had seemed to do from their first proper meeting at the café in the Barbican. He felt very sure of Billy, despite the brevity of their friendship, but he knew the relationship with Mr Masters senior had to work too; otherwise any future partnership would be doomed before it had even started. There was so much to discuss and the fine details had to be agreed before he returned home. Still, there were three more days yet before Tomkins was due back at the railway terminus.

He had decided to offer £150 for a quarter share in the business. That would give him a quarter share of the profits too, which would be about £80 a year if Billy's assertions were borne out by the ledgers he would ask to see. And he believed Billy implicitly. He knew the investment would stretch his resources but he had made up his mind that it was worth the risk. He had worked out that his ceiling was £200; he knew he could not offer more than that. You had to speculate to accumulate, he said to himself, as he pulled on a clean pair of socks and took a last look in the mirror before closing the bedroom door behind him.

'Come on, Billy, are yer ready?' he called cheerfully as he reached the parlour door, 'let's be off shall we?'

They let themselves out of the front door before Mrs Flanagan had a chance to appear from the kitchen, stepping out into the cold morning air. 'This'll blow the cobwebs away,' commented Billy as he buttoned up his short blue overcoat.

'Just as well,' said Max, 'I'll need me wits about me today.'

Billy gave Max a friendly punch on his arm. 'He's not an ogre, yer know!' he chuckled, 'an' I've told 'im all about yer.'

'That's settled it then, sunk before we start!' replied Max wryly.

They walked on in companionable silence and were soon threading their way through the winding streets on the outskirts of the Barbican.

'We've got time ter go ter the quay first. I'll show yer the boats if yer like,' suggested Billy. 'It'll be fairly quiet there at this time o' day.'

Max smiled his assent as Billy led the way. They passed the café where they had stopped for lunch before reaching the cobbled quayside. Billy stopped to point out the Tablet that had been erected in 1891 in the mayoralty of J. T. Bond to commemorate the departure of the *Mayflower* in 1620, but Max only had eyes for the boats. He spotted *The Mermaid* almost immediately, tied up next to the quay itself.

'That's one o' ours, isn't it?' he asked, before correcting himself hastily. 'I mean, one o' yers.'

'Yep, she is,' confirmed Billy, 'one o' ours.'

Max looked at him and smiled.

'Next ter 'er is the *Girl Jennifer*, an' over there,' he said, pointing to his left, 'is *Northern Star*. Them's the three trawlers. The yawl will be out fishin' fer pilchards. We call 'er *Faith*. She'll be back in later this afternoon.' Then, nudging his arm, Billy pointed further round to his left. 'Yer see that boat just beyond the buoy there, slightly smaller than ours? That's a trawl sloop. What I was tellin' yer about last night?'

'Yes, I remember. Surprised yer do though!' ribbed Max, invigorated by the sea air and the thought of the meeting to come. 'Where's the ware'ouse yer mentioned, is it far from 'ere?'

'Just round the corner,' replied Billy, with a nod in the direction of the police station.

The sign on the front of the building boasted large black letters neatly painted on a white background. 'H. & W. Masters.' In his mind's eye Max could see the words 'purveyors of fresh fish and fine foods' in smaller lettering underneath, as the seeds of a new idea started to germinate in his mind. The two-storey building was in a row of four that adjoined each other at right angles to the quayside. It did not look particularly big from the outside but, as they turned the corner, Max could see that a single storey extended a fair way back at the rear.

'Welcome to H. & W. Masters,' said Billy with a theatrical flourish of his arm. 'Me Dad will be out the back I expect,' he said, as he unlocked the front door. 'Dad, we're 'ere,' he shouted as he led the way in and along the narrow corridor leading from the front. 'The ware'ouse is through 'ere,' he explained as he reached a double set of doors at the end of the passageway. He pushed the left one open with his shoulder and motioned Max inside.

'Dad, this is Max Chambers,' he said to the old man standing in front of him.

Chapter 18

'Pleased ter meet yer, Mr Masters,' said Max, holding out his hand and looking the older man straight in the eye.

'Harold Masters, call me Harry,' said the old man, taking it in his firm grasp. 'Billy has told me about you. Welcome.'

'Thank yer, 'Arry. Billy 'as just been showin' me yer boats.' Max smiled tentatively.

'Has he? Oh, good. What do you think? I don't get around as much as I used to,' he said as he gestured towards some chairs. 'Shall we sit down?' he suggested, moving slowly and rather awkwardly towards them. There were four clustered around a small square table.

Harry Masters looked older than his years. He was 61 and in failing health. He suffered painfully from arthritis, which had prematurely aged him, but despite that he was still a formidable looking man. His face was heavily lined, like the seat of a well-used leather armchair. His hair was thinning but he sported a beard that was thick and bushy. Both had already turned completely silver. He must have been over six foot in his prime, thought Max, but he was stooped now, which made him appear somewhat shorter. His eyes were a distinctive grey-green colour and twinkled brightly under equally bushy eyebrows, although these remained jet black without a trace of silver to be seen.

'Billy has been telling me you'd like to buy into our business, Max, is that right?' he asked without preamble.

'Yes, 'Arry, I'm very interested,' he replied, trying not to show his surprise at the direct approach. He would come to learn that it was typical of Harry Masters. 'If the terms are right o' course,' he added quickly, not wanting to appear too keen.

'If we like each other, Max, we'll not fall out over money,' he said. 'Has Billy described what we do in any detail?' He looked unwaveringly at Max as he spoke. 'He tells me you are aware of my reluctance to allow an outsider into my business.' Max nodded. 'Billy is third generation and I want him to have something to pass down to his children. I could sell it lock, stock and barrel tomorrow you know; one or two of my competitors are constantly knocking on the door but they always get the same answer.'

He spoke quietly and Max had to concentrate carefully to hear what he was saying. His manner commanded respect. In fact Max was beginning to get the impression that Harry was not particularly in favour of taking on an outside partner after all. He was worried, but determined not to show it, and so he fixed him with a warm and confident smile.

'I feel exactly the same about my business, 'Arry,' he said, 'so I do understand what yer tellin' me. But that is precisely why yer should consider me.'

There was a short silence while Harry appeared to think about what Max had just said. He was also a man who followed his instincts. 'Billy, could you fetch some drinks please, son?' He looked enquiringly at the two young men. 'I'm sorry, Max; I should have offered you a drink. Please forgive my bad manners.'

Billy smiled to himself as he got up from the table. This was the signal he had been waiting for. Once given, it never failed. It was the sign that his father had passed judgement; the sign of his acceptance. Now it was up to Max.

'Tell me about yourself then, Max. You seem very young to be in business,' said Harry, as he shifted uncomfortably in his chair in an attempt to ease the pressure on his arthritic hip. It was said in his usual blunt fashion.

'I am young I s'pose,' began Max, 'but that is...'

He was interrupted by Billy returning with three brimming tankards, which he put down rather messily on the table.

'Got the shakes I see, from last night no doubt...' observed Harry dryly, as he looked from one to the other in amusement. 'Hair of the dog, lads, it'll do you the power of good!' he chuckled and his deep throaty laugh, which was in marked contrast to his quietly spoken manner, filled the empty room.

Max relaxed slightly but was careful to maintain his guard. He was beginning to get the measure of this well-spoken man who was now watching him with eyes that seemed to be partially obscured by unruly hairs trailing from his luxuriant eyebrows. But Max was not fooled, sensing Harry's penetrating gaze hold him like a fly caught in a spider's web.

'If yer say so, Dad,' said Billy, looking ruefully at Max. 'Sorry, Max,' he muttered, taking a sip and feeling it settle uneasily on his empty stomach.

'You were about to say, Max?' said Harry.

'Yes, I may be only twenty-three but I 'ave been runnin' my business in Lee Moor long enough ter understand a thing or two, an' my success should speak fer itself.' He watched Harry's reaction carefully. 'Not as much as yer good self of course, 'Arry,' he added quickly, lest he gave offence. 'I'm now sellin' ter a wide area around this part o' Devon and I'm set ter expand inter Plymouth.'

'This is your fine foods trade I take it?' asked Harry.

'Yes, that's right.' He glanced at Billy, pleased to know that he had briefed his father well. 'My impression is that there are good prospects fer it 'ere. There is the potential ter expand the range fer some o' the shops an' grand 'ouses as well. I make some of it meself and I buy other products ter sell on. I 'ave regular customers who buy from me an' it's makin' steady profits. Then there's the business at The Wheelwrights. That's the pub in the village. I 'ave a profit-sharing arrangement with the landlord and I want ter open my own independent establishment. Plymouth would be ideal I reckon. Both o' them fit tergether nicely.'

'A profit-sharing arrangement you say,' remarked Harry. 'So why are you interested in us?'

'Because I want more, 'Arry, *much more*!' said Max, with a conviction that was startling. 'An' I see our two businesses 'elpin' each other, a bit like a marriage if yer like.'

Harry was impressed with his honesty, although in truth Max could have been more forthright. It was not that he had been in any way dishonest; it was rather that he had chosen not to reveal the full extent of his ideas for maximising the benefit of a shareholding in 'H. & W. Masters'.

'I'm not seeking someone to come in and run the show. You would need to understand that.'

Max sensed that he was making progress. 'I don't want ter do that, 'Arry. I need ter concentrate on my own affairs. I have plans fer the next few years yer see, but we can 'elp each other.'

'We'd need to put a clear agreement in place to guarantee that,' he replied slowly. 'You say that now, Max, and I'm willing to take your word for it, but things do change. I've seen it happen too many times and that's when arrangements start to go wrong.'

Max nodded. 'I'd need ter see yer books of course,' he suggested in a businesslike manner, 'if we're ter talk money that is...'

Harry sat back in his chair and picked up his drink, pleased with what he had heard. Billy had been right. He seemed straightforward and had a direct way of speaking. He liked that in a man, having a similar approach himself. It was rare to meet someone as self-possessed at the age he was and he was certainly businesslike. It did inspire a certain confidence, he had to admit.

'I only want to sell a portion of my shares, mind you,' he warned, 'I meant what I said about keeping it in the family.'

'I don't doubt yer, 'Arry,' Max said firmly. 'I was thinking of perhaps a quarter holding.' He leaned forwards as if to emphasise his next point. 'With profits shared in the same proportion of course.'

'No, no!' he exclaimed in disbelief, the surprise evident in his voice, 'I was thinking more like ten per cent, fifteen at the most!' He certainly has nerve, I'll say that for him, thought Harry, staring across the table.

'But, 'Arry, the return on my investment must be big enough ter be worthwhile!' replied Max instantly.

'A quarter share would give you too much of a say in our affairs ... too much influence.'

'Yer can set the limits that make yer comfortable. I suggest yer write 'em inter our agreement,' countered Max, conscious that Harry was wavering.

'No, lad, you must think I'm simple!'

Max chose to ignore that, sensing the crucial moment had arrived. Without hesitating he said, 'I am able ter offer fifty pounds fer fifteen per cent or one hundred pounds fer a quarter share.' He sat back and saw Harry raise an eyebrow at Billy who nodded imperceptibly.

'And the profits, Max...'

'Shared every six months in proportion to shareholding,' he replied in a steady voice.

'One hundred and fifty pounds for a quarter share and I agree.'

'One hundred and twenty-five and it's a deal,' said Max, trying hard not to let his eagerness show.

Harry was silent for a minute and then, raising himself to his feet, he held out his hand. 'Very well, one hundred and twenty-five it is, subject to contract of course.'

'Of course,' said Max, 'and review of the books...' he added, with admirable aplomb.

A huge beam of excitement and relief spread across his face, which he did not bother to hide. *He could scarcely believe it!* He shook Harry's hand first and then Billy's, with such enthusiasm that Harry felt obliged to point out with a smile that he had only bought a share in the business and not the whole thing.

'Just make sure I don't regret it, Max, that's all I ask.'

'Yer won't, 'Arry, yer won't, I can promise yer,' said Max, as his mind already began to plot and plan his next moves. All he wanted to do now was to go home, back to Lee Moor, and Rosie. He could not wait to tell her the good news but there was so much to be done to seal the deal before then.

'I must be getting back to your mother, Billy,' announced Harry, interrupting Max's thoughts, 'I'll leave you to show Max around.'

'Right yer are, Dad,' answered Billy, his face brimming over with pleasure. 'I'll be 'ome later. Come on, Max, let's start upstairs,' he said, leading the way back into the corridor and up the stairs.

Chapter 19

It was late by the time Max got back to Treville Street. He opened the front door quietly and saw to his dismay a light still burning at the end of the hallway, which signified that Mrs Flanagan was in the kitchen. He tiptoed softly towards the stairs and had barely gone two steps when the door opened and Mrs Flanagan appeared, bearing down on him like a galleon in full sail.

'Good evening, Mr Chambers,' she said, coming to rest at the bottom of the stairs.

'Good evenin', Mrs Flanagan,' replied Max, with a gentle nod of his head.

'You're back late, Mr Chambers. I was just beginning to get worried about you as you hadn't said.'

Max stifled a smile as he ignored the admonishment. 'I 'ope yer didn't wait up fer me, Mrs Flanagan. There was no need,' he said, trying to keep the amusement from his voice.

'Oh no, I was just tidying for the morning,' she fibbed smoothly. 'Good meeting was it?' she asked.

Max knew she would have been sitting in wait for his return, realising she must have jumped up the minute she heard his key in the lock. 'Very good thank yer.' He smiled at her as he began to climb the stairs. 'Well, I'll say goodnight, Mrs Flanagan. Busy day tomorrow.'

'Oh!' is all she could say as Max reached the landing and the sanctity of his bedroom.

He yawned. What a day it had been, he thought to himself as he started to undress. He still could not quite believe that he was the possessor of a quarter share in a flourishing fishing business and all because of a chance meeting outside the railway terminus. He would really know it was for real when he signed the purchase contract that Harry was sending round in the morning. He was meeting Billy first of all to go through the trading accounts, which he fully expected would enable him to confirm his offer. In fact he was even more delighted, and a little surprised, that he had not been pushed to his maximum price, which meant that there was some money left over to fund his development plans for the fine food range. These were now an urgent priority. He also wanted to amass the capital required to buy and equip his first eating house but he knew that he had to recoup the investment he had just made in 'H. & W. Masters' first. Six months, he said to himself, as he slipped out of his shirt, six months is all he would allow himself to do that and then he could use the revenues from both the fine foods and his new fishing interests to build up the capital.

He shivered as he laid his clothes out neatly on the chair ready for the morning. The fire in his bedroom had not been lit and the room was cold. The matches would be in the kitchen but he did not fancy running the gauntlet of Mrs Flanagan's curiosity again so he quickly got into bed, jumping slightly as the touch of the cold sheets sent goose-pimples rushing over his naked body. He pulled the sheets up under his chin and stretched out his legs, exploring the freezing recesses of the neatly made bed as he did so. By this time on Thursday he would be home. He smiled to himself as he closed his eyes, feeling the familiar stirrings of desire begin to creep over him as he thought about Rosie, wishing that she was there next to him.

Billy reached his front door at around the same time as Max was warding off Mrs Flanagan. He turned his key in the lock and let himself in as gently as he could so as not to wake his mother who would be asleep upstairs. He knew Harry would be dozing in front of the fire in the back parlour, waiting up to see him. He was overjoyed that his father had agreed to sell a portion of their shares. The strain of running the company was adding to the pain of his worsening arthritis and Billy hated to see him struggle to cope, even though he would have bawled out anyone who dared to suggest he might take things a little easier. Billy was also champing at the bit to take over, eager to prove his worth just as his father had done before him. The lack of ready cash necessary to secure a comfortable retirement had long been a barrier to his succession, but thanks now to his persistence his father had at last succumbed and opened the door to an outsider.

Billy was a shrewd judge of character for a young man and was very confident that Max was the right choice. He had felt that ever since their shared plate of mackerel in the café. The business needed an injection of new energy and enthusiasm and he thought that Max was just the man to give it that. There was a potency about him that was tangible and he seemed driven by a desperate need to succeed. It was as if he was locked like a prisoner into his vision for the future, from which he would only break free when he had reached his ultimate goal. He thought he had discovered part of the reason for its intensity the previous evening when Max was talking about his background, but he was not sure he yet understood it. He was an ambitious man himself, just like Max, and he too wanted money and the satisfaction that would come from enhancing the success of the family business, but he was also a realist and he knew that he could not manage it alone. Pragmatism was one of his great strengths and a true sign of his maturity. His desire for wealth was strong too but it was not the same. He had other, more personal, motives; he did not possess the pure hunger for money itself that so inspired Max.

'Dad, are you awake,' he whispered softly as he entered the room where his mother spent most of her waking hours when she was not occupied in the kitchen beyond. He sat down in the armchair opposite Harry and whispered again. There was no response save for the rhythmic snoring that Billy had heard so many times before. He looked at his father with a mixture of amusement and compassion. He had been lucky with his parents; listening to Max describe his own life at Fern Cottage had made him realise they shared that common bond, except that is where the similarities in their circumstances ended. His mother had never really recovered her vitality and zest for life after the death of his twin brother James in a boating accident three years previously and his father's arthritis had seemed to worsen more rapidly since that tragic day.

They had been together on the deck of *The Nightingale*, one of their older trawlers at the time, when strong winds unexpectedly blew a fresh gale, whipping up the sea and sending waves crashing over the deck. They were dressed in heavy oilskins trying to stow the nets when a freak wave hit them broadside on, sweeping them overboard as the boat heeled over. It had all happened so quickly but the skipper had been magnificent, managing to get a lifebelt to them within minutes. James was the stronger swimmer and had forced the belt over Billy's head, gripping tightly on to his hand as the skipper tried to manoeuvre the wildly pitching boat near enough to them to throw a line. The combination of the cold water and cumbersome oilskins made it impossible to get a firm hold of the line when they caught it and it was too late for James. He lost consciousness and, although Billy had done his desperate best to support him, the cold and shock had removed all feeling in his upper body and James just slipped from his grasp. Billy blamed himself for his brother's death and was consumed by guilt, despite Harry's heartrending attempts to persuade him that there was nothing more he could have done; even the skipper was unsuccessful in convincing him that it was a tragic accident, and when he had attempted to shoulder the responsibility himself, Billy would not listen; it was his fault, he had let James go and that was all there was to it. He had withdrawn from normal life for almost a year, taking no interest in anything or anybody, least of all himself. It took the realisation that his behaviour was destroying the remains of his mother's already shattered spirit to gradually drag him out of his decline. The guilt was still there and would never leave him, but it had been overtaken by an overwhelming need to prove his worth to his parents and, subconsciously to himself, through his role in the business. It was as if James's death would not be completely in vain if he could make an even greater success of the business than his father had done, and his grandfather before him. He also believed that Harry's determined reluctance to dilute family control and preserve the legacy for future generations stemmed from the same sentiments.

He leaned forward to gently nudge his father and then hesitated. Instead, he softly prodded the glowing embers in the grate with the iron poker he and his brother had made between them from the remains of an old metal boat hook, and settled back in the chair. The fire flared up, sending the tiny remnants of a burning log crackling on to the hearth. He usually looked forward to this quiet time alone with his father and it had certainly been a momentous day, but his mind was too full of the ideas he and Max had discussed during their tour of the warehouse and he was not yet ready to share them with his father.

Billy stared at the flames as they guttered and died, lost in concentration. He had to hand it to Max, he lost no time in spotting the business potential of a situation. They had been looking at the empty space on the first floor that had once been his home when they 'had lived above the shop', as his mother was fond of saying. It had been used for storage since they had moved out but latterly it had lain empty. Max had suggested it would be ideal as a base for the expansion of his fine food lines, beginning to see the combined benefits that their new relationship might bring. His enthusiasm was infectious and they had eagerly debated the possibilities, both concluding that it made good sense. 'No point in wastin' valuable resources, Billy,' Max had said, 'an' I could sell some of yer catch as part of a new fresh produce range,' he had added, his thoughts racing off at a tangent almost at once. He had been encouraged at how readily and easily they had agreed the basic framework of the idea, which augured well for the future, and the rent Max would pay for the space would please his father, of that he had no doubt. It would provide some of the finance necessary for the purchase of the new sloop. In fact it was this thought that had decided it for him. 'Money should be used to make more money,' his grandfather had once told him, not long before he died. How right he had been.

His concentration was disturbed by the chiming of the clock. 'Dad, Dad, wake up,' he said gently, 'it's gone two o'clock.'

Max could not sleep. He sat up and rearranged his pillow for the second time in as many minutes and lay back down again, fidgeting restlessly as he peered at the first light of dawn filtering through the curtains. He had run through the events of the day in his mind over and over again, unable to relax and let sleep overtake him. It was no good, he thought, as he pushed the bedclothes back, he could not sleep. He padded over to the window and pulled the curtains back, looking out on to the deserted street below. The milkman would soon be starting his rounds and the first of the day's delivery men would begin knocking on doors, but until then all was quiet. It was the perfect time to draw up his plans for the additions to his fine foods so he could show Billy what he had in mind. He reached out for a blanket from the top of the bed and wrapped it around his shoulders and pulled a pen from his bag. 'Chambers Fine Food Emporium' he wrote, 'Specialities for all occasions delivered to your door'. For the next hour he proceeded to commit his thoughts to paper, organising and refining them as he wrote until he finally sat back, satisfied that he had thought of everything. He rubbed his eyes and listened to the early signs of life rising from downstairs. Mrs Flanagan must be up and stoking the range, he thought, as he heard the muffled sound of footsteps clattering from the direction of the kitchen below. He stood up and wrapped the blanket tightly around him, deciding to go in search of matches to light the fire already made up in the grate. He crept lightly down the stairs, not wanting to wake the household, and through into the rear parlour, where the unmistakable sounds of Mrs Flanagan could be heard from behind the kitchen door.

'Mrs Flanagan, do yer have...'

'Oh!' gasped Mrs Flanagan as she turned round with a start, 'Mr Chambers, you gave me a fright!' Her hand flew to her cheek as Max started to apologise.

'I'm sorry, Mrs Flanagan, I didn't mean ter.' He stood in the doorway and smiled at her. 'I was wonderin' if yer 'ad any matches so I can light the fire in my room?'

'It's cold all right, I'll grant yer that,' she replied, 'yer up bright and early this morning, Mr Chambers.'

'Yes, Mrs Flanagan,' Max replied, 'yes I am.' He shivered as she opened the back door to put a bag of rubbish out into the yard.

'Yer'll catch yer death, walking around like that,' she remarked with raised eyebrows as she stared at him.

Max blushed and gripped the blanket more tightly around his waist with one hand, conscious of Mrs Flanagan's eyes boring into him. 'The matches, Mrs Flanagan...'

'There's some in the drawer here. Ah yes, here you are, Mr Chambers,' she said, handing him a small box, which he took with his free hand. 'There should be enough kindlin' up there to set it off.'

'Thank yer, Mrs Flanagan, I'm sure it'll be fine,' he answered with relief as he turned to go, suddenly anxious to be back in the privacy of his room.

Chapter 20

The following two days passed in a whirl of activity, which left Max barely time to draw breath. He had reviewed the trading accounts on Monday morning with Billy, who had been very fulsome in his explanations of the cashbook and balance sheet. These revealed the business to be both healthily profitable and securely financed, which had given Max the confidence to sign the purchase agreement with Harry later the same day. He had been delighted when Harry had insisted on adding his name to that of the company, and touched when he had immediately instructed that a new sign be made for the front of their premises. Henceforth they would be known as 'Masters, Masters and Chambers Ltd,' which soon became abbreviated by most people in the industry to 'MMC Ltd'.

Tuesday was spent with Billy, learning as much as he could about the workings of the business. He had met the boats' crews and sailed around the bay on the *Girl Jennifer*. The sea had been calm but, despite that, his brief familiarisation trip had left him full of admiration for the work they did. He could only imagine how difficult it must be to rig the nets and haul them in on to a pitching deck when the seas were rough. Billy had described their customer list in some detail and, between them, they had begun to identify those who might have an interest in his emporium service.

The plans that Max had set out were ambitious but he was convinced that they were realistic and Billy had been very enthusiastic when he began to see the opportunities they presented. With Harry's blessing they spent a productive few hours deciding how to make best use of the vacant space above the warehouse, after which Billy had cheerfully offered to obtain estimates for the alterations that would be required. The necessary storage areas for the enhanced range of foods would have to be built, and a preparation area for the fresh foods that would need to be made ready for onward delivery was essential if they were to ensure that these items reached the customer in the best possible state. 'I'm only as good as my last delivery, Billy,' Max had said, 'each one has to be as perfect as I can make it.'

Max whistled happily to himself this morning as he walked purposefully along Gunter Lane, his mind full of thoughts of home and Rosie. He had slept soundly and woken refreshed and eager to enjoy the last day of his trip to Plymouth. He felt he had earned these few hours off considering all that he had accomplished and there was one more thing he wanted to do before Mr Tomkins picked him up in the morning. This was no ordinary task, however; in fact it was probably the most important one he would ever undertake in his whole life. The streets were fairly empty but, even so, he slowed to a gentle stroll and began to look in the shop windows. The shop he was looking for was near 'Webber and Sons', which was just up ahead. He had noticed it on his way back to Treville Street the previous evening, by which time he had already made his decision. He spotted the awning first. It was a deep green, which contrasted brightly with the majority of the others stretching across the pavement on this side of the lane and the words 'Benyamin Abrahams, Jewellers of Distinction' were ornately scripted in a semi-circle of gold letters on the wide glass of the front window. As he pushed open the door a bell jangled above his head and the grey-haired man bending over a display cabinet at the rear of the shop looked up and smiled.

'Good morning, sir,' he said, straightening up, 'what a pleasant morning it is too. Benyamin Abrahams at your service.'

'Good morning, Mr Abrahams,' replied Max, returning the smile. 'Yes it is a lovely morning.' He smiled back and glanced round at the carefully arranged displays in the cabinets and on the shelves that ran around the length of each wall.

'Is there something in particular I can help you with?' asked Benyamin Abrahams, moving out from behind the cabinet, 'or are you happy just to look?'

'I'll look fer the moment thanks,' said Max, turning towards the trays that were sparkling brightly beneath the gleaming glass counter nearest to him and feeling slightly uncomfortable in such unfamiliar territory.

'Papa, can you come and check this clasp for me?' a voice called out from the rear of the shop.

'Excuse me for a moment,' said Benyamin, rolling his eyes towards the ceiling, 'my daughter, she's in the workshop. Please take your time. I won't be long.' He gave Max a friendly nod. 'I'm coming, my dear, just a moment...'

The first display of trays held a fine selection of gold and silver necklaces and bracelets. Many had stones delicately arranged in a variety of different settings and Max was captivated by the intricacy of some of the designs and the vivid colours of the twinkling stones. He imagined some of them to be diamonds by the way they sparkled because they reminded him of the times when, as a small boy, he had seen Lady Constance dressed for a ball with dazzling gems blazing around her neck and wrists. But, lovely as they were, he had not come to look at necklaces. He moved on to the next cabinet, which contained rows of stunning brooches and earrings that were carefully arranged to show them at their very best. A couple of paces further, in the cabinets ranged along the far wall, he saw what he had been looking for. He bent over the polished glass to get a closer look and his eyes were instantly drawn to a tray that held some of the most beautiful rings he knew he had ever seen. He gazed at them, lost in thought.

'Have you seen something you like, sir?' enquired Benyamin quietly. He had reappeared without Max noticing.

'Yes I think so,' replied Max slowly. 'Can yer tell me what these are please?' asked Max, pointing to the tray that had caught his attention.

Benyamin took a small ring of keys from his waistcoat pocket and unlocked the back of the cabinet. He lifted the tray out gently, handling it as if it were a precious newborn child. 'These are diamonds and the blue stones are sapphires,' he explained, pointing with a neatly manicured index finger as he spoke. 'All the blue stones you see on this tray are sapphires, set in eighteen-carat yellow gold. This one here,' he went on, 'matches the eighteen-carat gold and sapphire locket *lavaliere* in the cabinet you might have seen over there.' He nodded towards the displays over by the door. 'It's part of a set. The others are individual pieces. Most of the diamonds are old cut with fifty-eight facets each. This gives them their particular fire and brilliance.' He looked at Max with a faint smile on his lips as their eyes met. 'Is it for someone special may I ask, sir?'

Max smiled back a little self-consciously. 'It's for my fiancée, Mr Abrahams. Someone very special.' He savoured those words. It was the first time he had used them and he felt a warm glow inside him as he did so. He did not reveal that he had not actually proposed to Rosie but he planned to do so as soon as he returned to Lee Moor the following morning. 'I like that one, second row down,' he said, 'the one with the sapphire in the middle and the smaller diamonds on either side.'

'Please, take it out and look more closely,' suggested Benyamin courteously. 'She's a very lucky lady if I may say so, sir. Does she like sapphires in particular? You know myth has it that they were once thought to protect the wearer from poisonous creatures.' He smiled to himself as he watched Max gingerly take the ring from the tray and place it in the palm of his left hand.

For a moment Max was nonplussed. He had chosen sapphires thinking they would match the beautiful blueness of Rosie's eyes, which was one of the first things he had noticed about her, but he realised he had no idea whether she liked them or not. 'Ter be truthful, Mr Abrahams, I'm not sure.'

Benyamin detected Max's uncertainty straightaway. He was used to the signs after his many years in the business. 'I'm sure she will. It's a beautiful piece, very simple but very elegant. Perfect for the younger lady. The diamonds are shoulder set and the sapphire is mounted in a six-prong coronet setting to allow the light to circulate all around in order to enhance its natural lustre.'

'I see,' said Max, impressed with the jeweller's sincerity and obvious enjoyment of his craft.

'Do you know the lady's finger size, sir?'

'Oh ... no ... I don't,' stammered Max. This thought had not occurred to him and he cursed himself; it was so obvious.

'I have a suggestion, sir.' It was one Benyamin had made many times before. 'My daughter will try it on for you, which might help.' He smiled and called through to the back of the shop. 'Eliza, my dear, would you come here for a moment please?'

A petite, dark-haired girl appeared almost immediately and smiled shyly in their direction. 'Yes, Papa?' she said sweetly.

'We need your help, my dear. Mr ... er,' he looked enquiringly at Max.

'Chambers, Max Chambers,' replied Max, 'I'm sorry ter be a nuisance.' He smiled warmly back at her.

'Not at all, Mr Chambers, not at all,' said Benyamin quickly. Turning back towards his daughter, he explained, 'Mr Chambers is interested in this ring for his fiancée and we wondered if you might try it on for us? We want to see what it would look like and get an idea of the size. Come over here by the window.'

Taking the ring from Max's hand, Eliza slipped it on to her engagement finger and held it up for them to see. It sparkled tantalisingly in the daylight and Max was immediately sure; this was the one.

'Thank yer, Miss Abrahams, thank yer very much,' he said as she removed it, being careful to avoid touching the stones so as not to dim their brightness.

'Thank you, my dear,' said Benyamin, watching as she disappeared back to the workshop. 'Did you like it, Mr Chambers, and the fit...?'

Chapter 21

'Good trip then, Max?' asked Alf Tomkins as he climbed aboard the estate wagon.

'Yes thanks, Mr Tomkins, better than I could ever 'ave 'oped,' said Max with a broad grin.

'Move on there, move on,' said the Gordons' head gardener as he firmly flicked the reins. The horses took the strain as he gently turned them around to head back to Lee Moor. They quickly found their stride as Max settled back in the seat alongside Alf, thinking only of Rosie and home, oblivious to all around him. All that broke the companionable silence between the two men was the rhythmic clip clop of metal shoes striking the road.

It was not until they reached the outskirts of town that Max shook himself out of his private dreams. Alf had been looking at him out of the corner of his eye since leaving the railway terminus, smiling to himself each time he saw the far away look on Max's face. He was not a betting man but he'd happily wager that Max was 'thinking about that lass of 'is'.

''Ow's things been at 'ome, Mr Tomkins?' asked Max at last, with just a hint of trepidation in his voice.

'Much the same as usual, lad, except for one thing. Caused quite a stir it 'as,' replied Alf. He chuckled as he saw the apprehensive look on Max's face before adding quickly, 'Young Rosie is fine, if that's what yer worried about! I hear from yer Ma she's been kept proper busy with that business o' yers.'

Max grinned with relief and relaxed, keener than ever to get home. He surreptitiously felt for the small square box at the bottom of his jacket pocket and smiled again, this time to himself, as his fingers closed around it. 'What do yer mean, Mr Tomkins? What's 'appened?' he asked curiously.

''Is Lordship's bought a motor car, that's what's 'appened. A Rover it's called, big black beast it is. Noisy and smelly if yer ask me. Lord William drives it mostly. 'E's none too careful either, yer 'ave ter get out o' 'is way when 'e's in the village I can tell yer. The grooms are already talkin' about it being the beginnin' of the end an' 'ow they're goin' ter get the sack!'

'A motor car!' he exclaimed excitedly, 'I've seen pictures in the papers but never one fer real! What's it like?'

Alf chuckled again at Max's reaction. 'Yer are the first person ter be excited about it, an' no mistake. There's been a right ter do at the 'ouse. Stable gossip is rife I can tell yer an' Lord William isn't 'elping things, parading around in it, drawin' attention ter 'imself, rubbin' people's noses in it.'

'That doesn't surprise me at all!' commented Max, unable to hide the bitterness in his voice. ''E'll be lovin' every minute of it too.' All of a sudden a thought dawned on him that threatened to deflate his excitement; how would it affect his father? But he pushed it to the back of his mind for the moment, no point in crossing that bridge unless it was necessary, he said to himself, and he couldn't help his enthusiasm at the news. He recognised the huge potential of the motor car. It would revolutionise people's lives, or at least those who could afford one, to say nothing of the world of commerce. He could not wait to see it.

'What about Lady 'Enrietta, 'as she been seen in it?' asked Max suddenly, thinking about his chance meeting with her in Plymouth.

'She's been away fer a few days, so we 'aven't seen 'er at all. She's due back tomorrow, so Makepiece informs us.'

'An' yer don't know the 'alf of it!' thought Max with a wry smile, and for the first time he was surprised to realise he did not feel any animosity when he spoke her name.

They chatted happily for the remainder of the journey back to Mount Royal until Max fell silent as the great walls of the estate came into view on the outskirts of the village. He began to experience the feelings of excitement and anticipation in the pit of his stomach as he always did whenever he was about to be reunited with Rosie after a short absence, only this time it was stronger than usual, much stronger. Sometimes he even felt it when he was walking home to Fern Cottage after a normal day's work at The Wheelwrights, and this time he had been away for a whole week, and there was so much to tell. Alf became aware of the change in Max as he reined the horses back to a slow walking pace along the high street. He sensed the tension just beneath the surface; it was controlled but, despite Max's attempts to conceal it, quite evident to him. It showed in his facial expressions but Alf wisely chose to ignore it.

'This is where I'll let yer off, Max,' he said, swivelling his head towards

Max, 'before I turn inter Home Park.' He smiled warmly as Max looked at him and brushed aside his thanks. 'Good to have yer back, lad. Say 'ello ter yer Ma an' Pa an' Rosie fer me won't yer?'

Max jumped down and reached up for his overnight bag. 'Yep, I will an' tell Mrs Castle ter 'ave the kettle on bright an' early in the morning, I'll be in ter see 'er,' he replied as he gave his friend a cheerful wave goodbye. He liked Alf Tomkins a great deal. In fact in his earlier years when he had spent many a day wandering the Mount Royal estate on his own, Alf had befriended him and had become almost a surrogate father figure. Now, in adulthood, Max no longer saw him as a father figure but he nevertheless retained strong feelings of affection and respect for him and, if he had ever asked Alf, he would have discovered that those sentiments were keenly reciprocated.

Walking quickly in his keenness to get home, he was consumed by an eagerness to see Rosie after their separation, which had seemed to him to last for ever, but he was strangely anxious at the same time. As he turned into his lane and he could see Fern Cottage up ahead, he slowed down and took several deep breaths to calm his nerves. For someone who was normally so confident and sure of himself, or at the very least, adept at concealing his anxieties when they existed, Max was unable to stop his hands from visibly trembling as he reached the garden gate.

He saw her before she saw him. She was standing by the fireplace in the front parlour with a bundle of papers in her hand and, as he fumbled with the latch of the garden gate, something made her look through the window and in that instant she saw him. His heart leapt as he saw her dash for the door, scattering the papers in her wake. He dropped his bag and began to run down the path, reaching the front door just as it opened. Then Rosie was in his arms, laughing and crying at the same time, her face resplendent with joy. He held her close, feeling her tears trickle down his cheek as they clung together, wrapped in a silent embrace, until Max gently released her. He smiled down into her eyes and dried them tenderly with the back of his hand.

She made to speak but he held his forefinger softly to her lips. 'Shh, darling, don't say anything,' he whispered softly, 'just let me look at you...'

He gazed into her eyes again and she felt herself mesmerized by his look of love for her, his eyes blazing with intensity. He ran one hand through the silken waves of her golden hair, smoothing away the tresses that were now spilling from the clips that secured them. His fingers came to rest in the nape of her neck, tantalisingly caressing her skin with the lightest of touches. His other hand cradled her face, firmly drawing her to him as his mouth sought hers. He kissed her deeply, urgently, her body responding willingly to his as they were both engulfed by their longing and desire for each other.

'I've missed yer so much, Rosie,' he groaned and he swept her up into his arms and carried her into the parlour. He kicked the front door shut behind them with his foot and laid her gently on the sofa. 'Me Ma an' Pa, where are they?' he asked hoarsely. 'At work?' Eyebrows raised, he smiled down at her shining face, his eyes burning into hers as he tugged at his jacket and then the buckle of his thick brown belt.

Rosie nodded quickly and reached up for him. 'Max ... Max...' she gasped, unable to control the tremor in her voice. Taking her hands in his he knelt down and drew her to him, fumbling with the clasp of her dress as she raised herself up and pulled at the buttons of his shirt. His lips met hers as he covered her body with his own, their kisses growing ever more desperate as they tugged at the remainder of their clothes. His mouth drifted across her shoulders and into the hollow of her neck. She quivered under his touch as his hands moved firmly, at first quickly and urgently, then slowly and teasingly as he caressed every part of her, reaching out to her with an infinite tenderness that carried her to the brink of desire. Her slender fingers ran across his broad shoulders and along his arms, lingering as they explored the ripples of muscle before finding his waist, pulling him ever more closely to her.

'I want us ter really know each other,' she cried softly as she reached down for him. Max groaned as the warmth of her touch enveloped him, sending a fiery heat rushing through his trembling body. He responded with growing passion, aching to please her, and she him; their bodies joined in their desperate need to possess each other, her arms encircling him, binding him to her as he moved swiftly until their bodies locked together, unable to resist the final overpowering moment of pure joy.

They lay there, entwined, neither wanting to be the first to move. Rosie opened her eyes and looked up at him as he gently stirred; her face flushed with an expression of sheer pleasure and contentment that almost took Max's breath away. As he kissed her tenderly she saw tears spring to his eyes. They were tears of adoration, mixed with a look of innocent vulnerability that she found irresistible. He made her feel safe and protected and she knew then that she wanted to spend the rest of her life with him.

'What are you thinking, darling?' asked Max quietly, without taking his eyes from her as he drew away and lay beside her.

She sighed languorously, struggling to find the words to describe how she was feeling. She laid her head on his shoulder and toyed with the hairs covering his chest, tracing the line running down to his navel with her finger. He laughed as it tickled. 'Hey!' he protested in mock indignation as he clutched her hand, 'that tickles!' They were both laughing together now and Rosie was filled with a sense of real peace for perhaps the first time in her life. She was overwhelmed by a feeling of fulfilment and belonging that she had not experienced before.

Max knew that the moment had arrived. 'Rosie.'

'Yes, darling?' She detected the change in his tone and turned to look at him with a quizzical expression on her face.

He put his arm out behind him and fumbled for his jacket. 'Rosie, I've got something ter say.' He could not feel his jacket and cursed silently as he gently slid his other arm from around Rosie's shoulders and stood up.

'Max, what's the matter? What have yer lost?' she asked, mystified.

'Nothing, sweet'art... Ah, 'ere it is,' he exclaimed. His voice shook slightly and he bent down to rummage in the pockets. Rosie leant towards him and started to smooth her hands up and down his legs. Her nails left little furrows in the hairs on his thighs.

'Whatever it is, darlin', it can wait,' she teased.

Max tensed as her hands crept higher and he knew he would be powerless to resist in another moment. 'Rosie, I'm trying ter be serious fer a second!' he protested as his fingers found the box at the bottom of the right-hand pocket. Found it! he said to himself triumphantly. He stood up and turned round, smiling down at her.

'I've been doin' a lot of thinkin' whilst I was in Plymouth, Rosie, an'...'

'Careful!' interrupted Rosie mischievously, with a gleam in her eye, but then she checked herself. There was something in Max's expression that told her he really was being serious.

'Rosie, I've got somethin' ter ask yer,' he began again, and all of a sudden a silence descended and Rosie felt her heart begin to race. 'Rosie, you 'ave become my whole world,' he stammered slightly and he wiped the palm of his left hand on his bare leg, not even noticing the quick pain as it tugged roughly on the hairs. He knelt down beside the sofa so his face was almost level with hers. 'I want yer ter be my wife so we can spend the rest of our lives tergether!' He opened the lid of the box to reveal the sapphire and diamond ring he had so lovingly chosen at Mr Abrahams'. She gasped and stared in wonderment as he handed it to her. 'Marry me, Rosie, please...'

Chapter 22

Rosie was speechless, unable to reply, so overcome was she by the strength of her emotions. Tears welled in her eyes and began to roll down her cheeks as she stared spellbound at the ring Max was slipping on her finger.

'Say something, darlin',' he urged anxiously and she smiled at him through her tears. She was incapable of speech and could only look at Max as he gathered her in his arms and held her tight. 'Hey ... hey,' he said softly.

'I love yer with all my heart, Max ... more than I ever thought possible ... but how can I?' she finally managed to whisper through trembling sobs in his ear. 'Oh, Max ... I can't!'

Max turned deathly pale. 'But ... I ... I don't understand...' he stammered, dazed by Rosie's response. 'I love yer ... more than yer'll ever know. I can't bear ter be without yer, Rosie...'

It was as if the whole world had come to a standstill in that moment and a stunned silence descended on the room. The only noise was the sound of Rosie's anguished sobbing. She drew away from him and buried her face in her hands, incapable of looking at the tortured expression on Max's face as he too struggled to hold back the tears. She turned away but he took hold of her arm and pulled her back towards him.

'But I thought yer loved me too, Rosie ... yer just said so!' Max's tone was insistent, almost harsh in its firmness.

'Oh, Max, I do! But...'

'Well then, that's all that matters!' he countered.

Rosie was beside herself with guilt for causing Max such heartache. In truth she was captivated by him, besotted by his boyish charm and protective presence. He was the first man she had ever known, or wanted to know, so completely, and she felt drawn to him in a way that was hard to describe, much less to understand. His compassionate kindness and caring spirit were enticing enough on their own, but when combined with the force of their powerful mutual attraction, they were irresistible.

Max had become her world. He had allowed her to see the man behind his handsome and beguiling veneer and, with each new revelation, her feelings for him deepened. His energy and vitality were impressive, his quick wit and mischievous sense of humour, infectious, his moments of vulnerability, bewitching, and his sharp mind – coupled with an extraordinary determination she had not witnessed in any other human being – astonishing. He excited her, enthralled her and compelled her to be with him.

Max was equally besotted. He lived for her and felt incomplete when they were apart. He thought she was the most beautiful woman he had ever seen; beautiful in both body and mind. He had never been in love before but he knew that his feelings for Rosie were genuine, all consuming and permanent. She fulfilled him in a way he would not have believed possible.

Rosie raised her head and looked into his eyes, seeing the hurt and bewilderment, which she found almost too great to bear. She gently pulled him down on to the sofa so they were sitting side by side.

'Max,' she began slowly, fighting to keep the tremor from her voice as she grasped his hand tightly, 'please let me try ter explain...' Max was silent. 'I love yer, darling, yer are my life.'

'Well then...'

'Shh, darling, let me finish,' she pleaded. 'I couldn't love yer more if I tried, but...'

'So...'

'*But* I can't hold yer back, Max, I couldn't do that, it's not fair!' she wailed as she lowered her eyes to the floor.

'Hold me back!' he exclaimed incredulously, 'what on earth do yer mean, Rosie?'

Rosie looked up quickly. 'Because of what 'appened ter me, darling!'

Max was really confused. 'D'yer mean the accident?' he asked, mystified. He called it an accident even though he was convinced it was *not* an accident at all. 'How could yer ever hold me back?'

'Don't yer see, Max, I can't stay 'ere, in Lee Moor! Not after what's 'appened. I'm frightened! Every time I go near the 'ouse, or see the family ... I've got ter leave ... go back ter London...' She paused. 'Anywhere ... I don't know!'

'But, Rosie,' cut in Max, 'we can go...'

'No!' said Rosie sharply, 'I won't take yer away from 'ere. Yer grew up 'ere an' yer business is based in this village. Yer going ter be successful, Max, an' I won't let yer throw it all away on me!' She looked at him, her eyes full of anguish and misery.

'*Throw it all away?*' said Max, beginning to understand. '*Hold me back?*'

He began to laugh softly as he put his arm around her shoulders and held her to him. He could feel the tension in her body as she fought to hold herself under control. He kissed her tenderly and very gently began to explain. 'I could never throw anything away fer yer, darling, because I'm doing this fer us, don't yer see? I haven't 'ad chance ter tell yer about Plymouth 'ave I but things 'appened there, good things, which means our future is away from 'ere anyway. The business is goin' ter be much too big fer the village, especially now, an' just because I grew up 'ere doesn't mean ter say that we 'ave ter stay 'ere for the rest of our lives!' He was looking intently at Rosie as she sat huddled against him. She was quiet now, her tears had subsided. 'We can go ter Plymouth, or ter London if yer want ... ter your family ... the business I've bought inter wants ter expand inter London an' we'll need somebody there fer that.' He paused and kissed her again, feeling her relax as she pressed her body to his. 'I know yer can't stay 'ere, Rosie, I've known that ever since the day we 'ad that picnic on the moor.'

Rosie's face crumpled and the tears came again as she listened to the earnestness of Max's tone, every word spoken with an urgency and suppressed passion that revealed the true depth of his feelings. This time they were tears of joy.

'Do yer really mean it, darling?' she cried. '*Is it really all right?*'

'Of course I do, sweet'art!' he whispered as he went down on one knee. 'Will yer marry me, Rosie?'

'*Oh yes Max, yes, I will!*' she gasped, her eyes brimming with the love she felt for him.

He saw the flush of pleasure on her face as he eased himself back on to the sofa and enfolded her in his arms, euphoric with relief and happiness and vowing never to let her go. Their kisses came quickly as Max cupped his hands underneath her chin, tilting her head towards him. She traced a line with her finger down his spine, which made him shudder as he stroked her thigh with one hand, grazing her neck with his lips as she began to moan lightly in his ear. Her hands smoothed the firm rounded outline of his buttocks as he caressed her breasts with his palm. They could wait no longer, their need for each other overpowering in its intensity. Rosie gripped his waist and pulled him to her. In one easy movement Max was enveloped by her desire; his mouth sought hers, kissing her deeply as they moved together, his hands brushing over her skin with mounting fervour as he carried her with him.

They lay in each other's arms, exhausted by the strength of their infatuation. They had discovered in each other the profound union that only exists when there is a meeting of parallel souls as well as bodies. Rosie nestled her head more closely against Max's shoulder and glanced dreamily at the clock on the mantelpiece. It was only three o'clock, plenty of time before Molly or Bert came home from work. She sighed contentedly and looked at her finger, as if to make sure she was not dreaming about the ring that adorned it.

'Penny fer 'em?' she teased as she caught sight of the far away expression on his face.

'Beg yer pardon, ma'am?' he grinned and touched his forelock as she hit him gently in the ribs. 'Actually, I was thinking I need ter own up ter yer about somethin'.'

'Oh, an' what might that be, Mr Chambers?' she asked coyly. As she said those words she suddenly thought of her new name, 'Mrs Chambers' and it sent a warm tingling feeling through her, which made her flush slightly.

'It's about yer ring, Rosie. Promise yer won't 'it me again...' Max looked at her warily out of the corner of his eye.

'Well now, that depends, Mr Chambers!' she replied, trying to sound menacing but, instead, collapsing in a fit of giggles.

'Yer know those are sapphires an' diamonds,' he began, 'well, ter be honest ... they're not ... real ... if yer know what I mean...' he confessed.

'Do yer mean ter say yer've asked me ter marry yer under false pretences!' she exclaimed in mock outrage. 'Well, I shall 'ave ter consult my lawyers, Mr Chambers!'

'If I promise ter replace it with the real thing when we're rich an' successful, will that do yer, madam?' asked Max in the best contrite tone he could manage.

'I'll think about it, Mr Chambers,' replied Rosie, 'but make sure yer do mind!'

'Oh thank yer, madam! I promise! I'm in yer debt for ever...'

'Yer are, Mr Chambers, yer are...' she warned with a huge smile as she playfully tweaked his ear. 'It's beautiful, real or not, an' I love it just as it is!'

'Ouch!' cried Max again, laughing and making a mental note to return to Benyamin Abrahams' shop at the earliest possible opportunity to replace it with the biggest sapphires and diamonds money could buy. He silently thanked the kindly jeweller once again for discreetly suggesting that he buy a paste ring when it had become apparent that the price of the one Max had so liked was beyond his means. 'A very appropriate solution to a situation that is more common than you might imagine,' Mr Abrahams had murmured sympathetically, almost to himself, to spare Max's embarrassment.

'Come on, lazybones, yer can't lie there all day!' ordered Max as he jumped up from the sofa. 'We don't want my Ma an' Pa ter find us like this do we! An' I've got so much ter tell yer...' He bent down to pick up his clothes from the floor and the muscles on his broad back and toned legs rippled, which made Rosie want to wrap her arms around him and never let him go. She watched as he pulled his shirt on and stepped into his trousers.

''Aven't yer ever seen a naked man before?' asked Max cheekily as she followed his every move from her position on the sofa. 'Yer must 'ave...'

'Scoundrel!' He ducked as one of her boots narrowly missed his head. He laughed delightedly. 'And yer a rotten shot!'

There was a loud clatter as it bounced off the mantelpiece behind him and he turned round to see the clock and photograph that stood next to it fall off on to the hearth.

'Oh no!' squealed Rosie in horror, 'look what yer made me do!'

'*What I made yer do?*' exclaimed Max in high amusement.

There was no harm done; the basket of logs Bert had filled up that morning before setting off for the stables had fortunately broken their fall. Rosie was beside him now and she breathed a sigh of relief as she picked them out of the basket.

'Yer'll catch yer death,' murmured Max, picking her dress up from the floor and passing it to her.

'Max, who is this?' asked Rosie curiously as she carefully placed the photograph back on the mantelpiece. 'I've wondered since I noticed it properly fer the first time when yer were in Plymouth.'

The young woman stared out of the little wooden frame at her. She was smiling, her long hair cascading prettily down to her shoulders. 'She's very beautiful,' added Rosie.

'Yes, she is, isn't she,' replied Max, 'it's been on the mantelpiece fer as long as I can remember but ter tell yer the truth, I don't know who she is.'

Rosie gave him a strange look.

Max shrugged his shoulders. 'I know, but me Ma 'as never really explained ter me. I've asked 'er a few times over the years, but...'

Rosie glanced at the photograph again, puzzled, but then said, 'Come on then, darling, I want ter know all about Plymouth.'

Chapter 23

It was a quiet spring wedding in the little village church in Lee Moor, attended by an inordinately proud Bert and Molly, Mrs Castle and Alf Tomkins, who would not have missed it for the world, Jack and Daisy from The Wheelwrights and one or two of the villagers who had known Max all of his life. Much to Max's delight, Billy made the journey from Plymouth, bringing Elizabeth, his new girlfriend with him. She was a tall, good-looking girl who knew how to make the best of herself, as Molly would say. Rosie warmed to her immediately.

The months leading up to it had been busier than ever and now, as Max and Rosie paused arm in arm at the small west door of the church to acknowledge the smiling group of well-wishers waiting to see them emerge, he turned to his new bride and whispered, '27th March 1909, the happiest day of my life.' Rosie looked into his eyes and replied, 'Mine too'.

Bert and Molly had taken the news that they were going to live in London surprisingly well after recovering from their initial shock. Molly, ever the practical and perceptive mother, understood exactly why Rosie could not remain in Lee Moor. Max and Rosie had discussed whether to move to Plymouth or London at great length, often talking long into the night without reaching a final conclusion. There was the business to consider first and foremost and Plymouth therefore seemed to be the logical choice, but Rosie's family were in London and Max knew she would like to live nearer to them; not that Rosie would ever have tried to influence him in that way. In the end it had been Billy who had decided it for them on one of Max's regular visits to see him. Chambers Fine Foods Emporium had been launched with help from Harry Masters and his network of customers and many other local contacts, and, after a slightly slow start, sales had grown steadily to the point at which Max had needed to appoint a produce manager far sooner than he had envisaged. Word of mouth had spread rapidly amongst the eating houses and grand residences in the town and it had proven far too much for him to handle from Lee Moor. Since Rebecca Fellowes had settled in, a young lady recommended for the job by Tommy Sullivan, Max had been travelling to Plymouth once a week to oversee the buying arrangements and review the figures. Billy had been eager to help oversee things too in between Max's visits and this arrangement had proven very satisfactory. Checking the long lines of entries in the sales ledger always gave Max a great sense of accomplishment, and, after calculating his profit each week, he would smile and thank Rebecca sincerely for her hard work and adroitly raise her targets for the following week, with the promise of a bonus if she achieved them.

On one particular trip Rosie had accompanied him and, over a drink in Billy's local they had told him of their dilemma. He had stared into his beer for a few minutes before announcing that, in his opinion, London was the answer. His reasoning, as Max later pointed out to Rosie, was both persuasive and well-founded. He told them that he could keep a careful eye on the emporium, in fact he would positively enjoy it, and still have enough time to manage the fishing fleet, meaning that Max would be free to move away. In turn he suggested that Max could manage the expansion of MMC Ltd into London. This was the next big step he had wanted to take with the business for a long while, reminding Max that he had mentioned this intention when they had first talked over dinner at Donovan's Dining Rooms. There was no better way to do it, he reasoned, especially as the two businesses were now working so well together; so London it was.

'Ladies an' Gentlemen, please welcome the bride an' groom!' proclaimed Jack from his position at the end of the main bar. All eyes turned towards the door as Max and Rosie walked in to loud cheers. The Wheelwrights was full to bursting point as the wedding party mingled with the regulars, whose numbers had been swelled by some of the staff from Mount Royal who had been granted an hour off to wish them good luck. Sam and Raymond had managed to inveigle the time off together from Makepiece on account of Jackson offering to stand in for them both. Even so it had taken Mrs Castle's stern entreaties to persuade the bad-tempered steward to sanction it, and now she was wondering if it had been such a good idea as they were at the forefront of the raucous comments that accompanied Max and Rosie's entrance.

'Never mind, Rosie, better luck next time,' came the loudest cry from the corner, where the two footmen were doing their best to charm Daisy with their latest servants' hall jokes, prompting howls of laughter and even louder expressions of sympathy from the assembled throng. Max and Rosie slowly made their way around the room, laughing and chatting animatedly as they greeted their guests, accepting good wishes and congratulations from all sides. Every now and then their eyes would meet and they would steal a secret glance before the next guest could interrupt their retreat into their own private world. At last they reached the bar where Jack was standing with Bert and Molly, waiting to hand Max a small white envelope carrying a familiar crest embossed upon it. 'Open it, Max,' said Jack, leaning forwards to make himself heard above the hubbub.

Max raised his eyebrows questioningly, looking first at Jack and then at his parents as he tore open the envelope. He unfolded the single sheet of heavy white notepaper, embossed at the top with the same crest, and read the neatly written words.

Dear Max
Congratulations to you and your bride. One good turn deserves another.
Good health to you both.
Henrietta Gordon.

'What is it, darling?' asked Rosie, seeing a frown crease Max's forehead.

He passed her the note and her eyes scanned the page as Jack mouthed the words 'In The White Lion' to Max, nodding in the direction of the door. Taking Rosie's arm, he gently led her back through the throng and across the hallway. Entering the snug, where earlier that morning Molly and Daisy had lovingly laid out the wedding breakfast, they both stopped and stared in amazement. Standing on a white clothed side table were four jeroboams of vintage Krug champagne.

'Jackson brought them in yesterday, with the note,' explained Jack as he appeared behind the bar counter. 'Apparently it was Lady Henrietta's idea an' His Lordship an' Her Ladyship insisted that Jackson brought them round 'imself.' Max looked at Rosie. 'Good of 'em, yer got ter say that. So what 'ave yer done ter deserve this special treatment?'

Max looked blankly at him. 'Search me,' he shrugged and caught Rosie's eye. 'Suffragettes,' he whispered with a wink.

Rosie could not suppress a giggle as she recalled Max's account of Lady Henrietta's encounter with the Plymouth police. 'Can we accept it?' she asked quietly.

Max was relieved to know that it came from Lady Henrietta and not her brother, as that would have been an entirely different matter. 'I suppose it would be wrong ter deny our guests...' he began as Molly appeared in the doorway.

'I see yer've found it then,' she said with just a hint of nervousness in her voice.

'It's all right, Ma,' said Max with a smile.

Relief flooded over Molly's face and she beamed back at them both. 'Is the food all right? Daisy 'as worked ever so 'ard, an' Jack 'as too.'

'It's luvely, Molly, really luvely!' exclaimed Rosie, 'an' so 'ave you an' Bert. Thank yer so much.' She threw her arms around Molly. 'Everyone is being so kind ter us,' she said in a voice choked with emotion.

'Now, now, lass, yer'll start us all off in a minute,' uttered Molly quickly, overcome by Rosie's expression of gratitude and her pride in the happy couple. 'Come on then, Jack, it must be time ter eat don't yer think?' she declared, almost sharply, as she turned towards the bar. Jack nodded in amused approval. It was not often he saw Molly almost lost for words.

Max softly brushed away the tears swimming in Rosie's eyes as he looked at her, his face full of tenderness and love. He took her hand and squeezed it gently as the first of their guests appeared from the hallway.

'Come on in, Elizabeth, an' Jim, 'elp yerselves,' said Molly as she began handing plates round. ''Ave some beef won't yer, Sam, there's mustard if yer want some. Frank, would yer like a piece of salmon?' She saw Billy standing behind him and winked as she added, 'It's best quality!'

Daisy soon appeared at Molly's side to help serve and Bert and Jack busied themselves topping up drinks before preparing the glasses for the champagne. 'Ma, Daisy, sit down an' 'ave something ter eat,' said Max as he and Rosie sat side by side, unable in their excitement to do anything other than pick at the food in front of them.

'It'll soon be time ter catch our train an' yer won't 'ave eaten anythin',' said Rosie, looking at the clock on the snug wall. 'Come on, everyone's 'appy fer the minute,' she said and patted the seat next to her insistently. 'Where's Bert an' Jack? They should be sat down too.'

The two women took one last look around the room and nodded with satisfaction to each other before doing as they were told. 'Your dress is beautiful, Rosie,' said Daisy as she spooned a generous portion of hollandaise sauce on to her plate, all the while secretly wishing it was she who was wearing Max's ring. 'The veil is exquisite.'

'Thank yer, Daisy!' said Rosie, touched by the barmaid's obvious sincerity as she knew that Daisy had held a torch for Max for a long time. 'Molly 'elped me and loaned me the lace fer it,' she explained.

'*Gave* yer the lace,' interrupted Molly firmly, 'an' every single stitch was my pleasure, an' that's a fact.' She silently prayed that neither Max nor Rosie would ever discover that the Countess had given her the lace with the express condition that her gift must remain a secret. She was to tell no one and so when Rosie had asked her where it had come from, she simply said that it had been in her possession forever and she had long since forgotten.

The persistent clink of metal on glass brought a hush to the bar as Jack stood up to begin the speeches. He was standing in for Rosie's father as none of her family had been able to make the long journey from London. When Rosie had hesitantly asked him several weeks earlier if he would be willing to make the father of the bride speech, he had been honoured to accept, and did so immediately. He had grown very fond of the 'young lass from London' as Rosie had first become known in the village, and he had watched happily as her relationship with Max had deepened as the months passed. He was going to miss them both and The Wheelwrights would be a sadder place without them, even though Daisy had vowed to keep the food side of his joint enterprise with Max going. Watching her now tucking into a heaped plateful of cold salmon and new potatoes, he could not doubt her enthusiasm for the task but worried about their future profits.

'Ladies an' Gentlemen, I am proud ter 'ave been asked by Mrs Rosie Chambers...' A loud cheer erupted in the room '...by Mrs Rosie Chambers, ter say a few words...'

'Make sure it is only a few!' came the slurred cry from a grinning Raymond, only to be silenced by a stern glare from Mrs Castle.

'...on behalf of 'er father, in honour of this auspicious occasion. We 'ave known Max as man an' boy, an' think of 'im as one of our own. Some of us 'ere terday 'ave watched 'im grow up from the small boy who used ter wander the estate and hills of Lee Moor inter the young man of independent means 'e is terday, a credit ter 'imself an' ter Bert an' Molly.' He looked at them and smiled broadly. Molly blushed and looked down at her hands, beaming with pleasure, as Bert stared fixedly into space. We 'ave known Rosie fer a much shorter time, but already we regard 'er in the same way.' Another cheer broke out, and this time Mrs Castle joined in. 'Those of us who 'ave 'ad the pleasure of working with 'em both an' know 'em well, can see 'ow perfectly matched they are tergether. As they now set out on a new stage in their lives, we wish 'em all the 'appiness in the world, good 'ealth and the best of luck.'

'Hear! hear!' The sound of hands thumping the tables in agreement drowned out those last few words and Jack had to wait until the noise had subsided before he could continue.

'An' so ... an' so will yer please stand an' raise yer glasses in a toast ter the bride an' groom, Rosie an' Max.'

The assembled guests were on their feet in an instant. 'The bride an' groom,' echoed clearly around the room as they drank from glasses filled with the Krug provided by Lady Henrietta.

Max rose to reply with a short but touching speech in which he thanked just about everyone in the room amid much barracking and laughter and then it was time to cut the magnificent wedding cake made for them by Mrs Castle.

'Keep an eye on the time,' whispered Bert to them both as they sat back down after the speeches. 'Yer don't want ter miss yer train.'

Overhearing what her husband had said, Molly glanced at the clock and suggested, 'Why don't yer get changed now, whilst the cake is being cut fer everyone?'

Max and Rosie looked at each other and nodded their assent, quietly slipping upstairs where their going-away outfits were waiting for them.

'Well, wife?' said Max with a broad grin as he sat down on the bed to untie his boot laces.

'Well, husband?' replied Rosie with raised eyebrows and a big smile as she sat down next to him.

'Give us a kiss,' teased Max, leaning towards her.

'Not now!' admonished Rosie playfully, 'there isn't time.'

'Everyone can wait,' protested Max in a rueful tone.

'Oh, all right,' said Rosie with an exaggerated sigh and she leant towards him before suddenly jumping up and skipping over to the wardrobe. 'But yer'll 'ave ter catch me first,' she giggled.

'Mrs Chambers, if yer think we've got time ter play silly games...' said Max as sternly as he could manage, bending down to reach for his laces.

'Spoilsport! Yer've missed yer chance now...'

'Well, there's plenty more where that one came from!' countered Max.

'Ooh, is there now!' exclaimed Rosie, trying not to giggle again, 'we might 'ave ter see about that...'

'Be quiet and get on with whatever it is yer supposed ter be doin',' said Max in his best schoolmasterly voice.

'Makin' myself beautiful, actually,' retorted Rosie tartly.

'There isn't time fer that,' said Max quickly, and then ducked as Rosie threw her underskirt at him. 'Missed!'

'Yer just wait!' warned Rosie.

'Good Lord, is that a promise?' replied Max innocently as he reached for the suit he had not worn since his first trip to Plymouth.

'Pig!' muttered Rosie, 'now come 'ere an' make yerself useful. 'Elp me with these buttons.'

Chapter 24

'Bye, darling! Write ter us!' cried Molly as the train started to pull out of the station. 'Bye, Rosie, love, look after yerselves!' She waved her scarf as hard as she could until the sight of Max and Rosie leaning out of the carriage window was obscured by billowing white clouds as the engine strained to gather momentum. She stood there for ages, with Bert by her side, until the last carriage had disappeared from view.

'Come on, love, they've gone now,' he said gently, touching her arm. 'Time ter 'ead back, it's gettin' dark.'

Molly nodded and slowly wrapped her scarf around her shoulders as she took one last look along the now empty line, reluctant to tear herself away. They were the last people remaining on the platform. 'It's goin' ter be strange without 'em,' she murmured softly in the silence that had descended, disturbed only by the sound of the stationmaster locking up the shutters of his tiny ticket office and the porter stacking his cart away in readiness for the next train.

'Yes, it is that,' replied Bert in a subdued voice, 'but they 'ad a good send off. It's been a grand day.'

'Over all too quickly, but yes, it 'as. One of the 'appiest of my life ... an' the saddest...' Her voice trailed off and she gathered up her skirts as Bert took her hand. He felt exactly the same but was trying to remain positive for Molly's sake.

'They'll not forget us, don't yer worry. An' maybe when they're settled we could take a trip ter London ourselves.'

'Yes, maybe...' said Molly in a small voice. She had been determined to hide her distress from Max and Rosie, but now that they were gone she could not help herself. She burst into tears and allowed herself to be led to the station bench, which stood underneath the ticket office window at the entrance to the station, where Bert did his best to comfort her.

'Shush, love, shush...' whispered Bert, 'cryin' won't 'elp.'

'I know...' said Molly through her tears, annoyed with herself for being so foolish, 'it's just that it seems so final.'

'Now don't be silly, love, course it isn't,' said Bert firmly, 'yer just upset...'

'Come on!' said Molly fiercely, standing up and making an effort to pull herself together, 'let's go 'ome.'

They began the long walk back to Fern Cottage, regretting now that they had not accepted Alf Tomkins' offer of transport. He had been willing to wait in the wagon for them, whilst they saw the newly-weds off, but Molly had declined, wanting to keep it a purely family affair. Bert had tried to persuade her to change her mind, but she was adamant. He knew very well that the real reason was Molly knew she would be upset and was loath to let Alf witness what she regarded as her weakness. He had reminded her that they had known Alf for many years, but to no avail.

They relived every moment of the day as they walked briskly along, swapping their impressions in the comfortable way that only old married couples can and Molly's spirits gradually began to rise. By the time they reached the outskirts of the village they had been walking for nearly an hour and were chatting and laughing contentedly, looking forward to putting their feet up with a warming cup of tea.

The driver of the motor car saw them too late as they rounded the bend. Dazzled and startled by the headlights speeding straight at them, Bert and Molly stood transfixed in its path, unable to move for a second.

'Look out!' screamed Bert in the next instant, as he lunged at Molly, pushing her with all his strength into the hedgerow.

The car was going too fast to stop, swerving violently as the driver braked hard, fighting to maintain control. It clipped the bushes on the opposite side of the narrow road but carried on.

151

PART TWO

LONDON

1909–1914

Chapter 25

''Ow about these, luv?' shouted Richie, holding up a large green apple for Mrs Cooper to see, 'perfect in a pie an' ready to eat! Only ha'penny a pound to you, Mrs Cooper.'

'Go on wiv you lad...' exclaimed the middle-aged woman from Number 24, 'a ha'penny for *them!*'

'Top quality, Mrs Cooper, you know me, no rubbish on 'ere, an' 'specially not for you!'

'Go on wiv yer! Oh ... all right, Rich, ha'penny it is,' she said grudgingly and handed over some coins.

'Ta, Mrs Cooper. I'm givin' 'em away at that price!' he replied with a winning smile, 'my assistant 'ere will bag 'em for you,' he added, nodding at Max who was standing behind the barrow, watching Richie at work.

''Ere yer are, Mrs Cooper,' said Max quickly, weighing out a pound of Bramleys he selected by reaching over to the front of the display. 'Never put soft fruits at the front of the barrer, always put 'em at the back, 'ard fruits an' veg go at the front' was what Richie had told him, 'that way they don't get bruised 'cause people can't 'andle 'em until they're paid for.'

'Thanks, luv,' said Mrs Cooper. 'Workin' you 'ard is he?' she asked with a grin.

'Somethin' terrible!' replied Max with a chuckle. 'But don't tell 'im I told yer! 'Ere's yer change,' he said, counting the coins into her outstretched hand.

Richie looked across at him and smiled. One of the first pieces of advice he had given Max, other than to show him the best way to set out the barrow, was to ensure that coins were always counted back into the individual's hand in order to avoid accusations of short changing; sleight of hand was common amongst their less scrupulous customers, and for the inexperienced costermonger it could prove costly.

They had formed an easy friendship since he and Rosie had arrived after their long train journey from Devon. When Richie had suggested that Max help him work the pitch along the Mile End Road, he had said yes immediately. Watching him at work, Max quickly realised that he was a natural, a born salesman with the ability to charm. He had an open and friendly manner but he was quick-witted with it. This was very clear when he negotiated with the traders at Covent Garden, holding them with a steady gaze as he shrewdly struck a good price for top quality produce. Despite the fact that he and Rosie had only been in London for a week, Max had already accompanied Richie on one of his early morning trips to market, eager to learn its workings as quickly as possible. The suppliers seemed to respect his brother-in-law and respond to his direct manner. His reputation for not suffering fools gladly seemed to be well-known and he did not hesitate to change suppliers if they let him down or abused his loyalty in any way.

The Black family had welcomed Max and Rosie with open arms from the minute they arrived, tired and hungry after their travelling, but still full of joy and high spirits from their wedding celebrations. Stan and Ivy were meeting Max for the first time as well as welcoming him into the family as their son-in-law and they went out of their way to make him feel at home. Ivy was the heart and soul of the family, holding everything together. She had a strong physical presence that was not immediately obvious because of her slight frame. In fact Max's first impression was one of frailty but he soon realised that one of her strongest attributes was an unflinching resilience and no-nonsense manner, which bolstered those around her. An innate warmth and good humour, revealed whenever she smiled, softened her rather gaunt and austere appearance. Her smile could transform a room, making the recipient of it feel special. Stan also had a commanding presence due to his height and stocky build, although it was now diminished somewhat by the lingering effects of his accident. He would have made a good prize-fighter in his youth. His mass of dark hair, greying at the temples, and large round eyes resembling dark saucers in his round face were characteristics he had passed on to his three sons. Grace, their adored daughter, who had died so young, had taken after Ivy and her spirit was still very much in evidence in the little house. Her battered rag doll sat on the window-sill in Stan and Ivy's bedroom and Ivy would say 'sleep tight' to her every night as if she was talking to Grace herself.

Stan was a proud man with a strong work ethic and had been beside himself with guilt and worry about keeping his family from poverty after his accident, which had meant that he could no longer work at Smithfield Market. The pay there had not been good but at least it was regular. At first he had blamed himself, sinking into a depression that made him more and more difficult to live with until finally Ivy, at her wit's end, had threatened to leave him. Only then did he start to pull himself together and become a proper father to his children once again. Ivy would not have carried out her threat but she could think of no other way of inspiring him to fight his malaise. Through it all, Richie, as the eldest, had assumed the role of chief breadwinner after Stan's best friend had asked him to help work the pitch along the Mile End Road. He had been learning his trade ever since and now, skilled at his craft, he longed to have his own barrow with his own name painted on the side.

'I don't know 'ow we'd manage if it wasn't for the money you two boys bring in,' Ivy would sometimes tell Richie and Len when Stan was out of earshot. But she knew Stan was not idle and saw to it that his fragile ego was protected whenever she sensed his depression was creeping back to afflict him. He was still the head of the family.

Money was always very tight, only alleviated occasionally when Stan found the odd day's work here and there, sometimes on the barrow, sometimes not, but always as a result of tramping the streets for hours on end. This allowed Ivy to buy extra coal for the fire so it could be lit earlier in the day, and a few small treats for the table, or, on very rare occasions, a plate of pie and mash with jellied eels for them all to share. Max was shocked by the meagreness of their lives and the extent of the deprivation he saw all around him in the East End. He had not experienced it on such a scale before, not even in Plymouth, which until their arrival in London had been his only real exposure to the world beyond Lee Moor. At least in the village the natural beauty of the estate and countryside dominated the senses instead of the squalor and destitution that threatened to engulf them here. There had always been food on the table and a fire in the grate at Fern Cottage, even if his Ma and Pa's lives were ruled by permanent servitude. He realised this with a feeling of detachment for he was no longer a part of it; through his endeavours, he and Rosie had broken free from the yoke of servility and it could no longer menace them.

He was beginning to feel safe from the clutches of the Gordon family and the power they held over the lives of so many people, his parents included. It was a good feeling, not one he had savoured before, and to his surprise he realised that their new geographical separation from his childhood home was the reason for acknowledging it now. But, as good as it was, it was not enough.

The family home in Globe Road, just along from the infirmary, was

157

in one of the poorest slums in London where local memories were still haunted by the notorious Jack the Ripper killings, even though they had occurred some 25 years earlier. It was a two-up and two-down terraced house barely able to accommodate everyone. Stan and Ivy slept in their own room and Richie, Len and their youngest brother Jimmy were crammed into the little room opposite on the other side of the narrow landing. There were two equally small rooms downstairs, one of which served as the scullery and the other as a living-room, or parlour, as Ivy liked to call it. Despite this lack of space, Stan and Ivy insisted that Max and Rosie stay with them for as long as they wished and had moved out of their bedroom into the parlour downstairs. 'Newlyweds need their own space,' said Ivy.

Max and Rosie were grateful to the Blacks for their hospitality because it gave them the time to look for somewhere more suitable to live, given their relative prosperity, and for Max especially, it provided the opportunity to learn first-hand about London's fruit and vegetable trade from Richie. However, they all knew it could only be a strictly temporary arrangement.

'She always tries it on, that one,' said Richie, nodding in Mrs Cooper's direction as she bustled away, 'but she's got an 'eart of gold when it matters.'

'If yer say so,' said Max with a grin. 'They all seem ter do the same though. It's different ter my business, Richie. My customers place an order fer me ter deliver ter 'em and they already know 'ow much it's goin' ter be, or they're paying fer a plate o' food with a clear price displayed before 'and.'

'Most of them round here are all right, an' you get to know who the ruffians are pretty well,' replied Richie. 'Come on then, it's about time ter pack up,' he said, looking up at the fading light, 'give us an 'and, Max, will yer?'

'Yeah, of course,' answered Max. 'Veg away first?' he asked, picking up a wooden crate from alongside the barrow. As the two men worked methodically to pack everything carefully away Max asked Richie a question that had been on his mind all day. ''Ave yer ever thought o' delivering produce ter people, instead o' always relying on 'em ter come ter yer?'

Richie was silent, taken aback by the question. 'It might be a way ter raise yer sales without needin' another barrer,' said Max when Richie did not reply.

'I've never thought about it ter be honest. Don't people want to see what they're buyin'?' he said after a while. 'An' it's not my barrer anyway, more's the pity,' he added.

'Some of 'em do, yeah, an' always will. But what about people who can't get out during the day, yer know, shopkeepers, small business owners, publicans … those sort o' people?'

Richie looked at Max out of the corner of his eye as he started to throw the cover over the now empty barrow. 'Catch 'old of the other side will you … that's it … pull it tight and tie the rope around the metal clip … well, I dunno, Max, yer might be right.' He pulled hard on the cover so that it was taught. 'That'll keep the rain out, just in case,' he explained. ''Ow would it work though? There's only me ter do everything an' I can't be in two places at once.'

'I know,' said Max thoughtfully, 'we would 'ave ter work somethin' out. But we can't do anything until this barrer's yers. Would yer Dad's mate consider sellin' do yer think?'

'It's the pitch that's worth more than the barrer, Max. Without that there's no point 'aving the barrer in the first place.'

'S'pose not,' responded Max quietly as he helped finish packing up.

'Let's get 'ome,' said Richie, thrusting his hands into the pockets of his old overcoat. 'Back to that new wife o' yours!' he said with a wink, grinning broadly.

'Yeah,' replied Max, smiling back. 'P'raps she's found us somewhere ter live so we can get out o' yer way.'

'So we stop crampin' your style more like!' rejoined Richie, this time with a loud chuckle. 'You know me mum an' dad mean it though, don't you?' he asked with a slightly worried look on his face, 'you can stay as long as yer need.'

'We know,' said Max softly, 'an' it's very kind o' yer all, but we…'

'… *are* crampin' your style,' interrupted Richie quickly, 'you don't 'ave to say it!'

They both laughed and walked on. Max considered himself lucky to have taken to all three of the Black brothers. He already felt he knew Richie well because they had spent most time together and he had seen how he put his natural charm and ability to get on with people to effective use working the pitch. He was an extrovert with a cheeky and confident personality but there was definitely a firm side to him; he had seen that at Covent Garden market. Len was the second oldest and was a little more reserved than his older brother, but for all that, no less confident and good humoured. He had learned his trade as a carpenter and was good at it. Rosie said that he had shown an interest in wood from an early age and as a young boy had collected odd pieces of wood he would find here and there. He had become known as the scavenger in the family, turning the wood he found into beautiful carved objects and small practical items for the house. It was clear that he had a natural talent for his work, handling wood as if it was a precious commodity deserving of love and care. He was particularly adept at joinery and could even turn his hand to cabinet making. Slightly shorter than Richie, he was nonetheless thickset like his brother and could look after himself in the rough back alleys of the neighbourhood.

The youngest of the family was Jimmy and he was altogether different to Richie and Len. Slender in build, he was quiet and studious and was never happier than when he had something to read. Being the junior of four, he had spent a lot of his time trying to be alone when he was growing up in order to avoid being treated as the baby of the family. He was still sensitive to that and detested it all the more because in a strange way he felt it usurped Grace's place in the family hierarchy. He was the most academically gifted of them all and excelled at the local school where Stan and Ivy were regular visitors to hear of his progress from his teachers. He worshipped his older brothers who were very protective of him, often denying themselves things in order to afford to buy him paper and pencils to write with, or books to read. If they found a newspaper discarded in the street they would pick it up and take it home for Jimmy to study. His face would light up when they handed it to him and he would spend the rest of the day trying to read every word, sometimes stumbling over the longer ones. When he encountered a word he had not heard of, or did not understand, he would write it down and take it to his teacher the following day and ask for help with it. Gradually, as time went on, this list got shorter, and his spelling better, until his need to do it at all became the exception rather than the norm. Even though he did not possess many of the physical attributes of his brothers, he was nevertheless courageous and determined and had always managed to stand up for himself whenever the occasion demanded it.

'It's only us, we're 'ome,' yelled Richie as he pushed open the front door.

'Tea's almost ready,' called Ivy and Rosie in unison from the scullery, 'come an' wash yer 'ands.'

Max followed Richie along the dark passage towards the scullery. The gas lamp had not been lit despite the gloom. 'It needs a new mantle,' explained Richie, nodding towards the wall, 'an' Ma won't waste money on 'em. Besides, I expect the meter needs feedin' too.'

''Ello, luv, 'ow did yer get on terday?' asked Max. He gave Rosie a big kiss and whispered, ''Ere's some money fer the meter,' pressing a couple of coins into her hand as he began to roll up his sleeves at the sink.

Rosie smiled discreetly at him and slipped out to the meter, which was in the cupboard under the stairs. She knew her mother would make a fuss so she went ahead and put them in without saying a word. 'There yer are, Ma, meter's fed,' she said firmly as she went back into the scullery.

''Ow many...'

'Now, Ma, it's done so don't go on!' She silenced Ivy with a look, and Max, busy at the sink, concentrated hard on his hands to hide the beginnings of a smile that he was having trouble controlling. He was getting used to being part of a larger family circle and enjoyed the easy banter and familiarity that went with it.

'I can't wait ter tell yer about a little 'ouse I saw terday, Max,' said Rosie enthusiastically, 'it'd be perfect fer us and I think we can afford the rent.'

Max saw the flush of excitement on her face as she passed him a cloth to dry his hands. 'Use this, luv,' she said.

'Ta. Whereabouts?' he asked.

'Pimlico,' replied Rosie.

Chapter 26

'It's cold sweet'art,' said Max, snuggling up to Rosie as the faint light of dawn found its way around the edges of the thin piece of material hanging in front of the window. He nuzzled her ear with his lips. 'Are yer asleep?'

'Ssh, darling,' mumbled Rosie drowsily, 'yer'll wake the 'ouse...'

'Be quiet then,' whispered Max in reply as his hand crept around her waist, his fingers softly lingering over her skin.

'Max, me brothers are only next door! Richie'll be awake soon...'

'We'll 'ave ter be quick then...' murmured Max mischievously.

Rosie stifled a yawn and caught hold of his hand and returned it firmly to his side. 'Be'ave yerself before we get inter trouble!'

'Too late...'

Max felt a sharp nudge from her elbow. 'Ouch!' he exclaimed, trying to sound put out and hurt as quietly as he could. 'Thought we were on 'oneymoon.'

'Patience, darling, patience...' soothed Rosie, 'wait till we get our 'ouse...'

'That'll be ages,' groaned Max resignedly.

'No it won't, we'll go round first thin' in the morning ter see the agent. Now go back ter sleep.' She turned her head towards him and smiled as she saw his eyes were already closed.

The letter arrived the next morning just as they were about to leave the house. Max was lacing up his boots in the scullery and Rosie was putting on her coat in the passageway when there was a loud knock on the front door. It startled her as it was too early for the coal or gas man and they were the only people who normally called at the front. The neighbours always came round the back.

'Was that somebody at the front door, luv?' called Ivy from upstairs where she was sweeping the floors.

'Yes, Ma,' shouted Rosie, holding a small envelope in her hand. 'It's the postman.'

'Postman?' exclaimed Ivy, her tone registering her surprise. 'What, *fer us?*' she said, appearing on the tiny landing between the two bedrooms.

'With a letter, addressed ter Max,' she said slowly. She recognised the handwriting on the envelope. 'Max, this 'as just come,' she called down the hallway as she turned round from the door, but Max had already heard and was behind her, holding out his hand.

Max looked at the envelope and knew who it was from straightaway. 'It's from...' he began as he tore it open, his eyes scanning the first few lines.

'*What is it, darling!*' cried Rosie in alarm, her hand flying to her mouth.

Max had turned deathly white. Ivy, sensing trouble, stood motionless at the top of the stairs.

My dearest Max and Rosie
I pray ter God that this reaches yer. Please come 'ome. Yer Pa 'as been badly 'urt by a motor car and is askin' fer yer. We were walkin' 'ome from seein' yer off at the station an' it came round the bend an' 'it us. Don't yer worry about me I'm all right but yer Pa is bad.
I'm sorry, Max, please come 'ome as quick as yer can.
Ma.

His hands were shaking as he handed the letter to Rosie. 'I must go sweet'art.' His voice trembled. '*She don't say how bad 'e is!*' His mind was a confusion of thoughts and he struggled to make sense of them.

'*What's 'appened ... what does it say?*' demanded Ivy, flying down the stairs.

Rosie handed her the letter without a word. 'I'm comin' with yer! It won't take a second ter pack a few things.'

'*No!*' he said agitatedly and stretched out a hand to touch her arm. 'Yer should stay 'ere, darling. No point in both o' us goin'.'

'*But what if...*' Her voice trailed off and she just looked desperately at Max, her eyes beseeching him to change his mind.

He was thinking more clearly now, frowning as he pulled himself together. 'It doesn't make sense fer both o' us ter go,' he said firmly. 'Yer stay 'ere and go ter Pimlico as we decided. I might only be gone a few days,' he said, with false optimism. 'Can yer 'elp me get my things...' *Why doesn't she say more?* he demanded silently as they ran upstairs to pack his bag, *like how bad 'e is ... is she 'urt? ... she says she's all right, but ... I should 'ave been there...* He knew it was pointless to think like that but, for once, his normal rational and practical mind was overwhelmed by the shocking unexpectedness of the news. *Think ... think!* he said savagely to himself.

163

Rosie had a shrewd guess about what was running through his mind. 'She would 'ave said if she was 'urt too, Max and she said she was all right didn't she … *I should be with yer,* or at least let me come fer Molly's sake?' Max shook his head as they threw some clothes into the brown overnight bag. Rosie knew it was pointless to argue. His mind was made up. 'Take these too, yer might need them,' she said, handing him some more clean socks, 'an' these.'

Max threw her a rather forced, thin smile as he fastened the bag. 'Thanks, luv. Now don't yer worry about me, I'll be back as quick as I can, promise. Just get that 'ouse yer've set yer 'eart on remember?'

He put his arms around her and held her tightly. She closed her eyes, willing herself to remain composed, not knowing whether the tears stinging the backs of them were for Max, Bert … Molly, or even herself.

'Be careful, darling,' is all she could manage to whisper before her voice broke.

Ivy was standing by the front door waiting to see him off. 'God speed,' she said softly, smiling gently as he kissed her on the cheek. 'Don't worry about things 'ere. I'll look after 'er for you…'

She closed the door behind him and made for the stairs. 'Now then, Rosie, 'aven't yer got an appointment, it won't do ter be late!' she called out in a decisive voice. 'Let's be 'aving yer!'

Max ran down Globe Road, thinking about his route back home. He knew he could catch the 'Zulu' express from Paddington, the London terminus of the Great Western Railway, to Plymouth via Exeter St Davids. It left at three o'clock but he hoped there might be an earlier one. At least he had enough time to make the later train if necessary. If he was lucky he might just make the connection on to Bickleigh, that would be the nearest station to Lee Moor, but he'd check to make sure at Paddington. From Bickleigh he could try and thumb a ride or, if the worst came to the worst, he would just have to walk. He paused briefly to catch his breath, feeling slightly more in control of the situation now that he had decided what to do. After a few more deep breaths he hitched his bag more firmly over his shoulder and set off again, this time at a sensible pace to give himself a chance to find his way as he suddenly realised he had no idea how to get to Paddington without Rosie to help him.

When at last the distinctive curved outline of Brunel's huge glazed roof that spanned the main train shed came into sight he breathed a sigh of relief and, turning into Praed Street, he found himself in more recognisable surroundings. The station was on his right, that much he recalled from their journey up from Devon, and just ahead of him was the tunnel entrance from the street to the Metropolitan Railway. He did not remember seeing that at the time but it had been dark when they had arrived. Rosie had told him about the railway that ran underground. He walked past the Great Western Hotel, which did not look nearly as splendid as The Royal in Plymouth, and entered what looked to be the main thoroughfare through to the trains.

Ever since leaving the house he had been thinking about the letter until finally his mind was numb with fatigue. There were no answers to the jumble of questions that kept darting through his head, but they kept on whirling round and round until he could no longer concentrate clearly. He found himself concocting wild theories about what might have happened but there was one persistent image that remained lodged at the forefront of his mind; that of his father lying injured, bleeding, and maybe even dying, in the road.

'What time is the next train ter Plymouth please, connecting ter Bickleigh?' he asked when he reached the ticket office. The queue had not been particularly long but the wait had seemed interminable to Max.

'Three o'clock, sir. Platform two,' came the reply from behind the small window.

'An' the connection please?' queried Max again, this time unable to conceal his impatience.

'*You* will have to ask when you get there, *sir. This* is the Great Western Railway. The line to Bickleigh is a separate company, *sir,*' said the man testily. He had detected the edge to Max's tone and did not like it. 'Bloody rude if you ask me,' he muttered under his breath, but just loud enough for Max to hear. Max was in no mood to argue and chose to ignore it.

'An' 'ow much is that?' he asked, handing over a one pound note and deliberately avoiding the man's eye.

The man mumbled the answer and abruptly pushed the change across the counter. Turning away, Max pocketed the coins and put the ticket in his coat pocket before looking for platform two. The station was crowded; there were groups of people milling around in search of their trains and to Max it all seemed like a world away from the relative tranquillity of the sleepy village halts he was used to. Ordinarily he would have felt exhilarated by the vibrant energy of the place, invigorated by the bustling activity around him, but today he was just desperate to be on his way back to Lee Moor.

'Excuse me, platform two please?' he asked a harassed looking man in uniform.

'Over there, sir, to the right of the clock,' said the assistant stationmaster, pointing over Max's left shoulder. Swivelling round, Max looked in the direction of the gold braided arm and located the clock. It was showing just after one o'clock. Turning back, he nodded and smiled his thanks but the man had already hurried on. '*Two hours yet!*' he groaned in despair. All he could think about was the last words of his mother's letter: ... *as quick as yer can.*

Chapter 27

It was late and the high street was deserted. He had been fortunate to find a lift on the outskirts of Bickleigh from a local farmer who had been out delivering cattle feed to a nearby farm, despite the lateness of the hour. It was not particularly unusual to find farmers helping each other out in this way and it was Max's good fortune to have spotted one such Good Samaritan as he walked down the lane leading from the station. The man had brought him almost halfway to Lee Moor before their paths diverged and now Max was relieved to be alone again. He was grateful for the ride and, above all, for the time he had saved because of it, but the man had talked incessantly, barely drawing a breath for the entire journey, which Max had found vexatious in his current state of mind.

The Wheelwrights was silent and shuttered for the night as he strode quickly past. He was relieved to have missed closing time and the inevitable band of hardcore regulars who would insist on propping up the bar until the last possible minute before being unceremoniously ejected into the street by a determined Daisy. Up ahead he could see a dim figure silhouetted against the light shining through the open door of Clarke's General Store. He crossed to the other side of the street and quickened his pace still further, hoping to avoid encountering anybody else before reaching home. He checked himself as that thought crossed his mind, Fern Cottage was not his home any more. London was where he belonged now, in London, with Rosie.

'Max ... is that you?' a voice called out as he drew level with the light. The figure took a few steps towards him, peering into the darkness until, out of the corner of his eye, Max could see it was Ed Clarke busy cleaning the empty display shelves alongside the shop window. Max hesitated, fighting the desire to pretend he had not heard and walk on. 'Hey, Max, *it's me, Eddie!*'

Max stopped and looked over to him. 'Eddie! 'Ow are yer? Didn't expect ter see yer still 'ard at it at this time o' night.' He took a couple of steps towards him.

'Spring cleanin', mate. Me dad wants all the window displays cleaned before the mornin',' he replied ruefully, 'an' me back's killin' me.'

At the mention of the word 'Dad' Max's heart lurched and he looked at the ground to hide his pained expression. 'Just like yer dad!' said Max trying hard to sound cheerful.

'That's true enough,' exclaimed Edward with feeling, but his tone was kind. 'They're all the same if yer ask me!'

Max averted his head. 'Yeah, you're probably right...' he mumbled. There was a silence before he looked up and said, 'I'd better let yer get on, it's late.' He smiled quickly and turned to go. 'Be seein' yer then, Ed, look after yerself,' he said in a clipped tone over his shoulder as he crossed back over the street.

Edward watched Max go, taken aback at his curtness. Then, suddenly, he swore under his breath as he realised how insensitive he had just been. He had opened his mouth without thinking. What a dreadful business it was ... poor Bert ... he thought to himself and shook his head sadly. 'It always 'appens ter the nice ones,' he sighed as he bent down to pick up his bucket.

Max hurried on, knowing he had appeared rude but he could not help himself. The torment of wondering about his father had been worsening the nearer he got to Lee Moor and it was now unbearable as he turned into the little lane of cottages. He could see lights burning in their parlour window and he broke into a run.

Molly was sat with her back to the door staring into the fire as he walked in. 'The kettle's on, Eileen,' she said in a quiet voice without turning round.

'Ma, it's not Mrs Mears, it's me,' panted Max as he slipped his bag from his shoulders, letting it drop on to the floor at his feet. The moment she heard his voice, Molly shot up out of her chair and rushed across the tiny room towards him. She flung her arms around him with such force that he stumbled backwards. 'Whoa, Ma, it's all right,' he gasped, nearly winded by her greeting.

She buried her head in his chest and held him close. 'I thought it was Eileen, she's been comin' in an' sittin' with me fer a bit these past few nights,' she sobbed.

'What do yer mean?' asked Max, alarmed and discomfited by her reaction. 'What's the matter, Ma?' Gently, he tried to raise her head. 'Look at me!' he demanded. 'Where's Dad?'

Before he could say anything else there was a knock on the door behind them and Mrs Mears appeared. 'Max! Thank the Lord yer 'ere,' she exclaimed, relief flooding across her face as soon as she saw him.

He looked helplessly over the top of Molly's head towards her. 'Come on, Molly, luv, 'e's 'ere now,' she said softly, taking hold of her neighbour's arms and gently prising her away. 'Yer see, I told yer 'e'd come,' she went on in the same soothing manner as she led her back to the chair. 'You sit by the fire an' I'll make us all some tea.'

'Dad will wonder what all the fuss is about,' said Max uneasily. Molly did not reply. She just sat there, crying so much that she could not speak. 'Is 'e upstairs, Ma? I'll just go up an' see 'im while the kettle's boilin' . . .'

'No, don't do that, Max,' cried Eileen sharply, swivelling round quickly from the range, 'Bert's not there . . . 'e's . . .'

'Well where is 'e then?' interrupted Max, his voice rising.

Mrs Mears looked uncomfortable and tried to busy herself with the teapot. Her throat had gone dry and she could not find the right words. What could she say? Her mind had gone blank.

'Come an' sit down, Max. Yer dad is dead,' said Molly suddenly. She said it bluntly and without warning, her voice barely audible.

'Dad, *dead*,' whispered Max incredulously. ''E can't be dead, Ma! I would 'ave known, would 'ave felt somethin'.' He lowered himself into the chair next to Molly, his face drained of all colour. Molly took his hand and tried to say something but the words would not come. 'I know I would . . .' But the expressions on their faces told him it was true. Tears welled in his eyes but he fought them, gripping tightly on to the arm of the chair with his free hand, determined to remain composed for her sake.

Mrs Mears looked from one to the other and bit her lip, her eyes blurring as she softly cleared her throat. She knew she would have to explain as Molly was too distraught to speak. They were like family to her; she had known them for over 20 years and Bert had always looked out for her, so now it was her turn.

'It was on the way 'ome from the station, as yer mum's letter said. Yer mum an' dad were walkin' round the bend by the chandlers . . . yer know, at the far end . . . and this motor car came straight at them, goin' fast it was . . .' She faltered and looked carefully at Molly. 'Shall I go on, Molly?'

Max answered for her. 'Yes please, Eileen,' he said steadily. 'I want ter know.' He used her Christian name for the first time. He had always called her Mrs Mears as it seemed the correct thing to do for some reason, but now it felt different. He gripped Molly's hand, trying to give her comfort through his grief.

'Yer mum saw it first I think and fer a moment they were blinded

by the 'eadlights and then Bert ... 'e must 'ave realised what was goin'
ter 'appen an' pushed yer mum out of the way. Just in time it was. The
motor car swerved across the road an'...' Her hand flew over her mouth
as she choked back a sob. Max stiffened as she took a deep breath and
continued... ''E did try ter miss 'em Max, really 'e did...' and her
voice trailed away.

They sat there in silence for a long time until Molly stirred in her
seat. Her sobbing had begun to subside and she tried to wipe her swollen
and red-rimmed eyes with her trembling hands.

''Ere yer are, Ma,' said Max, offering her his handkerchief. She took
it gratefully and dabbed at the tears still rolling down her flushed cheeks.

'Thanks, luv,' she said tremulously. Her voice was drained and desperate
with sadness. ''E saved me, yer dad, 'e pushed me out o' the way, inter
the bushes but then it must 'ave been too ... 'e couldn't get out o' the
way 'imself before the car...'

Max turned even paler and felt sick with anguish. 'Who was it?
Driving, I mean?' asked Max between clenched teeth, his eyes motionless
as he waited for the answer.

Molly looked at him, sitting bolt upright in his chair, holding himself
under control with a rigid determination. At that moment all she could
see was her tough little boy who used to run to his father shouting
'Daddy!' at the top of his voice as soon as Bert walked through the
door at the end of a hard day's work, demanding to be swung high in
his father's arms, giggling delightedly as he swayed through the air before
coming to rest happily on his father's lap where he would want to stay
for the rest of the evening until bedtime. How Bert had loved that. She
stared into space, that picture lingering in her mind, until she finally
managed to say, 'They're not sure, but there aren't that many folk round
'ere that 'as a motor car...'

'They...? Who...? The police, yer mean?' asked Max slowly. His
blood had run cold. His features were impassively set, as if carved from
stone, as he looked from Molly to Eileen, unyielding in his resolve to
know everything, however heartrending it was.

'Yes, luv, Constable Terry came after we'd been found an'...'

'*Been found!*' Max exclaimed in disbelief, '*yer mean the car didn't stop!*'
This time his voice was loud, full of pent-up fury and distress. He felt
physically crushed, shuddering with horror as he imagined the suffering
his father must have endured after the car drove off, leaving them lying
in the road, mutilated and bleeding in the darkness. He found himself
praying the end had been quick.

As if reading his mind, Eileen said, 'Doctor Roley assured us 'e wouldn't 'ave felt much pain, Max, it would all 'ave been very quick, with the force o' the impact yer see.'

Max nodded, steeling himself to ask the question to which he already knew the answer. 'It was 'im wasn't it?' His face was inscrutable, betraying no sign of emotion whatsoever as he spoke. It was more of a statement than a question but he spat out the words as if they were poison.

'The police investigation 'asn't finished yet, luv,' said Molly slowly, 'Constable Terry 'as called in 'elp from the station at Princetown so we can't be sure, an' it 'appened so quick I didn't see ... but ... yes...' Molly hesitated. 'It might 'ave been 'is Lordship's motor car. They 'ave been up at the 'ouse two or three times.' She looked at Eileen and then at Max. 'We'll know soon enough...' She grimaced as she leant forward.

'Ma, are yer all right?' asked Max quickly in a choked voice. His grief was now tinged with guilt. 'Sorry, Ma, I 'aven't asked how yer are yet, are yer in pain?'

'Now, lad,' replied Molly in a stronger voice, which brought a strangled sob to his throat for that was the expression his father had always used, 'I'm perfectly all right, just a few scrapes an' bruises, nothing that time won't 'eal.' She was beginning to recover a semblance of composure now.

Max glanced at Eileen and she looked back at him reassuringly. 'Yer Ma will be all right with lots of care an' rest, an' that's what I'm 'ere for. Doctor Roley says so, Max. There's no need fer yer ter worry, 'onestly.'

Max closed his eyes and leant back in the chair, inwardly breathing a sigh of relief. He was dreading hearing more but he could not help himself, he had to know everything. He took a deep breath, not wishing to set Molly crying again. 'Where is 'e now, Ma?' He stared straight ahead at the flames flickering in the grate and his mouth quivered but still he did not give in to the tears that were stinging his eyes.

''E's in the chapel, luv ... 'e's very peaceful an' the flowers are...'

'Can I see 'im?' he asked in a low voice that was devoid of all spark.

'Course yer can, luv, if yer sure that's what yer want, but ... the lid is closed...' Max looked at her. 'On the casket...'

Molly could see he did not understand, that he wanted to see his Dad one more time, ter say goodbye. 'On account of 'is...' She was silent for a moment. 'On account of ... the injuries yer see...'

Max looked blankly at her. 'An' the funeral, Ma?'

'The day after termorrow, it's all arranged. Eileen 'elped me.' She looked across at her neighbour and smiled gratefully. 'So yer can bury 'im, luv, like 'e would 'ave wanted,' she finished softly.

Chapter 28

Max was exhausted but he only managed to sleep fitfully. He had lain awake in the darkness listening to the sound of his mother crying in her room, not knowing whether to go to her or leave her to her own private grief. He felt suffocated and incapable of rest and by the time the first hint of dawn crept through the curtains he could stand it no longer. He rose and dressed swiftly and crept down the stairs, quietly scribbling a note to say he would be back later before letting himself out of the front door.

He followed the path he knew so well, past Jolly Lane Cottage and granite cross, walking purposefully without pause for breath as his route took him up into the sloping hills of his childhood that he used to call his own. He paid no heed to the beauty of the emerging spring morning, conscious only of his feelings of devastation and despair. The grass in the field was long and wet underfoot and by the time he reached the stile next to the road, the dampness had begun to soak through the leather of his boots. He took no notice, not even when he lost his footing on the slippery blanket of moss covering the first wooden step, catching his shin hard on the attached upright support. He climbed the steep path up to his vantage spot, to the place where he had brought Rosie the first time they had made love.

He looked down at Mount Royal in the distance and his feelings of grief were replaced for a moment by pure hatred, an all-consuming sense of loathing for the Gordon family, and for Lord William in particular. It must have been their motor car that killed his father, and, but for the grace of God, his mother too. *He knew it and Molly knew it*, although she had been unwilling to say so last night despite admitting that there were not many other people with cars in the neighbourhood. That bastard of a son was driving, undoubtedly, only he could have been so callous as to drive off and leave them for dead! That made it cold-blooded murder as far as he was concerned. But he'd get away with it, he always did. Driving fast, Eileen had said, too fast, he'd wager, just like the way he drove his carriage through the village. It was well known in these parts.

Why did she persist in defending them? It was the same when Rosie had had her accident ... *some accident* ... he was absolutely sure Lord William was behind that too, somehow or other. Don't jump to conclusions, Molly had said then. If it was not for the fact that it would disquiet Rosie even more, who just wanted to try to blank it from her mind, he would... He really did not understand his mother's inexplicable desire to protect them. *Why was she being so reasonable?* He shook his head savagely and tore his eyes away from the house, unable to deal with the bitterness of his thoughts on top of the unrelieved heartache he felt for his father.

The funeral was tomorrow and there were decisions to be made. He looked across the valley to the church and thought of his father lying in the little chapel. He would go to see him there later in the day to say goodbye. He wanted him to know what he would have said if he had been there at the end, to express all the things that a devoted son should say to an adored father. It did not matter that the coffin was already closed. He wanted to remember him as he had been in life, caring, loyal and utterly dependable, so full of spirit and kindness. He shut his eyes and took a deep breath to steady himself, deriving some small comfort that he had at least arrived in time to be able to do that.

He sat down on a rock that was jutting out from a clump of bushes behind him. It was now almost fully light and the whistle would soon be sounding at the mine. Mrs Castle would be busy in her kitchen and no doubt the rest of his friends below stairs would be occupied in preparing for *their* annual migration to Chesterfield Square in a few weeks' time. Sitting there, in this place he knew so well, it could almost have seemed like old times except that so much had happened in the intervening years, which had changed their lives for ever. He could ... no, *would,* never go back to the life he had led as a child and to which his mother was still bound.

His father's untimely death had taught Max one important lesson, which he was never to forget; he was no longer simply just his mother's son, he had now to fulfil the role of parent to her as well, to look after and protect her as Bert had always done for him. He had realised that the previous evening when he had tried to soothe and comfort her, just as a parent does to a child who is upset, and as he lay awake during the night listening to the torment of her crying for his father. He vowed that his love would give her hope, hope for the future, just as her love had done for him whenever he was sick or frightened as a little boy.

The revelations of the previous evening had also served as the catalyst for another decision, which would have far reaching effects for the rest of his life. The time spent with Richie on the barrow, albeit brief, had set him thinking about the direction of the emporium in London, and their trip to Covent Garden had shown him that an idea he had been mulling over was worth exploring. He had asked Richie if he had ever thought about delivering produce to customers instead of expecting them to buy from the barrow. It was no idle question at the time and now, with more thought, he believed the future of the emporium lay in the wholesale delivery of fresh produce and fine foods to businesses, as well as to private households. London had astounded him with its multitude of public houses, hotels, restaurants and other eating houses, all of which needed daily supplies of fruit and vegetables, fresh meat, fish and a whole myriad of fine foods, *and* these establishments would buy it in greater quantities than the private households would ever do, however grand they may be. He had seen the demand for his range in Plymouth quadruple under Rebecca's stewardship since the early days and the addition of fresh fish and, more recently, a limited range of fresh meat and poultry butchered daily in their premises in the Barbican, had produced profits comfortably exceeding £200 per week. This was due largely to Billy's shrewd management. The potential in London could be almost limitless but he would need premises, delivery vehicles, and more staff before he could put his hunch to the test.

He shifted his weight on to his right leg to ease the ache in his back caused by sitting for too long on the hard, uneven surface of the rock. His left leg had turned numb and he rubbed it vigorously to revive some feeling. He felt a little better now that he had reached a conclusion about these outstanding business matters, particularly as they were vital to the future direction of the company. He would have to discuss them with Billy because MMC Ltd and the emporium would be drawn ever more closely together if they were to succeed, as he believed they could. The first step was to talk to Jack to see if he had considered a proposition Max had put to him on the eve of his wedding.

The unmistakable sound of the whistle broke his concentration. The village was waking up and it was time to go back to Fern Cottage and Molly. He stood up and stamped his feet once or twice in the damp grass to fully restore the circulation. He had forgotten how much he liked this time of year and, as he took one last look at the beauty of the surrounding countryside, a sensation of peace crept over him and, for the first time since receiving Molly's letter, he felt better equipped to deal with his turbulent emotions. The great dark clouds of misery that had been sweeping over him began to subside and he set off on the walk home with renewed spirit for the harrowing days ahead.

'Ma, I'm back,' he cried softly as he opened the front door.

'I'll be down in a minute,' called Molly from upstairs, 'I'm just gettin' dressed. Put the kettle on fer us, luv, will yer?'

A few minutes later Molly appeared and smiled bravely at Max who was busy at the range. 'Yer must go back 'ome ter Rosie, luv, straight after yer dad's funeral. She'll be missin' yer,' she said in a tone that brook no dissent, but nonetheless expected to receive some.

Max looked at her pale features and noticed the ends of a crumpled white handkerchief protruding from the sleeve of her black dress. He opened his mouth to remonstrate but she raised a finger to silence him.

'Now, it's no good yer arguin', Max, me mind is made up. I've got ter start sometime an' it might as well be now.' She gave him a reassuring look but it did not deceive him. Max knew the effort it was costing her to put on such a brave face and she was glad when the kettle started to whistle and he turned round to fill up the teapot. He did not notice her mouth quiver and the tears spring to her eyes, which she quickly wiped away with the handkerchief before he had a chance to see them.

'I'm not sure, Ma,' he began uncertainly, 'why don't yer come back ter London with me? Rosie's found an 'ouse in Pimlico, which would be big enough fer all of us.'

'Pimlico?' replied Molly, shaking her head, 'where's that, luv?'

'Ter tell yer the truth, I'm not sure,' he confessed. 'London is like no place yer've ever seen.' He poured out the tea and put two sugars in Molly's cup, stirred it and then handed it to her. 'I got 'opelessly lost trying ter find Paddington station an' 'ad ter ask several people the way. Some idiot sent me in completely the wrong direction an' it was ages before I realised . . .'

Molly smiled, and this time she meant it. 'Tell me about the Blacks, luv. Nice, are they?'

Max proceeded to describe the family to her, giving her his impressions of each of Rosie's brothers: Richie's cheeky charm and easy but sure manner; Len's artistic talent and quiet but confident personality; and Jimmy's studious and determined character. Molly smiled again when Max told her that Ivy reminded him of her in so many ways and it made him glad that he had managed to cheer her up, however briefly.

175

He told her about Stan's accident and his subsequent tendency to depression and the difficulties the family had faced as a result of it.

'At least yer dad was taken quickly,' murmured Molly quietly, almost to herself, ''e couldn't 'ave stood being a cripple,' and Max knew she was right, but it did not make the pain any easier to bear. 'I see yer went up ter the hills,' said Molly, 'ter that place of yers,' referring to Max's early morning departure, which she had witnessed from her bedroom as she sat in her little white rocking chair in the corner of the room, staring out of the window, praying silently for Bert's soul. 'Did it 'elp?' she asked perceptively.

Max smiled. 'Yer don't miss much, Ma, do yer?' he replied. 'Yeah, I think it did. I'm goin' ter see Dad this afternoon.' He looked at her as he said that. 'I thought I'd go on my own ... unless yer wanted to come, that is,' he added hesitatingly, feeling slightly uncomfortable, but he did want to go alone. Molly just smiled gently and nodded her head imperceptibly. 'I thought a lot about *them*, Ma, and I really do think yer should come back ter London with me an' Rosie. They've been the cause of so much grief fer us, first there was Rosie, now Dad, an' yer've given 'em the best years of yer life ... what's goin' ter be next, I ask myself?' He could hear his voice becoming strident, so he stopped, making himself calm down.

Molly reached out her hand and looked at him, her face full of compassion and concern. 'I can't do that, darlin'. It's a really kind thought an' yer don't know 'ow much it means ter me, but my place is 'ere, where I've always been.' She held his arm more firmly as she went on, 'Yer really musn't take on so about the family...'

'But, Ma...'

'I know, luv,' interrupted Molly before he had the chance to say more, 'yer've always 'ated 'em but they've been good ter yer dad an' me, looked after us an' that.'

''Ow can yer say that, Ma!' exclaimed Max in amazement, 'with Dad not yet...' He stopped himself from finishing the sentence, realising that it was neither the time nor the place to have this conversation.

'I know ... I know, Max,' she responded gently, 'but blame isn't goin' ter bring 'im back an' yer musn't jump ter conclusions. I told yer last night, the police...'

'It's no good expectin' the police ter do anythin',' he said dismissively, with a hint of bitterness, 'they'll get away with it, their sort always do!' He looked away for a moment. Not if I have anything to do with it, he said fiercely to himself, however long it takes. He turned back to

176

Molly. 'I just don't understand it, Ma, that's all. Why yer keep defending 'em.'

'I know, luv,' said Molly again, 'but I can't explain it, yer just 'ave ter accept it, that's all.' Now it was Molly who turned away so he would not see the tortured look on her face and the anguish in her eyes as she said it. 'Now, tell me 'ow things are goin' with the business, luv, yer must be all right if yer are getting yer own 'ouse?' she asked, deliberately changing the subject and trying to sound more cheeful.

Max knew it would be pointless to continue with his questions and the last thing he wanted to do was upset her further. 'Things are goin' well, Ma, very well in fact,' he said, unable to hide a smile of satisfaction. 'Overall, the business is clearing five hundred pounds profit every week at the moment; it's the big 'ouses in Plymouth that make the difference yer know.'

Molly was astounded at that sum. 'Good Lord! What, every week? That's a huge amount of money, Max!' She was genuinely taken aback. 'Why, it would take me years ter earn that, and yer tellin' me it's every week!' She was flabbergasted at the full extent of her son's success.

'An' the fishing business is thrivin' an' I've now recouped the cost of buyin' my shares in the first place. Best decision I've made in a long time that was. I'm 'opin' that Billy will like my idea of workin' more closely tergether in London because the way I see it, there's a goldmine there just waitin' fer someone ter realise it.'

Molly leant forward and felt the side of the teapot. It was still warm. She motioned to Max to pass her his cup. ''E's a good one, that Billy. I liked 'im straightaway at yer weddin' an' she seemed nice too...'

'Who Ma, Elizabeth yer mean?' he said, taking the full cup from her.

'Yes, that was it. I couldn't remember 'er name. They seemed very 'appy tergether I thought, an' Billy spoke very highly of yer, darling.'

'I think they are, Ma. I'm goin' ter ask Rosie to invite them ter London as soon as we move inter our own place. I want 'im ter see the potential fer 'imself because there's a lot of investment needed if we're ter make a proper go of it.'

Molly smiled at him. How she wished Bert could have heard him say that and, to her surprise, that thought made her happy rather than sad.

Chapter 29

The chapel was one of the earliest to be erected after the passing of the Burial Act of 1855, which permitted for the first time burials to be made somewhere other than in a churchyard. The little chapel of Lee Moor, tucked into the southern corner of the village cemetery, was funded by a generous donation from the eighth earl and consecrated by the bishop in May of that year.

Max had rarely ventured into the cemetery and he walked up the narrow gravel path through the headstones with a feeling of mounting apprehension. He was beginning to wish he had not insisted on coming alone but it was too late to change his mind and he knew it was something he had to do. He stopped at the heavy wooden door and glanced up at the circular window in the front wall, which was a fine example of Victorian craftsmanship, before tentatively pushing it open. He was immediately struck by the peacefulness of the interior and the sweet scent of flowers hanging in the air. His boots echoed on the tiles and the sound bounced off the thick stone walls. As he carefully closed the door, the only light to brighten the gloom came from large candles burning silently in their tall metal stands and the meagre afternoon sunlight drifting in through the windows that were set into each wall.

He slowly peered around, not really knowing what he expected to find. He glanced upwards and strained to read the sentences inscribed on the string course under the plate of the stained deal roof. He could barely make them out but managed to read just two of them: 'Blessed are the dead which die in the Lord' and 'I know that my redeemer liveth'. Max was not a religious man but these words sent a shiver down his spine, despite the fact that he did not really comprehend their meaning.

Then he saw it. The coffin was resting on its bier, surrounded by four large candles positioned at each corner, which had clearly been burning for some time. A large spray of brightly coloured spring flowers had been placed on top of the lid, which, as Molly had told him, was firmly sealed. Max surreptitiously wiped the palms of his hands on his trousers as he felt his pulse begin to quicken. He was struck by the powerful serenity of the scene and the natural dignity of his surroundings, which seemed to be entirely appropriate. He felt unsure and a little self-conscious as he approached the simple catafalque, swallowing hard as the sinking feeling in the pit of his stomach grew stronger. But he reminded himself that this was something he had to do, no ... wanted to do ... for his father, and for himself, and it was the one and only opportunity he would have.

'Dad, it's me, Max,' he whispered as he knelt down in front of the coffin. 'I'm here, Dad, 'cause I've got things ter say ter yer...' An image of his father flashed into his mind, at first upright, strong and vital as he had been in life, and then battered, bleeding and prostrated in the road as he was in death. It momentarily paralysed him as he envisaged his father's pain and terrible suffering and his mother's torment, and, for the first time in his life, he began to pray.

It seemed as if time had abruptly stopped and he was conscious only of his immediate surroundings in the chapel, and the smell of the flowers. 'I should 'ave been there, Dad, with yer. I would 'ave 'elped yer...' His words, slow and hesitant at first, became like a torrent as he sought to tell his father everything that was in his heart, desperate to feel the dead man's loving presence surround him for one final time.

He knelt there, motionless, ignoring the numbness that gradually invaded his legs, and when at last there was nothing left to say, he felt relieved and grateful that he had been able to express all that he had planned, but at the same time regretful that he had not done so often enough when his father had been alive. It was a feeling that he had not experienced before, but it was strangely moving and comforting. He felt a trickle run down his cheek and was surprised to find that he was crying and yet there was no sound. He stared straight ahead but saw nothing as the silent tears rolled unchecked down his face.

Then the anger came. It was a different kind of anger to the one he harboured for Lord William. It was more akin to a fierce and contemptuous disbelief. Max was not religious and yet he had just been praying to God, to something or someone that he did not believe in. How could God exist? His father would still be alive if He did because, surely, God would not allow someone to be taken as cruelly as his father had been? Slowly, he rose to his feet, mentally exhausted and too drained of emotion to try to make any sense of that. He stood in front of the coffin for a few moments longer and then reached over to gently straighten the flower arrangement on its top. As he did so his hand knocked the small white card that had been placed in the centre of the blooms and it fell on to the floor. He bent down to retrieve it and recognised his mother's neatly formed handwriting on the front. Feeling as if he was intruding on something very personal and intimate, but unable to stop himself, he read her last message to the husband she adored.

To my darling Bert
You were my life
In joyful and everlasting gratitude
Mol

His hands shook as he read it over and again. He found the very simplicity of her words uplifting despite the desperate sadness of their finality and, for the second time since entering the chapel, he felt oddly comforted as he carefully put the card back in its place.

It was time to go, he had done what he came to do. He turned round and walked out, pulling open the wooden door without a backwards glance. Once outside, his feet crunched briskly on the gravel as he followed the path through the cemetery, heading for The Wheelwrights. He looked neither right nor left, his mind now set on the future. It was almost as if a guillotine had descended to prevent him thinking about the past. There was still the next day to contend with, but he had said his goodbyes now and he regarded the funeral as little more than the public ritual that had to be observed. He did not know if his mother felt the same but he would be there for her sake and her sake alone.

As far as Max was concerned, it was only the future that was important now and he determined to bury his grief deep within himself in his relentless pursuit of the plans he had made up in the hills that morning.

There was a lull in the conversation as he entered the main bar of The Wheelwrights in search of Jack. One or two of the men gathered there sympathetically nodded in his direction and Max returned their gestures with a brief tight-lipped smile, relieved that they made no attempt to engage him in conversation or to offer any words of condolence. Daisy had her back to the door, tidying the bottles on the shelves in front of the mirrors and she saw his reflection in them as he approached the long mahogany counter. In an instant she was out from behind it with outstretched arms, gathering him in an embrace full of compassion and concern. The scent of lavender water emanating from her ample cleavage enveloped him as she led the way through to the back.

'Max, we knew yer'd come, 'ow are yer? When did yer get back?

'Ow's Molly, and Rosie? We're so sorry...' She was firing the questions at him one after the other until she suddenly stopped, her hand flying to her mouth as she realised what she was doing.

'Shh, Daisy, luv, it's all right,' reassured Max, brushing smudges of rouge from his cheek, 'thanks fer your concern, sweet'art. We'll be all right, don't yer worry. Ma's bein' very brave an' is bearin' up I think. Tomorrow will be 'ard fer 'er but I'm trying ter persuade 'er ter come back ter London fer a bit once Rosie an' me are settled.'

'Will she, do yer think?'

'She says not but we'll 'ave ter see. We're takin' one day at a time. So 'ow 'ave yer been then, Dais, are yer managing all right?'

'Without yer, yer mean!' said Daisy smiling gently at him. Max smiled back. 'We all miss yer bein' around, an' Rosie too. Jack's out in the yard I think, 'e'll want ter see yer I know.' Just then a familiar voice called out from the bar demanding attention. 'I'm comin'! Patience is a virtue yer know, Ted!' she called out. 'Sorry, Max, back in a mo,' she said apologetically as she bustled away.

Max chuckled softly to himself. Daisy always managed to cheer him up with her no-nonsense, happy-go-lucky attitude whatever the circumstances. He was about to go out into the yard when he heard the back door open and he turned round to see Jack walk in.

'Max! When did yer get back, mate?' cried Jack in surprise. 'I wasn't expectin' ter see yer in 'ere!' He stretched out his arm and they shook hands warmly. 'I am so sorry about Bert,' he said quietly, 'I've been up ter see yer ma a few times but I don't want ter intrude...'

'Thank yer, Jack, I know an' Ma's appreciated it,' replied Max simply. 'Yer welcome anytime, yer know that.' There was a momentary and companionable silence as both men looked at each other before Jack added, 'We'll all be there tomorrow an' I'm sending some food over ter the cottage fer afterwards. It's all arranged with Eileen so Molly needn't worry 'erself about it.'

'Thank yer, Jack,' said Max again. 'Actually I wanted ter ask if yer'd thought about that offer?' he added, changing the subject.

'I 'ave, Max, an' I think we can do something. Daisy seems ter 'ave taken ter it like a duck ter water.' A mental picture of Daisy as a plump duck instantly flashed into both their heads and they laughed out loud. 'Let's 'ave a drink in the snug ter talk about it,' suggested Jack, 'what'll yer 'ave, Max?'

Daisy found them still deep in conversation an hour later when she pulled up a chair and sat down next to them with a sigh of relief. 'Ooh, me achin' feet,' she said, 'not interruptin' am I?' In fact she rather hoped she was as she had been struggling to contain her curiosity about what they had been talking about for so long, huddled together in the relative privacy of the snug.

'No, we've finished talkin' shop. Max was just tellin' me about London,' explained Jack. 'Yer'd better sort those feet of yer's out because you'll be needin' 'em even more now.'

Daisy groaned exaggeratedly. 'Don't tell me yer've gone an' done it, Jack!'

'Of course I 'ave so we're on our own now, girl,' laughed Jack. 'Get yer apron ready 'cause we've got ter make the money back it's just cost me fer Max's share.'

'Don't listen ter 'im, Dais, I've just given it away!' protested Max feeling very satisfied at the agreement they had come to for the sale of his share of The Wheelwrights' food business back to Jack, who laughed and said, 'Yer never give anythin' away, Max Chambers!' in return.

In fact he was pleased on two counts. First of all, and most importantly, he had now raised enough cash to fund the first part of his plan for the new wholesale business, which necessitated the immediate purchase of a delivery vehicle. He needed the payment in cash instead of a loan note because he intended to buy the van outright in his own name before transferring it to the new company he was going to form to handle all future transactions on his and Rosie's behalf. He intended establishing a holding company, which would also in time control his shares in MMC Ltd and his outright ownership of The Fine Foods Emporium. If the potential in London was as limitless as he believed it to be Max knew how essential it was to establish ownership and control of the new venture at the outset before involving the others. These would naturally include Billy, who was after all still the majority shareholder in MMC Ltd, and Richie, who he also planned to ask as soon as the necessary arrangements could be made.

He was pleased too because Jack had told him that he was going to split some of the future food profits with Daisy as a reward for her loyalty and hard work over the years. Apart from genuinely liking Daisy, Max appreciated loyalty in a person and believed it should always be recognised and rewarded.

Chapter 30

Rosie put the last of the invoices in date order and closed the drawer, breathing a silent sigh of relief. Max would be home soon and it was almost time to start dinner. It had taken her most of the afternoon to catch up with the backlog of filing but it was her own fault, she had been putting it off for much too long. There seemed to be a constantly increasing number of them these days but she knew she should not grumble. It was a tangible sign that Max's belief in the limitless possibilities for them in London was well placed.

She straightened the remaining papers on the desk in front of her and promised herself that she would not get so far behind again. Despite her dislike of filing, she actually rather enjoyed dealing with the administration for Rosima Holdings, which Max had set up in 1910 as a holding company for their shares in Chambers & Co, the new London wholesale business. She liked being involved in their commercial affairs, which consumed such a major part of Max's life, although they had both agreed that she would stop when they had children. During the past year it had often seemed as if she had hardly seen him as he and Billy worked all hours of the day and night to establish themselves in the capital. Recently though, the pressure had begun to ease a little when Richie had joined them to manage the day-to-day operations; this at least allowed Max to get home to Gloucester Street for dinner most evenings and, because their time together had become so precious, she liked things to be just so when he did.

She glanced at her watch. She wanted to check the acceptances that had arrived in the morning's post for the party they were shortly to give at The Coburg Hotel to celebrate Chambers & Co's first anniversary. She had spent part of the morning on the telephone, discussing the menu with the hotel's general manager who was also their latest customer on a list that now included some of the best hotels in town. The Ritz, Claridges and The Savoy were buying daily and Max hoped they would soon be joined by The Berkeley, another prestigious hotel in The Savoy Group. He wanted the food at the celebration to be a showcase for their produce but other than insisting that their Whitstable oysters and the new Cheddar cheese from the Isle of Mull be featured somewhere on the menu, he was leaving the arrangements entirely up to Rosie. She had discussed the details at length with the general manager who had been very accommodating and had made a number of interesting suggestions.

Between them they had decided that the oysters would be baked and served as a canapé to accompany the Perrier-Jouët Brut on arrival. A venison terrine with junipers or hot-smoked mackerel pâté would follow and the main course was to be a choice of either prime roast beef from their Hereford range or fillet of turbot, which Billy had told her was fishing particularly well at the moment. There would not be a savoury but instead a selection of their finest cheeses from the emporium range would be offered. This left just the wines to be chosen (and the head sommelier was going to help with those), the flower arrangements for the tables to be ordered and final numbers to be confirmed.

'Eighty-one, eighty-two,' she counted as she cross-matched the morning's responses with the running total on her list. 'Oh, good,' she thought to herself, going through them, 'Max will be pleased, Rules Restaurant in Covent Garden say yes, making eighty-three, The Athenaeum has declined, that's a pity and...' she paused as she added up the responses yet to be received, 'twenty-six still to reply.'

She looked at her watch again as she hurriedly shuffled the replies into some semblance of order. It was incredible to think how greatly their lives had changed since moving to London and sometimes she still could not quite believe it. She fingered the delicate string of milky white pearls at her throat as she got up from the chair, smoothing the creases from the skirt of her finely tailored pale-blue day dress as she went out into the hallway. The wide collar and turned-back cuffs were contrasted in deep navy and whenever she wore this dress Max never failed to say that the shade perfectly complimented the colour of her eyes, as he would no doubt do when he got home this evening. The necklace had been a Christmas present from him that year and was the first piece of real jewellery he had ever bought her. Consequently, it held great sentimental value but it was also a symbol of how relatively affluent their lives had become.

Rosie quickly climbed the stairs from the hall to the first-floor drawing-room to check that it was clean and tidy before going down to the kitchen. She had heard Mary, their daily, dusting in there before going home, and sometimes she did not leave things as she found them, which never failed to irritate them both. She looked at the photograph of Bert and Molly in its little silver frame on the console table next to the fireplace and was pleased to see that it was exactly where it should be, which usually meant that the other photographs and ornaments would be in their proper places too. Mary was 18 and the daughter of one of Ivy's friends; Rosie had known her since she was a little girl living in the street around the corner from Globe Road. She was a godsend really, and in the 18 months that she had been working for them, had rarely put a foot wrong.

When Max had first suggested that they employ some domestic help, at around the same time as she started taking care of the administration for Rosima Holdings, Rosie had been reluctant to engage anyone at all, but Max had insisted and now she did not know how she would manage their increasingly busy lives without her. If she sometimes did not put things back in their proper place, it really was a price worth paying.

The generously proportioned room was immaculate and Rosie silently thanked Mary for her efforts. Rose velvet cushions had been neatly arranged on the comfortably upholstered armchairs and sofas, which were positioned in the centre of a rich, dark-green carpet that covered the greater part of the polished parquet floor. Bookshelves were set into the oak-panelled walls on either side of the white marble fireplace on which rows of red and black leather-bound books were displayed in precision straight lines. They were the sort of books that looked as if they could have been handed down from one generation to the next but had, in fact, cost Rosie £5 in a job lot at Borough Market. Mary had even carefully laid a fire in the grate in readiness for the evening chill, and the burnished copper coal scuttle was freshly filled. Pale-green curtains, elaborately draped in swags and tails, and fringed with a cord of deeper green to match the carpet, adorned the front windows and gave the room a character that was elegant but homely. A modest crystal chandelier hung from the high white ceiling, and four delicate side tables, inlaid with marquetry, completed the room. The whole effect was a world away from Fern Cottage and Globe Road.

Just as she was turning to go, she heard the faint sound of the telephone ringing on her desk on the floor below. Cursing whoever it was at this hour, she hurried back down to the morning room and lifted the receiver.

'Hello, Pimlico 2356.'

'That you, darling?' Max's unmistakable voice crackled down the line. 'I'm going to be late and Billy and Richie are with me. Can we stretch dinner?'

185

'Of course...'

'We've got to sort...' The crackling got worse.

'I can't hear you, luv...' she shouted into the phone, 'ah, that's better,' she said as the interference subsided.

'We've got to finalise the purchase of the new vans so Billy is going to stay over and go back to Plymouth tomorrow,' explained Max, 'we'll be home in about an hour, sweetheart.'

'All right, darling. Tell Billy the spare room is all ready for him. Richie can stay too if he wants.'

'Thanks, sweetheart, won't be long,' said Max as he hung up.

Rosie replaced the receiver in its cradle and smiled, relieved that she had more time now to prepare for their unexpected guests. As she headed for the kitchen she thought she'd better change for dinner if Billy was staying because Elizabeth was always so smartly dressed and well turned out. The first thing she saw as she descended the backstairs into the basement was the largest of their heavy cast-iron saucepans standing on the side next to the range with a piece of paper propped up against it.

Hope you like my stew, not sure if I've done it right but Ma says it's the one thing I can do. See you in the morning.
Mary.
P.S. Hope you don't mind my making this but I had a spare half hour.

Rosie found herself silently thanking Mary for the second time that day as she lifted the lid off the pan and gave the contents a stir with the wooden spoon that Mary had thoughtfully hooked through the handle. Max had been saying for a while that they should look for a cook on a live-in basis and perhaps he was right. She made a mental note to talk to him about it later; there was the little room off the kitchen that would be ideal as a bedroom. The beef stew smelled delicious and she quickly prepared some potatoes and vegetables to go with it and decided that they would have cheese for afterwards. If the boys were still hungry after that she would make them a savoury on toast. Putting the stew on a low heat to warm through, she got the cheese out of the larder so it could rest in the warmth of the kitchen to bring out its full flavour, and then she went back upstairs to set the table.

The dining-room was on the ground floor at the back of the four-storey house. At one end were double doors leading through to the morning room, and at the other, a tall window looked out over the tiny rear garden. A single door at that end opened on to the hallway. It was not large but could seat eight people around the polished mahogany table, which took up almost its entire length. Lennie had acquired this table and the chairs to go with it through his contacts in the rag and bone trade, telling Rosie not to ask too many questions when she wanted to know where it had come from. It had been in dire need of attention when she first saw it but after a week of Lennie's skilful and painstaking restoration, it had been transformed into a shining and graceful centrepiece for the room. She and Max always made a point of using it every Friday evening if he was home in time for dinner; otherwise they ate very simply on trays in the drawing-room. Quickly selecting the necessary cutlery and china from the sideboard, she laid it neatly at each place setting before going upstairs to change.

She stepped out of her shoes and dress and slipped on the black silk robe that had been another present from Max, before going into the bathroom to draw her bath. Whilst she was waiting for the tub to fill, she tied her hair back with a silk scarf that she had made to match her robe and quickly removed her make up in the large circular mirror. This was opposite the bath and hung above a narrow glass-topped table on which she kept her small bottles of perfume and her various creams and lotions. Max was forever fiddling with these when he was in a mischievous mood, which always seemed to be when she was busy trying to get ready. She then selected a dress from one of the wardrobes lining the walls of the small dressing area that separated their bedroom from the bathroom, and laid it out carefully on the bed before going back into the bathroom.

She particularly liked these two rooms which she regarded as the private heart of the house. The decor cleverly combined the femininity of the pale pink and cream colour scheme with the masculinity of the rich, dark wood of the bedroom furniture. She liked nothing better than when the two of them could spend a leisurely hour luxuriating in the deep tub at the end of a long day, which they often did, or when she could talk to Max from the bedroom as she changed for dinner whilst he unwound in a hot bath after a busy day.

Rosie removed her robe and underwear and stepped into the hot water, deciding that she could allow herself ten minutes rest whilst Mary's stew warmed through. She lay back and closed her eyes, thinking about the telephone conversation with Max. It was so thoughtful of him to call and let her know he would be late and to check if Billy and Richie could stay for dinner. Billy was their oldest and closest friend, closer almost than family, and Max knew he could stay whenever he wanted to but he still took the trouble to call and ask. She was so lucky. She sat up and reached for the bar of Pears' soap from the little china soap dish that stood on the corner of the tub, her thoughts turning to the new vehicles Max had mentioned. Chambers & Co delivery vans, supplied by the Associated Equipment Company, had become a common sight in the more affluent parts of London. The company name painted on both sides in distinctive gold lettering against the deep burgundy bodywork made them easily recognisable and set them apart from the competition, which was exactly what Max had planned. He had also insisted that they were washed at the end of each day so that they appeared clean and shiny on the road every morning.

The drivers had grumbled at first when Max had told them it was their job to do it, but he wanted every man to take responsibility for his own vehicle and they soon began to take a pride in their work. This quickly spread to all aspects of the delivery service for which they were individually responsible; it was an inspired decision, which served the company well. From the very first model, purchased with the proceeds of the sale of his share in The Wheelwrights' food business, Max had steadily added to the fleet until now, nearly two years later, it numbered 34. He reasoned that Chambers & Co must become renowned for the quality of its service and one way to ensure that was to limit the size of each delivery round in order to maximize speed and reliability. Whilst this meant that delivery costs would be higher than they might otherwise be, because of the greater number of vehicles and drivers required, Max argued that they would attract more customers because of it, and, moreover, keep each one for longer, which would mean that their profits would be derived from high growth and secure volume. It had certainly proven successful so far as they were continuing to win business from their competition, and their reputation continued to flourish.

Looking at her watch, which was balanced rather precariously on the side of the tub, Rosie realised that Max would be home very shortly and she needed to check on the dinner. She climbed out of the bath and energetically towelled herself dry before skipping through into the bedroom. She quickly removed the scarf and brushed her hair vigorously before deftly pinning it up so that it was arranged high at the back. She held it in place with her tortoiseshell comb inlaid with gold filigree in a style reminiscent of one she had seen in *The Delineator Magazine*. She usually wore her hair like this in the evenings, particularly if they had company, although she was always careful to make sure that the scar from her accident was well hidden. Sometimes she wore a Grecian band in the style of the times, which more easily concealed it, but she did not have time to curl her hair for that this evening.

Sitting down at her dressing-table, Rosie gently applied a little Papier Poudré and a light dusting of rouge, a little mascara and then finally her favourite shade of lipstick. She sat back and turned her head from one side to the other in front of the mirror and decided that she would have to do. She stood up and quickly pulled on a clean pair of silk stockings before stepping into the dress she had laid out on the bed, and when she was finished, she paused to look at herself in the long mirror of the armoire. The graceful simplicity of her deep-aquamarine dress perfectly emphasized her narrow waist and slender hips, and the soft, fluid draping of the skirt, shortened to just above her ankles, swayed gently as she moved. She decided that her plain jet necklace and earrings were the only jewellery she needed and, with a quick dab of Edwardian Bouquet by Floris behind each ear, she went downstairs as the carriage clock on the hall table was chiming seven.

Chapter 31

'That was a lovely dinner, darling,' whispered Max in Rosie's ear as he got up from the table. 'I thought the baked oysters were particularly good!' He smiled into Rosie's eyes as she leant back and raised her head to look up at him, her appreciation and delight in his comments clearly evident in her expression.

'Thank you, Max,' she replied softly. 'It's going rather well isn't it?'

'Yes I think it is,' said Max, listening to the lively babble of conversation in the room that seemed to endorse their belief. 'All down to the organisation of course,' he joked, 'and my insistence on the oysters!'

Rosie laughed with him, her face radiant with happiness at her husband. Her eyes were sparkling to match the diamond clips that twinkled at her ears. She knew how important the evening was to him and to the business, and when Max had surprised her with the clips as they were dressing for the party earlier in the evening, she was touched beyond measure. 'Just something to say thank you, darling, for what you've done,' he had said, kissing her deeply before she had had a chance to say anything.

'Will you excuse me for a minute, love, Miles Brandon wants a quiet word, in private. He's going to meet me in the ante-room,' he said. 'Go and rescue Billy, I think he could do with some help, look...' He nodded in Billy's direction and giggled. Their friend was being monopolised by the portly buyer from Simpson's-in-the-Strand. 'I won't be long.'

Rosie looked across at the next table and giggled too. Billy had an expression on his face that only those who knew him well would realise was one of desperation.

'You're right, darling, I'll go over,' she said, touching Max's arm.

She rose from her chair and watched as Max walked across the room towards a pair of double doors that led into the small antechamber adjoining the main room. She thought how handsome he looked in his new evening dress bought especially for the occasion, even though he had complained that the bow-tie was much too uncomfortable as she had been trying valiantly to tie it for him in front of the armoire mirror whilst the taxi was waiting impatiently outside to take them to the hotel.

* * *

190

'Close the doors, Max, I don't want anyone to overhear this,' said Miles without preamble as Max entered the room.

Max looked quizzically at the man who was Chambers & Co's very first customer, but did as he was asked. 'We shouldn't be interrupted now, Miles.'

Miles Brandon was a friend as well as a long-standing business associate, and the two men got on well. He was short and stocky with greying hair and always full of energy. He was a self-made man and owned a large chain of restaurants in the City and West End, which made him well known in the trade. He had achieved his success through sheer hard work and determination from humble beginnings, and it was those traits that he had recognised in Max at their first meeting.

'Have you heard of "Williams and Abel", Max?'

'Of course, been in the business for twenty years or more I think, Charlie Williams took over from his father about three years ago didn't he? Got a big place in Chelsea.'

'Well, they're in trouble.' Miles clipped off the end of a cigar he took from his inside pocket and lit it slowly, sending puffs of sweet-smelling smoke into the air. He fixed his eyes on Max. 'Had you heard?'

'No, I hadn't, Miles, but they have lost a few customers recently, *that* I had heard. My drivers keep their ears to the ground you know!'

'It seems that Charlie has got in over his head and is having difficulty repaying a loan. His father died about eight or nine months ago and I suppose with no one there to keep him in check ... Charlie always had grand ideas...' He puffed on his cigar and waited for Max to reply.

'How do you know all this?' His heart had lurched at the mention of the death of Charlie's father. It was always the same; it made him immediately think of Bert, he could not help it. But there was also something in Miles' tone that made Max inhale slowly; alert for whatever was coming next. He studied Miles carefully.

'I had lunch yesterday with a good friend of mine. He's not in the business, nothing to do with it at all but he has contacts at Covent Garden. I can't tell you his name, Max; I gave him my word on that. It seems that Charlie is not paying his bills on time and he's being refused credit. So I asked around and the rumour is that he is struggling to meet repayments on a loan he took out, which is secured on the company.'

Max wondered why Miles was telling him all this but he knew him well enough to know there would be good reason, which Miles would have already thought very carefully about.

'How much is the loan, do you know? And what was it for? If he's not paying his bills in the market, he's in serious trouble. You know how quickly bad news spreads there.'

'Exactly, Max. The loan is for fifty thousand pounds and I gather he is three thousand pounds behind with the repayments, which I suppose represents about six payments, wouldn't you...?' Max nodded. 'Now here is the interesting part. The loan is not with a bank.' He paused and looked at Max. 'The funds were advanced by a private moneylender in Manchester who is now about to call in the whole loan and Charlie can't pay, and you know the most ridiculous part of this is that he borrowed the money to finance the construction of some grand country house in Wiltshire. Pure vanity!'

Max now thought he knew where the conversation was leading but he waited for Miles to finish the story. 'Williams and Abel are a respected name and his father must be turning in his grave as we speak.' Max felt a stab of anguish at those words. 'You see this kind of situation all the time, a successful father hands over the reins to the son who then, through immaturity, or some kind of irresponsible behaviour, very quickly squanders his inheritance and good name.'

Max instantly thought of the Gordons and the likely parallels with their situation but he impatiently dismissed them from his mind to concentrate on the opportunity that he suspected was about to be revealed.

'How much is the company worth, Miles? It must be somewhere in the region of twice that, around one hundred thousand pounds, wouldn't you say?'

'Well, you would know better than I, but I imagine it must be about that, yes,' replied Miles, 'and that's the point. Charlie is about to forfeit his business for only half of its real value unless someone can help him.'

'And that someone might be me, you're thinking,' said Max slowly.

'Think of what it could mean to Chambers & Co, Max!' exclaimed Miles quickly. 'By the way, this is all in the strictest confidence. I have given my word.'

Max nodded, his mind already working on the possibilities. Williams and Abel had an extensive customer base and the potential benefits to Chambers & Co were immediately obvious, but £100,000 was a lot of money and, moreover, it was money he did not have. However, over the years he had learned never to reveal what was on his mind until he was ready, and never to show weakness even when it existed.

'There's no need to worry, Miles. I wouldn't want it any other way.

There isn't much time if the rumour is out in the market and he's defaulting on his obligations. Where do you come in though, Miles, if you don't mind me asking?'

'You'll find out soon enough so you might as well know now, I'm a shareholder in Williams and Abel.'

Now it began to make sense. 'So, forgive me, but why don't you step in?' asked Max curiously, 'if that isn't a rude question?' Even if it was, Max would still have asked it and expected to receive the answer. This was business.

'No, it isn't a rude question, Max, we've known each other a long time and I've always trusted you. That's why we're talking now. I'm not in a position to help him financially with my new restaurant in Piccadilly opening soon, as you know, and, actually, Charlie and I have never seen eye to eye. In fact, I've found out about his problems from this friend of mine. Charlie has not mentioned anything to me at all, which I find incredible ... but then we hardly speak.'

'So why are you in business with him?'

'I was originally in business with his father. James and I went back a long way. He used to supply me with fruit and veg in my early days. I didn't ever get on particularly well with Charlie, even when he was younger. I should have got rid of my shares when Jimmy died but the right moment never seemed to come along.' He shrugged his shoulders and took another puff of his cigar. 'But I'm damned if I'm going to stand by and let some moneylender steal the business from under my nose!'

'Give me two days, Miles. Can you do that?'

Miles smiled. 'I think I can keep the wolves at bay until Thursday.'

'Let's meet here for lunch at, say, one o'clock?' suggested Max.

'Yes, but come to my place in Knightsbridge, my treat,' said Miles, 'and you can see just how good your produce is!'

The two men laughed and shook hands. 'Let's rejoin the party. Your lovely wife will be wondering where you've got to.'

It was after midnight when the last of their guests finally departed with profuse thanks for a wonderful evening. It had certainly seemed to go well if success could be measured by the number of new enquiries Billy was already in possession of and which he would give to Richie to follow up in the morning. Max was pleased that the general manager of The Berkeley had confirmed his intention to transfer his account to them, and Billy proudly announced to their amusement that 'portly Peter', as he had already nicknamed the buyer from Simpson's, had asked for someone to call and see him at their earliest convenience. But these developments, good though they were, paled into insignificance when Max began to recount his conversation with Miles Brandon in the taxi-cab on the way back to Gloucester Street. When he mentioned the figure of £100,000 Billy let out a low whistle.

'Gawd, Max, that's a hell of a lot of money!' he exclaimed.

'I know, I know,' agreed Max, 'more than we can afford and that's a fact.' He looked at Rosie. 'But there must be another solution. I suggest we talk about it in the morning once we've slept on it.'

He yawned and settled back next to Rosie who was struggling with the soporific effect of the vehicle's motion. Billy too was fighting a losing battle to keep his eyes open, having been up since before dawn to travel up from Plymouth. They soon lapsed into a contented silence, each lost in their own thoughts. It was not long before the taxi driver was pulling up outside their front door, and having paid him off and seen Billy comfortably into the spare room, Max and Rosie collapsed happily on to their bed.

'Well I'm glad that's over!' said Rosie with feeling as she sat up to undo her shoes. 'Ooh, that's better, my feet are killing me.'

Max reached over and kissed her gently on the side of her face. 'Help me with this damned bow-tie, will you, darling? It's stuck!'

Rosie giggled. 'No it isn't, you silly thing, you're pulling on the wrong end … there you are you see … it's simple.' She took off his bow tie and undid the top button of his dress shirt to reveal the familiar whirls of curly black hair. 'Is that better now?' she asked teasingly, as a mother might do to a young child.

'A little,' said Max languorously, pulling her closer to him, the heavy shadow on his chin contrasting darkly with the starched white collar of his winged shirt. He was relaxed and deliberate as his fingers sought the buttons on the back of her dress, and the persistent fragrance of Edwardian Bouquet that he loved so much, drifted over him.

'Max,' whispered Rosie, holding her face close to his, 'we don't have to be careful tonight, not if you don't want to be.'

For a moment he was uncertain, his nerves were tingling and the hairs on the back of his neck started to rise. 'Are you sure, darling, really sure?'

'Yes,' she murmured, 'absolutely sure.'

Chapter 32

Max had formed Rosima Holdings almost two years previously for two reasons. The first was simply to act as a holding company for his shares in Chambers & Co, into which he also intended to place his 25 per cent shareholding of MMC Ltd and his outright ownership of The Fine Foods Emporium, and the second reason was both shrewd and forward thinking: he planned to use it as an acquisitions company through which he would channel future share purchases in other companies. Now, with that framework in place, Miles Brandon's revelations gave him the opportunity to put his strategy into effect.

Williams and Abel represented a sound investment, even though it was likely to fall into the hands of the moneylender at any moment. The essentials of the business were strong even though greed and vanity had brought it almost to the point of bankruptcy. Charlie Williams' mismanagement of his inheritance revealed a fundamental weakness of character and, as far as Max was concerned, made him unfit to continue as managing director. However, they remained a respected company in the wholesale market place and one that could triple the size of Chambers & Co almost overnight. In addition, the Williams and Abel warehouse in Chelsea would enable him to consolidate his own distribution operations and provide him with new capacity for future expansion. It also occupied a valuable piece of land that was only ever likely to increase in value. Max and Billy had discussed their ideas in preparation for his lunch appointment with Miles, and Richie was already working on an outline plan to merge the two companies. Max knew that time would be of the essence if an agreement could be reached.

'I want fifty-one per cent of the shares, Miles, in return for assuming the liability for the loan and bringing it back within terms.' Miles raised his eyebrows but said nothing. 'I also want a two-year option to purchase the remainder of his holding, effective from the date of the final loan instalment.'

Miles brushed some imaginary crumbs from the starched white tablecloth. 'Those are pretty steep terms, Max, I doubt that Charlie will agree.'

'That's his prerogative, Miles, and those are my terms. He can take them or leave them.'

Miles was typical of a certain type of working-class northern man who had dragged himself up by the bootstraps; he respected straight talking when straight talking was needed.

'He is unlikely to be able to raise the money elsewhere. He's about to see the loan called in and his business seized as a result. The ensuing damage to his reputation will mean he won't be able to secure credit in the market ever again. He'll be finished, we both know that. I am offering him a solution to all his problems.' Max then laughed sardonically. 'Incidentally, he'll be able to finish building his house ... in Wiltshire, wasn't it?'

Miles smiled. 'I can see you've done your homework.' He slowly took a drink from his glass of claret. 'And what would you see happening to my shares?'

'Whatever you wish, Miles. I would hope that in time you might want to sell them to me but the choice is entirely yours of course. Perhaps I'd go as far as to ask for a first refusal clause to be included in the sale and purchase agreement. If my plan works, you'll make a handsome profit when you do.'

Miles nodded thoughtfully. 'I see. You've thought about what would happen to Charlie I imagine?'

'Of course. I'd want him to remain as a figurehead for, say, twelve months or as long as it takes us to settle the business down. But only for appearances sake with his customers, nothing more. Billy Masters would assume direct overall control during the transitional phase as we merge their operations with Chambers & Co, and he would then head up the new enterprise. Richie Black, my brother-in-law, would be in day-to-day charge. Charlie could be non-executive chairman of Williams and Abel I suppose, but his hands would be tied. When I say a figurehead, that's exactly what I mean. I don't want him to damage the business any further.'

There was a pause as both men looked at each other across the table. A waiter appeared to clear the main course plates and leave the sweet menus.

'Just coffee for me please,' said Max, 'I'm watching my waistline,' he explained ruefully. Miles looked at him in amusement. At 28 there was not an ounce of spare flesh on him and his waistline was as trim as it had always been.

'I gave up worrying about that years ago!' laughed Miles. He quickly

196

scanned the menu and ordered the Pierrot Pudding with hot chocolate sauce. 'I'll put your proposal to Charlie and tell him it has my support.'

'Thank you, Miles. Will he speak to you?'

'He'll have to, Max; he's got no choice has he?'

'No, he hasn't,' said Max firmly, allowing himself a discreet smile of satisfaction.

That evening, when he was recounting his meeting to Rosie, he felt confident that the deal would not only transform the future of Chambers & Co but, with the greater financial muscle it would create, doors to other parts of the country would be opened too. It was all happening much sooner than he had imagined possible.

It took Charlie Williams a little longer than Max had thought to agree to the terms. He was reluctant to sell his shares despite the fact that he was teetering on the brink of professional and personal disaster, but the prospect of having to abandon construction on his country home was even less appealing. The lure of an easy life as a figurehead chairman was also attractive and pandered to his love of status and ostentation. Max had cleverly exploited his opponent's weaknesses from a position of strength, although there was a point later in the week when he worried that the moneylender was going to foreclose and Charlie's dithering would cost them all dearly.

He had heard rumours coming back from his drivers that Charlie was blundering around the marketplace endeavouring to raise the money to pay off the loan, without success. That sort of gossip was unhelpful and unsettling for the company's customers, and so Max moved swiftly to deliver an ultimatum. Agree by the end of the day or the deal was off and he would open negotiations with the moneylender instead. This sent Charlie into a blind panic, as Max intended it should, and it had the desired effect. The sale and purchase agreement was signed the following morning and, through Rosima Holdings, Max became the majority shareholder in Williams and Abel. The process of merger and consolidation started immediately.

Within days, the blue and green vans of the Williams and Abel fleet were repainted in the distinctive burgundy and gold livery to match the existing Chambers & Co vehicles, and they became a regular sight in almost every area of London. Richie shrewdly paired up his drivers with their new colleagues to speed up the process of integration, and very soon Williams and Abel customers were commenting on the much improved service they were now receiving. As a result, orders increased and not a single customer was lost. It helped that Billy and Max had strongly supported Richie from the outset, holding a meeting with the workers in the Chelsea depot on the morning after the agreement was signed.

They had been forthright. 'You are probably very aware from the rumours that have been circulating that Williams and Abel has been in serious financial trouble. Well, we can confirm that those rumours were true and were first brought to our attention by one of the company's shareholders. I am not able to be more specific because it was done in the strictest confidence and we are men of our word, but we can tell you that although the problems were actually quite simple, they threatened to have catastrophic consequences for everyone here today. However, we are pleased to say that yesterday we agreed a deal with Charlie Williams to purchase fifty-one per cent of the business with an irrevocable option to purchase the remainder in due course, so your futures are now secure.' A ripple of relief spread through the assembled men. 'Charlie will remain with the company as chairman for a period of twelve months and Richie Black will assume day-to-day responsibility with immediate effect. With Chambers & Co we have built a solid reputation for both the quality of our produce and our service and we can now offer an enhanced range of goods to our new Williams and Abel customers through our two sister companies, MMC Ltd and The Chambers Fine Foods Emporium. We will be relying on your co-operation and support to ensure this period of transition goes smoothly and we want each one of you to feel able to approach us at any time if you have any questions or concerns.'

There were several knowing looks amongst some of the audience at this last comment. A man at the front cried, 'We've 'eard you're gonna cut our wages!' which was swiftly followed by vigorous nods and loud groans.

Max held up his hand for silence. 'Let me make one thing perfectly clear, right now. If you don't hear something directly from either Richie, Billy here, or me, then it isn't true! We intend to make a success of this business and are committed to its future, and your futures, one hundred per cent!' A few cheers broke out. 'There will be changes but these will be carefully planned and made for the benefit of the company, and none of you will lose your jobs as a result of them. In fact, I hope to be taking on more men as we win new customers, so there may well be bigger opportunities for some of you in due course. That is all we want to say today other than to thank you for your loyalty and hard work and to remind you that you can approach any one of us at any time if you have any questions. Thank you and now we have orders to fulfil and customers to look after!'

The cheers gave way to applause and this groundswell of goodwill set the tone for the following months. Max was as good as his word about Charlie and kept him on, but Billy kept a very close eye on his activities. It quickly became clear that he rather enjoyed his new role, free from the stresses and strains of running the company and trying to meet his crippling debt repayments. Without the threat of bankruptcy hanging over him, he began to relax and in fact proved to be very helpful, not least because of his knowledge of the marketplace beyond London. He had contacts with the proprietors of a number of regionally based companies, which had originally been established in his father's time, and with deliberate but subtle nurturing, Billy became the recipient of a great deal of interesting information, which would be useful in the future.

As he became more and more comfortable, Charlie spent an increasing amount of time in Wiltshire, which Max was quite happy to accept as it kept him out of harm's way, and on the days when he did appear in Chelsea, he liked nothing better than to gossip indiscreetly about his London associates. In this way Billy also discovered much about their closest competitors, which was swiftly put to good use.

Chapter 33

'I'd like to propose a toast,' Billy said, looking around the table at the assembled company, 'to us and our continued success in 1912.'

Broad smiles spread across their faces and they raised their glasses in approbation. 'To us, 1912', came the replies. They had promised themselves the luxury of a celebration lunch if the half-year trading results following the merger were good, and as Max put down his glass he felt an enormous sense of pride in their achievements. The figures were ahead of their best expectations and new orders continued to pour in. He was extremely grateful to Billy and Richie who had both been instrumental in managing the tricky process of consolidation so smoothly, and consequently he had wanted this occasion to be a great success.

He had booked a table at The Savoy Hotel and, at Rosie's suggestion, had invited Elizabeth and Marjorie, Richie's new girlfriend, to join them. Elizabeth and Billy had been quietly married in a simple ceremony the preceding month following the not-unexpected death of Harry Masters, whose health had been failing for the last two or three years. A bigger wedding was originally planned but Billy had thought it inappropriate under the circumstances, and Elizabeth had readily agreed. She was a quiet woman who had had a strict and moral upbringing, and she knew her own mind, learning to take care of herself after being orphaned at the age of 18. She disliked fuss and had a tendency to be shy on first meeting, but, as Rosie had quickly discovered, was warm and friendly after the ice was broken. So a low-key wedding it was, with Max as best man and only a handful of guests. Max smiled as he watched her chatting to Rosie with Billy sitting opposite, looking proudly on. He caught Billy's eye across the table and raised his glass to him in silent appreciation.

Richie was holding court at the other end of the table with Marjorie hanging on his every word. She was darkly pretty, her deep-brown eyes gleaming brightly against a faultless strawberries-and-cream complexion. She wore her auburn hair naturally styled beneath a striking grey toque adorned with a large ostrich feather in the fashion of a hussar's plume. She was laughing gaily with Richie and seemed very at home in their company. Max was pleased; her engaging, extrovert personality and youthful warmth were a good match for Richie's happy-go-lucky approach to life and they clearly enjoyed each other's company.

Arriving on the stroke of one, Max had been aware of the admiring glances from the other diners as the ladies had been ushered to their table in the grill room by the deferential maître d'hôtel. Rosie looked ravishing in the outfit she had bought especially for the occasion and, as he watched her chatting easily to Elizabeth, he was still as captivated by her beauty and charm as he had been when he had first set eyes on her in Mrs Castle's kitchen. He shook his head, marvelling at how much she had changed since those days and yet, underneath her poised and enchanting exterior, she was still the Rosie he had fallen in love with and, if it were possible, was even more in love with today.

As he gazed at her she became aware of him and turned, her blue eyes laughingly catching his. She held his gaze for a moment and a faint blush rose to her cheeks before she turned away to resume her conversation with Elizabeth.

Max leant back, lost in his own thoughts, as the chatter continued around him. A letter from Molly had arrived that morning, which threatened to reignite an argument with Rosie that had first arisen some three weeks earlier and which he was still struggling to cast from his mind. It was rare for them to argue about anything; in fact he could not remember the last time they had done so, but the subject had been the cause of some harsh words between them.

He had been studying the Williams and Abel overdue accounts list with Billy in the office at the Chelsea warehouse when he had spotted an entry in the 60-day column that caused him to catch his breath:

Gordon, Lord & Lady,   Invoice 13297   30th August 1911   £10.15.09
1 Chesterfield Square

The Earl and Countess were customers of Williams and Abel, and greater investigation revealed that they had been supplying produce to the Chesterfield Square mansion for many years. Max had always assumed, if indeed he had ever really thought about it, that provisions were sent up from Mount Royal during the family's annual migration for the London Season. However, they clearly purchased some of their household requirements from local merchants and, in the case of Williams and Abel, were not particularly prompt in settling their bills.

The discovery of this coincidental link to the Gordon family was

201

oddly disquieting to Max, but he could not understand why that was so. It was, after all, a matter of such little significance as to have no meaning, but the effect it had on him was compelling. It had preyed on his mind to the extent that at times he found it difficult to concentrate on matters in hand, and it rekindled the feelings of enmity that had resurfaced with his father's death, but which had then lain dormant since finding real success with Chambers & Co. Finally, after days of trying to rid his head of these thoughts, he decided that he must see the house for himself in the hope that his curiosity would then be satisfied and he would somehow find peace of mind.

That evening he told Rosie about his discovery and intentions over supper in the drawing-room and he had been completely taken aback by her instant and hostile reaction. She was vehement in her objection to his idea. 'Let sleeping dogs lie,' she had insisted, her blue eyes flashing as she challenged him, refusing to countenance the prospect of reopening old wounds. Max was stunned into silence, and when he saw the fear in her eyes, he was reminded of her reaction on seeing Mount Royal heave into view on the way home from that first picnic together after her accident, all those years ago. She was adamant that the Gordon family were a part of their past life and had no place in their lives now. She would not let the matter rest until Max had promised to drop the idea of going to Chesterfield Square, but the arrival of Molly's letter that morning, as they were getting ready to leave for The Savoy, threatened to fan the flames of those fevered emotions.

She had written to tell them that the Earl and Countess were sailing for America on the RMS *Titanic* in April and they would not therefore be in residence at Chesterfield Square for the Season. They would be away for three months and, during that time, she would be staying in Chesterfield Square to supervise the redecoration of the ballroom, before returning to Mount Royal to oversee the spring cleaning that always took place there when the family were away. She was therefore looking forward to being able to spend some time with them, having enjoyed her last visit to Gloucester Street in the summer.

It would be the ideal time to see the house for himself with his mother staying there without the family, but Rosie's angry words reverberated in his head now as he watched her chatting happily to Elizabeth and Billy. Molly did not mention the whereabouts of Lady Henrietta or her brother but, ever since his encounter with Lady Henrietta in Plymouth and her thoughtful gesture at their wedding four years ago, he had relented a little in his attitude towards her. However, he could not think of Lord William without his mood darkening and an icy fury overtaking him. He sighed, not wanting to allow the man to spoil his enjoyment of their celebration; perhaps Rosie had been right and they should put all that firmly behind them. And, in any case, there was so much to be done, which demanded his full attention.

There were Charlie Williams' regional contacts in Birmingham and Leeds to follow up now that the merger with Williams and Abel was complete. He was also determined to acquire the remaining 49 per cent of the shares as soon as it was possible to do so. He was confident that Miles would be prepared to release his holding for the right price, which would be undeniably more than he would otherwise have been offered for them, and Charlie had no choice in the matter. The sale and purchase agreement made certain of that. Then there was the question of the future of MMC Ltd following the death of Harry Masters. Billy's father had always been opposed to the gradual integration of his business with the emporium and, latterly, Chambers & Co, but he had never prevented it from happening, accepting with good grace the success of the strategy Billy had always championed. Now he was gone and Billy had inherited all of Harry's shares, so there was nothing holding them back from fully combining the two businesses, which is why Billy had presented proposals to do just that at their board meeting the previous week.

His suggestion was for Rosima Holdings to purchase the remaining 75 per cent of MMC Ltd at an equitable price, to be agreed by an independent valuation, and in return he would become a director of Rosima Holdings with director's fees and a share of the annual profits. He further proposed that Rebecca Fellowes be promoted to take overall charge of their operations in Plymouth so that he and Elizabeth would be free to move permanently to London in order that he could assist in a nationwide expansion of Chambers & Co. Max had agreed immediately, saying that it was more than acceptable to him, and he had also insisted that Billy become managing director of Chambers & Co with Richie as his right-hand man, in addition to his seat on the Rosima Holdings board. He and Billy were a good team and had built up much of the current business together and it was no more than he deserved.

In fact, Max now employed the whole of the Black family and he was delighted to do so. Stan had learned to drive and now worked one of the delivery rounds, Ivy helped out at the office in Chelsea on Tuesdays and Wednesdays and Lennie looked after all of the handyman jobs in the warehouse, whilst he was apprenticed to a local builder and joiner. Even Jimmy washed vans on a Friday evening to earn five shillings, which was a ridiculously generous amount of money but it allowed him to buy new books and writing materials, which he promptly did every Saturday.

The only member of the family not engaged with the businesses in some way or another was Molly. Apart from regular trips to London to stay with Max and Rosie in Pimlico, she had resolutely refused to leave Lee Moor, and Max despaired of ever persuading her to retire and live a more comfortable life with them.

'Yer just as much a slave ter yer master as I am, luv,' she had once said, 'except yer master is the business and mine is the family who 'ave looked after me all me life, an' it's what I know.'

'But, Ma,' Max had protested, 'it's not slavery, nothing like it. I enjoy it and I'm free!'

'Well, yer not at someone's beck an' call, I'll give yer that, but it's a funny sort o' freedom if yer ask me, always out at work, never at 'ome, albeit when yer are, it's in luxury,' she had replied and left it at that.

'Darling, you're miles away,' said Rosie as the waiter topped up their glasses with the remainder of the Château Léoville-Poyferré 1887.

'Sorry, sweetheart, just thinking about the business ... and watching you...'

She really did possess an unaffected grace and charm that radiated from within and captivated those around her, and yet she seemed refreshingly unaware that this was so. She retained a curious innocence beneath her growing sophistication that seemed to magnify her natural beauty, and her generosity of spirit was never far from the surface. Today she was so alive, so vital and bubbling with energy and good humour that Max thought he had never seen her look more alluring.

She smiled coyly at him and lowered her eyes for a moment, instantly reminding Max of the endearing mannerisms of their courtship. 'Whatever do you mean?'

'I was just thinking that you are the most beautiful woman in the room, that's all, and that I hope our children turn out to look like you.'

Rosie blushed. 'Shh, Max,' she protested shyly, reaching for his hand under the table.

His reference to children made her feel slightly anxious for a moment, but the sensation was fleeting. 'Don't be silly,' she told herself, 'it will happen soon,' but she was secretly rather anxious that she had not managed to conceive yet. They both longed to have a family together to make their happiness complete but there had been times since they had first started trying for a baby when she worried they were being greedy, wanting to have too much when they did not deserve it. It was as if they were somehow tempting fate, although she had not shared her fears with Max, knowing that he would gently, but firmly, brush them aside. All the same, she did sometimes worry about it even though she knew she was being irrational.

Chapter 34

The opening months of 1912 were particularly busy ones for Max and Billy as they worked hard to sustain progress at Chambers & Co following the successful completion of the merger. Billy had settled into his new role as managing director with his customary enthusiasm and drive and Richie was in his element ensuring the business ran like clockwork. Their reputation for the speed and reliability of their delivery service continued unassailably as they added additional routes to their schedules to meet demand for the new lines they had introduced from France. These had been launched with an auspicious advertising campaign masterfully put together by Max to tempt jaded taste buds in the post Christmas lull and had been an instant success. The *duck* and *goose foie gras, rillettes, confits* and *terrines* were in great demand and the fine *truffles* and *ceps* were proving almost as popular, particularly with their hotel customers. Richie found that he had needed to increase the order from their French suppliers twice in the first two weeks.

Then, as Easter approached, Rosie and Elizabeth had collaborated on an idea to offer a gift and packaging service, the like of which had not been seen before. It caught their competitors by surprise and left them trailing in their wake. The merchandise ranged from individual pots of fancy jams, marmalades and bottled fruits and vegetables to presentation hampers filled with a selection of seasonal fayre, all of which the customer could individually choose to satisfy their own unique requirements. Two of the most requested items were a dainty china jar filled with crystallised ginger and the tray of glazed fruits from Cherbourg, which was prettily wrapped in pink and white paper and tied with navy ribbons edged in gold. Billy had taken on six more warehouse men and two new drivers especially to cope with the orders for this new line, and their distinctive burgundy delivery vans were constantly travelling to and fro between the grand squares of Mayfair and Belgravia and the Chelsea depot.

Max still rose early to be at his desk at the warehouse before the last of the drivers left on their rounds. He liked to keep a close eye on what he described as the public face of the business, and he found that by arriving at seven each morning he could do exactly that. He could see for himself whether the delivery vans had been properly washed at the end of the previous day, he could inspect the produce for freshness and presentation as it was being picked from the warehouse shelves and loaded on to the vehicles, and in a glance he could check the appearance of the smart black and green uniforms he had designed especially for the drivers. He would then have two hours of relative peace before the office staff arrived to begin work, when he went through the accounts in minute detail. His concentration during this time was absolute so that by the end of it he would be fully aware of the company's latest financial position and therefore be able to act accordingly, with a promptness and fleetness of foot that sometimes astounded his bank manager.

Less than a year after his original conversation with Miles Brandon, Max was at the helm of a business that dominated the market in London and the south west and was poised to expand into the Midlands and beyond. He was comfortably in the black, after absorbing the acquisition and merger costs from Williams and Abel, and profits were soaring. He also had growing reserves of cash that he judged should be sufficient to see him through the next stage of expansion.

But on this fine April morning, having put aside the last of the ledgers, he could not settle. In three days' time Molly would be travelling with the Earl and Countess to Southampton to assist with their embarkation, and then the chauffeur was driving her on to Chesterfield Square in time for the decorators to commence on the 11th, the day after the RMS *Titanic* was to sail for New York. Max knew that in the end he would be unable to resist the temptation of Chesterfield Square once Molly had arrived from Mount Royal, despite Rosie's passionately voiced objections and his promises to the contrary.

Since his discovery of that overdue account the previous autumn, he had been keeping an eye on the orders from Chesterfield Square and consequently was aware that regular requests continued to come in from Monsieur Renard, the chef in charge who deputised for Mrs Castle when Lord and Lady Gordon were not in residence. She only travelled to London when the Earl and Countess stayed there for the Season. Occasionally the order would increase in value, which Max presumed indicated that a member of the family was in town, but in the main there was only the skeleton household staff to cater for.

Max was loath to broach the subject with Rosie again, but Molly's imminent arrival had reawakened the anxiety that had beset him since first discovering the Gordons' name in the ledger. He glanced out of

207

the window and saw one of the new drivers pulling into the parking bays in front of the loading area. Looking at his watch, he pushed the chair away from his desk and stood up.

'I'm just going out for an hour, would you let Mr Masters know please, Jenny,' he called decisively to his secretary, 'I'll be back before eleven.'

'Very good, Mr Chambers,' she replied as Max strode out in the direction of the yard. He walked briskly past the goods inwards area towards the loading bays as Jim Walton brought his van to a halt in front of bay number 4.

'Good morning, Jim, are you out again in a minute?'

'Yes, Mr Chambers,' replied the new man as he jumped down from the driver's seat, 'I'm off to Mayfair, Grosvenor Square first I think.'

'Mind if I come with you? I'd like to see the new gift service working for myself.'

'Of course, Mr Chambers, sit up front if you like, I won't be long.'

'Thanks, Jim,' smiled Max, 'I'll keep out of your way, unless I can help?'

'Oh, no thank you, Mr Chambers, that's all right! I can manage,' said Jim quickly, as he started to pack the first of the waiting parcels into the back of the van.

Max noticed the anxiety on Jim's face. He probably thinks I'm checking up on him, thought Max with a chuckle. 'If you're sure then, Jim,' he replied, opening the passenger door and putting his foot on the running board as he smiled broadly in order to put the man at ease.

In no more than 15 minutes, which was one of Jim Walton's fastest turn rounds since starting work for Chambers & Co two weeks previously, they were turning out of the large black warehouse gates in the direction of Hyde Park.

'The customers can't seem to get enough of these new lines, Mr Chambers,' said Jim as he steered the heavy vehicle through the busy streets. 'I've got two more trips to do after this one.'

Max nodded. 'Yes, you're right, Jim; the gift range is selling well. An instant success you might say. We'll have to introduce new products and seasonal specialities as we go on mind you. Richie Black is working on those at the moment. It's all about keeping ahead of the competition, Jim.'

'Well we're certainly doing that I'd say.'

'Good!' exclaimed Max, feeling very satisfied that their gamble was paying off so quickly.

They lapsed into silence for a while and soon the streets became enclosed by rows of large stuccoed houses and tall red brick Georgian mansions, which were the preserve of the rich in this part of London.

'So where are we going this morning?'

'Grosvenor Square, number 19 and number 5, 60 Duke Street, 39 Hill Street, four stops in St James Square, on to Chesterfield Square, there's six deliveries to do there, and then back out to Piccadilly, numbers 147 and 154 and finally Kensington Church Street.'

Chesterfield Square, thought Max to himself, what a stroke of luck! 'What numbers in Chesterfield Square, Jim?' he asked, turning towards him.

'Numbers 4, 7, 9 and...' he glanced at his list, '12, 24 ... oh yes, and number 1.'

Max was silent and looked away. His face was inscrutable and displayed no hint of what was running through his mind. Jim looked at him out of the corner of his eye, puzzled at Max's reaction.

It was just before half past ten when Jim turned into Chesterfield Square and pulled up outside number 24. He jumped down from the cab and went round to the back of the van where he selected three neatly wrapped boxes from the solid wooden storage crates that Richie had installed in each van to protect the gifts whilst they were in transit. He checked them against his order list and disappeared cheerfully down the area steps leading to the tradesman's door. Max remained in the passenger seat, staring across at the long oblong building fronting the pavement on the opposite side of the square. His view was partially obscured by the trees and bushes rising up from the gardens in the centre of the square, but the scale and grandeur of the house were unmistakable. It dominated that whole side of the square and in an instant Max knew it must be theirs, the grandiose symbol of the Gordons' power and prestige which he had heard so much about in his childhood but had never seen, until this day.

The sound of the driver's door slamming shut startled Max from his reverie. He turned quickly to Jim who was putting his list back in his pocket. 'They want four more of the glazed fruits and some of those chocolate fondants for Friday, Mr Chambers, cook says they're the best she's ever seen and the mistress has asked for them when the Italian Ambassador comes to tea. Cheaper than making them herself, she says, but if you ask me, she passes them off as her own!'

Max laughed. He did not care if she did. In fact, he took it as a compliment.

'I'll just finish here and we can head back out to Piccadilly. Soon be done, Mr Chambers.'

Max nodded as Jim cranked the engine and edged away from the kerb. Minutes later he was pulling up in front of number 1. The house looked even more stately close too and Jim flashed Max a curious look as he turned the engine off. 'Is everything all right, Mr Chambers?'

'Yes thanks, Jim, I was just thinking what a huge house this is, that's all.' And beautiful, he had to admit to himself.

'One of the grandest in London, I wouldn't be surprised. Equal to some of them ducal palaces, easy. Chef here is a bit of a gossip but he's harmless. He told me last week Lord and Lady Whatsit are off to America on that new liner ... what's it called now? ... The *Titanic*, that's it ... meant to be unsinkable they say. So I don't imagine we'll be getting much in the way of orders from him for a while. The young master is going to be in town though. Chef says he gambles you know ... poker I think ... and apparently he's forever getting into debt because of it.' He hopped out of his seat. 'All right for some!'

Max smiled grimly to himself. So he's still losing at cards, he said to himself, and no doubt his father is still bailing him out. 'As you say, all right for some,' is all he could reply as Jim whistled happily to himself as he reached for his list.

Chapter 35

'Rosie, Rosie!' cried Max as he rushed in through the front door, 'have you seen the evening paper?'

'Hello, darling, I'm just coming,' called Rosie from the first-floor drawing-room.

'Has the evening paper arrived?' he shouted again as he shrugged off his overcoat.

Rosie appeared at the top of the stairs. 'I'm coming, whatever is the matter, Max?'

'The evening paper...'

'Mary will have put it in the morning room, darling, as she always does before she leaves,' she said, mystified by Max's behaviour. 'Whatever is the matter?' she asked again.

'You haven't heard then?' he answered over his shoulder as he opened the morning room door, 'The *Titanic* has sunk! I saw the headlines on a newsboy's billboard as I drove along the river. It said *Titanic Disaster, Great Loss of Life!* Where is it! What's Mary done with it?'

'Oh, Max! But it can't have done, surely? She's the largest ship in the world. They said she's unsinkable!' exclaimed Rosie, aghast. 'Here it is,' she said, picking up the paper from her writing table.

They scanned the front page together and looked at each other in horror; it was true. They were shocked that the great liner could sink despite all her technological advances. The reports suggested that there was no loss of life, which contradicted the newsboy's headline, but it was unconfirmed.

'The morning papers will be full of it,' said Max, 'we'll find out more then. It's just so incredible ... unbelievable isn't it! God, I could do with a drink.'

The telephone rang before he had a chance to reach for the decanter, and he lifted the receiver to hear Molly's voice on the other end.

''Ello, 'ello, are yer there?'

'Ma, it's me, Max.' He mouthed 'Molly' to Rosie who was pouring him out a whisky.

'I'm ringin' from Chesterfield Square, 'ave yer seen the evening papers, Max, that boat 'as gone down!'

211

She sounded panicked. 'Ma, calm down. We were just reading the front page when you called. We can't believe it! Are you there on your own?'

'The staff is 'ere of course but the decorators left about an hour ago...'

'I meant Lady Henrietta or her brother.' He could not bring himself to refer to Lord William by name.

'Lord William is due termorrow until the end o' the week but Lady 'Enrietta is at Mount Royal. Oh, Max, those pour souls ... an' the master an' the mistress...'

'Do you know anything yet?'

'No, darlin', we've been telephonin' the White Star offices but we can't get through, so we're just waitin'. I don't know what else ter do. 'Er Ladyship spoke ter me earlier an' that's all she said we can do fer the moment. We 'aven't 'eard from Lord William.'

That doesn't surprise me in the least, thought Max; he'll be too busy thinking of himself to care about anybody else, even his own parents. 'Do you want to stay here tonight, Ma? You sound upset and I can come and get you in the car.'

'No, darlin', my place is 'ere in case they need me. I'm fine, 'onestly, but thank yer. Is Rosie all right, Max?'

'She's fine, Ma, thanks, she's standing next to me and sends her love.' Max smiled at Rosie as he said it. 'We'll know more in the morning I'm sure, it'll be all over the papers. Let me know if you hear anything, won't you?'

'I will, darlin', give my luv ter Rosie, bye, darlin', bye.'

The line went dead as Molly hung up.

'Well, come on, love, what did she say?' demanded Rosie impatiently.

'You heard most of it I think,' replied Max, taking a long drink from his glass, 'she doesn't know anything more than it says in the papers. Lady Henrietta is in Devon but has spoken to them on the telephone. Neither sight nor sound from *you know who* and, as you can guess, she insists on staying in Chesterfield Square. She'll call if there's any more news.'

DISASTER TO THE TITANIC
World's largest liner sinks after colliding with an iceberg during her maiden voyage.

The next day's headline in the the *Daily Mirror* stared out at them as they sat at the breakfast table. The evening paper's report of no loss of life had clearly been tragically wrong but it would be some while before an accurate picture of the number of fatalities emerged. There were many famous people on board, including Benjamin Guggenheim and Colonel John Jacob Astor IV, the American property magnate, sailing with his new young wife Madeleine; in fact the first-class passenger list read like the pages of *Who's Who*. The atmosphere in the dining-room was subdued as Violet, their new live-in maid, hired to help Mary, offered Max some more coffee.

'No thank you, Violet,' he said kindly as he rose from the table. 'I must go, sweetheart, they'll wonder where I am. Ma said she would telephone if she hears anything.' He leant over and kissed Rosie goodbye. 'John Henderson is coming down from Leeds to see me and I'm going to be late. I'm supposed to be picking him up from his hotel in half an hour.'

Rosie smiled up at him. 'Be careful, darling. See you tonight. I thought we'd invite Molly to dinner.'

'Yes, that's a good idea, if she'll come ... bye, love.' With that he was gone, the front door slamming in his wake.

BAND PLAYED TILL END

There was no news for two days save for the endless coverage in the newspapers. The tales of desperation and horror were heartrending, interspersed with reports of breathtaking heroism and gallantry. The whole country was shocked, or so it seemed, and nobody could talk of anything else. Then the telegram arrived. The doorbell rang in Chesterfield Square as Molly was replacing the flower arrangement on the round pedestal table that stood in the centre of the vast inner hallway underneath the coved and painted ceiling by the Venetian Giovanni Antonio Pellegrini. The tall antique crystal vase was always full of brightly coloured flowers whenever a member of the family was in residence, in accordance with Lady Constance's wishes, despite the fact that Lord William neither noticed nor commented upon their presence.

With her feet echoing on the elaborate chequered pattern of the marble floor, she opened the glazed doors that led into the entrance hall, tut-tutting quietly to herself as the doorbell rang again.

'I'm coming, I'm coming,' she muttered as she reached the front door.

'Telegram for you,' said the boy standing on the door step and holding out an envelope to her.

213

Molly's blood ran cold. It was addressed to 'The Viscount Bickleigh' and carried the White Star Line's crest.

'Thank you, son,' she said, handing him a farthing, which he promptly pocketed before handing Molly the envelope.

She uttered the words as if they were choking her. Slowly, she closed the door, unable to take her eyes from the envelope she held in her trembling hand. 'Now, don't be silly,' she told herself firmly, 'it might be good news,' but she knew that was probably a vain wish as she placed it on a silver salver to take to Lord William. So many people had perished according to the newspapers.

'Come!' barked William as Molly knocked on the tall mahogany library doors.

'Beg yer pardon, milord, this 'as just arrived fer yer,' said Molly, struggling to keep her voice strong as she held the salver in front of her. Lord William was sitting in one of the sofas reading the morning paper and he looked up, irritated at being disturbed. Molly approached him across the great expanse of Aubusson carpet that had been specially woven to match the very fine tapestry hanging on the wall above the fireplace.

'Well, what is it?' he demanded peremptorily.

'It's a telegram, milord.' Molly hesitated. 'From the White Star Line, milord.'

William did not look at her as he snatched it from the salver and impatiently tore it open. He betrayed no hint of emotion whatsoever as he quickly scanned the words, the flint-like greyness of his eyes cold and unfeeling as they held her then in a compassionless stare. He placed the envelope back on the salver and returned to the paper. Molly was almost trembling with trepidation, unsure of what to say or do. Without glancing from his page he dismissed her with a curt 'That will be all.'

She waited until she had closed the doors behind her, letting out an audible gasp, shocked and bewildered at his callous behaviour. For a moment she thought she might faint and she leant against the wall for support. She had to sit down and so she walked unsteadily across to the staircase and sank down on the bottom step. Her fingers were clumsy as she fumbled with the envelope in her haste to read its contents. Her eyes skimmed the first words until they came to rest on one line:

Deeply regret to advise you The Earl Gordon missing, presumed drowned.

The remaining words were a blur but they confirmed her worst fears.

214

But what about Her Ladyship? thought Molly desperately; there is no mention of Her Ladyship! A mixture of distress and almost physical pain assailed her and she buried her head in her hands. She was stunned into disbelief at Lord William's cold-hearted reaction to the news. The words continued to sink in as she read them again, frozen to the spot. The master gone! she cried to herself and, for all we know, Her Ladyship too! Shock rocked her without mercy as she imagined the icy water claiming its victims, the vicious cold overwhelming the desperate casualties on the stricken liner. Death had no respect for rank or position.

One of the housemaids found her still huddled there a quarter of an hour later as she was on her way up to the ballroom with a tray of tea for the decorators, and gently helped her to her feet.

It was another two days before word of Lady Constance reached Chesterfield Square and this time, mercifully, it was good news. She was alive, having been forced into a lifeboat by Lord Hugo, and had been rescued along with the other survivors by the RMS *Carpathia*.

Chapter 36

There was a knock on the door and Jenny came in.

'It's only me, Mr Chambers, Andrew Latchmere is here and I've finished the amendments you wanted to those contracts.'

'Thank you, Jenny, put them on my desk would you and show him in. Could we have some tea please?'

'Yes, Mr Chambers.'

Max stood up and walked across to the door to welcome the senior partner of Latchmere & Latimer, who had been his trusted solicitor for the past four years. At 30 Max was a shrewd and successful figure with a commanding presence, inspiring respect from both colleagues and business adversaries alike. He was at the height of his powers and carried his success well. He dressed smartly, but discreetly, and without succumbing to vanity, and had developed a degree of sophistication, which sat perfectly with his natural warmth and charm.

'Good morning, Andrew, how are you?'

'Good morning, Max, very well, thank you, and you?' Andrew took his outstretched hand and shook it firmly.

'I'm fine, thank you, Andrew, Jenny is bringing us some tea,' replied Max with a smile as he showed him to a chair. 'I have the amended Henderson contracts here to go through and I'd also like to discuss another personal matter with you before we finish.'

Andrew Latchmere nodded his head, intrigued by Max's reference to a personal matter, which he had not mentioned when they had spoken on the telephone the day before. But he said nothing because he knew Max well enough to realise that he would reveal whatever it was in his own good time.

'Let's start with Henderson then shall we?' said Andrew. 'You explained the background to the deal yesterday but perhaps it would be a good idea to go back to the beginning before I take a look at the contract so we can be sure I don't miss anything, seeing as I haven't been involved up until now.'

Max smiled at the gentle rebuke. 'I have been discussing the possibility of buying John Henderson's company since March and we started serious negotiations about six weeks ago, towards the end of August. He is one of James Williams' old contacts; Charlie Williams introduced me to him last year. Merchant Wholesale Provisions is the leading provider of wholesale foodstuffs to the catering and commercial retailers in the north of England. They act as the middleman between the manufacturers and retailers, as we do here in the south. John has wanted to sell for some while because he suffers from a medical condition that has been getting steadily worse and he wants to enjoy what time he has left without the burden of running his business. He doesn't have any family to hand the business on to and in my opinion he's left it rather late to sort out his future. He's rather desperate to sell in fact.'

'So you could acquire it for a good price?' interrupted Andrew, more in the way of a statement than a question.

Max looked at him. 'Yes, of course, otherwise I wouldn't be interested.' It was Andrew's turn to smile at the gentle admonishment. 'There is significant potential to increase revenues by tapping into the private marketplace in Leeds as well, again just as we do here in the south, and I think Henderson has allowed his commercial sales force to become complacent. That's what happens when you take your eye off the ball.' Max's face broke into its broadest smile yet. 'However, the main reason for agreeing to buy the company is to secure the buildings and vehicle fleet that will provide us with a ready made base from which to extend our activities immediately. I estimate this will save us at least a year compared to starting from scratch, and it will cost much less in the long run.'

'I can see you've done your homework, Max,' he said, 'which is no more than I would expect,' he added quickly. 'How much is he asking?'

'I have agreed forty thousand pounds in cash on signing, with a further twenty thousand payable in two instalments, the first in six months and the second three months after that.'

Andrew raised his eyebrows in alarm. 'Forty thousand in cash, Max, that's a lot of money! It would be more normal to offer a third on signing, with perhaps the remaining balance in equal instalments after six months and twelve months. Are you sure you can afford it? I mean … I know Chambers & Co is booming but you've just completed the purchase of Billy Masters' MMC shares, through Rosima Holdings, and…'

Max held up his hand. 'I should have said, Andrew, this will be channelled through Rosima Holdings as well.'

'Well then,' cut in Andrew, 'even more reason to spread the cost more evenly. I'm not sure it is advisable to extend yourself like this.'

'I'm not taking risks and I'm certainly not over-extending myself. I could easily go to the bank for the money if I was worried about cash, but I'm not. Chambers & Co produces more cash than we need and I'd rather put the surplus to good use than place it on deposit,' he replied firmly. 'That has always been my policy and I'll have more than sufficient working capital for both Chambers & Co and MMC even with this purchase, and you know my opinions of the banks! Their only motivation is to make money out of their customers from the outrageous interest they demand in return for a loan, and the control they require is out of all proportion to their risk. Why should I allow them to do that? Besides, this is a golden opportunity to turn Chambers & Co into a national company and I'm not going to let it pass us by for the sake of a few thousand pounds of cash upfront. I want to strike quickly whilst the iron's hot. Henderson needs the cash now and he'll be unable to walk away from my offer.'

'Maybe you're right, Max,' conceded Andrew cautiously.

'I'm sure I am, Andrew, and I want the contract with him by the end of the week. Can you do that please?'

Andrew reached for the document that Max was holding out to him. 'Of course, but why the hurry?'

'No sense in taking longer than is absolutely necessary,' said Max decisively, 'a deal isn't a deal until the ink is on the paper, you've always told me that and I don't want him to change his mind!'

Andrew laughed softly. 'You could probably rely on your verbal agreement if you had to, seeing as you've discussed the fine detail in this case, but you're right, there's no substitute for a signature. I'll go through this as soon as I get back to my office and telephone you in the morning if I have any queries,' he promised, sliding the contract into his briefcase. 'If everything is in order I'll have it typed up and two copies sent over to you by the end of the day.'

'That will be excellent, Andrew, thank you,' said Max, clearing his throat. 'Now, moving on to the other matter I mentioned when you arrived.'

'Yes,' said Andrew, 'I am intrigued I must admit.'

Max grinned easily, delighted to have aroused his solid and reliable solicitor's curiosity. 'I want to offer someone a job and I need your help.'

Andrew raised his eyebrows. 'You need my help to offer someone a job? Isn't that a little unusual?' he asked. 'It isn't customary to employ a solicitor to do that.' He smiled. 'But then you know that! Oh well, I daresay the fees will come in handy,' he said roguishly.

Max chuckled at this sudden display of wit. 'I want to keep my identity a secret for the moment, not from the man concerned of course, as we have been speaking for a while now, but from other interested parties shall we say. This man is concerned to ensure that his current employer remains unaware of his contact with me. I'd like you to act as my intermediary and handle all the correspondence on your firm's letterhead if you would?'

'I'd be pleased to, Max, just give me the details and I'll make contact with him.'

'His name is Jim Edwardes and he manages the Gordon family mining and quarrying interests. I have spoken with him very recently and I know he is keen to leave their employ, now that the son has inherited.' His voice was steady but Andrew was not fooled. He was aware of Max's feelings of enmity towards the new Earl Gordon.

'Ah, I see,' he said slowly. 'So things are not the same since the ninth earl went down with the *Titanic* I take it?'

'No, far from it I hear. Wholesale changes throughout the estate, old loyal retainers dismissed without as much as a thank you, unrest at the mines, tenants evicted from estate cottages if they cannot pay the new rents, even the Dowager Countess has been pushed into the Dower House with indecent haste.'

'Your mother tells you all this I presume ... is she all right?'

'Yes, that's how I know what has been going on. She has remained with the Countess and insists on staying despite my efforts to persuade her to the contrary. I understand the sister, Lady Henrietta, has moved with her mother too and is refusing to have anything to do with her brother. The estate trustees have apparently intervened where they can but their powers seem to be limited.'

Andrew nodded. 'They will only be able to act within the parameters laid down by the old earl's will. But getting back to your man, what will he be doing for you?'

'I have asked him to take charge of things in Leeds if my offer for Merchant Wholesale Provisions goes through but I want him to start as soon as possible. He will need to familiarise himself with how we do things in London and Plymouth before he moves up north. His employment will be with Chambers & Co but is not to be conditional upon the successful conclusion of the acquisition; however, it is another reason why I want the contract to be signed without delay.'

Andrew regarded Max carefully, seeing the look of determination on his face. 'Are you sure he can do the job, Max, after all your business isn't exactly mining is it?'

'No it's not, but Jim is an extremely able manager who has been known to me for many years and has served the Gordon family with great loyalty during that time. He is a gifted leader of men who like and respect him, which is exactly what I need. I must have someone I can rely on implicitly to act on his own initiative and who I can trust to make the right decisions because I will be so far away. I have offered him more money than he would get elsewhere and am willing to compensate him for moving north. I know he will accept.'

Andrew smiled appreciatively at Max. 'You've left nothing to chance as usual!'

'I can't afford to, Andrew, not if I intend for this to work, which I do!'

'I'll draw up his contract and letter of appointment and have it sent round to you later today. If you're happy with it I will send it to him this evening and suggest he starts ... shall we say ... a week from tomorrow?'

'Yes please, that will be fine.'

'Good, thank you, Max, I'd better be going then as I've lots to be getting on with!' said Andrew with a chuckle as he snapped his briefcase shut and stood up, 'unless there's anything else I can help you with?'

'No thank you, Andrew, that's all for the moment. I appreciate your help, as always.' He held out his hand as he reminded himself how fortunate he was to have a solicitor as good as Andrew Latchmere to take care of his legal matters.

Shaking Max's hand, Andrew said, 'Oh, by the way, I nearly forgot. How is Rosie, I hear congratulations are in order?'

Max grinned from ear to ear. 'Thanks, Andrew, yes, we're over the moon of course. She's due in February.'

'Give her my regards won't you.'

'I will, thanks again, Andrew,' said Max and he walked him to the door.

When he had gone and Max had settled back behind his desk, he looked out of the window and thought about Jim Edwardes. He was certain Jim was the right man for the job but he had to admit that he was equally as pleased to contemplate the chaos that would ensue after Jim's departure. It was Jim who kept things running smoothly at the mine and quarries, Jim and the men's residual loyalty to Lord Hugo. Without Jim there, Lord William would turn the men against himself in no time at all, and in so doing, he would irreparably damage one of the family's main sources of income. He smiled satisfyingly to himself. 'Serves him right,' he swore softly, 'and not before time.'

Chapter 37

'How dare you do this!' screamed Henrietta, her hazel-brown eyes blazing with rage. 'It is unforgivable!'

William lounged back in the chair that had been his father's favourite and stared disinterestedly out of the study window, an expression of pure disdain on his face. 'Actually I can do whatever I choose,' he said calmly, without bothering to look at his sister.

'Papa would never have...'

'Papa is dead and buried and I am the master now,' cut in William, his tone controlled and uncompromising. Only two small circles reddening on his cheeks betrayed any hint of emotion. He laughed sardonically. 'You and Mama have not quite grasped that fact yet, have you?'

'Leave Mama out of this,' spat Henrietta, 'she has enough to cope with already.' Her heart lurched as she thought of Lady Constance. The trauma of her ordeal on the *Titanic* and her devastation at Lord Hugo's death were still so acute that she would spend days secluded in her rooms, unable to receive anybody, and, at times, even to summon her maid to help her dress and set her hair. William's behaviour since succeeding to the title had proven to be much worse than even Henrietta had imagined, and she had repeatedly been forced to watch as her brother wreaked havoc with much of what the family had held dear for generations. She was been powerless to halt his increasingly irresponsible and mean-spirited behaviour, and when she had appealed to the trustees for help, they too were impotent and unable to stand in his way.

'The men at the mine deserve better! Can't you see that? They have served this family loyally for years, generations in some cases, and you just cast them aside as if they count for nothing. They're people ... human beings, with families to support ... children to feed...' She was almost speechless with disbelief.

William turned to look at her, his eyebrows raised in arrogant appraisal of his sister. 'Blame Edwardes, not me! If he hadn't left me in the lurch everything would be running smoothly. As it is...'

'Don't blame Jim Edwardes for *your* incompetence,' fumed Henrietta. 'That's typical of you, isn't it. You lose the best manager we've ever had and then make the situation worse by cutting the men's pay *and*, as if that isn't enough, you refuse to meet with them to listen to their grievances.' She stared contemptuously at him. 'And those who live on the estate have been hit by your increases to their rent as well. No wonder there's trouble. All done to cover your gambling debts I daresay! Papa must be turning in his grave.'

William snorted with derision. 'If Papa had reviewed the rents when he was alive, as I wanted, then I wouldn't have had to do so now. They've been allowed to fall behind for years and we've been gradually bled dry as a result.'

'So that is his fault is it?' she snapped, '*I might have known!*'

'I blame Chambers if you really want to know, he is the cause of all this.'

'*Who…?* You mean Max Chambers, the housekeeper's son? How on earth…'

'She is no longer the housekeeper here and if Mama had any sense, she wouldn't be in her employ either!'

We'll come on to that in a minute, thought Henrietta grimly, but she was determined to stick to the point. 'Max Chambers is a successful businessman, very successful I gather, and rich. He lives in London and I haven't seen him in these parts for a long time!' He's clearly a far better businessman than you'll ever be, she almost added, but instead she snapped icily, 'You'll have to think of a better excuse than that, William.'

'Chambers lured him away with the offer of a job in Leeds at a ridiculous salary and of course Edwardes, being the greedy man he is, jumped at the chance. He didn't care that he was throwing our business into chaos, and if he thought he could blackmail me by demanding more money to stay, then he was greatly mistaken. Good riddance I say! It was a deliberate attempt by Chambers to harm our interests if you ask me.'

'If it was, which I very much doubt, then he's succeeded, hasn't he!' she retorted scathingly. She glared scornfully at her brother and truly thought she did not know him any more. 'You always treated Jim Edwardes like he was some kind of animal, even in Papa's day, so there's no point in denying it. It's little wonder he seized the first opportunity he could to leave and now Max Chambers has got a very good man, which will no doubt make him richer still, and what have you got…?'

William's mouth contorted in fury and, for a moment, Henrietta felt the urge to laugh. He really believed he was the wronged man. 'I'm warning you, William, you've gone too far this time. Don't force me to do something we'll both regret...'

The menace in her tone caused William to pause. He looked at her face and saw the tell-tale signs that he had learned to be wary of. For all his bravado and ill-conceived spitefulness, he knew when to tread carefully. 'I have absolutely no idea what you mean,' he said circumspectly, 'and you certainly can't threaten me.'

'Oh, I'm not threatening you, William, and I think we both know what I mean,' she said quietly. William looked blankly at her. 'I know what happened all those years ago, and it broke Mama's heart.'

He let out a hollow laugh. 'I don't know what you're talking about...'

'Oh, I think you do ... and before you tell me it was a long time ago, I also know how you tried to repeat it all over again, only this time someone intervened, which nearly caused another tragedy. I overheard you at the time, plotting in the long gallery, embroiling Makepiece in your nasty, wicked scheme.' She paused. 'You look surprised, William! You didn't know I was nearby did you? I was standing on the stairs and I heard everything. I didn't understand to begin with, but I soon worked it out. I should have done something about it then, in fact I shall never forgive myself for keeping quiet.' The memory was etched on her mind. 'If it had not of been for...'

'*For what!*' interrupted William harshly, 'for the good of the family name...?'

'No!' hissed Henrietta, 'for the sake of Mama and Papa, but now I have only Mama to worry about.'

'And yourself,' said William sarcastically, 'you can prove *nothing*, because there is nothing *to* prove, and I'd see you in hell first.' He stood up abruptly.

Henrietta stood her ground as he brushed belligerently past her, clenching her hands at her sides, knowing that her words had struck home. She held him in a piercing gaze as he strode out of the study and slammed the door behind him. Then her legs began to tremble and she sat down quickly on one of the chesterfield sofas flanking the fireplace. She had known for some months that this confrontation had become inevitable, and even though she had prepared herself for it, now that it was over she felt no sense of satisfaction whatsoever. In fact she felt worse than before their spat, realising that she had not achieved any success at all in her attempt to curb her brother's behaviour. He seemed intent on feeding his own selfish and miserable greed whatever the cost to his family and their future, and that knowledge appalled her. I shall have to enlist Mama's help, she said to herself, but until her mother was stronger she dared not burden her with yet more bad news. She stared at the painting on the wall, of the storm clouds swirling across the leaden sky, and thought how aptly the scene captured her mood. She allowed herself a wry smile, despairing of the further damage William would do in the meantime.

She sat there for nearly an hour until she was disturbed by a knock on the door. She looked up to see Jackson standing in the doorway. 'Excuse me, milady, may I draw the curtains?'

Rousing herself from her musing, she realised that the light was failing rapidly and it was time she returned to the Dower House. 'Of course, Jackson, thank you. Gosh, is that the time? I must be getting back.'

The butler smiled warmly at her. 'Milady. May I ring for the chauffeur, milady, it is getting dark.'

Henrietta smiled back. 'Thank you, Jackson, but I shall be fine. The fresh air will do me good.'

'Very well, milady.' He hesitated, unsure of what to say next. Henrietta noticed his uncertainty and she smiled again. 'Was there something else, Jackson?' she asked gently.

'Well, milady,' he began as he cleared his throat nervously, 'it's just that we ... I mean the rest of the staff ... and myself of course, well ... we were wondering if there was anything we could do to help you and Her Ladyship, seeing as you don't live here any more...'

'That is very kind of you, Jackson,' she murmured softly, 'all of you. Will you please thank everyone downstairs for me?' He nodded immediately. 'Her Ladyship and I are only on the other side of Home Park so we haven't gone away. There are lots of changes happening on the estate, which I was just discussing with Lord William,' and that is an understatement, she thought dryly, 'but things are far from settled I know.' She looked at him standing respectfully before her and was struck by the almost overwhelming feeling that she should be the one offering to protect and care for them. 'How are things in the servants' hall, Jackson?' she asked in a kindly tone. 'I want you and the others to know that you can always speak to me, or to Her Ladyship, if you need to, at any time. Please don't forget that, Jackson.'

A look of relief and gratitude swept across the butler's face. 'They are not so bad, thank you, milady. We're bearing up. Will that be all, milady?'

'Yes, thank you, Jackson.'

After he had gone, Henrietta began to gather her things together and, as she did so, she looked wistfully around the study. It had been one of her father's favourite rooms and it reflected his character perfectly. There was a patrician air about it, with the well-used and familiar furniture providing that comfortable feeling of continuity that she had so relished when it had been her father occupying the broad leather chair behind the desk. Even the Earl's preferred magazines and newspapers were still arranged daily on the ebony library table next to the fireplace. At least that's something *he* hasn't changed, she muttered bitterly to herself, and she found herself crying tears of longing for her father, for the old order that he had nurtured so diligently all his life, and which now seemed to be crashing down around them. But most of all she cried tears of rage for the folly of her brother.

Chapter 38

It was still dark when Max quietly switched off the bathroom light and crept back over to the bed. He was being careful not to wake Rosie who had only just dozed off again after an uncomfortable night. The baby was due in a little over four months and she was beginning to find it difficult to sleep undisturbed through the night.

'Bye, darling, see you later on,' whispered Max as he leant over and gently kissed her goodbye. She did not stir.

Creeping silently out of the house, Max walked briskly round to the mews and opened the garage doors. It was at times like this, when he was tired from his trip to Leeds and with a very full day ahead of him, that he questioned the wisdom of refusing to employ the services of a chauffeur. However, on this cold November morning, he decided a bracing drive through the quiet London streets was just what he needed to sharpen his senses.

The engine of the Rolls-Royce sprang into life as he cranked it two or three times before confidently reversing it out of the garage. He loved the rhythmic hum of the six-cylinder motor as he accelerated towards the Embankment, and with little traffic around at this time of the morning he was on the outskirts of Chelsea in no time at all. The Silver Ghost handled superbly well and Max could not understand why anyone would want to deny themselves the pleasure of driving such a fine vehicle by having someone else do so for them. With 40/50 horsepower surging under the bonnet he could see why the model had recently won four prizes at the Austrian Alpine Trials, and by the time he turned through the heavy black gates into the warehouse yard, in his mind's eye he was one of those victorious rally drivers crossing the finishing line.

He pulled into one of the parking spaces in front of the offices, exhilarated by the cool air and the thrill of the brisk drive. The warehouse was still in darkness and only the night-watchman was on duty at this early hour. Unlocking the front door, Max switched on the lights and went up to his office to organise himself for the first of the day's meetings. He had arranged to meet Billy and Richie at half past seven and it was already a quarter past six. He had the plans for the enlargements to the

Leeds warehouse in his briefcase, which he had taken up with him to Leeds to discuss with Jim, and he wanted to review the comments Jim had made once more before Billy and Richie arrived. Time was pressing if Lennie was to start the building work immediately after Christmas. They then had an operational meeting to agree the December schedules, and Rosie and Elizabeth were joining them at eleven o'clock for a last run through of the Christmas gift and party lines, which the two of them had been working on since the autumn. The morning room at Gloucester Street had been littered with samples of all manner of festive specialities for weeks, and today was the final decision day if orders were to be placed with the manufacturers for end of the month deliveries. Customers were already enquiring about their Christmas ranges and demand promised to be buoyant from Plymouth right the way through to Leeds. He also had to check the ledgers, which he had not been able to look at for several days whilst up in Leeds, although Billy had telephoned him daily with the latest sales and cash receipts figures.

In no time at all he was engrossed in the papers laid out on the desk in front of him, poring over the fine detail of Lennie's quotations to estimate how they would change if all of Jim's suggestions were to be incorporated. The sound of loud footsteps on the stairs disturbed him whilst he was in the middle of adding up a long column of figures and he cursed under his breath as he lost his place. He glanced at his watch, almost seven o'clock, Billy must be early.

'In here, Billy,' he called without looking up, 'I'm just checking Lennie's costs for the Leeds work.'

He was startled as the office door was flung open with a crash and William Gordon appeared on the threshold. Max was caught unawares for a moment and he remained immobile behind his desk. Then, in an instant, he was on his feet. 'What the...' he said coldly before William cut him off.

'So this is where the great Max Chambers hides himself is it?' sneered William in a superior tone. His voice was slightly slurred and it was clear from his evening dress that he had been out all night. He advanced a few paces into the room.

'How did you get in?' demanded Max. 'I've got nothing to say to you! I suggest you leave now before I throw you out!'

'No, not until I'm ready,' jeered William. 'Where's Edwardes?'

Max tensed and clenched his fists by his sides, coming out from behind the desk. 'Don't force me to throw you out, you bastard!' he warned again, eyes narrowing as they met his.

227

William stared back at him with a mixture of arrogance and malevolence. 'I'll ask you again, where is Edwardes!' He swayed unsteadily on his feet.

'Jim Edwardes has nothing to say to you, and I for one don't blame him,' asserted Max with glacial coldness.

'Don't you now, and what business is it of yours?' His sarcasm was biting.

'Jim left Lee Moor months ago, which was not a moment too soon. He works for me now so it is...'

'I know he works for you now! You stole him from me and I intend to get him back,' shouted William, 'after all, my family has done for him, and as for you ... you've leeched off us for years, you and your lazy, good-for-nothing parents. And as for that bitch of a kitchen maid...' His face was turning a bright reddish purple and his breathing was becoming increasingly laboured.

Max was speechless, unable for a moment to take in what had just been said. Then, as his eyes blazed with hatred, he grabbed the paper knife from his desk and menacingly took a step forwards. William was a big man, several inches taller than him, but Max felt an overpowering urge to use it. 'Don't you ever mention my family again,' he hissed with a deadly finality as his grip tightened on the knife.

William glanced down at Max's right hand and recoiled involuntarily. The man's a coward, thought Max, as he fought to control his rage. 'You're not worth hanging for, Gordon!'

A smirk formed on William's face. 'Your sort is all the same,' he raged, 'you get ideas above your station and think you're as good as us. Edwardes is just the same...'

'Jim Edwardes is a fine man and he is doing an excellent job *for me*. He left because you treated him like dirt, but that's how you treat everybody isn't it! You bring your troubles upon yourself.'

'Troubles...'

'Oh I know all about your problems at the mine and the quarries and I hear they're going to get worse.' Max could not keep the flash of satisfaction from his voice. 'And you deserve every one one of them!'

'*Worse!* What do you mean?' demanded William, caught off guard.

Max laughed disparagingly and ignored him. 'I promise you, Gordon, if I ever set eyes on you again, you will regret it for the rest of your life! If I hear so much as a whisper from Molly that...' William snorted derisively. 'So much as a whisper, I will kill you, so help me. Do you hear me?' Max spoke calmly, in a low and even tone, and one that was full of venom. He looked down at the knife, which was still in his hand, and then his eyes travelled slowly and deliberately to William's face and fixed him with an unyielding stare.

William opened his mouth to answer but swivelled round quickly as he heard someone coming up the stairs, and before he had the chance to say anything Billy appeared in the doorway. There was a momentary silence as a dawning realisation appeared on Billy's shocked features.

'Bloody hell, Max, what's he doing here?' he gasped.

'He was just leaving and he won't be coming back.' William did not move. 'I'll have to throw him out then,' said Max, looking at Billy. 'Or, better still ... telephone the police would you, Billy, and tell them we have an intruder on the premises. They can take him away in handcuffs.'

'Right away, Max,' replied Billy quickly, his eyes never once leaving William's face, which was now perspiring heavily. He moved across to the desk and lifted the receiver.

'You haven't heard the last of this!' threatened William but Max just stared back and took another pace towards him, raising the knife just enough for William to notice.

'Max, no!' cried Billy, but he did not need to worry. The office door slammed shut as William left. Max and Billy looked at each other. 'It's a long story,' began Max as Billy went over to the window.

'Just checking he's really gone,' said Billy, watching the retreating figure stride across the yard towards the gates. 'God, I think I need a drink!'

Max sank down in his chair and exhaled deeply, releasing his grip on the paper knife. He looked down at the deep outline of the handle imprinted on his palm and grimaced, flexing his fingers to restore the circulation.

'It's a good job you weren't late, otherwise I'm not sure what would have happened,' he said quietly. He was shaken and did not mind admitting it as he reached down and opened the bottom drawer to pull out an almost full bottle of whisky. 'I think I'll join you,' he murmured as he poured a generous measure into two glass tumblers. In his mind he was remembering the childhood incident with Lord William in the kitchen garden at Mount Royal, which had caused him nightmares for weeks afterwards. He could still recall the malicious look on Lord William's face as if it had happened yesterday and he had seen it again this morning. He thought about putting a call through to Molly, but then told himself he was being foolish because that would only upset her. But the man was stupid and reckless enough to do just about anything and that knowledge worried him. He began to tell Billy what had happened.

'It's a bit early wouldn't you say?' said Richie with a grin as he appeared about ten minutes later, nodding at the opened bottle and half empty glasses on the desk, 'don't tell me Lennie's figures are that bad!' The two men laughed for the first time that morning but Max knew that a line had been crossed and the bad feeling that had always existed between him and Lord William had now been brought out into the open; if it was not personal before, it had certainly become so now.

'Sit down, Richie and I'll tell you what's been going on,' said Max, raising the bottle of whisky in his direction.

Richie smiled and nodded, reaching over for a fresh glass from the tray that always stood in the middle of the long meeting table. Max was as brief as possible because there were still the Leeds plans to finalise before the operational meeting, and the warehouse supervisors who attended these scheduling meetings could not afford to be kept waiting, otherwise the deliveries for the day would be affected. Christmas was approaching and there was a lot of work to do. However, by the time he had finished, the three of them had agreed that security at the warehouse needed to be tightened, and for good measure they decided to do so in Plymouth and Leeds as well, but, most importantly as far as Max was concerned, Rosie and Elizabeth were not to be told anything. Billy was in complete agreement with this; neither man was prepared to allow anything, or anybody, to put the health of their unborn babies at risk.

Chapter 39

The ornaments decorating the Christmas tree in the corner of the drawing-room twinkled brightly against the pale-green curtains that were drawn against the dark coldness outside, casting a magical spell as they caught the light from the softly glowing table lamps.

'Thank you, Mary, thank you, Violet,' said Rosie with a warm smile to the two parlourmaids as they finished laying out the supper trays. 'We'll look after ourselves now.'

'Very good, Mrs Chambers,' they replied, almost in unison as they cast their eyes over them one last time to make sure nothing had been forgotten.

'But before you go there is something under the tree, which Mr Chambers and I would like you to have. I'll just ring for Mrs Walsh to come up too.'

'Let me do that, darling,' offered Max quickly, rising from the sofa.

'Oh, Max, I'm not an invalid you know,' said Rosie in mock exasperation as she eased herself to her feet and went over to the bell to call for Mrs Walsh.

By the time they were all gathered next to the tree Rosie had selected a parcel for each of them from the small collection of prettily wrapped presents that were arranged in a semi circle around it. 'This one is for you, Mrs Walsh,' said Rosie to their cook, who smiled shyly as she handed it to her.

'Oh thank you, Mrs Chambers, Mr Chambers,' she gushed, looking at each of them in turn. 'May I open it now?' she asked, sounding almost as excited as a young child would be.

'Of course you may,' smiled Rosie, 'it's with our very best wishes for Christmas and with our gratitude for all your hard work throughout the year.'

'It's a pleasure I'm sure, madam,' replied Mrs Walsh, blushing furiously as her fingers fumbled with the red velvet bow on top of the box. 'It's a shame to tear the lovely paper,' she remarked as she unwrapped it carefully, placing the length of velvet in her apron pocket, thinking it was bound to come in very handy for something else. Years of thrift had left their mark. She gasped with delight as she held up a beautiful deep-brown leather handbag. 'Oh, it's lovely! Thank you! And my old one is splitting down the seams too! However did you know, madam?'

Rosie smiled happily. 'I'm so glad you like it, Mrs Walsh, and thank you again for such a splendid luncheon today.' Exquisitely wrapped gifts were then presented to each member of staff in turn: Mary, the young parlourmaid, and Violet, the newest member of their household staff. Both were delighted.

'We have something for you too, Mrs Chambers, and for Mr Chambers,' Violet said hesitantly, 'we know it's a bit premature but it seems like the right time to ask you to accept this.'

Rosie and Max looked at each other in surprise as she darted out on to the landing and came back in with a small parcel wrapped in brown paper. 'I'm afraid it's not as nicely wrapped as yours,' she said apologetically, 'but we all thought this might come in handy when the baby comes.'

Rosie took the proffered gift and stammered her thanks as she unwrapped the paper with shaking hands. 'Oh, Max, look at this, it's beautiful!' she exclaimed softly, 'thank you all so much! You really shouldn't have!' The three women looked pleased. 'Max, look,' she said as she handed him a small leather-bound Bible, 'isn't it lovely darling?'

'Yes it certainly is,' he said, genuinely touched by their thoughtfulness. 'It's very kind and we shall treasure it always. Thank you!'

'It's our pleasure, sir,' said Mrs Walsh. 'Now then girls, we should go back downstairs, if you have everything you need, madam?'

'Yes we do, thank you. More than enough I'm sure.'

'Goodnight then, Mrs Chambers, goodnight, Mr Chambers.'

'Goodnight girls and Merry Christmas once again,' said Max. 'And we hope you'll have your own celebration downstairs now.'

'Yes of course, you must,' added Rosie quickly. 'Goodnight.'

'And please help yourselves to a bottle of something from the cellar with our best wishes,' instructed Max kindly. God knows they've earned it, he thought to himself.

After they had gone, Rosie asked, 'I think they liked them, don't you, love?' as they sat back down on one of the sofas to wait for Molly to rejoin them from upstairs.

Max stretched his legs out in front of the fire and pulled her close. 'Yes, I'm sure they did, darling, and I'm glad. They deserve it and we'd be lost without them, wouldn't we? Especially now with the baby due in a few weeks. You know, I was just thinking, it takes me back to Christmas at Mount Royal. It was never like this ... I mean, I know

Ma and Pa used to receive a gift and you did, didn't you? But it wasn't as if they meant anything.'

'What do you mean?'

'Well, I mean it didn't ever seem sincere, more that it was what was expected … because of etiquette I suppose. There was no feeling of benevolence or anything was there?'

'I don't know, Max,' sighed Rosie comfortably, 'but it doesn't matter now, it was all a long time ago.' She looked over at the trays of food. 'Where's Molly? She's taking a long time and I'm starving!'

Max laughed. 'How on earth can you be hungry after such a huge lunch?'

Rosie grinned and looked guiltily at him. 'Must be on account of whoever is in here,' she said, patting her stomach.

It certainly had been a large gathering with masses of food and drink. They had squeezed eleven round the dining-room table, which had been a very tight fit indeed, but they had managed it. All of her family had come, and Richie had brought his partner Marjorie too. Molly was able to stay with them for the Christmas week because the Dowager Countess and Lady Henrietta were visiting friends and the Dower House was closed up, and Billy and Elizabeth had accepted their invitation to the family party, being told they were as good as family anyway. Mrs Walsh had excelled herself with the food and Max had selected some of the best champagne and wines from his cellar to accompany it. He had also made sure there was a plentiful supply of beer for Stan and Lennie.

The festivities had started with the present giving in the drawing-room as soon as everyone had arrived. Rosie had spent weeks choosing singularly thoughtful gifts that she hoped would surprise and delight each recipient and she had roped Max into helping with the wrapping up, so that by the time Christmas morning arrived the tree was surrounded by an array of parcels of varying shapes and sizes, each one carefully concealed in gaily coloured paper with bows and ribbons neatly tied in velvet and gauze.

When, at last, all the gifts had been exchanged and opened, with much merriment and whoops of delight and repeated cries of 'Thank you! Thank you!' it was time to hand out the special decorations from the tree. Mrs Walsh had made some tiny cakes and sweetmeats, which Rosie had dotted around the branches, together with little ribboned bags of sweets and sugared almonds from the Chambers & Co festive range. These were intended to be taken home but Jimmy, for one, opened them straightaway, causing Ivy to warn him that he'd ruin his appetite if he ate them all at once. They had all then trooped downstairs to the dining-room for lunch, where they remained at the table for the rest of the afternoon until it was time to go home.

'It's been a lovely day hasn't it?' said Rosie as she rested her head on Max's shoulder.

'Yes, it has, our last Christmas as just the two of us,' replied Max reflectively, 'and next year will be even better won't it? I wonder if he'd like a train set, or maybe some toy soldiers...'

'Steady on, darling!' He's going to make a wonderful father she thought lovingly to herself. 'And anyway, it might be a girl you know!'

'Well all right then, a doll's house or rocking horse perhaps?'

'Honestly, Max!' she said, laughing contentedly and reaching over to plant a kiss on his forehead, 'this child had better not grow up to be spoiled.'

'Spoiled? Did I 'ear yer say spoiled?' asked Molly as she came into the room. 'Of course my grandchild is going ter be spoiled. It's a grandmother's duty!'

'Ah, that's different, Molly,' said Rosie, smiling at her mother-in-law as she sat down in the armchair opposite them, 'grandparents are allowed to do that.'

'Just as long as he or she is healthy, that's all that matters for the moment,' said Max.

'Oh do stop worrying, darling, everything is going to be fine, I promise you. I've had a trouble free pregnancy so far, haven't I? Now then, who would like some supper?'

'Before we 'ave anything ter eat,' said Molly quietly, 'I've got something here fer yer that I've been keeping safe fer a while now, ever since yer dad died actually...' She paused to look at the two of them. 'It's something 'e wanted yer both ter 'ave.' She held out a small plain box, which Max reached over and took from her, his face a picture of curious surprise. 'We always said that we would give yer this when yer 'ad a family of yer own and so now seems ter be the right time. But, before yer open it,' she went on, her voice steady and clear as Max began to open the box, 'there'll be questions yer will want ter ask me so I've written this letter ter go with it.' She produced a sealed envelope, which she handed to Rosie. 'But it is not ter be opened until after my death. Yer father was insistent about that.' Both Rosie and Max were looking increasingly puzzled as she continued. 'I know it all sounds odd and I'm sorry about that, I really am, but that's the way yer dad wanted it so yer must both promise me that yer will do as I ask.'

There was silence as her words sank in. 'Well, go on then, open the box,' suggested Molly, 'then we can 'ave some supper!' she added, attempting to lighten the atmosphere, which had grown solemn.

Max did so without saying a word and he looked at Molly in amazement as he pulled out the picture of the young girl that had always stood on the mantelpiece at Fern Cottage for as long as he could remember.

Chapter 40

Bickleigh Manor on the Mount Royal Estate had served as the dower accommodation for three successive generations of the Gordon family. The ten-bedroomed house was situated on the edge of Home Park and stood within 50 acres of its own grounds. It was, to all intents and purposes, a separate small estate in its own right with private carriage access to the village, which meant that visitors did not need to pass by the main lodge at the gates to Mount Royal unless they chose to do so. The seventh earl's young widow had ordered the construction of this discreet entrance when she was in the throes of an adulterous affair with a neighbouring landowner in order that she could come and go as she pleased, without scrutiny from either the main household staff or her family.

Molly had preferred to use this route ever since she had started working solely for Lady Constance and living for part of the week at Bickleigh Manor itself. At the Dowager Countess's bidding she had taken to sleeping in one of the attic bedrooms for four nights of the week before returning to Fern Cottage early on a Friday evening to spend the weekend there. This suited her well because it gave her company for much of the time whilst allowing her to retain the tenure of the cottage where she and Bert had lived for most of their married life. Lady Constance had been particularly supportive of her after Bert was killed and had since gone out of her way to ensure she was protected from the changes wrought by William after Lord Hugo's death. If it had not been for the Countess's iron-willed intervention the new Earl would have seen her dismissed from her position as housekeeper at Mount Royal and evicted from Fern Cottage.

Lady Constance had put an end to William's witch hunt, as she bitterly called it, by asking Molly to combine the duties of lady's maid and housekeeper at the manor house. She had gratefully accepted despite Max's persuasive efforts at the time to convince her to move to London. She wanted above all to remain in Lee Moor, where she felt close to Bert. The Countess had also taken Mrs Castle with her to the manor when William had forced his mother to move from Mount Royal within weeks of Lord Hugo's funeral.

On this February morning Molly was deep in thought as she walked briskly through the carriage gates. The house stood majestically before her in the distance at the end of the long tree-lined drive. She shivered, drawing her coat more closely around her. A late winter frost covered the ground with its blanket of white, making the grass crunch underfoot as she quickened her pace. It was still early and Lady Constance would only just have received her morning tea but she did not want to be late, knowing it took ten minutes to reach the house from this point and she had a busy day ahead. She had to be on hand to help Her Ladyship bathe and dress and, as it was Monday, it was also linen day so there were all the beds to change before lunchtime.

The wintry scene reminded her of Christmas and for a moment memories of the joyous week she had spent in London pushed thoughts of all that needed to be done to the back of her mind. Gloucester Street was such a warm and happy house where she always felt welcomed and cherished in Max and Rosie's company. She was particularly glad that this year she had been able to fulfil one of Bert's long-held wishes by giving them the picture from the mantelpiece at Fern Cottage. 'It's only right,' he used to say whenever they discussed it. She thought Lady Constance would want to know she had done so too and she made a mental note to tell her as soon as the opportunity arose. She hoped Her Ladyship would be pleased.

Lady Constance had aged considerably since her husband's death. Despite the fact that she was nearing 80, she had always been very spry and full of life, but the tragedy of the *Titanic* had changed all that. She now leant heavily on a cane when she walked, which made her seem rather frail and delicate, and her once dark hair had turned completely white and was thinning rapidly. Her mind, however, was still razor sharp and her appearance belied her resilience and strength of character, which remained undimmed. Since recovering from the initial overwhelming shock of Lord Hugo's death, her determination to limit the excesses of her son's behaviour as far as she could was testimony to that. She had resisted William's charmless attempts to evict her from Mount Royal at first, but now, having settled comfortably with Lady Henrietta in the Dower House, she was actually enjoying her new surroundings.

Although with ten bedrooms the house was rather large, it was small compared to Mount Royal where she had been chatelaine for so many years. She regarded it as cosy and far more manageable and had gathered a small but loyal household around her, drawn from her retinue of personal servants who had always looked after her well. In addition to Molly and Mrs Castle, she had taken two of the housemaids and Raymond with her. Raymond had been promoted to the position of butler and Jackson's teachings over the years were paying off handsomely; he had settled into his new role with ease. Two new kitchen maids had been engaged to help Mrs Castle, and Lady Henrietta had brought Hazel, her lady's maid, with her. Hazel also helped Molly with Lady Constance, and all in all it was a happy household compared to Mount Royal, where the servants lived in fear of Lord William, and Makepiece still ruled below stairs with a rod of iron.

'Morning, Mrs Chambers,' said Hazel as Molly came into the kitchen through the back door, 'it's a cold one this morning.'

'Mornin', Molly,' called Mrs Castle from the stove.

'Mornin', Elizabeth, mornin', Hazel, it is that,' replied Molly with a shiver. She took off her coat and carried it through to the servants' hall. 'Everythin' all right with 'er Ladyship?'

'Yes she's had her morning tea, took it up about twenty minutes ago,' confirmed Hazel. 'There's a pot just brewed on the stove if you'd like one.'

'Oh ta, luv,' said Molly gratefully, 'I've just got time fer a quick one before I go up; she'll be ringing in a minute.' She went over to the stove where Mrs Castle poured her a cup of steaming hot tea, which she took back to the kitchen table. ''Ow was she?'

'She seemed much better than yesterday. Her cold has nearly gone by the look of things and Lady Henrietta returns from Plymouth today so that must be cheering her up. She's having breakfast in the dining-room too.'

'Hello, Molly,' said Raymond cheerfully as he came into the kitchen carrying an empty tray. 'Dining-room is all set up, Mrs Castle, an' the warmin' plates are on.'

'Thank you, Raymond. Ours is nearly ready. No news from Rosie yet then, Molly?'

'No, nothing yet,' said Molly slightly ruefully, 'and she's five days overdue now so it must come soon!'

Mrs Castle laughed. 'Nature 'as an 'abit of taking 'er time. 'Ere we are then, breakfast is ready. Are the girls finished upstairs yet do we know?'

Just as she said that the two housemaids came clattering down the stairs that led from the main entrance hall. 'We're 'ere, Mrs Castle,' cried Emily. ''Ere, Elsie, could yer put these in the scullery whilst I lay the table fer breakfast?' she added, handing her a broom and dustpan and brush before the younger girl had the chance to protest. 'Won't be a tick, Mrs Castle!'

Raymond looked at Mrs Castle and rolled his eyes heavenwards. 'Behind again then, girls, I see...'

'But...'

'Take no notice, Emily, he's only teasin' yer!' placated Mrs Castle, thinking how different he was to Makepiece who would have been in a rage by now, 'but be quick otherwise it'll get cold. I reckon yer've just got time fer a quick bite, Moll?'

In no time at all they were all sat round the long oblong table in the servants' hall tucking into bacon and eggs and more tea. Molly had just put down her knife and fork when the bell rang.

'That'll be 'er Ladyship, right on cue,' said Molly, looking up at the board to check. 'Right, I must be going up. Emily, Elsie, bring up the clean linen please when yer done.'

'Right oh, Mrs Chambers,' said Emily with her mouth full of bread and butter.

'An' don't speak with yer mouth full,' admonished Raymond, and Elsie did her best not to giggle.

Molly quickly climbed the stone stairs up to the entrance hall and pushed open the green baize door at the top. She crossed the hallway, casting her eyes around to check that everything was in order before the Countess came down. She had one foot on the first step of the main staircase when she noticed a dead bloom lying next to the flower arrangement on the hall table. The Countess was a stickler for fresh flowers and would be bound to spot it immediately. Age had certainly not dimmed her eyesight, or her attention to detail. The housemaids would need to be more careful, she said to herself, hurriedly sweeping it into the pocket of her dress. Climbing the main staircase, she ran her fingers along the frames of the paintings hanging on the staircase wall to check for dust and, to her satisfaction, found there was none to be seen.

Lady Constance's bedroom and private sitting room occupied the left hand side of the house and her sitting-room windows looked out over the front drive, which meant that they caught the morning sun. On a fine day it was a very cheerful and pleasant place to spend the morning as the Countess was apt to do; she did not usually appear downstairs until after eleven o'clock other than on the days when she breakfasted in the dining-room. Her normal habit was to breakfast in bed, especially when Lady Henrietta was away, and so Molly had been surprised to learn that she was going to eat in the dining-room this morning. She knocked gently on the bedroom door.

'May I come in, milady?'

Lady Constance opened her eyes with a start. 'Yes please, Mrs Chambers,' she smiled as she struggled to sit up.

'Oh I'm sorry, milady, did I wake you?'

'No, that's quite all right, Mrs Chambers, I was only dozing, that's all,' replied Lady Constance, betraying her impatience with her efforts to sit up. 'It's time to get up.'

'Very good, milady, I'll just draw yer bath.' Molly went through into the adjoining bathroom and began to run hot water into the large iron bath tub. Whilst it was filling up she went into the next room beyond the bathroom, which served as the Countess's dressing-room. She swiftly pulled back the curtains to let in the morning light and then opened the doors of one of the large mahogany wardrobes that lined the walls. She selected two long woollen dresses and took them through to the bedroom where she showed them to Lady Constance.

'I think the blue one, Mrs Chambers, don't you?' said Lady Constance, peering at them through her spectacles, 'it's so much brighter than the brown one on a day like today.'

'Very good, milady,' said Molly, laying the blue one carefully on the *chaise-longue* that stood at the end of the four-poster bed. 'Your bath is almost ready, milady.' She checked the temperature of the water on her way back to the dressing-room and decided it was just a little too hot so she turned on the cold tap, leaving it to run whilst she hung the brown dress back in the wardrobe. Then she selected the remainder of the garments Lady Constance would need and went back into the bathroom to lay out the soaps and lotions that the Countess liked to use. 'Everything's ready, milady,' she announced as she returned to the bedroom. 'May I 'elp yer, milady?'

'I shall be fine, thank you, Mrs Chambers,' said Lady Constance as she slowly walked across the room, her cane tapping on the polished wooden floor between the edge of the fine Savonnerie carpet and the bathroom door, 'and I think I'll wear the navy shoes from Worth with the gold buckles.'

The bedroom was huge and classically square in proportion with tall rectangular windows set majestically into two of the four walls. These were hung with splendidly draped pale blue silk curtains that provided the room with an air of restrained and graceful elegance. The high ceiling was painted a brilliant white and embellished with an exquisitely moulded cornice, and set with panels embossed with intricately moulded plaster leaves and flower petals. The room was undeniably grand but, at the same time, simple and understated in its furnishings.

Two armchairs upholstered in the palest eau-de-nil silk to match the chaise longue were arranged around three highly polished occasional tables. These, together with a glazed armoire that stood along one wall, and which displayed the Countess's priceless collection of porcelain and Fabergé, were of a rich, deep mahogany to match the large four-poster bed. The only other pieces of furniture in the room were an antique dressing table and mirror positioned between two of the tall windows facing the bed, on top of which was arranged a silver, gilt, gold and tortoiseshell hand mirror and brush set that had been a ruby wedding present from Lord Hugo. A multitude of silver-framed photographs of him and Lady Henrietta were dotted around the room, but the only ones of Lord William dated back to when he was a small boy. It was as if the vindictiveness of his more recent years had caused Lady Constance to erase him from her presence, preferring instead to see images of him as a child. A delicate chandelier of twinkling crystal hung from the centre of the ceiling and a fire blazed strongly in the grate of the pristine white marble fireplace which was set in the wall opposite the armoire. Above the fireplace hung a gleaming mirror that reflected the shimmering rays of light from the chandelier. The overall effect was so unlike the fashion of the times, which tended towards excessive clutter. Anyone entering the room immediately felt at ease despite its grandeur and it reflected the character of its occupant perfectly; grand, elegant and devoid of pretension.

Molly had just finished laying the Countess's clothes neatly on the bed when Lady Constance appeared from the bathroom. 'Are yer ready ter dress, milady?' she asked.

'I think I'd like my hair done first,' replied Lady Constance with a smile as she went slowly over to the dressing-table.

Molly moved quickly to pull out the chair to enable her to sit down. When she had done so and made herself comfortable, the Countess held out one of the tortoiseshell brushes, which Molly took and gently began to brush her long white hair.

'These were a present from Lord Gordon on our fortieth wedding anniversary you know,' said Lady Constance wistfully.

'They're beautiful, milady,' replied Molly.

'Fifty-three years we were married...'

'Yes, I know, milady,' said Molly softly, 'fifty-three years of 'appy memories.'

Lady Constance smiled and nodded gently. 'How long were you and Mr Chambers married?' she asked suddenly, looking at Molly's reflection in the mirror in front of her.

Molly paused for a moment, surprised by the question. The Countess did not often enquire about her servants' personal lives. 'It was thirty-nine years, milady, it would 'ave been our ruby anniversary three months after...' Her voice drifted away and the sentence hung in the air.

'After he was killed, I know,' said Lady Constance quietly. 'By the car my son was driving.'

There was silence and Molly looked away, unsure of what to do or say. The memory came flooding back and she wanted to cry out, but with a supreme effort of will she managed to stop herself. It was as if the two women could read each other's minds. Lady Constance did not once take her eyes from Molly's reflection as she continued.

'You knew, didn't you, but you never said a word to anyone.'

Molly nodded and met her gaze. 'It was an accident ... a dreadful an' tragic accident...' she mumbled hesitatingly.

'No!' said Lady Constance sharply, 'he was driving recklessly, much too fast for the lanes around here and as a result your husband was killed! A man who had served my family faithfully for years. I have never forgiven him for that and I reproach myself constantly for it.' Then she added, in a quiet voice as if she was speaking to herself, 'For that and many other things.'

'But, milady, yer 'ave nothing ter reproach yerself fer!'

'Oh but I do, Mrs Chambers, I should have told the police when they asked, instead of which I kept quiet and, as a consequence, he has continued to bring misery to people's lives!'

'Milady, yer musn't say that!' said Molly, aghast at the frankness of Lady Constance's words.

'I'm getting old and there are things that should be said...'

'We can't be responsible fer our sons all their lives an' the police would still 'ave concluded it was an accident!'

Lady Constance turned to look at her. 'My son has turned out to be a great disappointment to me.' Molly made to protest but Lady Constance held up her hand.

'No, Mrs Chambers, it's true. I just thank God his father was spared these last two years; it would have broken his heart.'

Molly could not think of anything to say, so instead she smiled sympathetically. Lady Constance smiled back and in that instant, when she thought about it later, it felt to Molly as if they were not mistress and servant but simply two old women with a bond between them that had never been articulated before, but which had been forged from a lifetime of knowledge and experience of each other's lives. It was an unfamiliar feeling but one that was surprisingly comforting in a way that she could not quite explain.

Lady Constance turned back to the mirror, which was the signal for Molly to resume her brushing. 'Tell me about Max, I hear he's doing rather well?' said Lady Constance after a short silence.

Molly's face lit up. 'Yes 'e is, milady, quite the businessman 'e is now.'

The Countess nodded. 'And the baby? Rosie must be due any day I imagine?'

It was strange to hear Lady Constance talk of them in this familiar manner, in the same way that she would talk of her own children.

'She's overdue by five days now, milady, so I'm expectin' the call at any moment.'

'Well, you must go to them as soon as it comes. Roberts will drive you to the railway station. I will inform Makepiece accordingly,' said Lady Constance firmly. 'After all, we both have a vested interest you might say.'

Their eyes met once again through the reflection in the dressing-table mirror as Molly began to set Lady Constance's hair up in its customary style, which was a little old-fashioned but suited her well.

'I gave them the picture, milady, do you remember? It always stood on the mantelpiece in Fern Cottage. The number of times Max 'as asked me questions about it over the years ... I also gave them a letter which is only to be opened after my death ... I made them promise about that...'

Lady Constance nodded her head slowly. 'As I say, there are things that need to be said before it's too late, loose ends you might say,' she murmured with quiet satisfaction.

Chapter 41

The telephone call came shortly after nine o'clock the following morning, 22 February 1914. Ivy dialled the number for Bickleigh Manor and spoke to Raymond who sent for Molly straightaway. She was busy in the laundry room sorting out the bed linen from the previous day. As soon as Emily approached her she knew that the time had come and immediately flew to the receiver on the wall outside Raymond's pantry. After a hurried conversation she put a call through to Roberts, the chauffeur at Mount Royal, and was soon on her way to the terminus in Plymouth to catch the morning train to Paddington. Lady Constance had been as good as her word, issuing instructions to Makepiece to the effect that when Molly telephoned, Roberts was to come over with the car at once.

Max had had a premonition that the baby would come when he had woken up that morning, but Rosie, with her usual practical common sense, had told him that there was no sense in him staying at home as things would happen in their own time. He was therefore at his desk at the warehouse when Ivy telephoned to tell him that Rosie's waters had broken, the doctor was on his way and he was to come home at once. Ivy had been staying with them since the beginning of the week to be on hand as Max did not like the thought of leaving Rosie on her own in the house.

He dashed through the front door of Gloucester Street after a breakneck drive from Chelsea, nearly bowling Mary over, who was busy sweeping the hall floor.

'The mistress is upstairs, sir,' she said quickly before Max had a chance to ask.

'Thank you, Mary,' cried Max as he dropped his briefcase and bounded up the stairs. As he reached the first floor landing Ivy appeared in the drawing-room doorway. 'She's upstairs with Doctor Mansell Max, she's askin' fer yer.'

Max barely paused. 'Thanks Ivy,' he said as he ran up the next flight, not stopping until he was outside their bedroom door. Then he drew breath and waited while he composed himself before knocking gently on the door.

'Ah, there you are, Mr Chambers,' said Dr Mansell, looking up from Rosie's side. 'Mrs Chambers has been asking for you. Everything is fine but it's going to be a while yet.' He smiled reassuringly. 'Nurse Andrews and I will look after her.'

The small red-haired nurse was in the middle of pouring some water into a bowl and she stopped and smiled. 'Aye, don't yer worry now, sir, everything is under control,' she said in a strong Scottish accent. 'Mrs Chambers is doing just fine.'

Max was relieved to hear their calm and confident words as he looked down at Rosie who was lying on the bed, propped up against the pillows. She smiled bravely at him as the doctor moved aside to let Max sit down.

'How are you, darling?' he asked softly, taking her hand in his.

'I'll be better when all this is over,' she replied drily and winced as another light contraction came and went.

Max bent over and kissed her cheek and smoothed her long blonde hair away from her face. Nurse Andrews was hovering at the other side of the bed, dabbing Rosie's forehead with a damp cloth. 'I think I'm in the way, darling,' he whispered.

'Why don't you wait downstairs with Mother?' she whispered, 'go on, love, it's all right.'

Max looked anxiously at Dr Mansell who nodded in agreement. 'All right, sweetheart, if you're sure,' he said, 'I'll come back in a little while.'

The hours passed slowly, broken only by Stan's arrival just before two o'clock and the occasional interruption from Mary and Violet as they went about their duties. Once or twice during the afternoon, Nurse Andrews appeared to let them know all was progressing slowly but well and at around three o'clock Mary collected the remains of a tray of half-eaten sandwiches that had been sent up by Mrs Walsh. Apart from that there was very little to disturb the heavy air of tension that pervaded the house.

Shortly after four Mary knocked on the door of the drawing-room to ask if she might draw the curtains and turn on the lamps and to enquire about dinner arrangements. Max looked at Ivy who suggested that something light on a tray might be suitable and then the interminable waiting resumed.

'Max! Max! Wake up!' said Ivy, urgently shaking his shoulder, 'Doctor Mansell is 'ere.'

Max jumped up with a start, blinking rapidly. 'What is it? I must have dozed off,' he said, looking confused.

'Yer've been asleep fer nearly three hours, Max, Doctor Mansell is 'ere an' 'as somethin' ter tell yer,' explained Ivy with a beaming smile.

'You have a little girl, Mr Chambers, a fine healthy baby girl,' said the doctor with a broad grin, 'Mrs Chambers is asking for you.'

'How is she?' asked Max quickly, barely able to contain himself. 'Is everything all right?'

'Mrs Chambers is very tired and quite weak, as is to be expected...'

'She is all right though isn't she?' interrupted Max, giving Dr Mansell a piercing stare.

'...as is only to be expected, Mr Chambers. It was a long birth and difficult at times, but your daughter is fine.'

'But my wife is all right, isn't she?' Max demanded again, his voice starting to rise.

'She needs to rest, Mr Chambers, to recover her strength,' replied the doctor. 'The nurse is with her. Let's go up and see her now.'

Ivy made to follow them out of the door of the drawing-room but the doctor turned and said, 'It would be better if Mrs Chambers didn't have too many visitors for the moment. I don't want her to get over excited, one person at a time, please, until she's had some rest.'

Ivy nodded. 'Yes, of course, I understand. Give 'er my love, Max, will yer?'

'As soon as Nurse Andrews has finished with your daughter, Mr Chambers, she can be brought down here for a short while.' He smiled. 'I'm sure you're all dying to see her.'

The doctor opened the door for Max and they climbed the stairs. When they reached the bedroom door, he quietly said, 'Please be brief, she's exhausted,' before ushering him into the room and closing the door gently behind him.

Max padded softly over to the bed and smiled down at Rosie who opened her eyes as he bent down to kiss her. 'Are you all right, darling?' whispered Max softly in her ear. 'I'm so proud of you.'

Rosie reached for his hand and smiled wanly, the fatigue etched on her face. 'I'm just a little tired, darling, and I have a headache, that's all. We have a beautiful baby daughter, Max, she looks so lovely.' Her eyes flickered. 'Eleanor we said didn't we?'

'Yes, darling,' replied Max as he stroked her face, 'Eleanor Rosemary

Chambers, Rosemary after her beautiful mother. What do you think of that, love?' He stared into her eyes and a faint smile flickered on her lips again. 'You must get some sleep, darling, the doctor says you must rest now.'

'Where is she?' asked Rosie, rousing herself with a supreme effort of will as she tried to sit up.

Max put his hand on her shoulder but he need not have bothered. Rosie did not have the energy to resist and she shrank back into the pillows with a sigh.

'Shh, darling, don't worry. She's with Nurse Andrews next door. I'll look after her while you rest,' said Max. He had never seen anybody look so exhausted, so totally drained of energy, and he was beginning to grow concerned.

Dr Mansell stepped forward and cleared his throat softly. 'I think that's enough for now, Mr Chambers.'

Max turned round and nodded. 'Yes, of course, doctor.'

He turned back to Rosie and smiled, 'I'm going back downstairs now, sweetheart, so you can get some sleep. Everyone sends their love.' He kissed her once more and whispered, 'I love you, darling, sleep tight.' With that, he gently stood up and straightened the bedclothes, tucking the blankets lightly around her. Her eyes were closed and there was a faint smile on her lips as he quietly left the room.

Dr Mansell followed him. 'All she needs is plenty of rest. I don't want her disturbed again tonight and we'll see how she is in the morning.'

'I've never seen anyone look so utterly exhausted in all my life,' said Max, not trying to hide the alarm in his voice now that he was out of the room.

'It was a difficult labour, Mr Chambers, and a long one too. But your wife is young and strong, and she'll be as right as rain in no time. Nurse Andrews will look after your daughter until Mrs Chambers is well enough.'

'Can I see her yet?' asked Max, 'if the nurse has finished with her?'

'Of course you may. She was just washing her and checking her over so I expect she's ready. Let's have a look shall we?' He led the way into the next bedroom and stood aside as Nurse Andrews held up the tiny bundle cradled in her arms.

'Six pounds, ten ounces and perfectly healthy,' she announced briskly.

Max gazed at the tiny infant wrapped in white. My daughter, he said to himself in wonderment, and he could not stop himself from smiling inanely as the tears came to his eyes. 'She's beautiful,' he murmured.

247

'She has the loveliest blue eyes,' said the nurse, 'would you like to hold her?'

'May I?' asked Max.

'Of course!' chuckled Dr Mansell.

Max gingerly took her from the nurse who patiently showed him how to position his arms. 'Eleanor Rosemary,' said Max, willing her to open her eyes so he could see them, 'with eyes like your mother,' he said softly as he bent down and gave her the gentlest of kisses.

'I'll bring her downstairs in a little while, Mr Chambers, I'm sure her grandparents are dying to meet her,' said Nurse Andrews, holding out her arms to take her back. 'Come on then, Eleanor,' she said, quietly engrossed in her new charge, 'let's get you ready shall we?'

'And I should get back to your wife,' said Dr Mansell.

Chapter 42

Max dozed fitfully in the bedroom chair. After Dr Mansell had left and the others had gone to bed he had crept back into their room to sit with Rosie. The sound of Nurse Andrews tending to Eleanor whenever she cried in the next room had kept him awake for much of the night but Rosie had not stirred. Once or twice he had poked his head round the door of the temporary nursery to see what was going on, only to be politely but firmly ushered away.

'What is it, nurse?' asked Max with a start. Dawn was breaking and Nurse Andrews had come in to check on Rosie. Max shivered, the fire had died down and only the last embers still glowed in the grate.

'Wake up, Mrs Chambers,' she said urgently, 'wake up!'

The concern in her voice was obvious. Max leapt out of his chair and was at her side in an instant. 'What is it?' he demanded.

'I can't wake her, Mr Chambers! Quickly, out of my way!'

Max jumped backwards as the nurse threw the bedclothes aside and reached for Rosie's pulse. 'Ring for Doctor Mansell, tell him to come at once!'

An awful sensation of panic struck Max as he stumbled to the door. 'Quickly!'

Max half stumbled and half fell down the stairs in the darkness as he rushed to the morning room telephone. Without pausing to switch on the lights, he blundered across the carpet to Rosie's desk. His hands were shaking as he snatched the receiver from its cradle.

'Belgravia 5782, please, hurry!' Come on ... come on... he muttered frantically to himself as he waited for the connection. 'Doctor Mansell, is that you? It's Max Chambers, please come at once, it's my wife, the nurse can't rouse her!'

He had just hung up when he was startled by the lights being switched on and he swivelled round to see Molly and Ivy standing in the doorway. His blood rang cold as he saw their ashen faces and an icy feeling of imminent catastrophe seized him.

'What is it, Ma?' Max stammered. His mouth was dry and his heart was pounding in his chest. He knew before Molly opened her mouth to reply.

'Sit down, Max,' she said quietly as they moved towards him. Her voice was shaking badly.

'What's happened to her? Just tell me!' he demanded hoarsely and he began to tremble.

Ivy began to say something but stopped as her voice faltered. Molly put a hand on her shoulder. 'It's all right, Ivy luv, it's my place ter tell 'im,' she said softly. Looking him squarely in the eye she said, 'Rosie's dead, Max ... the nurse says she's passed away ... sometime in 'er sleep.'

Max stared at them, numb with disbelief. He was completely stunned. 'What do you mean? She can't be dead!'

He had turned deathly pale and his knees felt as if they would buckle. Molly and Ivy jumped forwards to steady him as he swayed unsteadily, and gently guided him to a chair. He sat down and buried his head in his hands. 'What do you mean, dead?' he mumbled again, 'I can't believe it.' He looked up at them blankly, the dazed expression on his face indicating his refusal to believe what they had told him. 'What about Eleanor...?'

Molly and Ivy sat down next to him, their own shock and anguish all too evident as they looked anxiously at him. 'Rosie ... .no ... it cannot be!' whispered Max, staring vacantly into space. 'The nurse must be mistaken! There's got to be a mistake!' he cried, his voice suddenly growing louder as he seemed to awaken from his confusion.

Both Molly and Ivy reached out to him, unable to think of what to say, searching for a way to soften the blow. There was a heavy silence as they sought the proper words but they would not come and Max began to groan.

'There is no mistake, Max,' said Ivy desolately and with great tenderness, 'it's true...'

Then her face crumpled and speech failed her as she wrestled with her own grief. It was overwhelming despite her usual implacable resilience. Tears trickled from her eyes and she only managed to stop herself from crying out by clamping her hand tightly over her mouth. It's Gracie all over again, she thought agonisingly to herself, how can it be fair? She shut her eyes in an attempt to drive those thoughts from her mind.

'I must go to her,' muttered Max decisively, rising from the chair. Molly's grip tightened on his arm and forced him back into his seat. 'No!' said Molly at once, 'the nurse is with her, wait fer...'

The sound of Eleanor's cries drifted down from upstairs. Ivy opened her eyes and looked at Molly, inclining her head towards the door. Molly nodded imperceptibly. 'Are yer sure, Ivy?' asked Molly tentatively, looking bleakly at her stricken friend and wishing there was something she could do to ease her pain.

'Yes,' said Ivy softly, 'I'll go up.'

She had just left the room when the sound of the front door bell startled them. 'That'll be Doctor Mansell, Max, yer wait 'ere while I let 'im in.' Molly stood up but before she reached the morning room door she saw Mrs Walsh hurry discreetly past to open it.

'I came as quickly as I could,' said Dr Mansell, stepping into the hall. 'Is Nurse Andrews with her?' he asked as Molly appeared in the doorway.

'Yes, doctor,' replied Molly quickly but he was already at the top of the stairs. Turning back into the morning room, she went over to the decanter and glasses that stood by the bookcase and poured out a generous measure of whisky. ''Ere yer are, luv, drink this,' she ordered and held it out to Max.

He did as he was told but his hand was shaking so much that some of the amber spirit splashed on to the carpet. He raised it to his lips and retched as he took a mouthful. He spluttered violently and put the glass down on the side table next to the chair with a loud crash which sent some more of the contents dripping on to the floor. Molly looked at him helplessly.

'I don't believe it,' he mumbled again and again, too distraught to comprehend. His face, normally so vibrant and handsome, was twisted in grotesque and abject misery.

It was light before Dr Mansell came back down. The sadness that he felt was etched on his face, and his footsteps carried an air of dejected finality. Ivy was pacing slowly up and down with Eleanor sleeping peacefully in her arms, innocently oblivious to the pain and wretchedness in the room. Molly was still sitting next to Max, doing her best to comfort him, but he was inconsolable, staring blankly in front of him. She rose rather shakily to her feet as Dr Mansell came in, desperately seeking some indication of hope from him.

'I'm so very sorry,' he said gently but firmly. 'Mrs Chambers passed away in her sleep sometime after midnight.'

Molly's hand flew to her throat, as if she was hearing the news for the first time. She gazed down at Max, who said nothing before looking up at her and then burying his head in his hands again. She wondered how Max was ever going to cope with this tragedy. They were so utterly devoted to each other, so completely happy together. He just adored her, and she him, and now she had been so suddenly and unexpectedly snatched away from him and from her newborn daughter who they had both longed for. Taken from all of them. She did not know whether Max would ever recover.

'Do yer know 'ow, doctor?'

Dr Mansell shook his head. 'I will inform the coroner and the police. There will have to be an autopsy.'

'The police!' exclaimed Molly in surprise.

'It is purely routine, Mrs Chambers, in these circumstances, when it is so unexpected. There is nothing to worry about,' he assured her. 'The post-mortem will tell us the cause of...' he hesitated and looked at Max, '... the cause of death. I have arranged the room and locked the door so nothing is disturbed. Nurse Andrews has the key and I have asked her to stay on for a while to look after Eleanor.'

'Thank yer, doctor,' said Ivy, ' 'ow long can she...?'

'For as long as you need her, Mrs Black,' he replied, 'but you don't have to decide now. That's all I can do for the moment. I am so sorry.' He paused. 'Before I go I can give you something to help you sleep, Mr Chambers, if you would like me to?'

Max looked up and shook his head vehemently. 'I want to know exactly what happened to her, doctor.' Silent tears trickled down his face.

'My son has to know, Doctor Mansell. We all do,' added Molly, looking at Ivy.

Dr Mansell nodded sympathetically. 'Yes, of course, I understand completely. If it helps I can tell you that Mrs Chambers won't have suffered. I can be sure of that ... right ... well, I'll be off now but I'll come back in after morning surgery to see you all. In the meantime Nurse Andrews will be able to take care of things, but please telephone me at any time if you need to.'

'Thank yer, doctor,' said Molly, 'I'll show yer out.'

PART THREE

FRANCE AND LONDON

1914–1925

Chapter 43

Max possessed an inexorably strong will and huge reserves of resilience, which had always helped him through the personal tragedies and testing times he had experienced in his life, but Rosie's sudden and calamitous death was different. It had struck without warning and at one of the happiest times of their lives. It left him utterly bereft.

He sat in the packed carriage of the train taking him to Scotland, oblivious to the raucous banter of the men surrounding him. A few were proudly turned out in uniform but most of them, like Max, were wearing civilian clothes. He glanced briefly around him. The majority were talking and laughing noisily but one or two were silent and withdrawn, seemingly alone amongst the animated throng. For a brief moment he wondered what thoughts were running through their minds before he drifted back to the despair of his own personal hell.

Seven months had passed since his beloved Rosie's death and, in that time, there had been many occasions when he did not care whether he lived or died. There was nothing left for him now except for the empty years ahead, until nature took its course and he was reunited with her. He had never been a religious man but he did believe he would see her again and this thought gave him great comfort. He clung desperately to it in the depths of his misery.

In the days leading up to the funeral he had been so completely crushed and debilitated by grief that even the simplest tasks had proven impossible. He had closeted himself in their bedroom where he lay almost deranged with shock, barely acknowledging the steady stream of visitors who all did their best to help him. Billy came at once, dashing over from the warehouse as soon as he received the call from Molly. Elizabeth, who was herself due to give birth in a matter of weeks, had rushed round too. They tried to talk to him but mostly they sat with him in a silence that was punctuated only by paroxysms of heartrending sobbing. These had been so bad that Molly had sent for Dr Mansell who prescribed sedatives. Max had refused to take them; fearful of what he might find when they wore off.

Richie came with Marjorie, and Lennie and Jimmy dropped everything to try and comfort him. They were all desperate to help but their kind and thoughtful efforts were in vain. Through those first awful days Stan had been a tower of strength, reaching out to Max, and Ivy, as well as to his boys, who were also grief-stricken for their sister. Molly found herself relying on him for support in making all the necessary arrangements because she had Eleanor to worry about too; without the calm and reassuring presence of Nurse Andrews she did not know how they would have managed.

Of them all, Molly was the best equipped to understand the trauma that beset Max. It had been the same for her when Bert had died, but not even she could reach him as he lay motionless for days, staring blindly into space, not eating or drinking and barely responding to anybody. Molly had tried to coax him downstairs but he preferred to remain shut in the room in which he felt closest to Rosie. The handbag she had been using stood open and untouched on the table by the bed, her black silk robe and scarf were draped over the chair in the corner of the room, where she had left them, and her perfumes and cosmetics rested neatly on the glass-topped table in the bathroom. On the third day Max said he could not remember her voice and had been overcome by a sudden feeling of panic. Molly had found him spraying her perfume around the room because he said it would help remind him of her presence. As Molly had told the others, there are no rules with grief, except that it is the price you pay for love, and Max had loved her so completely.

Each day seemed to bring fresh distress. A man from Cartier, the jewellers, had arrived at the front door on the afternoon of Rosie's passing with a small package addressed to her. Stan and Molly had looked at each other nervously, unsure of what to do, until finally Stan opened it to find a small black leather box containing an enormous sapphire and diamond ring, dazzling in its magnificence. It was an exact copy of the paste engagement ring Max had bought Rosie on his first trip to Plymouth. There was a note from Max nestling inside the lid, which Stan read out in a quiet, doleful voice:

My Darling Rosie
I never forget a promise
On the arrival of our first-born
Love you forever
Max

He had been planning this surprise with Cartier for months but now it would be weeks before he could even bring himself to look at the box.

They had all hoped that Eleanor's presence might provide Max with a reason for living when all sense of purpose seemed to have deserted him, but it was his resistance to involve himself with her that gave Molly the greatest cause for concern in those early days. He barely looked at the infant whenever Nurse Andrews brought her into the room and he would refuse to hold her. No amount of cajoling could persuade him otherwise. It was as if he wanted nothing whatsoever to do with her.

This alarming reaction was born out of the long, lonely hours he spent lying awake at night, listening to the sounds of Nurse Andrews tending to her in the next room. Unable to find any respite from his suffering in sleep, he would stare helplessly into the darkness as irrational thoughts raged unchecked through his mind, all sense of reason abandoned. The turmoil he felt was at its worst in the early hours before dawn, when all sense of proportion can so easily be lost. He decided that he was responsible for Rosie's death because it was his idea to start a family in the first place, and he blamed himself for forcing her to endure the pain of childbirth, which had proven too much for her.

Sometimes, when the sound of Molly's voice gently singing lullabies to soothe Eleanor back to sleep came floating softly through the half open bedroom door, it provoked a fierce and unexpected anger in him. This he directed towards Eleanor. It was all Eleanor's fault. The child that he had longed for had killed the woman he loved. His guilt at these thoughts was overwhelming and remained with him constantly, but in the tumult of his emotions he was incapable of dismissing them for what they were – the incoherent symptoms of grief.

The coroner's report arrived just before the funeral with the results of the post-mortem and it had sent Molly into a blind panic. The letter was addressed to Max but she had opened it to read the contents with mounting unease. She had then handed the papers to Stan without a word, but it was not until she asked Dr Mansell later that same day to explain exactly what the findings meant that she had realised their full significance. The report concluded that Rosie had suffered a massive brain haemorrhage whilst she slept, brought on by the bursting of one of the arteries close to the surface of her brain. She undoubtedly died without regaining consciousness and would not have known anything about it. Dr Mansell explained that it was similar to a heart attack, only centred in the brain and that there was often no warning. He did recall, however, that Rosie had complained of a headache after the birth and he thought that it was reasonable to presume that the haemorrhage had been triggered by the strain of her lengthy labour.

Molly thanked God she would not have suffered any pain and was just thinking this knowledge might provide Max with some comfort when he went on to admit that he was, nevertheless, surprised because Rosie was still young and in good health. The report drew attention to evidence of a serious head injury sustained some time in the past and, whilst it was not possible to be conclusive, suggested that it might have been a contributing factor in the weakening of the artery.

Molly's blood ran cold as Dr Mansell told her that the head injury could indeed account for the weakness as it was most unusual for it to occur naturally in someone of Rosie's age.

'Got a light, mate?' said the cockney voice next to him.

Max looked round with a start. He shook his head. 'No, sorry mate, I don't smoke,' he replied, dragging himself out of his day-dream.

The curtness of his reply did not seem to deter further questions. 'So where yer from?'

'London,' said Max, wishing the man would be quiet.

'Same 'ere, mate. Name's Edward Samuels. People call me Eddie.' He thrust out his hand.

'Max, Max Chambers.'

Max smiled, feeling a pang of remorse at his rudeness as he stared at his new companion. The lad was barely out of his teens and seemed eager to talk.

'Which part of London, Max?' he asked loudly above the noise of the train and the din from their fellow travellers.

'Pimlico. And you?'

Before Eddie could reply he was distracted by the offer of a light from the man sitting on the other side of him and he turned away with his cigarette hanging from his lips. Max breathed a sigh of relief and sank back into silence, glad to be left alone again with his thoughts. He felt for the letter, which he always carried with him in the inside pocket of his jacket, and slowly took it out, unfolding it in front of him as he did so. It was a copy of the one he had written on the eve of Rosie's funeral, in time for it to be placed in her coffin.

My dearest Rosie,

Never in my wildest dreams did I ever imagine I would be writing this letter to you but you left without giving me the chance to say goodbye. I don't blame you for that, my darling, I know you couldn't help it.

I don't know where to begin other than to say that I loved you with all my heart. It would not have been possible for me to have loved you any more than I did, than I still do, and the pain and horror of losing you is indescribable. It is so difficult to put my feelings into words, but I will try.

I still cannot believe that you are gone. I keep expecting you to walk through the door as if nothing has happened, I reach out for you when I wake up in the morning but you're not lying beside me, where you belong. I hear something and think to myself: Oh I must tell Rosie, but you're not there. I wish with all my heart that you were.

It was the most wonderful moment of my life when you agreed to marry me and people have said that the love between us was infectious, touching those around us with its warmth. It touched me every day sweetheart, and I long for it to do so again now. You always made me feel so special and you were the reason for my happiness. I hope you know how much joy you brought me and I want you also to know how thankful I am that the wonderful memories you have left behind are such happy ones. I will cherish them forever.

I am sorry that I was not there to hold you in your final moments as I desperately wish I had been. You see, my darling, I didn't know you were leaving, but I am holding you now, in my heart, and will never let you go.

Thank you for making my life complete.

I miss you so much, darling. Sleep tight and God bless.

Forever,

Max.

When he had finished reading, he carefully refolded it and put it back in his pocket. He found that the words gave him a curious sense of comfort, which is why he always carried it with him. It helped.

'Reading a letter from your girlfriend, mate?' shouted the youth from the seat opposite him.

'More like his mistress, I bet!' someone else bellowed good-naturedly, which prompted loud laughter from those around him.

Max was silent and stared out of the carriage window, studiously ignoring the well-intentioned gibes. If only you knew, he thought sorrowfully to himself, as he turned back and stared balefully at the perpetrators.

'Hey, Max, it were only a joke!' said Eddie quickly, sensing the blackness of his mood. 'They didn't mean no 'arm.'

Max did his best to smile. 'Which part of London did you say you were from, Eddie?'

Chapter 44

During the late summer of 1914 train stations all over Europe resonated with the heavy sound of army boots and the clattering of rifles as thousands upon thousands of young men were mobilised for what many predicted would be the most glorious conflict since the Napoleonic Wars. At this stage, before the slaughter on the battlefields turned naive belief into the horrific reality of the war to end all wars, the excitement of adventure mingled with national pride and zealous determination.

The train finally arrived at its destination after a brief stop to take on more coal and water, and hundreds of tired and hungry men spilled out on to the platform. The success of Lord Kitchener's first call to arms had been an almost overnight sensation following Parliament's sanction on 6th August of an increase in the army's strength of half a million men, and, as Max looked around him, all he could see was a swirling mass of patriotic fervour. A band was playing 'It's a Long Way to Tipperary' loudly in the background and a crowd of cheering well-wishers was waving wildly as a group of NCOs were trying to make themselves heard above the noise.

Slowly, and with some confusion, they were shepherded into groups and led off into an area in front of the station away from the worst of the noise where Max heard the young officer in charge issue instructions to the sergeant-major to 'carry on.'

'Right, let's 'ave you in line!' he bellowed, 'quickly now!' His wide medal-strewn chest heaved with the effort of marshalling the chaotic band of recruits into some semblance of order and Max found himself thinking wryly that it was a long time since he had taken orders from anyone, let alone obeyed them. Still, it was his idea to volunteer and he had better do as he was told, he thought quickly, as he felt himself jostled into position.

'Come on, move yourselves!'

The sergeant-major did not look like a man who was used to being ignored.

'All present and correct, sir,' said Sergeant-Major Wilkins finally, with a smart salute to the officer.

'Thank you, sergeant-major,' said the young man, returning the salute with precision timing.

He was fresh faced and immaculately turned out and Max wondered if he had ever seen action on the battlefield. However, in spite of his youth, he seemed perfectly at ease in front of them all, displaying an air of restrained arrogance, which was distinctly at odds with the controlled aggression of the obviously battle-hardened Wilkins.

'I am Captain Manvers, the battalion adjutant,' he began, 'and I will be responsible for you whilst you are stationed here in Scotland. We will shortly be marching to the barracks where you will bed down for the night. Supper is at twenty hundred hours sharp and lights out will be at twenty one hundred hours. You have a busy day ahead of you tomorrow, starting with the issue of your uniforms so you can begin to look like representatives of His Majesty's fighting forces instead of the motley bunch I see before me now.'

'Bloody cheek,' muttered the man next but one to Max, 'who does he think he is!'

'Reveille will sound at zero five hundred hours. You will rise for breakfast before beginning your training at zero six hundred. This will form the basic pattern of your time with us over the next twelve weeks, at the end of which we will have turned you into fighting men ready to face the enemy on the battlefields of France.' He paused for effect. 'Sergeant-Major Wilkins here will be the senior warrant officer in charge during your training and I suggest you follow his orders very carefully at all times. They might just save your lives. He last saw action at the Battle of Mons, where he was decorated for his bravery, and so he knows very well what you will face when you are ready for active service. Listen to him carefully and good luck.' He turned to his left. 'Carry on please, sergeant-major.'

'Thank you, sir,' said Sergeant-Major Wilkins immediately. 'Right, you heard Captain Manvers, let's be 'aving you then!' he barked.

They were marched swiftly through the streets to their makeshift quarters for the next three months, which turned out to be a huge stately home that reminded Max uncomfortably of Mount Royal. The ballroom had been turned into a huge dormitory where rows of narrow beds were lined up in straight lines barely two feet apart. There was a rush for them as the NCOs opened the tall double doors at either end of the vast high-ceilinged room, and when Max reached one of the middle rows and sat down firmly on the nearest bed to claim it as his own, he found himself next to Eddie Samuels.

'Hello again, Max,' said Eddie cheerfully, ''ere, 'ave yer felt these mattresses?'

Max laughed ruefully. 'I've seen better, I have to admit,' he said, thinking of Gloucester Street before clamping his mind shut to avoid its inevitable wanderings.

'Still, they say it'll all be over before Christmas don't they?'

'Yes, they do but I wouldn't be so sure and twelve weeks is going to feel like an awfully long time on these!' asserted Max, looking at the meagre sheet and single pillow resting neatly at one end.

'What time did 'e say was dinner? I'm starvin' 'ungry!'

Max looked at his watch. 'In about twenty minutes so we'd better get a move on if we're going to be sorted out by then,' he said, looking around at the other men who were busy unpacking their belongings and making their beds.

After a meal of boiled brisket and one small spoonful of mashed potato they returned to the dormitory to await lights out. As he lay on his bed, Max found himself glad to be distracted by his new companion. 'So what made you join up then, Eddie?' he asked.

'I wanted ter escape I s'pose, an' I saw the posters of Lord Kitchener so I thought it would be a good idea, serve me country an' all that. Me mam was furious with me but me dad didn't say much when I came 'ome an' told 'em.'

'They must be really proud deep down,' said Max. Eddie's eyes were downcast as he was explaining his motives until Max said that, whereupon his mouth broke into a broad smile as he looked up. 'Yeah, I think they were really. Me younger sister burst inter tears mind yer.'

'How many sisters have you got?'

'Two,' he replied. 'One's sixteen, two years younger than me and the older one's twenty.'

'Two years younger?' said Max slowly, 'that makes you eighteen...'

'Shh!' said Eddie quickly, 'don't tell anybody will yer?' he implored. 'The man at the recruiting office believed me easy enough.'

Max smiled at him. 'Don't worry, Eddie, your secret is safe with me.'

'Thanks, Max,' said Eddie with relief, 'so what about yer then, what made yer volunteer ter get shot ter pieces?'

Max sat up and hesitated for a moment. 'I guess ... to escape ... like you.' Then he lapsed into silence and looked away.

Eddie's youthful curiosity made him continue although Max's demeanour warned him not to. 'Escape, from what?'

'My wife died in February,' said Max flatly.

263

Eddie immediately regretted asking and recalled his father always telling him that he did not know when to keep his mouth shut. 'I'm sorry, Max, I shouldn't 'ave asked,' he mumbled awkwardly, his face reddening.

Max turned back and smiled reassuringly at him. 'That's all right, Eddie, you weren't to know.' He took a deep breath and continued, wanting to make Eddie feel better. 'It's a long story. She died after giving birth to our daughter Eleanor and I still can't believe it's happened. People say time is a great healer but I can't say as I agree with them yet...'

'Yer've got a daughter ... and yer *volunteered* fer this?' Eddie could not keep the surprise from his voice.

'I know,' replied Max guiltily.

Max did feel guilty but he could not help it. His decision to enlist had caused great consternation but he knew that for once in his life he needed to be selfish and consider his own needs first. He needed to get away, from Gloucester Street, from the business and even from the people who loved him the most. Molly in particular had watched him for weeks with mounting alarm, fearing the worst until those fears were realised on the day he announced that he had enlisted in the Middlesex Regiment and would be leaving for basic training in Scotland at the end of the week. He had placed the business in the capable hands of Billy and Richie, reasoning that as they had really been running things for months, there was nothing to stop that state of affairs continuing for the foreseeable future; in fact, they had already taken some prudent steps to cope with the effects they envisaged the war would have on their trade.

The prospect of leaving Eleanor could not deter him either, because, in truth, his feelings for his daughter remained ambivalent. The immediate and unconditional love he felt for her when he had first seen her cradled in Nurse Andrews' arms had given way to sentiments verging on antipathy in the aftermath of Rosie's death, and he had struggled to come to terms with them ever since. He knew it was wrong to feel the way he did towards an innocent and defenceless child; *she was his flesh and blood for God's sake!* He knew his attitude was entirely without justification but, as hard as he tried, he could not bring himself to love her in the way a father should. Not even the certain knowledge that Rosie would have been aghast at his behaviour seemed to have any positive effect. He had obviously made certain that she was well looked after and Molly, Ivy and Stan were doting grandparents, but even they had been forced to resign themselves to the hope that things would change in time as he slowly began to pick up the threads of his life.

On the day before he went to the recruiting office he had arranged for Eleanor to live with Billy and Elizabeth, neither of whom had ever stopped offering to help with her since Rosie's passing. Their own little boy, Alexander, had been born three weeks after Eleanor, and Elizabeth had insisted that she would be absolutely fine with them in their new home in Mayfair for the duration of the war. The house in Curzon Street was big enough to accommodate Nurse Andrews as well, so Eleanor's nurse-cum-nanny had gone with her young charge. Nurse Andrews had agreed to remain at Gloucester Street in that role after Rosie's funeral, in return for a generous salary, and she had become a surrogate mother to the little girl, much to Max's relief. This left Max free to close up Gloucester Street, leaving just Mrs Walsh, Mary and Violet to look after things in his absence. There would only be Molly staying there whenever she travelled to London to see her granddaughter, which she liked to do on a regular basis.

'She's being cared for by my oldest and closest friends who have a little boy of the same age, and her nanny has gone with her too. She won't come to any harm,' said Max rather sheepishly. He knew his explanation sounded lame, even to a young man of barely 18 years of age.

'A nanny? Bloody 'ell, Max!' exclaimed Eddie, quickly changing the subject, 'where do yer live then, Buckingham Palace!'

'Not quite,' replied Max, breaking into a grin.

'So what do yer do?'

'I own a wholesale business supplying food to individuals and the catering trade.'

'Blimey,' said Eddie, not really understanding what Max meant but thinking it sounded impressive. 'Which part of London?'

'Actually we supply all over the country, from Devon right the way up to Leeds and beyond...'

Eddie interrupted Max by whistling through his teeth. 'No wonder yer've got a nanny. I bet there's an 'ole 'ouse full o' 'em!'

Max laughed. 'Only the one, Eddie. So what about you, what do you do?'

'I were about ter be articled in a shippin' company near the docks, learnin' the books an' that. That's why me mam was so cross, said I'm throwin' me future away ... oh, look sharp, 'ere they come.'

Max turned round to see the duty sergeant and a corporal stride through the doors at the far end of the room.

'Lights out, lads! Come on, let's be 'aving yer! Reveille at zero five hundred sharp.' This reminder was met with loud groans. 'And woe betides the last man out of bed!' threatened the sergeant with glee as he turned down the gas lamps.

Chapter 45

Max woke feeling remarkably refreshed after an uninterrupted night's sleep. To his surprise the bed had turned out to be more comfortable than it looked. It was still dark when he swung his feet out from underneath the thin sheet on to the bare wooden floor, taking care not to disturb the sleeping figures around him. The silence was punctuated by the sound of snoring and the occasional grunt coming from some of the beds as he wound his way through them to the communal wash-basins lined up against the far wall of the dormitory. He was used to getting up early, and sunrise remained one of his favourite times of the day. It still reminded him of the many hours spent in the hills around Lee Moor, although that all seemed such a long time ago now. There would be no opportunity to watch it here, he thought dryly to himself.

It was too dark to see the hands on his watch clearly but he sensed he had better hurry if he was to wash and dress before everyone else. He did not relish the prospect of queuing for a wash-basin and he had heard someone say that the water was only changed after every fourth man. He flinched as the freezing cold water hit his face, but when the bugle sounded at reveille he was already washed and dressed.

'Up, lads! Rise and shine, up, get up!'

The corporal was shouting his orders before the bugler had even finished, which elicited loud groans and mutterings throughout the room.

'Last man up is on report!'

He strode along the rows of beds kicking each one as he went by, which very quickly had their occupants jumping up and rushing for the wash-basins.

'Get a move on or you'll miss breakfast,' said Max as Eddie looked drowsily around the room.

'If it's like dinner, it'll not be any loss,' muttered Eddie as he searched for his boots.

They filed out into the grounds where two large tents had been erected to accommodate the cookhouse and mess hall. There was a chill in the air and many of the men stamped their feet on the ground as they waited in line for their food.

'Wait 'til there's six inches of snow on the ground,' said someone sardonically.

'Not exactly The Ritz, is it?' declared a short man near the back of the queue in a very good imitation of an aristocratic accent.

'I'd complain ter the management if I were yer,' came the instant riposte in a broad cockney accent.

'Quiet in line!' bawled the duty corporal.

'Sorry, corp,' they said cheerfully to barely suppressed laughter.

Breakfast was a quick and meagre affair. Max held his mess tin out when he reached the front of the queue and received a spoonful of overcooked scrambled egg, a lukewarm cup of tea and some dry bread. The army could do with a decent wholesaler, he thought grimly as he took a mouthful of the unedifying mess in front of him, but nobody seemed to mind. The atmosphere was light-hearted and eager and the excited chatter round the long tables bore witness to the camaraderie that was already developing.

'Hurry up, lads, back to yer quarters. Bed inspection in ten minutes!' shouted the corporal.

'Come on, lads, be quick. 'E sounds as if 'e means it,' said an anxious voice further along the table.

'But I 'aven't finished me grub,' grumbled his neighbour.

'Looks like yer could do with losing a few pounds, Scottie,' said another.

At six o'clock they were gathered outside the front of the house in the area that had been taken over for the parade ground. Sergeant-Major Wilkins appeared as an air of expectation hung over them.

'Morning, lads, trust yer all slept well,' he shouted but he did not smile. 'This is where the 'ard work begins. I want yer lined up into four columns now. Move!'

He watched with a resigned expression on his face as they milled around trying to organise themselves as he wanted.

'You'll 'ave ter do better than that next time. We 'aven't got all day! The Bosche won't wait yer know.'

They marched up and down the rectangular ground for three hours without a break. One or two of the less physically fit collapsed and were dragged away to recover, their remaining colleagues told 'ter close up!' without pause. The NCOs marching alongside them kept shouting 'Keep in step! Look lively now!' in an effort to maintain some degree of formation until, at last, they were allowed to rest for ten minutes. Most of them just sank to the ground exhausted.

268

Eddie leant forward and eased the laces on his boots. 'Me feet are killin' me,' he said, 'Even me blisters 'ave got blisters.'

Max looked at him sympathetically. 'Try wearing an extra pair of socks, it might stop the boots rubbing.' His legs and feet were aching badly even though he was probably amongst the fittest of them there, but by no means the youngest. 'This is harder than I'd imagined,' he admitted as he rubbed his calves.

'I could murder a pint,' moaned Eddie, examining his right heel.

'Looks like tea will have to do,' laughed Max as orderlies appeared with two large urns.

The rest of the morning was spent on the parade ground marching relentlessly up and down until Sergeant-Major Wilkins called a halt to the proceedings.

'We don't want ter tire yer out on yer first day do we?' he gloated as the men stumbled with fatigue back to the mess tent where they devoured an indescribable looking stew as if it was finest fillet steak.

'I could eat an 'orse,' said the dark-haired man next to Max, hungrily wiping a piece of stale bread around the inside of his mess tin to soak up every last drop of gravy.

'Yer probably are,' said Eddie acerbically. Max laughed.

They were fitted with their uniforms that afternoon and given 20 minutes to return to the dormitory to put them on and pack away their civilian clothing before being ordered back on to the parade ground.

'Bloody sadist,' muttered Robbo, a thin, sallow-faced recruit from Stepney, only to be overheard by one of the ever present corporals.

'What was that, lad?' he demanded so that everyone could hear.

'Nothin', corp,' said Robbo hastily, turning bright red.

'Didn't sound like nothing to me, lad!' bawled the corporal. 'Report for latrine duty, nineteen hundred hours sharp.'

'But, corp I were only jok...'

'Don't but me, lad, nineteen hundred hours sharp!'

'Yes, corp,' said Robbo sullenly.

Max slept even more soundly that night but was still up and dressed by the time reveille was sounded the following morning. Their second day in His Majesty's army consisted of more marching drill until Max thought his feet would drop off. His regulation heavy leather boots fitted him reasonably well but his toes were beginning to swell up nevertheless.

However, it seemed he was no worse off than the others and in a better state than many.

'When do we get ter see a rifle, corporal?' asked Eddie during their lunch break, which was spent huddled on the side of the parade ground.

'Termorrow, lad, and God 'elp us all then,' he replied. 'I only 'ope yer can 'andle a gun better than yer can march, that's all.'

'Yes, corp,' said Eddie meekly, exchanging a knowing look with Max. He had learnt when to keep his mouth shut.

The days were filled with an unrelenting schedule of instruction to prepare them as far as was humanly possible for the rigours of the battlefield. Their spirit rarely faltered despite the gruelling hours of physical and mental exertion that tested them to the limit. They learnt how to handle their Lee Enfield rifles and were shown how to operate a Lewis machine-gun. They came to realise that their lives would depend on their ability to maintain the weapons in efficient working order, so they spent many hours stripping them down, cleaning them, practising how to clear blockages, and reassembling them in double quick time. Bayonet and target practice, map reading and basic first-aid skills featured on an almost daily basis, and kit and mess inspections became second nature as Sergeant-Major Wilkins and Captain Manvers drove them harder and harder with each passing week.

The initial trivial moans and groans gradually gave way to a willing acceptance of the remorseless discipline and a fierce pride in the regiment. One of the clearest signs that they were achieving the high standards demanded of them was the marked decline in the number of recruits put on Report. In the first weeks of training it seemed that there was a constant stream of men detailed for fatigue duties, but this had now dwindled to almost nothing. The comradeship that had developed was felt by everyone and manifested itself most obviously in their single-minded and united determination to trounce the Germans. The challenges of basic training had shaped a disparate group of men into a competent and homogeneous fighting unit, which, to many, had looked impossible at the outset. Not only did they now function effectively as a group, but, as individuals, they had also learnt to rely on one another when in need of help and support.

They were allowed out of barracks once a week although this freedom was restricted. Generally Captain Manvers granted them two or three hours' leave on the condition that they stayed within three miles of the barracks and behaved in a manner befitting the Middlesex Regiment at all times. Sergeant-Major Wilkins had made clear that this privilege would in future be denied any man reporting back drunk or as much as one minute late.

Max had been reluctant to take advantage of the first such opportunity and remained in the mess writing letters home to Molly and Billy. He felt that he would in some way be disloyal to Rosie if he went out to enjoy himself but he had to admit to being tempted. Eddie had been unable to persuade him otherwise on that occasion but for an 18-year-old lad he was perceptive and thoughtful beyond his years. He spent the following week convincing Max that he should accompany them the next time leave was granted, persuading him that he must live in the present and for the future and, by so doing, he would not be dishonouring the past. By the end of that week, when company orders confirmed leave for the forthcoming Saturday evening, Max had succumbed to Eddie's trenchant entreaties and agreed to go.

For the first time since Rosie's death, he forgot about the past just for a few hours and felt glad to be alive. He had Eddie to thank for that.

Chapter 46

The passing out parade was held on 25th November 1914 and for Max it marked more than just official recognition that they were now ready for active combat. The twelve weeks spent in the company of his fellow volunteers, united in the common aim of fighting for King and Country, had inspired him to reassess his attitude towards the future.

Molly was the first to notice the change. The battalion had been sent on leave for a week before sailing to join the regiment on the Western Front and she had travelled up to London to spend it with him in Gloucester Street. He arrived home late on the first day after the long train journey south from Scotland. The atmosphere had been one of jubilant anticipation after the rigours of the endless drill and instruction. As they passed through station after station, they had been cheered by local well-wishers as if they were conquering heroes, and this time they felt that they were almost worthy of this outpouring of goodwill.

'God, that was exhaustin', wasn't it?' Eddie sighed as they disembarked wearily from the carriage just before midnight. 'Me arms feel like they're going ter fall off from all that wavin'!'

Max laughed. 'I'm just relieved it's all over, that's all. I'm looking forward to a hot bath and clean sheets, I don't know about you. Come on, let's find a taxi.'

'Blimey, Max, a taxi! Yer a millionaire or what?' exclaimed Eddie. He had never ridden in a taxi-cab before.

'It's a long walk otherwise at this time of night and I, for one, have had enough marching to last me a lifetime,' joked Max. 'Look smart, there's one. Taxi!' yelled Max as he picked up his rucksack and began to run.

'Pimlico please, driver, Gloucester Street,' said Max as he opened the door and signalled for Eddie to get in.

'Are yer sure this is all right, Max?' said Eddie a little anxiously, 'stoppin' over at yours I mean? I don't want ter intrude or anythin'.'

Max smiled. 'I insist you do, Eddie. You don't want to be going all the way to your house at this time of night. A good night's sleep and a hearty breakfast and you'll be walking in your front door tomorrow morning before you know it.' He yawned. God, I'm tired, he thought, as he watched Eddie's eyelids begin to droop as he too fought sleep. The driver looked in his mirror a little while later when he turned into Gloucester Street and smiled. They were both fast asleep.

'What number, sir?' he called over his shoulder, half turning as he did so.

Max woke with a start and sat up. 'It's the one up there on the right, with the black front door,' he answered, looking quickly around him. He nudged Eddie. 'Wake up, Eddie, we're here.'

The taxi pulled into the side of the road and stopped. 'How much do I owe you?' asked Max reaching into his tunic pocket.

'No charge sir, always happy to help our fighting lads.'

Max and Eddie looked at each other in surprise. 'Are you sure?' asked Max.

'Of course, sir, only wish I was twenty years younger myself. Mind how you go now.'

'Thanks,' said Eddie quickly, before the man had a chance to change his mind. 'Christ, Max, it's a bloody mansion!' he exclaimed looking up at the house.

Max laughed. 'Come on, I'll show you round as long as you don't get your mucky hands on the furniture,' he joked, 'you'll be in the west wing.'

'Very funny!' replied Eddie sarcastically.

The light was on in the morning room, which meant that Molly was still up and, hearing the taxi outside, she had come to the front door just as Max was fishing for his key.

' 'Ello, darling,' said Molly with a beaming smile as she opened the door and held out her arms. Then she spotted Eddie hovering nervously behind Max. 'Oh, yer've brought someone with yer ... sorry, I didn't see yer there, lad, 'ello, I'm Molly, come on in then both of yer.'

'Ma, this is Eddie ... Eddie, this is my mother, Molly,' he said, introducing them on the doorstep. 'Eddie is spending the night here before going on to his folks in the morning Ma.'

'Of course, yer very welcome, Eddie. Yer both look exhausted, 'ave yer 'ad anything ter eat? Mrs Walsh 'as left something out fer yer. We're in 'ere,' she explained, indicating the morning room, 'because the drawing-room is all dust-sheeted. I said it would be all right.'

'Of course it is, Ma,' said Max. 'Is everything all right here? Is Eleanor all right? Did you get my letters?'

'Everything is fine, darling. Eleanor is a delight and growing all the time. She's missin' 'er father though…' She looked carefully at him as she said that. 'I want ter 'ear all yer news, but the morning will do, yer look dead on yer feet, both of yer.'

'Do you want something to eat, Eddie?' Eddie shook his head and yawned again. 'Come on then, I'll show you your room. Are they all made up, Ma?'

'Yes, love. I'll say goodnight then.'

'Goodnight, Mrs Chambers,' said Eddie.

'Goodnight, Eddie, an' please call me Molly. I'll see you in the mornin' an' just let me know if there's anything yer need.'

'Thanks, Molly.'

Molly watched them climb the stairs and thought how proud it made her to see Max in the King's uniform. It would have made Bert proud, although she could not help but worry about his safety, especially as there was bad news of losses amongst the British Expeditionary Force on the Western Front. It had been a disaster for Eleanor to lose one parent, to lose both would be a complete catastrophe. She went back into the morning room and turned off the lights before she too went up to bed. She was looking forward to spending a few days on her own with Max; she was sure she had detected a change in his demeanour. He seemed more like his old self, brighter, more positive and in charge of things. She prayed that she was right.

The following morning, over breakfast, Max insisted that he drive Eddie back to his home. He was relishing the prospect of getting behind the wheel again. Eddie was astonished when Max brought the Rolls round to the front door from the mews and spent the entire journey to Stepney open-mouthed, marvelling at the opulence of the car.

'Yer not at all like I would 'ave imagined yer to be if I'd just seen yer driving past in yer fancy car,' he said when they were nearing their destination. 'Drop me anywhere 'ere, Max, I can walk the rest.'

Max looked at him out of the corner of his eye as he looked for a place to pull over. 'What do you mean by that?' he asked, half amused and half mystified.

'No offence, mate, but I'd 'ave thought yer were stuck up, hoity toity like, but yer not at all are yer?'

Max brought the car to a stop and roared with laughter. 'I'm very pleased to hear it, Eddie, and no offence taken! I'm just an ordinary man, like you, but I had an ambition that I was determined to follow.' He paused reflectively for a moment. 'And I still am for lots of reasons, despite everything,' he went on quietly, 'life can be very cruel at times but you've just got to get on with things. It's for living, these last twelve weeks and you have taught me that.'

'Me?' burst out Eddie incredulously. ''Ow do yer work that one out fer Chrissake!'

'Oh you just have, that's all,' he replied, not wanting to be drawn on the subject. 'See you bright and early on Saturday then, enjoy your leave. Cheerio.'

'Yes, eight o'clock an' all ready fer France,' said Eddie with a hint of trepidation in his voice as he slung his kitbag over his shoulder and started to walk off down the street. 'Bye, Max, thanks fer the lift.'

Max drove back to Gloucester Street feeling more cheerful than he had done for a long time. It *was* good to be back in London and he was looking forward to catching up with Billy and Richie and the business, but before that, most of all, he was looking forward to seeing Eleanor. Stopping briefly at the house to collect Molly, they were soon on their way to see Elizabeth.

'Mr Chambers, Mrs Chambers, good morning,' said Mannings, the butler in Curzon Street, 'Mrs Masters is in the morning room, sir.' He led the way across the large hallway and knocked gently on a shiny mahogany-panelled door facing the main staircase. 'Mr Max and Mrs Molly Chambers, madam,' he announced.

Elizabeth looked up from her writing table. 'Max, Molly,' she cried, beaming with happiness. 'It's so good to see you both. How are you, Max? Back from the war already.'

Max laughed easily. 'It was only basic training but yes, I got back from Scotland last night. It's lovely to see you,' he said, kissing her warmly on both cheeks. 'How's Billy?'

'Oh he's fine, he said to tell you hello and he's looking forward to seeing you. He suggested dinner here on Thursday?' she said. 'Nothing fancy and no talk about the business mind you,' she warned, laughing, 'he said he's sure you'll have found out all you want to know well before then!'

'We'd luv ter, Elizabeth, thank yer,' said Molly, 'wouldn't we, darling?' she asked, looking at Max.

'Of course, that would be splendid, thank you. Now, where's that daughter of mine?'

Molly and Elizabeth exchanged delighted glances. 'She's upstairs in the nursery with Alexander. It must be nearly time for her morning walk actually,' explained Elizabeth, checking her watch. 'Nurse Andrews takes her out for some fresh air in her perambulator around about now. Would you like to go up straightaway?'

Max nodded. 'Yes please, I would, if I'm allowed.'

Elizabeth laughed again. 'Just mind out for your nurse, she's very protective of her you know! It's the door on the left, right at the top of the last flight of stairs. Molly knows, don't you, Molly?'

'Why don't you go on up on your own, Max, I'll be up in a minute?' Molly suggested, 'I just want ter ask Elizabeth something.'

'All right, all right, I can recognise a set-up when I see one,' agreed Max with a grin.

Molly and Elizabeth exchanged more delighted looks, relieved that their idea had worked, and when they both peeped round the door of the nursery 30 minutes later they found Max sitting on the floor with his back against the wall, bouncing Eleanor up and down on his knees to her obvious delight. She had the most startling blue eyes, which were staring with wonder at Max's smiling face, and her strawberry-blonde curls were tousled prettily atop her giggling, dimpled face. Alexander was asleep in his cot and Nurse Andrews was looking on disapprovingly, muttering about the dangers of interfering with a baby's routine.

'There's coffee downstairs when you're ready, Max,' said Elizabeth, smiling from the doorway.

'Oh no, not for me thanks. I'm taking Eleanor out for her morning air. We thought we'd go to Green Park, didn't we, sweetheart?' he said, opening his eyes wide and smiling broadly as he looked down at Eleanor. 'Nurse Andrews said I could as long as I was back in time for her lunch, didn't you, Nanny?' he asked, trying very hard to look serious.

She looked back at him with a deadpan expression on her face. 'As long as yer keep her wrapped up warm mind,' she said. 'There's a chill in the air this morning.'

'I promise,' said Max meekly, feeling very much like an errant child himself.

The week passed in a whirlwind of fun and laughter, largely centred around Eleanor, with Max trying very hard to make up for lost time, revelling in his new found enjoyment of his daughter. He cursed himself repeatedly for having been so selfish and irresponsible for nine months; so much so that Molly had to work hard to persuade him that it was only symptomatic of the grieving process and she was much too young for it to have any lasting ill-effects. She told him that it was the future that was important now.

He devoted some of his precious hours to Billy and Richie on business matters but mainly he just delighted in being with Eleanor. On the Wednesday he took her to see Rosie's grave and as he sat there peacefully amongst the headstones, with Eleanor gurgling contentedly on his lap, he began to tell her all about her mother until he looked down and found that she had fallen quietly asleep. It was, to his surprise, an uplifting experience, which he vowed to repeat on his next leave.

As the day of his departure drew nearer, the appreciation of what lay ahead dawned ever more harshly as he read the headlines of the morning newspapers with their reports of mounting Allied losses in Belgium and elsewhere along the Western Front. The excitement and glory originally felt by the thousands of enthusiastic volunteers as they flocked to the recruiting stations was rapidly being replaced by unimaginable horror and anonymous death as each week passed. This uncomfortable realisation caused Max to send for Andrew Latchmere to make sure his affairs were in order and, over dinner with Molly, the Blacks and Billy and Elizabeth, on his last night in London, he insisted on explaining the arrangements he had made, particularly with regard to Eleanor. It was a subdued, but necessary task, which cast a shadow over the evening that still lingered the following morning as he set off to join Eddie for the trip to Dover.

Chapter 47

Max and Eddie sailed for France accompanied by 500 other men aboard a cramped troop-ship en route to join their various regiments. It was three weeks before Christmas and the first Battle of Ypres had ended with an Allied victory whilst they had been on leave. The human cost had been enormous with 58,000 casualties amongst the seven British infantry divisions and three cavalry divisions alone. The defeated German army under the command of Erich von Falkenhayn had been halted at the Passchendaele Ridge, to the east of the town of Ypres, by the advancing British Expeditionary Force led by Field Marshal Sir John French. Both sides had dug in for trench warfare and the town had been quickly demolished by artillery and air attack. The Germans lost over 100,000 soldiers in the fierce fighting, many of whom were young volunteers. This was the main topic of conversation amongst the men on deck as the English coastline gradually disappeared from view and the ship began to roll atrociously in the mounting swell.

'They were mainly volunteers, just like us accordin' ter the papers.'

'Serves 'em bloody right!'

'Can't wait ter get stuck in meself!'

'But they were just kids.'

'Yeah, an' they were attackin' our boys!'

Max looked at Eddie who was standing miserably by the guardrail. 'Are you all right, Eddie?' he asked.

'I wish this boat would keep still,' he moaned, 'I've never been on one before. Think I'm goin' ter be sick.'

Max grimaced sympathetically and turned up the collar of his greatcoat. 'It's been a while since I was on one too.'

'Not taken the yacht across ter Cannes fer a bit then?' mimicked Eddie, doing his best to smile.

'Ha bloody ha,' said Max, 'only another ten hours or so an' we'll be there.'

'Oh Christ, is that all,' groaned Eddie before he lapsed into silence. 'You frightened?' he asked a minute or two later.

'Frightened, Eddie?' asked Max, 'no, I'm not frightened, I'm absolutely terrified.'

'Me too,' said Eddie.

The voyage across the Channel was interminable as the ship ploughed through heavy seas with many of the men remaining miserably huddled near the rails, trying to find what little shelter they could. When at last the coast of France hove into view a muted cheer went up and Max breathed a sigh of relief.

'See that, Eddie, dry land,' said Max, nudging him awake. 'We'll soon be off here now.'

Eddie looked blearily around him and closed his eyes again. 'Wake me up when we are then,' he muttered and went back to trying to keep his breakfast down.

Disembarkation was swiftly accomplished as soon as they were docked and Sergeant-Major Wilkins gathered them all together for a quick briefing.

'Listen up, lads. Tonight we march five miles east before setting up camp for the night. Reveille will be at zero six hundred tomorrow morning. Prepare yourselves for a week of battle training. Further orders will be issued in due course. That's all. Form up, at the double!'

They marched for two hours through pouring rain, which had long since turned the ground to mud, passing columns of men and animals heading in the opposite direction. Occasionally locals came out to stare as they went past, a few saluting and shouting words of support that Max did not recognise, but generally there was not much to see other than the rain slanting through the woods bordering their route. By the time they reached their destination the bad weather had mercifully eased and they set about pitching their tents in preparation for turning in.

'Chambers, you and Samuels take the first watch. We'll split the night into four-hour shifts. Challenge anybody who approaches and report it immediately. Do you understand?' ordered Corporal Granby who was in charge of their platoon.

'Yes, corporal,' they both said smartly.

'Keep yer eyes peeled. This isn't a drill now yer know.'

'Yes, corp!'

Max and Eddie positioned themselves at the end of their row of tents and slung their rifles over their shoulders. It was cold and damp, although the rain had stopped, and Max buttoned up his coat and stamped his feet on the wet grass to keep warm.

'What do we do now then?' asked Eddie quietly.

'Your guess is as good as mine,' replied Max, 'keep a good look out I suppose,' he said.

'There's no one around fer miles! If this is France I think I prefer 'ome,' said Eddie with feeling as his boots squelched in the mud.

Max laughed. 'The locals seemed friendly enough.'

'Yeah, but they could 'ave been shoutin' anything fer all I could 'ear. Probably bein' rude.'

Max laughed again. 'Cor blimey, it's cold.' He rubbed his hands together vigorously. 'I could do with a cup of something hot.'

'Me too,' said Eddie, 'I'll go find us somethin'.' He looked behind him at the rows of tents and could just make out the cookhouse at the far end of the camp. 'I'll be as quick as I can. If the Bosche come, duck.'

He walked off into the gloom and came back a quarter of an hour later with two steaming mugs of tea. 'Best I could do I'm afraid, clean out o' champagne. Told 'em it was fer you but it made no difference.'

Max smiled in the darkness. 'We shall have to take our custom elsewhere if things don't improve.' He cupped his hands around the hot mug. 'Ah, that's better,' he said, savouring the warming sensation and willing it to last for ever.

The night passed uneventfully and Max managed to get some sleep after their watch had ended until the bugle sounded reveille promptly at six o'clock. The day dawned bright and cold and he shivered as they packed away before the signal for breakfast sounded and he and Eddie joined the long queue snaking back from the entrance to the cookhouse. This set the pattern of their nights for the week, and their days were spent in intensive training in readiness for their move up to the trenches. On the last afternoon, after a particularly long session of rifle practice, the whole camp was summoned to a briefing by Captain Manvers and the commanding officer, Lieutenant-Colonel Sir Richard Hatchard VC DSO.

They were to march for Belgium at zero eight hundred hours the following morning and they were told they could expect to see action by Christmas. It took eight days of steady marching before they reached the war zone. The first indications that they were nearing the battlefield came with an increase in the amount of traffic on the narrow roads. They began to encounter all manner of motorized vehicles, some of which were carrying groups of soldiers, but it was the steady stream of horses and carts trundling slowly towards a collection of large tents emblazoned with red crosses that really caught their attention. These carts were loaded with stretchers bearing the wounded to the forward medical station, where orderlies were constantly rushing in and out to help the nurses unload each one as gently as possible in order to take them inside. Many of the nurses were wearing blood-stained uniforms. There were more of the injured walking slowly and awkwardly with the help of their comrades in the same direction.

Max swallowed hard. They passed close enough to the walking wounded to see the look of pain and despair ingrained on their faces and to hear the cries of agony coming from many of the stretchers.

'Eyes front,' shouted Sergeant-Major Wilkins as heads turned to witness the bloodshed and suffering.

They marched on but the earlier air of confident bravado had evaporated to be replaced by a feeling of subdued melancholy.

'Did yer see that?' whispered Eddie.

'Quiet in the ranks!' shouted Corporal Granby. 'Eyes front as the sergeant-major said!'

The distant noise of artillery fire drifted towards them and shortly afterwards they heard the intermittent staccato sound of gunfire. Sergeant-Major Wilkins brought them to a halt as Captain Manvers rode up to the front of the forward platoon to confer with him. They were soon directed across the fields on their left where they found an empty area alongside row upon row of tents that had already been erected.

'This'll be 'ome then,' said Eddie, 'they saved us some room.'

'Nice ter feel welcome at least. Bit too near that gunfire if yer ask me,' said somebody else. Nobody laughed.

They had been told that the front line was just under a third of a mile up ahead and Max could clearly hear the ugly sound of intermittent artillery bombardments as he and Eddie pitched their tent, which they could now do with their eyes shut; they had put it up so many times in the past two weeks that it took them less than 15 minutes from start to finish. The camp was bordered on three sides by thick woods and the battalion had been granted two hours rest and relaxation before a briefing by the adjutant planned for eighteen hundred hours. Most of the men chose to remain in their tents but Max was restless and unable to settle.

'I'm going for a walk, Eddie, won't be long,' he announced, 'do you want to come?'

'No, ta, I'm goin' ter put me feet up an' call fer room service,' quipped Eddie with forced jocularity, 'bring me back a present though.'

'Don't count on it,' replied Max.

He set out in the direction of the trees where he found a maze of well-trodden paths disappearing into the densely packed undergrowth. He followed these through to the other side without any difficulty, emerging to find himself staring upon a series of trenches dug into the ground in a zigzag shape about 200 yards in front of him. These must be the reserve trenches they had been told about, he said to himself, as he gingerly made his way towards them. They were joined to the front line by a series of communication trenches, which were used to ferry fresh troops, supplies and food to the front in addition to vital information about the enemy's movements. Reaching the nearest trench, Max suddenly fell to his knees as a particularly loud round of shelling startled him. He felt foolish as the noise abated and he looked up to see smoke drifting up into the air far away to his right.

'Yer'll get used ter it, soldier,' said a voice from the trench. 'They get a lot nearer than that I can tell yer.'

The sight and smell that confronted him was indescribable.

'Holy Mother of God,' muttered Max in disbelief.

Mud and water came up over the top of his boots as he slithered down into the dugout. The duckboards covering the ground to protect the soldiers' feet from the mud and slime were completely submerged, and therefore useless, and the jute sandbags stacked high on either side of him were sodden and offered scant protection from stray bullets. Max stood there, rooted to the spot, trying to take in the scene of utter filth and chaos as all around him men were standing alone or in small groups, engaged in the endless task of bailing water out of the trench only to see more take its place, bayonetting rats and mice, which appeared to be everywhere, and trying to brew tea on tiny stoves.

'Bet they didn't tell yer it was like this, did they?' said a young mud-streaked man near him.

'No, not exactly,' said Max, looking at him in astonishment. He could not have been a day over 20 but looked at least twice that. 'How long have you been here?'

'Got back from the advance trenches this morning. Four days back 'ere until we go up ter the front again.' His hands were shaking and then his voice cracked as he began to cry.

'It's all right, Tommy,' said one of his mates helplessly, 'it'll be over soon.'

He was led gently away while someone explained to Max that his best hope was to pick up a minor wound so that he would be sent to the medical station and hopefully, from there, be repatriated back to England.

'Shell-shock, mate,' explained an older man with three stripes on his sleeve, 'poor blighter'll be done fer cowardice if they catch 'im.'

Max had seen more than enough. It was time to be heading back for the briefing. He scrambled out of the dugout and headed back to the camp.

'Yer can't go ter the briefing lookin' like that, Max!' exclaimed Eddie when Max lifted up the tent flap and crawled in. 'Look at yer! Where the 'ell 'ave yer been?'

Max did not answer straightaway. He was covered in mud and ashen-faced but slowly, and quietly, he began to tell Eddie what he had witnessed as he did his best to clean himself up in the confined space. When he had finished, and they were on their way across to the far side of the field where the briefing was to be held, he looked around at his companions thinking they were in for the biggest shock of their lives.

Captain Manvers addressed the assembled company for 20 minutes and ended with the words, '... and so we move up to engage the enemy at zero four hundred hours tomorrow. May we bring glory to the name of the regiment and good luck to you all. God save the King.'

'And 'appy bleedin' Christmas ter you too,' said the platoon wag as they slowly dispersed in sombre contemplation of the fact that they might not live to see the following night.

Chapter 48

When day dawned, Max was astounded by the sight before him. The platoons had taken up their positions in the forward trenches as ordered and he was balanced precariously on the muddy fire step to the front of the trench as first light gradually appeared. He was full of nervous anticipation and his heart was pounding, every muscle tensed; this was the unspoken but favourite time for the beginning of an enemy attack. No man's land stretching out in front of him, beyond the barbed-wire fence, seemed nothing more than a series of enormous shell holes, filled with scraps of uniforms, weapons and dead bodies. The entire ground had been ploughed up by falling shells, leaving not a single blade of grass to be seen. It was a ghastly sight and beyond his worst imagination.

'Keep yer eyes peeled, lads,' warned Corporal Granby steadily, 'if they're comin' it'll be sometime soon.'

They needed no encouragement. The previous night's attack had been ferocious with enemy shells raining down for a full two hours before the German infantry loomed out of the darkness. These night-time attacks were the worst and the British defence had been fierce. By the time the advancing army had been beaten back behind their own lines 2,000 men lay dead, mown down by successive walls of shrapnel unleashed by the Lewis guns ranged along the front line. The sentries keeping watch had raised the alarm as soon as the first German soldier had appeared from behind their own barbed wire and a counter attack had been ordered, which had continued until gone two o'clock.

Consequently there had been no time for the fatigue parties to strengthen the trenches or repair the barbed wire before Max and his platoon arrived to take up their posts. Spent cartridges lay everywhere and the ammunition ledge just below the top of the trench, in front of Max, was almost empty. Platoon after platoon had been sent in to hold the line and most of them had been steadily annihilated. The dead lay uncovered, stacked in layers, one on top of another, with no time to bury them before daybreak.

'Come on then, yer bastards, if yer comin',' muttered Eddie who was huddled next to Max, straining his eyes to peer through the dim light.

They remained at readiness for an hour before the order came to stand down. There was no sign of activity from across no man's land and all seemed to be quiet so they got to work to dig graves for their fallen comrades in readiness for the simple burial service that was held just before midday as respectfully as possible. The afternoon passed without incident except for the rain, which started shortly after noon and continued unabated until the light began to fail.

'Jesus Christ, we're going to drown in this stuff before we get out of here,' said Max as he fell against the sandbags, having lost his footing for the hundredth time. His boots sank deeper into the mire, which now rose to his kneecaps before gradually beginning to seep halfway up his thighs. The stench was unspeakable; the mud had a pungency all of its own, revolting in its putridness, and mixed with it was the choking smell of decaying flesh and vomit.

'We'll be getting trench foot next,' grumbled Jamie, at 39, the oldest member of the platoon.

'No we won't,' said Eddie quickly, 'the Bosche'll get us first.'

In fact he had been worrying about that too because they had been told it made the foot change colour and swell up and he had heard of soldiers sticking their bayonets into their infected feet in an effort to dull the pain and avoid the need for amputation. He did not relish the prospect of being a cripple for the rest of his life.

Later in the evening they received a small helping of sodden bread and cheese and some plum jam and they huddled together for shelter as they did their best to eat it, but no one had much appetite for food.

'Christmas Eve tomorrow,' said a voice in the darkness.

Max immediately thought of home and the wonderful last Christmas he and Rosie had enjoyed before Eleanor was born, but he determinedly blocked that train of thought from his mind as suddenly as it had started.

'Anyone remember the decorations?' asked the same voice mirthlessly.

Max peered into the darkness, unable to identify who it belonged to. 'What a way to spend Christmas eh, Eddie?' he muttered. 'Goodwill to all men, what a joke.'

'Yer can say that again,' he replied, the sound of his feet squelching in the mud and water very loud in the still, dank air.

The rest of the night passed without incident. They were organised into four-hour watches for sentry duty and warned that the penalty for falling asleep on duty was death. Christ, thought Eddie miserably, if the Bosche don't get yer, yer own side do. Dawn found them at readiness again in preparation for a German attack, which, like the previous morning, failed to materialise. No orders for an offensive came down the line and so the day was spent in much the same way as before: bailing water out of the trenches, which was a never ending task with no visible result, checking and then double checking their equipment, brewing tea with chlorinated water, which tasted disgusting, waiting for the order to mount an assault and alert to the ever present risk of a German attack.

Each platoon spent four days in the front trenches followed by four days in the reserves until granted a brief respite back at camp, after which they were moved up to the reserve trenches again. This routine continued unchanged for weeks, sometimes months, in between attack and counter-attack. If an enemy bullet didn't end their lives in an instant, disease or gangrene probably did, but if they were amongst the fortunate few to survive, the rampant spread of lice caused epidemics of typhus and trench fever. A rumour was circulated by the old lags to the effect that more men died of disease caught in the trenches than from enemy fire. Max was not about to dispute it.

'Another two days of this before we get out of 'ere,' said Eddie mournfully as night fell. 'The excitement's killin' me.'

'There'll be excitement soon enough, lad,' said Corporal Granby, 'yer mark my words!'

'I wasn't complainin', corp!' said Eddie hastily, 'just commentin', that's all.'

'Stille Nacht, heilige Nacht,
Alles schläft, einsam wacht,'

'What the bloody hell...' exclaimed Max as the faint sound of German voices drifted across no man's land in the darkness.

'Nur das traute, hochheilige Paar,
Holder Knabe im lockigen Haar,'

'They're singing...'

'Look out, lads, it might be a trap!' shouted Sergeant-Major Wilkins who was slithering his way towards them. 'Rifles at the ready!'

'Schlaf in himmlischer Ruh'!
Schlaf in himmlischer Ruh'!'

'Can yer make it out, Max?' asked Eddie anxiously, squinting into the distance.

'It sounds like "Silent Night",' replied Max incredulously, 'if I didn't know any better I'd say they were singing carols!'

'Shh,' snapped Corporal Granby, 'listen out.'

They stood silently on the fire step looking over the top of the trench, rifles cocked and ready to open fire the moment they saw German soldiers come charging towards them, but none came.

'What's that I can see?' said Jamie suddenly, 'looks like lights or something...'

'I can see them,' cried Max, pointing away to his right. 'Look, corp, over there.'

'Silent night, holy night,
All is calm, all is bright,
Round yon virgin Mother and Child
Holy infant so tender and mild...'

'Cut that out!' hollered the Sergeant-Major to a group of men further down the trench but his command was drowned out as more soldiers joined in until only the sound of Christmas carols filled the air.

'They're bleedin' Christmas lights! The Bosche are decorating the bleedin' trees!' shouted Eddie in Max's ear, nudging him hard on his right shoulder.

It was true and then, in a lull between verses, both sides began to shout greetings to each other. This continued throughout the night, and as dawn broke there were calls to venture out into no man's land.

'It's a trap! Don't move!' bellowed Sergeant-Major Wilkins, glancing quickly up and down the trench.

They watched as a handful of German soldiers cautiously clambered out of their dugouts, waving their arms enthusiastically to show that they were not armed. Soon more of their comrades followed bearing small gifts of tobacco and chocolate until it became clear that this was not a plan to lure them all out into the open. The carols stopped and the artillery fire in the distance fell silent as soldiers from both sides slowly began to edge their way around the barbed wire and out into the muddy desolation of no man's land.

287

'I think I've seen everything now,' muttered Sergeant-Major Wilkins in disbelief, a veteran of the Sudan and Boer conflicts.

This unexpected and unexplained truce lasted throughout Christmas Day, which allowed both sides time to collect their recently fallen comrades. Captain Manvers organised burial parties and, for the first time in weeks, proper committals took place as both sides mourned their dead together. Max straightened up, put down his spade and stood to attention as the regimental chaplain read a passage from the 23rd Psalm:

The Lord is my shepherd. I shall not want. He maketh me to lie down in green pastures. He leadeth me beside the still waters. He restoreth my soul. He leadeth me in the path of righteousness for his name's sake. Yea, though I walk through the valley of the shadow of death, I will fear no evil.

As he bent down to begin shovelling the mud and earth back into the shallow grave in front of him, he could find no comfort whatsoever in the words, however hard he tried. It had been the same at Rosie's funeral and now, amidst the scenes of death and destruction, they seemed even more incongruous than ever.

At midnight the big guns started again and all feelings of goodwill vanished within minutes. This time their section was targeted and the shells rained down.

'Tin hats, lads,' shouted Corporal Granby, 'we're fer it this time.'

Max pushed his hat down hard and looked swiftly around at the other men in the trench, seeking out the rest of his platoon. They were all there, huddled below the top of the muddy wall, fear etched on their faces as shell after shell landed in their vicinity with one mighty crump after another. There was nothing to do but sit it out and hope for the best.

'Jesus Christ, that was a close one,' yelled Eddie. 'Do yer reckon they've got Big Bertha over there?'

'Christ knows, the ruddy things sound big enough!' said Jamie.

Those were the last words he ever uttered as he was thrown against the sandbags like a rag doll from the blast of a shell dropping nearby. Max struggled to clamber out of the muck and water in the bottom of the trench where he had landed as the shell struck, his helmet hanging loosely around his neck as pandemonium raged above him. Dripping with water, filthy and disorientated, he shook his head in a frantic attempt to clear his mind. Eddie! Where was Eddie? He looked wildly around and saw Jamie slumped against the side of the trench, a jagged hole ripped across the front of his tunic. He was staring wide-eyed in front of him and his mouth was moving in a twisted fashion as he struggled to say something. Max slithered over to him and knelt down and took him in his arms, cradling him like a baby.

'Shh, mate, try not ter speak,' he murmured. He turned quickly round. 'Medical officer, we need a medical officer over here now!' he shouted desperately as the blood oozed out of the gaping hole in Jamie's chest.

Jamie continued to stare blankly and gripped Max's arm tightly. 'Jesus Christ!' swore Max silently, he felt so helpless. 'Help's coming, mate,' he said softly, bending down so Jamie could hear him above the chaotic noise of the shells, which continued to rain down. 'Help's coming.'

Jamie sighed deeply and his grip loosened as his body went limp. He was dead. His eyes were still staring blindly as Max gently brushed the palm of his hand over the lids to close them, cursing bitterly to himself at the futility of it all. He gazed at Jamie's blood seeping into his own uniform and quietly muttered, 'You're well out if it, mate,' as he laid him gently down against the sandbags and covered his face with an oil sheet. He straightened up, afraid of what he would see when he turned round.

'Max! Max! Are yer all right, mate?' shouted a familiar voice.

Thank God for that he sighed. 'I'm all right, Eddie. Jamie's had it,' he said, nodding at the body lying motionless under the sheet.

'Poor sod ... corp's been blown ter pieces and I saw Jacko go down like a ninepin. Smashed ter bits too.' He began to curse.

'Stop that, lad! Take it easy!' said Sergeant-Major Wilkins coming towards them. 'Save it fer the Bosche.'

Eddie leaned back against the sandbags and closed his eyes, his young face grey and haggard and streaked with blood and filth.

'You hit, Eddie?' asked Max anxiously, noticing the blood for the first time.

'No, just wishin' I were somewhere else, that's all,' replied Eddie.

Chapter 49

They came back to camp in sombre mood, recalled from the front line after ten gruelling weeks of hell, which had seen many more of their comrades slain, often without firing a single shot in anger. Miraculously, with an average life expectancy at the front of less than two months, both Max and Eddie had survived.

The camp was much as they had left it apart from the new faces of the recruits who were arriving constantly to replace the men who had been lost.

'I feel like an old hand,' said Max as they stood in the queue waiting for the staff officer to distribute letters from home, which had arrived whilst they had been at the front.

'Me too,' said Eddie, 'did we really look that green do yer think?'

'Must have done...'

'Private Chambers, two for you!' The lieutenant handed him the envelopes, one of which he could see was addressed in Molly's handwriting. 'Private Metcalfe...'

Max took his letters and turned to go. 'See you back there, Ed,' he said as he ripped open the one from Molly and began to quickly scan the first page, eager for news. When he was settled comfortably on the grass in front of the tent he read it thoroughly, devouring gossip about the happenings in Lee Moor and Gloucester Street until he reached her news of Eleanor. Slowly, and savouring every word, he read of how she had changed since he had left for France, how she had taken her first faltering steps in the last week of January, how she spent her days with Nurse Andrews and how well she played with Alexander. Max sat back and closed his eyes, reliving the time he had spent with Eleanor on his leave as he had discovered the joys of fatherhood for the first time.

He had been a fool but he would make up for it, of that he was determined. He smiled, glad to be free from the horrors of the trenches, if only for a short while until they received their new orders from Colonel Hatchard who was no doubt safely ensconced in his headquarters well behind enemy lines.

Opening his eyes, he reread the paragraph about her first steps, laughing to himself as he imagined her attempts to totter across the nursery floor in Curzon Street and silently thanking Billy and Elizabeth for taking such good care of her. He read on and learned that Lady Henrietta had been posted to France after completing her nursing training with distinction, leaving just Molly and Mrs Castle and a housemaid to care for Lady Constance since Raymond had recently joined up and was in the middle of his basic training somewhere in the West Country.

When he had finished reading, he carefully folded it back into its envelope and opened the second letter, which was from Billy. This one was full of reassuringly good news of the business. It seemed that the war had been beneficial for trade so far as businesses and private individuals were stockpiling food in expectation of shortages. Rationing was now being threatened but prices were beginning to rise, which Billy thought might compensate for the rumoured restrictions on availability. To his surprise Max realised he had not given the business a moment's thought since joining the army, which only made him realise how fortunate he was to have Billy and Richie looking after things in his absence.

'You look pleased with yerself, Max, good news in yer letters was it?' asked Eddie as he returned from the cookhouse with two cups of cocoa.

'Oh ta,' said Max with a smile as Eddie handed him a cup, 'all's fine thanks. How about you?'

'Much the same as usual, Ma's still moaning about me joinin' up and me sister's pleased ter 'ave more room at 'ome with me not there, says me dad. It's nice ter feel wanted isn't it.'

They laughed, relishing the relative peace and tranquillity of the camp after the turmoil of the trenches.

''Ave yer seen Daily Orders?'

'No, why?'

'Briefing tonight at nineteen hundred hours, by Hatchard no less.'

'Hmm,' replied Max, 'that means something's brewing if you ask me. Come on, let's go and watch the boxing shall we?'

A makeshift ring had been set up in one corner of the field, alongside the woods, where boxing matches organised by the recreation committee were held three times a week between volunteers eager to prove their prowess. There was a small crowd of onlookers cheering on the two combatants as Max and Eddie strolled over to have a look.

'Go on, Mac!'

'Let 'im 'ave it, Frenchie!'

A loud groan went up as Lance-Corporal Mackenzie staggered against the ropes, caught by a glancing blow to the side of his chin.

'He's yers, Mac.'

'C'mon, man, get up!'

Max watched in amusement as Mac shook his head in bewilderment. He was a good foot taller and probably a stone heavier than his opponent, but he had not seen the punch coming. The smaller man was much lighter on his feet, ducking and diving around the ring as the section leader of 'B' Platoon tried to land a decisive blow.

'Hey, Cookie, yer dancin' like a bird. Yer'll never catch 'im, Mac.'

'Do you know who he is?' asked Max, turning towards Eddie who was in the process of cupping his hands around his mouth, intent on shouting louder than the others.

'Anton Duchamps ... or somethin' like that.'

'Who?' exclaimed Max.

'Anton Duchamps, one of the French liaison team seconded ter the regiment accordin' ter the Daily Orders board,' replied Eddie, shrugging his shoulders.

Max looked at Eddie and raised his eyebrows. Well, whoever he is, he can certainly box, thought Max as Lance-Corporal Mackenzie fell against the ropes before slumping to the floor, where he then remained. A loud cry went up as the referee held the Frenchman's arm aloft in triumph.

'Why are they calling him Cookie then?'

Eddie shrugged his shoulders. 'Dunno, but 'e'd be 'andy ter 'ave on our side in 'and ter 'and combat wouldn't 'e?' said Eddie as a few of the onlookers began to drift away whilst the next contestants climbed into the ring.

'He certainly would,' replied Max, for whom the prospect of watching two more men knock the living daylights out of each other was beginning to pall. 'I'm going to write some letters home, I'll see you in the mess tent later.'

Eddie turned and smiled quickly before turning back to the ring as the bell for Round One sounded and the loud shouts of encouragement began all over again. Max eased his way out through the ranks of spectators behind them and walked back across the field to the tents, already composing his letter to Molly as he did so. He had so much to tell her but at the same time he wanted to spare her the horrific details of life at the front. Settling comfortably on the grass in front of the tent, it took him two or three attempts to find the right words before he reached the end of the first page.

'Chambers!'

Max looked up with a start; he had not seen the Sergeant-Major approaching. Wilkins' imposing figure loomed above him.

'Sorry, sir, I didn't see you there,' he explained as he scrambled quickly to his feet, dropping his pen and paper in the process.

'The adjutant wants to see yer. Follow me.'

'Yes, sir, but...'

'Don't argue, lad, just follow me at the double.'

Max wondered what on earth he could have done to be summoned to see Captain Manvers. He did not have long to wait as they stopped outside the adjutant's tent.

'Stand to attention, Chambers, remain one pace behind me and only speak when yer spoken to, is that clear?'

'Yes, sergeant-major.'

The tent flap rose, as if by magic, and an orderly appeared. 'Captain Manvers will see you now.'

The two men marched in and halted in front of the captain's desk. Sergeant-Major Wilkins saluted. 'Private Chambers, 6893047, reporting as ordered, *sir*,' he barked in clipped tones.

Captain Manvers looked up from his pile of papers and regarded Max coolly. His boyish features were careworn, quite unlike the first time Max had seen the young adjutant standing in front of the volunteers in the station yard on their arrival in Scotland. He still displayed, however, the same nonchalant arrogance that Max so disliked. It was reminiscent of William Gordon.

'Thank you, sergeant-major. Well now, Chambers, the sergeant-major here has been watching you closely since our arrival at the front and tells me you have acquitted yourself particularly well.'

He looked back down at his desk and began to sign his name at the bottom of each piece of paper in front of him. They're probably letters home to grieving mothers, thought Max grimly, only half aware of what the captain was saying.

'As a result of which he has put your name forward for promotion to lance-corporal.'

Max was caught out by this unexpected turn of events and looked sharply at the sergeant-major, whose face was inscrutable. 'Eyes front, Chambers!' he bellowed.

'I am willing to accept his suggestion,' Manvers continued, without bothering to look up from his desk. 'I take it you will accept?'

There was silence as Max wondered what to say, although he did not imagine he had any choice.

'Well?' boomed Sergeant-Major Wilkins.

'Yes, sir!' answered Max promptly, 'thank you, sir.'

Captain Manvers glanced up and nodded curtly. 'You're the greengrocer from London aren't you, lance-corporal?' he asked without much interest. Max was about to correct him but thought better of it. 'There's someone I want you to meet and show around the place. You should have a lot in common.' He leant over to his right and looked at the orderly standing to attention inside the entrance to the tent. 'Stepson, see that Lance-Corporal Chambers finds that Frenchman ... whatshisname...?'

'Anton Duchamps, sir,' replied the orderly.

'Yes, well, whatever,' said Manvers impatiently. 'Damn waste of time if you ask me.'

'About turn, quick march, left, right, left, right.'

Chapter 50

They gathered around the piano in the village hostelry at the behest of the patron, who was proud to have the British fighting forces under his roof.

'Do you know "A Bicycle Built for Two"?' shouted Max in Anton's ear, trying to make himself heard above the din as Monsieur Bellevie played the first few notes.

Anton shook his head. 'Non, Max, but I will learn.' He laughed easily and raised his glass to his mouth, savouring the fiery liquor as he swallowed heavily. 'Another of your quaint English songs?'

Eddie squinted through the swathes of cigarette smoke swirling up from the overflowing ashtrays scattered along the top of the piano. 'Yer could call it that,' he laughed, 'just wait, "Alexander's Ragtime Band" is next, I 'eard Scottie ask fer that just now.'

They were enjoying a riotous evening in the little bar, which was nestled in a narrow side street just off the village square. Monsieur Bellevie had welcomed them with open arms as Max and his new section had peered in through the wide plate-glass window at the front. '*Entrez! Entrez!*' he had demanded from the doorway, and in no time at all they were seated around the well-scrubbed wooden tables with glasses of amber liquor being pressed into their hands before they could protest.

It had been Eddie's idea to venture into the village after Colonel Hatchard's briefing in order to celebrate Max's promotion and their forthcoming departure for the British base camp at Étaples. They were being sent there for a period of refresher training, after which they were to take up position along the Ypres salient, where they had been ordered to join the British, French and Canadian forces already stationed there. The briefing had been short and to the point, but the fact that it was delivered by the colonel himself signified the importance of their new orders. Anton and the other members of the French liaison team were to be attached to the regiment in preparation for the move.

'Hey, corp, or should I say lance-corp!' yelled Scottie mischievously from across the other side of the room, 'what did you have to do to persuade the adj. to give you a stripe then?'

The good-natured ribbing had persisted all evening and Max had relished every second of it. Their spirits were high and the few hours they had spent together in Monsieur Bellevie's bar had done wonders for their feeling of camaraderie. Anton's swarthy face was all smiles as he and Max edged away from the revelry around the piano and pulled two chairs up to a table near the window. His teeth, which were surprisingly white considering he rarely seemed to be without a cigarette hanging from the corner of his mouth, gleamed brightly against his dark skin, accentuated further by the mass of jet-black curls on top of his head, which he wore rather too long for Sergeant-Major Wilkins' liking.

He reached in to his tunic pocket and took out a small and well-worn leather pouch containing his tobacco and rolling papers. 'You know, Max, we are the only army in this war not to issue cigarettes and hence I have to do this all the time.' He revealed a thin packet of papers and a small quantity of sweet-smelling tobacco, which he held between nicotine-stained thumb and forefinger. '*Merde!*' he exclaimed sharply as he spilt some of the tobacco into his lap. 'We don't get enough to waste.'

'You can have my ration if you like, Anton, I don't smoke,' said Max with an amused expression on his face. 'They give us real coffin nails.' The Frenchman raised his eyebrows. 'Sorry, that's slang for cigarettes,' explained Max, 'I normally just give mine away to anybody who wants them.'

'Ah, I couldn't live without this ... what did you say ... this coffin nail?' said Anton triumphantly as he held up a fresh roll-up. 'So what do you do back home then, Max?' asked Anton, taking a deep draught of the cigarette.

'I buy and sell food, acting a bit like a middleman between the manufacturer and the consumer. We make some of the items ourselves, others we order in from other parts of the country, and from abroad, including France as it happens. We also have a fishing and butchery business in the south west of England, near where I was born.' He could see that he had Anton's attention. 'What about you, what do you do?'

'I am a chef. We have a restaurant in Paris so we are, as you might say, related.'

Max nodded and chuckled. 'Now I know why they were calling you 'Cookie' in the ring, and,' he continued quickly, 'why Manvers said we had something in common. What made you decide to be a chef?'

'It's what I've always wanted to do, ever since I can remember. My mama encouraged me to go off and learn my trade so I've travelled a fair bit too. I trained under the great Auguste Escoffier for a while at your Savoy Hotel in London.'

'I've eaten there,' said Max quietly, instantly recalling the lunch party he and Rosie had given in 1911 to celebrate the completion of the merger with Williams and Abel. God that seems like an age ago, he thought sadly to himself.

'What is it, Max, didn't you like the food?' asked Anton, noticing his pensive expression and the faraway look in his eyes.

'No, it wasn't that.' He cleared his throat. 'It's a long story, but not for tonight.' He signalled to the waiter. 'Let's have another drink and I want to hear all about your restaurant. It's something I've often thought about having. How many covers does it have...?'

They made it back to camp two minutes before curfew and awoke the following morning with the biggest hangovers imaginable.

'Not reveille already,' groaned Max through gritted teeth. 'My head's about to fall off.' He grimaced as he struggled to his feet, rubbing his shoulder to ease the stiffness in his joints.

'Mine just did,' grunted Eddie, who looked as white as a sheet. 'Oh hell, we've got ter pack up today. Why did yer make me do it, corp? A man with your responsibility should know better.'

It was a bright April day when Max brought his men to a halt in front of the forward camp where they were to rest for two days before moving up to the trenches. They felt curiously rejuvenated after their spell of refresher training in Étaples, and the team spirit amongst Max's section, born during the evening spent in Monsieur Bellevie's bar, had grown steadily as a result of the continuous exercising they had undergone. The many hours of instruction they had received in the art of hand to hand combat had indicated what the future might have in store for them and, now, days of steady marching had brought them to the eastern part of the Ypres salient, which was already heavily defended by one Canadian division and two British divisions. The Belgians were away to the north and two French divisions were covering the northern part of the salient itself. The Allied line followed the path of the canal around the town of Ypres and the Middlesex Regiment had been ordered to reinforce the British contingent.

The routine of camp life was second nature to them all after so many months at the front and the two days passed quickly. Max spent the spare hours ensuring his men checked their kit and rifles, cleaning and oiling them until they were in perfect order. Then he made them check everything over again. They practised fixing bayonets, trying to shave fractions of a second off the time each man took to do it; Max knew their lives might depend on speed and nobody complained. On the eve of their departure a calmness descended on the camp as most of them spent their last few hours of relative safety writing letters home, knowing that it might be their final opportunity to do so. Max wrote a long letter to Molly, reconfirming the arrangements he had made for Eleanor's future and that of the business and a slightly shorter one to Billy, mainly to do with the company. After these had been given to the orderly there was nothing left to do other than to snatch some sleep.

Max received orders to move his men up into the town of Ypres itself to assist with the forward movement of ammunition at zero seven hundred hours the following morning. There they spent a tense day waiting for the command to advance to the front line but, as the afternoon wore on, it became increasingly apparent that nothing would happen that day until, at seventeen hundred hours, the Germans unexpectedly opened up with a single shell from their Big Bertha gun, located away in the Houthulst Forest. This landed in the centre of the town and marked the beginning of the German offensive. It was quickly followed by a heavy bombardment from other long-range German howitzers and more shells from Big Bertha. At the same time clouds of chlorine gas were released from cylinders positioned along their front trenches towards the north of the salient, and the French troops, with no protection against the gas, retreated in panic. The Germans had caught them unawares and unprepared.

Max ran down the middle of Market Street at the head of his section as the shells rained down. 'Jesus! Watch out, lads,' he shouted, 'they're...'

His voice was drowned out by the sound of explosion after explosion as the Germans showered the road with artillery fire, creating a wall of shrapnel that obliterated everything in its path.

'Take cover!' yelled Max, gesticulating wildly to a group of civilians cowering by a clump of trees. 'Eddie, get them down into that ditch by the canal. Move! Now!' he ordered as his friend landed heavily on the ground beside him. 'Anton, go with him, quickly. The rest of you follow me,' he shouted, struggling to make himself heard above the frenzy.

He looked around as they ran towards the canal. The road was littered with dead and dying horses and splintered wagons. Terrified women and children were fleeing in confusion from their homes, making desperate attempts to reach the open fields surrounding the town. A group of screaming schoolchildren was being shepherded in that direction by their frantic teachers, who were trying pitifully to shield the youngsters from the maelstrom as they ran.

'Oh God no!' screamed Scottie, as a shell landed right beside them. When the smoke from the explosion cleared, all that was left was a gaping hole in the ground. He made to dash towards it. 'Sweet Jesus, the little sods couldn't 'ave been more than six or seven years old.'

'Leave it!' snapped Max, 'nothing can help them now.'

The shelling was ferocious in its intensity, striking people and animals indiscriminately, sending them hurtling through the air. Buildings were reduced to rubble from scores of direct hits, and terrified townsfolk were killed before they even had the chance to flee.

'Have you seen the lieutenant, Scottie?' asked Max suddenly. It must have been over 30 minutes since they had last seen him.

'Last I saw of him he was charging for the woods. Reckon he's safe in there somewhere.'

'Thank God. I thought he'd copped it,' replied Max as Eddie and Anton came tumbling down the slope towards them.

'No, don't think he did but I saw a number of our lads mown down like bloody ninepins. Poor bastards! A shell landed next to Jacko and blew him to smithereens and Archie caught it in the face and neck. Nothing left from the neck up.'

'Holy Christ!' swore Max savagely, 'Archie's got a young wife and newborn back home.' He closed his eyes and tried to shut out the chaos and destruction that raged all around him. In that moment he thought of Eleanor and Rosie and his heart bled for the young man's widow.

'Are yer all right, Max?' asked Eddie quickly.

Max wiped a grimy hand across his aching forehead. The futile barbarity of war struck him so forcibly that he thought he was going to be sick.

'Here, take it easy, my friend,' said Anton.

'I'm okay, just taking a breather for a second that's all.' He looked at them all. 'We've got to make for those woods over there,' he said, pointing into the distance. 'We can join up with the rest of the platoon on the other side of the trees, there's precious little ammunition left here to worry about now.' They looked at the devastated landscape ahead of them. 'All set then, lads? Right, follow me!'

They ran for their lives, into the eye of the inferno that raged on in its never ending hunger for more victims. The ground beneath them was blown asunder and scattered with the remains of soldiers and civilians felled by the cataclysmic storm of shells unleashed by the German guns. Men lay dead or dying on the ravaged earth and in the yawning shell holes but through this, caked in mud and splattered with blood from their fallen comrades, they made it to the outer fringes of the trees. There they collapsed, gasping, on the ground.

Max blinked rapidly and pushed back his helmet as he caught his breath, wiping the sweat from his eyes. 'Come on!' he urged, 'we're almost there.'

They scrambled to their feet again and half ran and half fell into the wood where they lay amongst the undergrowth, hidden from view, desperate for a respite, however brief, from the atrocious carnage, but with spirits undimmed and indomitable in their will to survive.

Suddenly Eddie grabbed Max's arm. 'Do yer notice something, Max?'

'No, what?'

'The bleedin' guns 'ave stopped.'

'Christ, so they have, Eddie.' Max sat up and peered through the trees. The only sounds he could hear were the distant explosions of munitions wagons caught by the artillery fire. 'This is our chance to rejoin the others, lads. The trenches must be the other side of these woods I reckon. Scottie, Anton, ready?' He looked knowingly at them and exchanged determined glances with Eddie as he got to his feet.

That was the last thing he remembered.

Chapter 51

The lucky ones lay on makeshift beds, others on the stretchers they had been carried in on. A few wandered about, dazed and disorientated. Some were so heavily bandaged that it was impossible to identify their features, and many cried out in pain. The suffering was intense.

Dusk was beginning to fall and Sister Fairchild, the sister in charge at the British Casualty Clearing Station, looked on in astonishment as Belgian civilians began to appear at the entrance to the tent with unusual and distressing symptoms, the like of which she had never seen before. One man came staggering in to be followed by a cartload of women and children. All of them had bleary red eyes and streaming noses and they were displaying all the signs of advanced pneumonia.

'Nurse, get these people to bed quickly. What on earth has happened to them?'

'Yes, sister,' replied Lady Henrietta, rushing forward to help the children who were cowering in misery behind the women's skirts.

'We need more space! Orderly, help me move these stretchers over there will you please, gently now,' barked Sister Fairchild, pointing to a row of casualties on her right. 'The children must be made comfortable first.'

More orderlies appeared and soon room was made for the new arrivals as doctors did their best to help them in the face of their baffling symptoms. Gradually it became clear from the halting and confusing gestures of the less seriously affected, who spoke only Flemish, that they were suffering from the effects of inhaling chlorine gas. Good God, thought Lady Henrietta in horror, as she took a little boy's hand and gently, but firmly, prised him away from the old lady he was clinging to, whatever depths of depravity will the Bosche sink to next!

'Stand aside! Stand aside!' came a cry from the entrance. 'Casualty arriving.'

Two nurses wearing bloodstained aprons turned to look as a man was carried in by two soldiers on a makeshift stretcher. Sister Fairchild took one glance at his bloodstained tunic and immediately gave instructions for him to be stripped and prepared for the doctors.

'Get me fresh water, cloths and more iodine. Quickly now! We need to stem the bleeding.'

The hospital tent was full to bursting point but still they came. The tally of the previous day's casualties exceeded 200, excluding the walking wounded, and so far today most of the nurses had been on their feet for 14 hours without a break. The odour in the operating room was terrible, what with the steam, the ether and the filthy clothes of the men, but the day was not over yet.

'Nurse Gordon, where is that iodine?'

In the midst of the mêlée the nurses concentrated on their tasks with grim determination, knowing that the soldiers' lives depended on them. The resilience of the hard-pressed doctors who worked quietly and systematically to remove the jagged pieces of shrapnel from the never ending stream of casualties, whilst the nurses sewed and tied and inserted drains, was pushed to the limits as the number of wounded threatened to overwhelm the station.

The sister ripped open the injured man's tunic and applied a thick wad of dressing to staunch the heavy flow of blood from the nasty wound to his right shoulder.

'Who brought this man in?' she asked without looking up.

She gently eased him on to his side to see if there was evidence of an exit wound and grimaced with relief when she saw the livid red gash on his back, just below his shoulder blade.

'The two soldiers are outside, sister, I can call them if you like,' said Lady Henrietta, appearing at her side with the iodine and a bowl of fresh water.

'Thank you, that won't be necessary,' she replied, 'there only appears to be one shrapnel wound to his right shoulder. He's one of the lucky ones. Clean him up and let the doctors know when he's ready for them please.'

'Very good, sis...' Lady Henrietta stopped in mid sentence and gasped audibly.

'Whatever is the matter, nurse?' exclaimed Sister Fairchild sharply.

Lady Henrietta was staring down at the man's face with an expression of amazement on her face. 'I know this man!' Even behind the thick layer of mud and filth, and with his eyes closed, she could see it was Max.

'Well, what of it?' demanded Sister Fairchild

These society girls really were the limit sometimes, she thought testily to herself, they seemed to know most of the soldiers on the Western

Front, although she had to admit that Lady Henrietta was not like most of them and she was a damn good nurse.

'Nothing, sister,' replied Henrietta quickly. 'I was just surprised that's all.'

'Well he's not in officer's uniform,' commented Sister Fairchild dryly before turning away to deal with the next group of arrivals.

Lady Henrietta bent over Max and gently began to wash around the edges of the gaping wound. 'Max, Max, can you hear me?' she asked quietly. 'It's Henrietta Gordon.' There was no reply. 'This might sting a little,' she said as she poured some iodine on to a cloth and began to apply it.

Max started as the burning sensation took hold and he opened his eyes. *Where was he? What was happening? Where were the others?* He immediately became conscious of the searing pain in his right shoulder and he winced involuntarily.

'It will hurt a little,' said the voice, 'but it will help.'

His eyelids fluttered briefly before they closed again and he drifted back into unconsciousness.

'This one's ready for surgery,' said Lady Henrietta to an orderly, 'can you place him in the line please but be careful of his shoulder.'

She indicated the row of stretchers lined up at the entrance to the operating room and then she moved on to the next man who was lying on the ground beside Max, groaning loudly, his leg a mass of soiled and bloody bandages.

Two days later Max woke up in the hospital tent alongside the Clearing Station where the recovering wounded were held until they were well enough to either return to the front line or to be sent home for a longer period of convalescence. His shoulder was heavily bandaged and his right arm was strapped tightly against his chest and his head ached badly. He lay still for a long time, trying to recall what had happened to him but his mind was a blank. He tried to sit up but the pain was too great.

'I see you're back with us, corporal,' said the young nurse on duty. 'How are you feeling?'

Max struggled to think clearly but his mind was muddled. 'Where am I? What happened?'

She smiled down at him, her youthful features a mixture of compassion and weariness. 'You're in hospital in the British sector. You've got a nasty shrapnel wound to your right shoulder, but you'll be as right as rain in no time.' She looked at her chart. 'Lance-Corporal Chambers isn't it?'

Max nodded, which sent a bolt of pain shooting through his head. He closed his eyes until it had passed and then asked, 'How did I get here?'

The nurse adjusted the thin blanket covering his bed. 'I don't know I'm afraid. You were brought to the Clearing Station next door where the doctors fixed your shoulder and then you were transferred in here. That was ... let me see ... two days ago.'

'What about the others ... the rest of my section?'

She smiled and put her chart down. 'Now that's enough questions for now. You must rest. I'll get you something to eat and drink in a little while.' She tucked the edges of the blanket more securely around him. 'Try and get some sleep.'

It was late afternoon when Max woke for the second time to find a different nurse on duty, who tried to persuade him to have some food. He felt as if he was waking from a dream as he attempted to piece together what had happened but he kept encountering large voids in his memory. He needed to talk to someone who could help him and he was desperate for news of the others.

'The doctor will be round when he can, Corporal Chambers. Maybe you'll find out more then,' soothed the nurse when Max asked the same questions again. 'I'm afraid I don't know any more than you've already been told.'

It was very frustrating and the doctor was of little help, other than to confirm that it was likely he would be repatriated home for a period of several weeks before he would be declared fit to return to the front, unless a temporary staff posting could be found for him behind the lines. It would all depend on the speed of his recovery, and meanwhile it was anticipated that it would be two or three weeks before he was well enough to leave the hospital. Max's feelings at learning this were mixed; he was delighted with the prospect of perhaps seeing Eleanor and Molly and to know he would be free of danger for a while, but at the same time he was reluctant to leave his men behind, particularly Eddie and Anton. He had grown close to the Frenchman in a short space of time, partly on account of their shared interests.

He was lying in bed on his left side to ease the discomfort on his injured shoulder, mulling over what the doctor had said, when he heard a quiet voice behind him saying, 'Max ... Max ... I've just looked in to see how you are. I imagine you're surprised to see me...'

That was an understatement. The voice was familiar but he could not quite place it as he turned over as quickly as his bandages would allow to find himself looking up at the smiling face of Lady Henrietta Gordon. He was lost for words.

'Of all the places to meet again,' Henrietta began. 'It's hardly Lee Moor or Plymouth is it?' The corners of her mouth twitched as she broke into a smile, which was warm and genuine in its friendliness.

Max's mind raced as he searched for a response. The years had been kind to her and even in the midst of these truly dreadful conditions she still carried herself well. The combination of her commanding presence and natural sensitivity and gentleness that Max remembered was much in evidence as she stood at the side of his bed whilst he slowly eased himself up against the pillows. She reached down to straighten them for him.

'Can you manage, Max? Let me help you.'

Max smiled at her and noticed the flecks of grey in her black hair. The last time he had seen her it was long and luxuriant, swept up in a fashionable style, but now it was cut much shorter and held in place by her uniform cap. She smiled back, and her smile was reflected in the brightness of her hazel-brown eyes. She was still a striking figure.

'All part of my duties,' she explained softly.

'And gratefully accepted,' said Max, 'Lady Hen...'

'Henrietta will do, Max, or even nurse. Anything but "Lady" thank you!'

Max chuckled, trying not to make the pain in his shoulder any worse. 'Very well then, Henrietta,' he replied. 'You're right; I certainly didn't expect to see you here!'

'No, I don't imagine you did,' she said. 'The same goes for me too. Actually I'm based in the Clearing Station so I saw you come in.'

Max immediately pricked up his ears. 'So you know what happened then? How did I get here? What happened to my men? Nobody seems to know.'

'You always did look out for everyone else didn't you, Max,' she observed gently. 'Two soldiers brought you in. I don't know their names. I'm sorry.'

'Did you see them though?' he asked anxiously.

'Well I didn't speak to them if that's what you mean, but yes, I saw them. One looked very young and the other had the curliest of dark hair.'

Max smiled.

'Two of your comrades?'

'Yes, I think so,' said Max, feeling much happier already. They must still be alive, he thought gladly, or, at least, they were then. 'I had heard you were a nurse, although I thought you had been posted to France.'

'I was initially, but I arrived here three weeks ago. You're very well informed I must say!' She sounded impressed, but not surprised. 'I suppose Mrs Chambers keeps you informed?'

'Yes, it was Molly who told me,' Max confessed.

Lady Henrietta had always known their housekeeper kept him abreast of her family's news. 'Mama would be lost without her,' she smiled. 'We all would.'

There was a moment's silence, almost an awkwardness between them, and then they both started to speak at the same time. 'Sorry. Please carry on,' said Max quickly.

Henrietta chuckled. 'I was just going to say that I have to get back but I just wanted to pop in and see that you were all right.'

'Thank you. I'll be as right as rain in a couple of weeks,' replied Max determinedly.

'I think it might take a little longer than that,' commented Henrietta slowly. 'I could look in again tomorrow...'

Max smiled and was surprised at how pleased he felt to hear her say that. 'Yes please, if you can spare the time. I'd like that.'

Chapter 52

Max began to look forward to Lady Henrietta's daily visits, which she managed to fit in between her long periods of duty. At first their conversation was peppered with slightly awkward pauses; it was almost as if they would suddenly become conscious of their circumstances and history, which inhibited the natural flow of conversation. They confined themselves to topics that were safe and neutral to begin with and so they talked of Max's condition and his recovery, about the war and their own experiences of it, about the people they had met whilst on active service and about the great resilience of the civilian people caught up in the barbarity. But gradually the more they chatted, the more they relaxed in each other's company, and by the end of Max's first week in hospital, the conversation flowed easily and they had moved on to more personal subjects.

'Mama tells me you have a baby daughter, Max?' said Henrietta. She had just finished a 15-hour stint with Sister Fairchild and felt exhausted, but her sense of duty would not allow her to go back to her damp and miserable quarters without first seeing Max and, besides, like him, she had begun to look forward to their daily chats.

'Yes I have,' said Max with a beaming smile. He was feeling a lot better and was sitting up in bed, having just had his dressings changed. 'We named her Eleanor; she's almost fifteen months old, which I find hard to believe! My last letter from home told me she's walking now, apparently there's no stopping her.'

Henrietta laughed, her eyes twinkling with amusement. 'I expect she's quite a handful, they usually are at that age I gather. She is certainly the apple of her grandmother's eye, I know that. Mama and your mother are always talking about her you know.' A wistful look crossed her face as she said that, which she could not hide. Max was quick to notice it.

'You never had children, did you?' he said, slightly hesitantly.

Goodness me, realised Henrietta suddenly, he thinks I'm disappointed about not having children! If only she could tell him the real reason for her melancholic expression. She was annoyed with herself for allowing him to see it, however fleetingly.

'No I didn't,' she sighed, 'it obviously wasn't meant to be. I would have liked them but...'

Her voice trailed off as she thought about James. He would have made a good father, she was certain of that. After all these years she still thought often of the man she had loved with all her heart, whose life had been ended so cruelly by a bomb on a railway line many thousands of miles from home. Her memories now were always happy ones because that first savage onslaught of grief, so raw that life did not feel worth living, when even the simplest of human tasks seemed impossible, had subsided a long time ago, to be replaced by a sad acceptance of her loneliness.

'You're so blessed to have brought a child into this world you know.'

Max nodded and looked closely at her. He sensed there was something she was holding back. He was usually a good judge of character but this last week had made him think he might have misunderstood Lady Henrietta and judged her too harshly. She was capable of an amazing power of expression, both in her face and in her whole being, and he knew that something was troubling her. He now realised that she had great generosity of spirit and behind the composed and self-assured façade, if you looked carefully enough for it, he recognised a rare softness and sincerity.

'I was sorry to hear about your wife, Max,' she said quietly, 'I feel guilty that I didn't get in touch when ... when she died. Forgive me, I should have done.'

Max was silent for a moment. 'Do you remember your wedding present to us? Those bottles of Krug?'

'Of course. It wasn't anything really.'

'Oh but it was. It was a great deal actually.' He laughed ruminatively. 'You know Rosie was worried about how I was going to react when I found out they were from you. So was Molly come to that.'

Henrietta smiled. 'And how did you?'

'Very well as I remember. In fact, looking back, it was probably the first time I wondered whether I might have misjudged you, you know.'

'Really?' said Henrietta tartly, but with a grin. 'And had you?'

'Possibly...' replied Max, deliberately and slowly, 'just possibly...' Then he laughed loudly, causing those around them to look over in their direction. 'I'm beginning to think I might have done.'

'Well, thank you,' she said, laughing too, 'we're not that bad you know.'

'Except for your brother!' said Max intensely and without thinking, but to his surprise, and interest, Henrietta did not disagree.

'You won't find me defending *him!*' she said bitterly. 'He is no brother of mine to have behaved in the way he has.' And for practically all of his life too, she added silently to herself. She had to stop herself from telling Max there and then, but it was neither the time nor the place, it was not fair and she had promised her mother that she would never betray the family; not like William! 'I just hope he gets his just rewards one day.' She could be imperious when she tried and the look on her face when she spoke of him would have sent shivers down a man's spine. As well as inheriting her father's strength of character, she had also inherited his temper, which was quick to erupt, but then equally quick to subside.

'Your intended died too, didn't he?' asked Max, hastily changing the subject.

'Yes ... yes he did. He was a soldier in the Boer War; he was killed in the siege of Ladysmith.' She smiled then, rather pensively. 'The pain never goes but you do learn to accept it, in time. I have only happy memories of James.'

Max nodded. 'As I do of Rosie...' He shifted his weight slightly in the bed to ease the ache in his shoulder.

'He was a ladies' man and he loved female attention and I know there were girlfriends before me, but he was very discreet about them. I never minded. I always knew I was the one he loved, right from the start.' She cleared her throat, 'It hasn't been very long for you, has it?'

'No ... no, it hasn't, but it seems like a lifetime.' He stared into space. 'But I have Eleanor and I thank God for that.'

'Tell me about Rosie, Max, I'd really like to know ... that is, if you want to.'

It was not often that anybody asked him to talk about Rosie any more and he welcomed the opportunity to do so. He laughed softly. 'It is bizarre isn't it, you and me I mean, having this conversation! Whatever would your mama say?'

Henrietta laughed back. If only I could tell him, she thought sadly, he has a right to know. For goodness sake, they might both be dead soon and then the truth would go to the grave and it would be too late.

'If I tell you that Rosie was my life and when she died I really did not want to go on living, it might put things into perspective for you. All that I've done, the business, everything, was to build a better life for us and without her it didn't seem worth it, not for a long time afterwards. But since I've been out here I've realised that the future

309

matters, it matters just as much as it did before, which is a bit odd in a way.'

'You know I always thought you've achieved what you have to spite us in some way, as if you felt we were responsible for your lot in life.'

Max looked slightly embarrassed. 'It was in a way, at least to start with. I used to look at my parents and think their lives were totally subservient to your family, without any prospect of freedom for themselves at all. Maybe that was too simple a view, I understand that now. But certainly I did not want that life for myself and I was determined to change it for the better.'

'You've managed to do that, haven't you, and I'm pleased for you. This war is changing everything you know, the old order as Mama describes it. What do you think is the secret of your success?'

'Determination, a bit of good luck and surrounding myself with the right people. I put it down to that.'

'Well, you certainly did that with Jim Edwardes. His resignation from the mine made William furious you know!' she chuckled.

'I know. He confronted me about Jim in my office, did you know that?'

'No, I did not. The fool! It served him right and I hope you told him so. He treated the man appallingly. Jim, and his father before him, had served our family loyally for years and William's behaviour towards him was a disgrace, as it has been to so many people.' Including your family, she said to herself. Her temper was clearly rising and she was doing her best to keep her voice down so as not to disturb the other patients.

'Where is he now?' asked Max. He had not thought much about William Gordon since Rosie's death but their conversation was reawakening those old, familiar feelings of enmity.

'We don't talk very much, Max, but I gather he has a cushy staff appointment with his old regiment.'

'That follows,' said Max caustically.

'He was in London the last time I heard. I don't go to Chesterfield Square any more and Mama is getting too old. I stay in hotels or with friends whenever I'm in town. I do miss the old house though, I have to admit.'

'I supply foodstuffs to you there actually, or did when I last checked.'

'I know.'

Max smiled. 'You know? I'm surprised about that to tell you the truth.'

'Well believe it or not, Papa and Mama were actually rather proud of the fact that they had an account with your company.'

Max looked quizzically at her but this time her expression was impassive.

'Although I suspect William doesn't know or he would cancel the account immediately,' said Henrietta.

'Why did he always hate me so much? I have never understood that, although God knows he's given me enough reason to hate *him*! Right from when I was a small child at Mount Royal I can remember him being nasty towards me.' Max could still recall the incident in the kitchen garden and he subconsciously ran a finger of his left hand over the small scar on his face.

'It's complicated,' said Henrietta uncomfortably, looking down at her lap, 'and it's all in the past. Besides, you have your own daughter now,' she said, changing the subject, 'she's a lucky girl, Max, and you must cherish her.'

'Yes I know and I do,' said Max softly, 'she is my future now.'

'And you might meet somebody else. You can never tell. It hasn't happened for me and I imagine that is the last thing on your mind, but time does heal in many ways, believe me...' She paused. 'You know, Max,' she said firmly, 'it is better to have loved and lost than never to have loved at all.'

Max looked at her and thought how unexpected life could be. He would never have believed that he would be having this sort of conversation, or any conversation for that matter, with Lady Henrietta Gordon and, moreover, listening to and valuing what she had to say.

He nodded slowly. 'I guess you're right, Henrietta. There must be a reason for what has happened, although for the life of me I can't think what it is.'

'Are you a religious man, Max?'

'No, not really. I don't know how I can be with all that's happened. I mean, why would God have taken Rosie from us, with all of her life ahead of her? Leaving a child without her mother? It just doesn't make any sense to me. And then there's this war. Thousands ... probably millions of innocent people being killed, and for what? Look at those Belgian civilians in the hospital, the ones you were telling me about, women and children gassed, in the most awful state. No, I don't believe in God.'

Henrietta was silent for a moment. She had the quick-witted intelligence of her father and she remembered Max as a good-looking, invigorating and confident young man who laughed a lot and enjoyed life, and who brought a single-minded determination and spirit to everything he did. No wonder Rosie fell for his charms. She thought of her Mama, and what she would think of him now. So much had changed.

'You know, Max, it's difficult to argue with what you say but I still believe in Him, despite everything. I suppose it's a matter of conviction that can't be thought of in terms of logic or common sense. He will prevail, however hopeless things may seem at the time. That's what I believe.'

Max shrugged his shoulders and then grimaced. For a moment he had forgotten his wound, in fact he had been so engrossed in their conversation that he had almost forgotten where they were. A look of sharp pain crossed his face.

'Are you all right?' asked Henrietta quickly. 'Here, let me have a look.' She made to stand up but Max gently held up his hand. 'I'm fine, really. I wasn't thinking, that's all.' He smiled at her to show her that he meant it and she smiled back, holding his gaze for a moment or two.

Mama would be very proud of him, as would Papa, she thought, and she ached to tell him.

Chapter 53

The banner across the top of the door read 'Welcome back, Mr C.' and Max had to duck to avoid it as he came in from the yard. The office staff were waiting to greet him at the top of the stairs just as the warehousemen and drivers had been five minutes earlier when the Rolls had pulled in through the heavy black gates.

'This is all your doing, Billy, you know how much I hate a fuss!' exclaimed Max, grinning broadly from ear to ear. It was good to be home; he felt invigorated and excited by the prospect of being back in the business and he had been bursting to ask Billy question after question on the drive from Curzon Street. His shoulder was much better and he had four weeks of uninterrupted leave ahead of him before he had to report back for duty. He was staying with Billy and Elizabeth at their invitation instead of opening up the house in Gloucester Street. 'It would mean less disruption for Eleanor,' suggested Elizabeth when he had telephoned them on arriving back from France, 'and we won't take "no" for an answer!' Besides which, Mrs Walsh was visiting her sick mother in Clacton and Violet and Mary were busy with their war work. 'There!' Elizabeth had pronounced triumphantly when Max had admitted that, 'It's easier all round.'

The second week of his recuperation in the hospital in Ypres had passed quickly. He had been delighted to see Eddie and Anton who managed to visit him two days before he was discharged for the journey back home. They explained what had happened because his memory was still blank. He had been shot by a German sniper who was part of a reconnaissance party hiding in the woods behind the British lines. A brief but fierce gun battle had ensued, which resulted in the Germans being captured without, miraculously, further casualties amongst Max's section. The three of them had spent a particularly happy hour together until it was time for Eddie and Anton to return to camp, parting with cries of 'Yer lucky sod' and 'See yer in a few weeks time', but each man knew they might never see one another again. Four weeks was an eternity at the front.

Lady Henrietta had continued to visit him on a daily basis, and in the midst of all the suffering and misery they had forged a genuine bond of friendship that was born out of their present circumstances and cemented by their shared but disparate backgrounds. On her last visit they had promised to get in touch after the war unless fate threw them together in the meantime.

'Can we have coffee in ten minutes in the boardroom please, Jenny?' asked Billy after the greetings were over and everyone had returned to their desks.

'Yes of course, Mr Masters,' said Jenny beaming with delight at seeing Max again. 'It is so good to have you back, Mr Chambers.'

'Thank you, Jenny, it's good to be back. I'm pleased to see you've kept Mr Masters here in order whilst I've been away.'

Jenny laughed and a faint blush rose to her cheeks.

The boardroom of Chambers & Co was a modest and businesslike room, very much in keeping with Max's approach to life. There was a complete absence of ostentation; visitors to the room would have been completely unaware that it represented the hub of a hugely profitable organisation spanning the length and breadth of the country. The company's half year accounts, just published, showed an interim net profit of £213,000 which was an excellent outcome considering the restrictions of war. The fishing fleets were doing especially well in compensating for a decline in the availability and demand for their fine foods, whilst, thanks to Billy's foresight, their temporary range of patriotic staples such as eggs, flour and home-grown vegetables were helping to support the figures. Recent contracts won to supply the Royal Navy and the army would also deliver benefits in the second half of the year.

An oval conference table stood in the centre of the room and this morning all the chairs around it were occupied apart from two empty ones positioned opposite each other in the middle of each side. All the faces Max expected to see were there – Jim Edwardes and Rebecca Florey, as she was now known since her marriage, were deep in conversation, Richie was glancing through a list of figures on the ink blotter in front of him and Patrick Jamieson and Charlie Warwick, who were in charge of purchasing and sales respectively, were sharing a joke together – and there was also one man he had yet to meet. Winston Griffiths had recently joined the board to take charge of their newly formed operations in Scotland. Max had heard much about him from Billy over dinner in Curzon Street the previous evening.

'Good morning, everyone, and thank you for coming,' said Billy from the doorway as everyone turned to look in their direction. A murmur of reply rumbled cheerily around the table. 'Shall we make a start straightaway as we have a lot to get through?' he added once they were settled in their seats. 'The purpose of this meeting is to brief Max on the current state of the company and our prospects for the remainder of the year. Jim, would you like to begin?' He nodded in a no-nonsense manner as Jim Edwardes cleared his throat and shuffled the papers in front of him.

'Good morning and welcome back, Max,' he began. Max looked at him and smiled with pleasure. 'I am pleased to report a buoyant half year overall with net profits ahead of the same period last year. This can be attributed...'

The presentations from each director were fulsome and encouraging. In summing up as the clock struck midday, Billy was able to confirm that the business was in robust health and looking forward with confidence to the remainder of the year. There were some clouds on the horizon, not least of which was a looming shortage of delivery drivers and warehousemen because of the increasing numbers of men who were joining up for war service, but that situation was being kept under close review.

'Well, there we are then, Max, that's about it I think,' said Billy, smiling at Max across the table, 'I believe you have something you wish to say...?'

Max nodded and looked around the table as all eyes turned in his direction. 'Yes I do and thank you, Billy. I must firstly thank you all for your enlightening and thorough reports, which leave me feeling very reassured about the future. It is a great relief for me to know that the company is in such capable hands during my absence and I thank you all for that. I have nothing to ask, or indeed to add, to what you have already told me in your impressive reviews so instead I would like to look ahead, to our future after the war is over. People are saying the world will be a better place when the enemy is defeated. Now I don't know whether that is true or not, but I do believe that people will want to enjoy their lives once again, only this time there will be opportunities for many more to do so as the society we have known changes. I am certain that this will bring us even greater opportunity than we have enjoyed so far and we must make sure the company is positioned to take advantage of it.

'We must continue to maximise our existing businesses and actively seek to increase our market share by investing in new equipment and products to keep us ahead of the competition, but I want us also to enter new markets; I want us to establish a number of restaurants that will enable us to showcase our wares in the high street. We must sell to customers at every stage of our supply chain, from private individuals, through to independent restaurants, public houses and hotels, as we do now, but then we must broaden our horizons to include the end customer, the men or the women in the street who will come into *our* restaurants.'

He paused to gaze around the table, pleased to note that he had their rapt attention. Billy was smiling quietly to himself. The two of them had discussed the idea long into the night and they had concluded that it was a good next step for the business to take, but they knew they would have to be patient until the war was over.

In fact the war news was not good. Britain and her Allies were losing thousands upon thousands of men, all of them slaughtered in the mud and gore of the trenches and the prospect of victory seemed remote, perhaps even impossible to contemplate. Speculation was growing about the introduction of compulsory military service for all single men and some of the papers were even suggesting that it might not end there. However, despite this grim news, Max and Billy had agreed that they should announce the idea at the board meeting, hoping that by so doing they would promote a feeling of confidence and optimism in their future.

The silence around the table was broken by Richie who was the first to ask a question and then everyone began to talk at once. Max held up his hand for order and then proceeded to answer each one in turn. By the time he had finished there was a palpable air of excitement and enthusiasm in the room and he had been persuaded that preliminary searches for suitable premises should begin with the objective of securing their first location in London by the end of 1916, although he was adamant that anything more must wait until the end of hostilities. This now left only one item on the agenda, which Billy had asked him to handle, even though it concerned Billy himself.

'Moving then to the last item on the agenda, I have been asked by Billy to announce that he will be stepping down temporarily as managing director to enable him to enlist in His Majesty's Royal Naval Reserve, and Richie will be stepping up into his role for the duration of his absence.'

Surprised expressions and exclamations greeted Max's pronouncement, as he knew they would, because Billy had been careful to keep his plans confidential until he had discussed them fully with Max and Richie. He had been agonising over this decision for weeks, trying to reconcile his conflicting emotions. Elizabeth was supportive but desperately worried; she knew he had to do what he felt was right and reluctantly understood why he saw it as his duty. He had chosen the Royal Naval Reserve because of his background in the fishing industry; his familiarity with the sea was eagerly seized upon by the recruiting commander, even though memories of his brother's death still haunted him. It would be safer than the trenches, he had reasoned with Elizabeth in an unsuccessful attempt to reassure her but it was the likelihood of compulsory conscription that had finally tipped the balance and convinced him that the time to do it was now.

He had told Max of his decision the previous night and suggested that Richie should assume responsibility for the company. He had been declared medically unfit by the recruiting office on account of poor eyesight and was therefore unable to join any of the services, much to his disgust. Max had been quick to accept both Billy's decision and suggestion and congratulated him at once, but it was with mixed emotions that he made the announcement to the board. In many ways he had been expecting it ever since he had enlisted himself and he certainly was not about to raise any objections, but inevitably he was worried for his best friend's safety.

Later that afternoon, back in Curzon Street, the two men spent a subdued hour playing with Eleanor and Alexander in the nursery. Max was leaving for Lee Moor with Eleanor to visit Molly the following morning and Billy was due to report for duty at the end of the week. They were outwardly cheerful and happily engaged with the children but they each suspected they knew what the other was thinking; in the same way that Max had parted from Eddie and Anton in the hospital in Ypres, they both wondered whether this might be the last time they saw one another alive. The casualties on the Western Front were truly calamitous but the war at sea was just as hazardous, especially as Billy, with his fisherman's background, was likely to be drafted to a minesweeper where mortality rates were much higher than in other warships.

Elizabeth had looked in on them, watching quietly from the door for a few moments without disturbing them, and even Nurse Andrews had discreetly vanished, finding something she needed to do in the night nursery, so it was just the two of them and the children.

317

'You know, Max,' said Billy reflectively, 'you can never foresee the future can you?'

'That's true enough,' replied Max with a grin, trying to be cheerful. 'No flies on you are there!'

Billy chuckled briefly. 'No, I just meant that I wonder where we'll be in another year's time. When I think back to this time last year...'

Max nodded. 'Yes, I know,' he said quietly, 'but you have to have faith, faith in the future. I suppose I've learnt that since Rosie died and you know, despite everything, I do. I did lose all faith for a while but in an odd way the war has allowed me to discover it again. It's hard to explain, considering all the horror and destruction I've witnessed, but my belief in the future is as strong as it ever was, if not stronger. I think it's partly because of this one here.' He smiled lovingly at Eleanor who was sitting next to him amidst a pile of colourful wooden building blocks. 'There has to be hope and better things to come for these two.'

Billy looked thoughtful. 'I hope you're right, Max. I've made you my trustee. I hope you don't mind. You and Andrew Latchmere. I asked Andrew too because ... well, you know ... just in case.' He looked across as Alexander tugged at his sleeve. 'My capital is in trust for Alexander but I want you to look after it for him, with full powers.'

Max caught his eye. 'I'd be honoured to, Billy,' was all he could bring himself to say as a lump formed in his throat.

'Elizabeth is well provided for of course and she would have my share of our annual profits for the remainder of her life but I want to make sure their futures are secured and in good hands. There is no one else I would trust.'

'But you will come back safely, Billy, you must tell yourself that. And just think of the future! There is Elizabeth and this little terror,' he said, leaning over to tickle Alexander, which made the little boy giggle delightedly, 'with perhaps a brother or sister for him, or maybe both!'

'And for you too, Max, you never know?' He said it carefully, as if he was testing an idea for the first time without being entirely sure of the outcome.

'I don't know,' replied Max steadily, 'we'll just have to see I suppose.' He took a breath before continuing. 'We've got so much to do with the business as well. There'll be some rebuilding to see to I'm sure and then there'll be the restaurants to open.'

'I hope so,' said Billy with feeling, 'I do hope so.'

Chapter 54

The village looked exactly the same as it had when he was last there. It never changed. On the journey down the previous day he had been trying to work out when he had last visited and he realised, to his surprise, he had not been back to Lee Moor for six years. In fact it was six years and two months almost to the day since his father's funeral and it still felt as if it was yesterday.

'Come on, darling, shall we go for a walk?' asked Molly. 'We might see some ducks so we'd better take some bread.' Eleanor looked up at her grandmother with her big blue eyes fixed on Molly's smiling face.

Max laughed. 'One of these days she'll answer you, Ma.'

'I can't wait,' replied Molly, 'she gets more beautiful every time I see 'er. I thought we'd stop at the grocery shop ter see if we can get some sweets. Will that be all right luv? I expect it'll be Ed serving today, 'e's engaged now yer know, ter the vicar's daughter no less. 'E seems ter 'ave taken over from 'is dad nowadays.'

'Yes that'll be lovely, Ma, Eleanor would like that.'

'I'll just run upstairs an' get 'er 'at an' coat, it can still be a bit chilly out this time of year. It'll give yer chance ter rest.'

'I'm fine, Ma,' he protested, 'I'm just a bit stiff now that's all. Another week or so and I'll be as right as rain.'

It was true. Max's wound had healed well and even the stiffness the doctor had told him to expect was lessening as each day passed. Being back in England was doing him the power of good although he could not help but wonder about the friends he had left behind in Belgium.

Max smiled to himself. He could only imagine how much Molly had been looking forward to their visit and her joy at seeing them was written all over her face. He looked around the parlour; it felt rather strange to be back in Fern Cottage. It seemed so small after the lofty spaciousness of Gloucester Street and, although it no longer felt like home, it was still the scene of so many of his happy childhood memories. It was also where he had proposed to Rosie on his return from his very first trip to Plymouth.

Molly interrupted his train of thought. 'We're off then, luv, shan't be long. Put the kettle on an' we'll 'ave some tea when we get back.'

'Actually I thought I'd pop along to The Wheelwrights when they open to see Daisy and Jack, so if I'm not here when you get back that's where I'll be. Why don't you come and join us?'

'What, an' bring Eleanor!' exclaimed Molly. 'A pub is no place fer a child.'

'Oh, Ma!' smiled Max, 'she'll be perfectly all right. Daisy will spoil her rotten!'

'Well I don't know,' said Molly dubiously, 'we'll see.'

After they had left, Max went upstairs to his old room to unpack Eleanor's things. Nurse Andrews had given him a list of what he had to do. 'It's the first time on your own with her, Mr Chambers, so you'll be needing this,' she had said firmly as she thrust two sheets of paper into his hand before he left London. The bag containing Eleanor's clothes was still on the white washstand in the corner of the room where he had left it the night before, with the papers sticking out of the top of it. Nurse Andrews' small and very neat handwriting filled both sides of each sheet from top to bottom and left nothing to chance.

As he took them out of the bag he heard footsteps outside and, imagining Molly must have forgotten something, he looked out of the bedroom window as he reached over to open it to ask what they wanted. However, to his surprise he saw the unmistakable figure of Mrs Castle receding down the front path and through the garden gate. He quickly undid the latch and leant out but he was too late, she was already disappearing along the lane.

He was disappointed to have missed her; she was one of the people he wanted to see above all others before he went back to London. Oh well, perhaps she thought there was no one at home, he said to himself with a shrug as he sat down on the bed to read Nurse Andrews' instructions. When he had finished, his mind was reeling and he realised how much he still had to learn about his daughter. The comprehensive lists contained, amongst many other things, precise details of the food Eleanor liked to eat, how long she should sleep in the afternoons and which were her favourite toys from amongst the small selection he had brought with him.

He saw the envelope lying on the front doormat as soon as he came back downstairs. It had landed address side up when Mrs Castle had pushed it through the letter-box and he could clearly see his name on it from where he was standing. He tore it open with a mystified expression

320

on his face, which deepened further as he read the contents. He had been invited to Bickleigh Manor for tea with the Dowager Countess at three o'clock that afternoon and she hoped he would be able to accept.

Max was intrigued. Suddenly, in the space of a few short weeks, he felt as if his life was becoming more entwined with the Gordon family than ever before. It was not something he had ever expected, much less sought, and he did not understand the reasons for it. He thought it odd that Molly had not mentioned anything to him and he was still pondering this when she and Eleanor returned from their walk.

'We 'ad a lovely time, didn't we, darling?' said Molly, brimming over with energy, 'although we couldn't find any ducks.' She bustled away to the tiny larder to put the bread back; she could not abide waste. 'You didn't go ter The Wheelwrights yet then, luv?' she called from the kitchen.

Max did not answer straightaway and Molly poked her head around the kitchen door. 'What's the matter, luv?' she asked, noticing Max's thoughtful expression.

'Mrs Castle called when you were out, Ma.'

'Oh, what did she want?'

'I didn't get to speak to her. I was upstairs but she delivered this.' He held up the Countess's letter as Molly came back into the room. She recognised the writing paper immediately.

'That's 'er Ladyship's paper,' said Molly with surprise. 'Whatever does she want, writing ter me 'ere?'

'It was addressed to me, Ma. I'm invited for tea this afternoon!'

'Yer what!' she blurted out. 'Whatever for?' She felt a sinking feeling in the pit of her stomach.

'I really don't know.'

'Are yer goin'?' asked Molly.

Her legs began to tremble. She thought she could probably guess what it was about and she hoped she was wrong. The Countess had become increasingly preoccupied with the past since war had broken out, and during recent conversations had spoken of the need to settle old issues before it was too late.

'I suppose it's the only way I'm going to find out what's behind it. I thought you might have some idea, Ma?'

Molly shook her head. 'No, no, not really,' she replied quickly. 'She 'as been a bit preoccupied of late though, I will say that.'

Max looked at his mother. There's something she's not telling me, he thought to himself, but he decided not to press her further. He would know soon enough. 'I haven't told you that I came across Lady Henrietta when I was in the hospital, have I?'

Molly shook her head again. 'No, luv, 'ow was that then?' she asked in surprise.

'She's stationed in the Clearing Centre, which is where all the casualties are taken to begin with and she saw me there. I must have been out of it because I didn't realise it was her, but after I was moved into the hospital tent she came in to visit me.'

'That must 'ave been a shock! Talk about coincidences. I knew she was a nurse, and a good one at that, but 'er Ladyship never told me exactly where she was.'

'Well that's where she is, Ma. I saw her every day actually.' He smiled as he recalled their bedside chats. 'I rather enjoyed our conversations to tell you the truth.'

Molly looked at him. 'I've always 'ad a lot of time fer Lady 'Enrietta. She's been very kind ter yer father and me over the years. More so since yer dad died. Yer don't suppose she's got anythin' ter do with the letter do yer?'

Max shrugged his shoulders and was pleased to notice there was no pain. He was recovering more quickly than the doctors had predicted. 'She might do I suppose, although I can't think how. Eleanor is invited too, you know.'

Molly stiffened when she heard that. As far as she was concerned that could only mean one thing and she prayed everything would be all right.

Chapter 55

Molly walked with Max and Eleanor to Bickleigh Manor and left them at the front door whilst she went round to the kitchen as usual. It would not do for her to enter by the front entrance.

The maid who opened the door within seconds of Max ringing the bell was not one of the old staff from Mount Royal. Max did not recognise her but by the speed of her response he suspected that she must have been waiting in the hall for the doorbell to ring.

'Good afternoon. It's Max and Eleanor Chambers for the Countess.' Max smiled warmly at her and she blushed.

'Yes, Her Ladyship is expecting you, sir,' she replied, trying not to look embarrassed but unable to avert her eyes as she opened the door wide. 'Please come in.' People had told her he was handsome and she could not take her eyes from his face.

'We're expected all right,' whispered Max discreetly to Eleanor, who was resting her head shyly against his shoulder. 'Now remember what I said, best behaviour my girl.' Eleanor whimpered quietly and increased her grip on his neck as she began to play with the buttons of his uniform tunic with her free hand.

'Her Ladyship asked me to show you into the drawing-room, sir. Please come this way.'

She led them across the warm, stone-flagged floor to an imposing set of mahogany double doors that were already open and shining brightly against the rich blue of the silk wallpaper in the large and elegant room beyond. She indicated that they should enter with a sweep of her hand.

'Please make yourselves comfortable. The Countess will be with you in a moment.'

'Thank you,' said Max, smiling again. She curtsied quickly and closed the doors silently behind her.

He shifted Eleanor's weight on to his left arm and looked around. He was pleasantly surprised to realise that the house had a comfortable and welcoming atmosphere and in that way it reminded him of Gloucester Street, although that was where the similarities ended. Bickleigh Manor was on a different scale entirely. He stood in the middle of the large

Persian carpet that covered the polished wooden floor, taking in the understated luxury that seemed to emanate from every corner of the tastefully furnished room. It was the first time he had ever set foot inside the house despite the many years he had spent on the estate and he already liked it much more than Mount Royal.

'Where shall we sit, sweetheart?' he asked, looking reassuringly at Eleanor. 'What a grand room isn't it?' He chose a long high-backed settee upholstered in palest blue brocade and sat down. 'Here we are, sit next to me,' he cajoled her gently, patting the cushion with his free hand, but Eleanor only held on to him more tightly. 'What's the matter, is it this strange place?' He smiled into her eyes. 'Don't worry, sweetheart, Daddy's here and there's nothing to be afraid of.'

He was looking around the room, trying to find something to distract her with when the doors opened and Lady Constance appeared, her tiny frame silhouetted against the high rectangular door frame. Max stood up as she slowly entered the room, walking carefully and leaning heavily on her cane. She carried herself well, her diminutive figure exuding an undeniably powerful aura despite her frailty. Behind her came the same maid who had let them in and this time she carried a box full of toys.

'Good afternoon, Mr Chambers, it is good of you to come, and to bring your beautiful daughter with you.' She stood on the edge of the carpet. 'It's Eleanor isn't it?' She inclined her head towards the little girl. 'Hello, Eleanor, look what we've got for you. Would you like to see?' She smiled kindly at Eleanor and turned to her maid. 'Would you place the toy box on the floor please Elsie? Thank you.'

The housemaid blushed furiously and put the box down in the middle of the carpet. She smiled shyly at Eleanor and curtsied before leaving the room, carefully closing the double doors behind her. Eleanor had been watching warily but when she saw the toys she looked at Max and pointed determinedly at them.

'Would you like to get down, darling?' asked Max as Eleanor started to wriggle. He looked at the Countess who smiled benignly. 'There you are then, why don't you see what's in the box?' Max nodded encouragingly at Eleanor who ran to it and began to take the toys out one by one, chattering to herself as she did so.

'It's so nice to see children having fun isn't it!' commented Lady Constance, obviously delighted. She came closer to Max and held out her right hand, holding firmly on to her silver-topped cane with her left. 'I am pleased to see you again, after so many years.' She smiled charmingly at him and Max noted that her eyes twinkled with sincerity.

Max took her hand and shook it gently. 'Thank you, Countess. It was very kind of you to invite Eleanor too.' He let go of her hand and thought how soft and delicately formed it was. 'And then to think of the toys...'

'Not at all, Mr Chambers, I remembered we had them in the old nursery. They have been there for years, gathering dust I imagine. My daughter used to play with them when she was a child.'

'Please call me Max, Lady Constance.'

'Very well then, Max it is. Thank you.' She smiled. 'Do sit down and I'll ring for tea.'

'Thank you.'

She slowly made her way over to the bell by the side of the fireplace as Max sat down again. He observed her closely from his position on the settee, the years falling away as he remembered her from his childhood days, when he used to roam the estate. She had always been a remote figure to him, although not an unkindly one, and her presence in the room now felt just as powerful as it always had. She was immaculately dressed in a mauve silk dress trimmed with silver fox and she wore diamonds at her ears and wrists. An amethyst and diamond brooch flashed brilliantly on her left shoulder and, as she seated herself in the chair opposite him, Max realised that her ability to mesmerise and command was undimmed by age.

'It has been a long time, Max,' she began when she was settled comfortably. Her voice was firm but quiet. 'I hope my letter did not surprise you too much.' Max was silent. 'Mrs Chambers told me you would be visiting at this time and so I thought it would be a good opportunity to meet.'

Max was watching Lady Constance's face carefully but she gave nothing away. 'Yes, I am home on leave for another three weeks before I go back to the front. London is my home now but it is always nice to come back to Lee Moor.'

'Ah yes, your mother has told me so much about London. She so enjoys her trips to ... Pimlico, I believe.'

Max nodded. 'Yes, that's correct, Lady Constance.'

'I admit to not being terribly familiar with Pimlico. Our London house is in Chesterfield Square, but you know that of course!' She was smiling. 'It is some time since I was last there. In fact I wonder if I shall ever go back now,' she added wistfully.

Max noticed the faraway look in her eyes and, much to his surprise, he felt a twinge of sympathy for her. 'Never say never, Countess.'

'This wretched war doesn't make life any easier does it? My daughter tells me she met you in Belgium.'

Max had wondered if Lady Henrietta was behind this meeting. 'Yes, she did. It was such a coincidence. I was in the hospital just outside Ypres. I discovered she is a very good nurse.' He chuckled, which made Eleanor turn round with a start. 'It's all right, darling,' Max reassured her with a big smile.

The doors opened before he could continue and Elsie and Emily appeared with the tea things, which they quickly and efficiently laid out on an antique walnut table, which stood to the side of the Countess's chair.

'Thank you, Elsie, thank you, Emily, we shall serve ourselves. That will be all,' said Lady Constance.

As soon as the housemaids had left the room as quietly as they had appeared, the Countess began to get up from her chair with a determined but obvious effort.

'Shall I pour, Lady Constance?' asked Max solicitously, rising from the settee before she had a chance to reply. He found himself warming to this calm and dignified old lady who so obviously had something she wanted to say to him.

The Countess looked gratefully at him. 'That would be very kind, Max, thank you. There is lemonade and some shortbread biscuits for Eleanor. Mrs Castle told me *you* used to like them as a small boy,' she said without a trace of condescension in her voice.

Max laughed easily as he poured the tea into a delicate china cup. 'I remember them to this day, Countess. I used to watch Mrs Castle make them in the kitchen at Mount Royal.'

'I know,' said Lady Constance softly, 'I always knew.' Max threw her an old-fashioned look but said nothing. 'I have asked your mother to join us after tea, Max; I hope that is all right?'

He nodded slowly. 'Why yes, of course.' He was unable to conceal his surprise.

Lady Constance smiled knowingly. 'I am sorry for the mystery, but there are some things that I want to say which concern you both. They have waited a long time but they will keep for a few moments more until we have finished our tea. Please do help yourself to some cake, won't you?'

Eleanor was munching happily on her biscuit and playing with a large china doll. 'Do you like her, Eleanor?' asked the Countess kindly. 'Her name is Mabel. She was my daughter's favourite you know. Perhaps Daddy will let you take her home with you when you go?' She looked across at Max. 'It would please me Max if you will allow it?'

Max put his cup down on the saucer. 'That is very generous of you, Lady Constance. I'm sure Eleanor would like that. You *are* a very lucky girl, sweetheart, aren't you?' He smiled at Eleanor who was much too engrossed in her biscuit to take much notice. 'It'll remind her of her visit here this afternoon.'

'Well I hope there will be many more,' replied the Countess. 'How is your shoulder, Max, have you recovered well?'

'It is fine now thank you. It was only really a superficial wound in the first place,' he said dismissively. 'I presume Lady Henrietta told you about it?'

The Countess nodded. 'My daughter told me it could have been very nasty. You were one of the lucky ones I think. So many of our fine young men are meeting their deaths on the battlefields. Tell me about the conditions, Max; are they really as awful as people say?'

'Worse, Countess, much worse. The newspapers don't begin to tell the real story!'

Lady Constance nodded slowly. 'My late husband had many friends in government you know, and I hear things, which maybe I shouldn't...'

'Well, whatever those things are, I suspect they are true and there is no end in sight as far as I can see. There'll be millions more killed before it all ends.' He sighed and turned his head to look out of the window. The peace and orderliness of the rolling lawns stretching into the distance seemed a world away from the brutality and chaos he had grown uncomfortably accustomed to.

'Quite,' said Lady Constance. 'Well, if you've finished your tea shall I ring for your mother to join us?' she asked in a decisive tone. 'It is time to tell you what you should know.' This time she did stand up with one resolute movement. 'She is expecting us to ring.'

Max was mystified and felt his heart begin to beat a little faster. He stood up and placed his empty cup back on the table by the Countess's chair and then moved over to bend down and wipe Eleanor's mouth and hands, which were covered in crumbs. 'It won't do to have you looking like that when Granny comes in, will it, young lady!' he remonstrated with mock alarm.

Lady Constance turned round from the bell by the fireplace and laughed. 'Mrs Chambers would never forgive either of us!'

Just then the doors opened and Molly came in. Max immediately noticed that she had changed into her best clothes and was looking apprehensive.

'Ah, Mrs Chambers, thank you. Won't you sit down?'

Lady Constance indicated the empty settee next to Max. Eleanor looked up and saw her grandmother and immediately scrambled to her feet and ran to her, holding the doll out in front of her for Molly to see.

''Ello, darling,' said Molly quietly, 'isn't that luvley!' She hoisted her on to her lap as she sat down, exchanging a worried glance with Max, who returned it with a quizzical look.

'Perhaps I should explain why we are all here, Max, and I must apologise again for the mystery but I hope you will forgive me when you hear what I have to say.' She looked intently at him. 'The circumstances are very painful but I am getting old and it is high time these things were said before it is too late. When I heard you had been wounded in the fighting, I knew that the time had come. You have a right to know and I can only apologise for not telling you sooner.'

Max looked from one to the other. 'I . . .'

The Countess held up her small and finely manicured hand. She was intent on telling him everything before he had a chance to interrupt. 'Please, let me explain and then hopefully it will be much clearer for you. I must begin by saying that my late husband and I were responsible for the decisions that were made in the matters I am about to reveal. Your mother and father came to our aid and I am indebted to them for all they have done over the years. You must remember that.'

There was an absolute silence in the room, broken only by the ticking of the grandfather clock standing against the wall behind the settee on which Max and Molly were sitting. Max's throat had gone dry.

'It was in 1885, I remember it as if it was yesterday. William came to his father in a state of panic. We had a young kitchen maid working for us at the time, her name was Florence Rathbone. She was a quiet, hard-working girl as I recall, very pretty and respectable, but always rather shy. Anyway, it seems that William had a relationship with her, as a result of which she found that she was expecting a baby. That baby, Max, was you.'

Lady Constance paused for a second to let the revelation sink in. Max was completely stunned and stared at her before slowly turning his head towards Molly. She looked distraught and was holding on tightly to Eleanor, who was very still. It was as if she could sense the atmosphere in the room.

'I know that this must come as a huge shock to you, and after all these years, but there was an agreement you see . . .'

'Agreement?' asked Max in bewilderment. 'So *he* is my father?' *It could not possibly be true!* He looked desperately at Molly, seeking some kind of reassurance that the Countess was wrong. Molly simply nodded imperceptibly and lowered her eyes. Lady Constance noticed the look.

'You must not blame your mother, Max, Lord Hugo and I asked your mother and father to look after you, to bring you up as if you were their own flesh and blood.'

'I could never 'ave children yer see, darling,' interjected Molly softly, 'and we loved yer like yer was our own...'

Even in his state of stunned shock he was acutely conscious of Molly's distress and he reached out to take her hand, holding it tightly.

'I am very aware of your feelings towards William and God knows he has given you just cause on many occasions, but my husband and I tried to do what we thought was right at the time, for everyone concerned,' explained Lady Constance as if in defence of their actions. 'I hope in time you might feel able to understand and to ... to forgive us.'

Max found to his surprise that he felt no animosity towards this proud and gracious lady who was doing her best to put matters right, matters that must have been deeply humiliating and distressing to her.

'Please, Lady Constance, I understand how difficult this must be for you...' he said evenly. The Countess looked at him with what appeared to be a mixture of sadness and gratitude. 'But I must know everything ... *everything!*' he insisted calmly.

'Yes, yes of course, my dear,' she replied compassionately.

'The girl who ... my mother...' It felt very strange to refer to someone other than Molly as his mother. She was his mother, not someone he had never met! 'What happened to her? Why did...'

'It was very sad, Max. Florence died in childbirth.' *My God!* thought Max to himself, just like his darling Rosie. 'There was never any question of my son marrying, you see, and so after much deliberation my husband and I approached your mother and father. It was Mrs Castle actually who suggested the idea.'

'Elizabeth knew we couldn't 'ave children of our own, darling,' said Molly almost to herself.

'It seemed to be a suitable arrangement, which guaranteed your well-being, here on the estate, and it meant that our grandchild would be raised in a secure and loving environment. The Rathbone family receive an annuity, which Lady Henrietta and I absolutely forbade my son to cancel when he inherited the title.' She sounded uncharacteristically bitter.

'Blood money?' asked Max sarcastically and then immediately regretted it.

'Max!' exclaimed Molly.

'I'm sorry,' said Max quickly, immediately feeling ashamed, 'that was uncalled for.'

Lady Constance shook her head. 'Not at all, it is a fair question.'

'What did she look like?'

The Countess looked at Molly who cleared her throat. 'Do yer remember the photograph that used ter sit on the mantelpiece at 'ome, darlin'?'

'The one you gave Rosie and me the Christmas before she died, Ma, along with that letter you told us not to open? Of course I remember. I've always wondered who she was. '

Molly nodded. 'Yes, I know yer 'ave, darlin', and as yer grew older I wanted to tell yer so very much, 'onestly I did, but we 'ad agreed yer see. It's a photograph of Florence that 'er Ladyship gave us. It was always meant fer yer.'

'It was I who originally insisted that you were not told, Max, and an agreement was signed to that effect; please don't blame your mother. I believe she wrote a letter to you at the time which was to remain sealed until after her death?' Max nodded. 'Well, that was because latterly we both decided we could not keep this secret for ever and we did not want the truth to go to the grave with us all. The letter explains everything.'

'But she looked so like Rosie, Ma!'

'I know,' whispered Molly with tears in her eyes.

'That brings me on to to something else,' said Lady Constance and then she paused. She had wondered whether to tell him this, but she was determined he should know the whole truth and there would be no second chance. It was now or never.

Chapter 56

The ticking of the clock behind Max intruded upon his thoughts as he looked at Lady Constance. Her silence hung awkwardly in the air as she appeared to be struggling to find her words. Max was unable to imagine what more she could be about to reveal but there was no mistaking the deep red flush that imbued her delicately rouged cheeks. This belied her outward composure and her eyes were downcast as her hands fidgeted restlessly in her lap. Suddenly she cleared her throat, lifted her head and began to speak once more.

'My husband and I were so delighted when you married Rosemary and we were equally happy that our daughter marked the occasion with that small gift from our cellars. But it was also a time of great sadness for us because we had always imagined that the marriage of a grandchild would be the cause of great family celebration. I longed for you to be able to celebrate your marriage at Mount Royal, but I know that would have been impossible. I often sensed you harboured great animosity towards my family and it broke my heart to think of what should have been, if only circumstances had been different.' She sighed heavily and appeared deflated. 'We have no one but ourselves to blame for that,' she said sorrowfully.

'It is not your fault, Lady Constance.' Max was perfectly calm. 'I don't blame you, or your late husband, for any of what you have told me. I admit that I did have the feelings you describe when I was younger, but all that changed a long time ago, at least as far as you and Lady Henrietta are concerned ... and Lord Hugo of course.' It was true: he was feeling genuine sympathy for the Countess who had clearly tried to do her best; he accepted that now. 'I am sure circumstances would have been wholly different without your intervention.'

'That is very generous of you, my dear. It is more than I can reasonably expect,' replied the Countess with relief. 'I was brought up to believe in duty and responsibility and my husband was an honourable and decent man. You are our grandson after all, but we were not destined to be a part of your life because of the stupidity of my son.' She swallowed hard. 'We had such high hopes for him but, if I'm honest, he has always been somewhat of a disappointment to us and I absolutely abhor his behaviour since he succeeded to the title.' There was a quiet steeliness to her voice now. 'It might seem a cruel thing to say about one's own flesh and blood, but I'm afraid that is what I think.'

Max looked at Eleanor who was sitting quietly on Molly's lap, and in that moment he had an intuitive inkling of what it must have cost her to be so brutally honest about her own child.

'My husband did not live to know that your wife was expecting Eleanor but he would have been so proud, proud but sad at the same time, as I was when I was given the news.' She reached for the handkerchief that was tucked into the sleeve of her dress and dabbed quickly at her eyes.

'Please, Countess, you have said enough. You don't have to go on, not just for my sake,' said Max.

'Oh but I do, Max,' she replied softly, 'there is more I must tell you. You have a right to know.'

Max nodded. 'Very well then, if you are sure?' He glanced at Molly who was still sitting quietly on the settee next to him, holding on to Eleanor who had dropped off to sleep. He squeezed Molly's hand and threw her a brief tight-lipped smile.

'Please forgive me for what I am about to say but it is important and I shall not rest until I've told you. It concerns William.'

A cold sensation gripped Max as he sensed a change in the Countess's manner. Molly's hand flew to her mouth as she guessed what Lady Constance was about to say.

'The night Mr Chambers was killed in that road accident, the night of your wedding I believe?'

Molly breathed a silent sigh of relief; she had been terrified that the Countess was going to tell Max of her suspicions about Rosie's accident. She really did not know what he would do if he ever found out that William was behind it.

'Yes it was,' said Max flatly.

'It was my son who was driving the motor car. He was going too fast I expect, driving it in the same way as he used to handle the horses. Reckless! We told him about it time and time again but he would never listen to his father, or to me. Once he got something into his mind there was no stopping him and we should have told the police.' An expression of guilt and anguish clouded her face. 'But, he was our ... I just couldn't...' she finished lamely. She looked up, having lowered her eyes in distress as she was speaking.

'I knew it was him! I've always known.' He stared at Lady Constance. 'But why are you telling me this now?' He spoke very steadily and quietly, betraying no sign of his raging emotions as all manner of vengeful thoughts flashed through his mind, all of them directed at *him*. Molly was not fooled. She knew exactly what he was thinking; his original hatred of the Gordon family had not dissipated at all, it was now merely directed at one man.

'I cannot close my eyes in peace until I have told the truth, Max. It is as simple as that and I regret not doing so sooner.'

Out of the corner of her eye Molly saw Lady Constance glance in her direction, and with an awful, sinking sensation, she knew what was about to be said. She closed her eyes in dread.

'I was so sorry to hear of your wife's passing, Max. I know that it was such an unexpected shock, and, having lost my husband in tragic and unexpected circumstances, I have some idea perhaps of what you have been through. I just thank God now that we were given so many happy years together, but you...' She paused and stared at Eleanor. 'You did not have that blessing. Do you remember the accident your wife had, here on the estate? It was before you were married and...'

She saw Max's expression and stopped herself.

'Of course you do, I'm sorry, how stupid of me! Well, I fear William was responsible for that too.'

Max sat bolt upright, his head swimming as her words struck at his consciouness like a thunderbolt. 'Can you explain why you believe that please, Lady Constance?' He managed to smile, but it was more akin to a thin and mirthless grimace.

'Florence Rathbone was a pretty girl, Max. You will have seen that from the photograph that is now in your possession and your late wife bore a striking resemblance to her, as you yourself said just now. It was not long after Rosemary had started working here that I began to notice my son taking an unusual interest in her. Henrietta commented on it too. I was worried about it of course and I had planned to take her to Chesterfield Square with us for the Season that year, where she would have been out of harm's way. I thought perhaps his interest might wane if he was unable to see her for a while. William rarely came to London for much of the Season you see, he always preferred to stay here. It was whilst we were in London that he had ... the liaison ... with ... with Florence. He must have got wind of my plans because Henrietta overheard a conversation between my son and Makepiece. It seems that William was attempting to find out if I had indeed decided to take Rosemary

333

to London, although I did not know about this until quite recently when Henrietta came to me to tell me what she had heard on that day.' She stopped and looked at Max who was sitting very still. 'Shall I continue?'

'Yes, Countess.' He was expressionless apart from the occasional flicker of his eyelids.

'Very well, if you are sure ... I can only conclude that William was intending to force himself upon her here whilst we were away. However, events overtook him, which resulted in the accident that befell your wife. It must have been her afternoon off and she was going into the village...'

'It was to meet me,' interrupted Max quietly. Molly reached across and touched his arm.

'The dogs had been let out of their kennels, deliberately mind you, and they chased after her. They were the estate guard dogs at the time, which we let out at night to roam the grounds. They were trained to alert the ground staff to strangers and although they responded well to their handlers, they would give chase if anybody ran from them. That is what Rosemary must have done. They caught up with her down by the lake...'

'Who let the dogs out?'

'I am not entirely certain. The identity of the culprit remains a matter for conjecture to this day but I think the objective was to frighten your late wife into leaving us. I cannot imagine the person responsible envisaged the near tragedy that followed. I do not believe it was William, that would make no sense at all because he wanted her to remain here, but I am sure it was done on purpose.'

'Makepiece,' muttered Max, his eyes glinting. 'It must have been Makepiece.'

'That is certainly possible but there is no evidence. I am aware that he had been unpleasant towards Rosemary for some time leading up to her accident. Mrs Castle told me that, in secret or course, but neither Henrietta nor I can say for sure.'

'Please go on,' said Max, taking a deep breath.

'I hope I am not about to break a confidence,' continued Lady Constance, glancing again towards Molly. 'I understand the coroner's report into your wife's sudden death concluded that she passed away as a result of a massive brain haemorrhage and I fear the blow to the head she suffered in that accident could have been responsible for it!'

Suddenly she stopped talking and sat back in her chair, momentarily closing her eyes as a sharp look of pain crossed her face. It was past in an instant but Molly noticed it with alarm.

'Milady, are yer all right?' she asked anxiously.

'Yes, yes I'm quite all right, thank you, Mrs Chambers,' said Lady Constance. 'It is just a little indigestion that's all.' She sat up and leaned forwards. 'I am truly sorry for what I have told you, Max.'

Max could not speak. Instead he got up from the settee and walked over to the windows and stood in front of them with his back to the room, staring out across the manicured lawns to the hills beyond, the hills where he had spent many hours as a young boy dreaming of his freedom and making plans for the future. He had not expected it to turn out like this.

Chapter 57

'I'm going out, Ma,' said Max at breakfast the next morning, 'I'm taking Eleanor up into the hills for a while.'

Molly smiled and put down her cup. It was what he always used to do when he had something on his mind. 'All right, luv. Do yer want some sandwiches ter take with yer? Eleanor will need somethin' if yer plan ter be out fer long.'

They had talked long into the night after leaving Bickleigh Manor. As soon as they had walked through the front door of Fern Cottage Max had told her, 'You and Dad are my parents, Ma, nothing has changed as far as I am concerned.' The enormity of what he had discovered that afternoon had thrown him into a state of shock, but as the night wore on he began to make some sense of the events of the past. By the time they had retired to bed they had said all that was necessary. However, there was no escaping the cruel irony of the situation; the man he regarded as his nemesis, for whom he had nothing but loathing and contempt, was actually his biological father.

The Countess had pressed them to stay for supper and had even invited Molly to eat with them in the dining-room, but Max had declined, graciously but firmly. Seeing the look of distress on her face, he had promised Lady Constance that he would bring Eleanor back to see her before he returned to London. He had assured her that he bore no ill will and thanked her for having the courage to be so frank with him. He also said that he hoped they would have the opportunity to get to know one another better, kissing her warmly on both cheeks as they left. Molly knew how much that generous gesture would have meant to the Countess and she had never been more proud of him than she was at that moment.

She felt an overwhelming sense of relief that the truth was out in the open at last; the secret that she had concealed for the past 30 years would no longer haunt her.

Since giving Max and Rosie the photograph of Florence Rathbone and the sealed letter in which she explained everything, Molly's feelings of guilt at continuing to conceal Max's true identity had intensified. As his hostility towards William had gathered pace over the years, so had her trepidation about his reaction to the disclosure of the truth. She was fearful too of his response to the realisation that she had withheld the facts for so many years and yet she did not regret for one moment agreeing to the Earl and Countess's original request to raise their illegitimate grandson as her own flesh and blood; to do so would be to regret Max himself. She was utterly devoted to him, and also now to Eleanor, and her emotional attachment to them both transcended all else in her life, especially since Bert's death. She loved him as a son and admired him for his achievements. In fact, her sense of pride in them was almost overwhelming, and since Rosie's untimely passing, these sentiments had only intensified. Quite simply, Max and Eleanor were the cornerstones of her existence, and the possibility of losing them was too awful to contemplate. Happily, all fears of that nature had been swept away by Max himself as soon as they had arrived back at Fern Cottage the previous night.

There was a knock on the door as she was getting ready to leave for the manor. 'Come in, luv, it's open,' she called, imagining it was Max and Eleanor returning to collect Eleanor's coat, which they had left over the back of the chair. 'I told yer it was chilly didn't I?'

'It's me, Moll,' said Elizabeth Castle in a rush, 'come quick! The Countess 'as 'ad a turn. We've sent fer Doctor Roley.' She stood on the threshold, red faced and panting.

'Whatever do yer mean?' cried Molly in alarm, jumping to her feet. 'What sort of turn?'

'I don't know exactly but Elsie came running downstairs about half an hour ago ter say she'd found 'er Ladyship lying on 'er bedroom floor.'

'Oh my God! Let me just get me coat.'

She quickly scribbled a note for Max and then the two old friends rushed back to Bickleigh Manor, where they found Doctor Roley's car outside the front door.

'He must still be 'ere then,' said Elizabeth, looking worriedly at Molly as they hastened round to the back and in through the kitchen door.

'Any news, Gladys?' demanded Molly immediately as she took off her coat. The young kitchen maid was distractedly peeling potatoes and looked relieved to see them. She shook her head. 'Doctor's still upstairs.'

Molly glanced at Elizabeth and motioned skywards with her eyes. 'I'll just go up and see what's 'appening then.'

She dashed up the backstairs that led from the kitchen to the main hallway and emerged through the green baize door just as Doctor Roley appeared on the half landing of the main staircase. She stopped and brushed her hands nervously along the front of her black dress.

'Ah there you are, Mrs Chambers,' said Doctor Roley, 'I was just coming down to speak to you.' He smiled pleasantly at her as he reached the bottom of the staircase. 'Is there somewhere we can go perhaps?'

'Yes, of course, doctor,' replied Molly quickly and she opened the morning room door. 'Please go in.' She stepped back to allow him to enter first and then she followed him in and closed the door behind her.

'I'll come straight to the point,' he said without preamble. 'The Countess has suffered a heart attack, quite a mild one I think, but there is a danger she might have another. The next day or two will be critical as far as that is concerned. I've given her a mild sedative to help her rest and she must stay in bed and not be disturbed. It's very important that she gets as much rest as possible. Is that understood?'

Molly nodded but she was unable to keep the anxiety from her voice. 'Yes, doctor, I understand. Ought we ter sit with 'er?'

'That's not strictly necessary, but she should be checked every half an hour or so just to be on the safe side.'

'She will be all right won't she?' Her concern was plainly evident.

'It's impossible to tell, Mrs Chambers, to be frank.' He sighed. 'She should be but it just depends. You can never tell with these things. I'm going to look in again this afternoon and we'll see how she is then. Did you know she had been suffering from chest pains?'

'No, doctor, I didn't. Oh ... wait a minute, she complained of a touch of indigestion when I was with her yesterday...'

'That was probably her heart and not indigestion at all. Hmm ... well, plenty of rest and I'll be back this afternoon. Call me in the meanwhile if you are at all worried.'

'Thank you, Doctor Roley, I'll show you out.'

After he had gone, Molly slipped upstairs to see Lady Constance and found her sleeping peacefully. She lingered at the bedroom door for a few moments, deep in thought as she gazed at the tiny figure who appeared lost and frail in the large four-poster bed. Molly's whole life had been entwined with that of the Gordon family, and the Dowager Countess in particular, and in recent years since the death of Lord Hugo she had sometimes felt as if she had become more than just a servant to Lady Constance. They had talked more freely than ever before, often about their personal lives, and always of course about Max. There remained, nevertheless, a respectful distance between them, which Molly had never abused.

She felt obligated to the Countess, and standing there listening to Lady Constance breathing softly in her sleep, she willed her to recover, fervently praying that the life she had known and loved in Lee Moor was not about to change. If the Countess were to die she knew that none of the downstairs staff, including herself, could expect any consideration whatsoever from Lord William. She sighed and, leaving the door ajar, she went back down to the kitchen to tell the others what the doctor had said.

It was late afternoon by the time Max and Eleanor reached the house and Doctor Roley's car was again outside the front entrance. They had found the note from Molly after a peaceful and cathartic time spent together in *his* hills and had come at once to Bickleigh Manor. Max did not waste time by ringing the front door bell but instead went straight round to the kitchen, opening it to find the small and closely knit household staff sitting around the well-scrubbed rectangular oak table, talking in subdued and mournful whispers. They looked round as soon as he entered.

'She's gone, Max,' said Mrs Castle quietly in a shocked tone.

'Gone?' exclaimed Max, 'you mean she's...'

'Yes, luv, 'er Ladyship died shortly after four o'clock. The second attack took 'er,' explained Molly. Her eyes were red and it was clear she had been crying, but now she was composed and trying to appear stoical.

Eleanor sensed the atmosphere in the room and began to cry. At just 18 months she was too young to understand but old enough to respond to the heavy air of sadness and upset.

'It's all right, darling,' whispered Max soothingly, and he held her to him, stroking her blonde curls with the palm of his right hand. 'It's all right.'

'Yer must be hungry, sweet'art,' said Mrs Castle, looking at the clock on the shelf above the range. She got up from the table. 'It must be past yer teatime. Let me see if I can find yer something nice to eat in the pantry ter be going on with.'

'Don't worry, Mrs Castle, I'll go,' said Max quickly.

'No, lad, I'll go. It'll give me something ter do.' She disappeared into the pantry and was back in no time with some of the shortbread biscuits she had made for Eleanor the previous day. 'How about this, luv?' she asked holding one up for her to see. 'Will they do?'

Eleanor eagerly held out her hand and her cries soon sudsided as she took a large bite from the triangular biscuit Mrs Castle gave her.

'Thank you, Mrs Castle,' said Max with a smile of appreciation. 'What happened, Ma, it must have been very sudden?'

'Come an' sit down, luv,' said Molly as the others made room for him at the table. 'She 'ad the first attack this mornin'. Elizabeth came ter fetch me just after yer had taken Eleanor up ter the hills. Elsie found 'er Ladyship collapsed on the bedroom floor...'

Molly was interrupted by Elsie bursting into tears. 'Come on, Else, crying won't 'elp,' soothed Mrs Castle as she put her arm around the young girl's shoulders.

'Doctor Roley told us bed rest an' peace an' quiet. We kept checkin' on 'er an' she seemed ter be sleeping all right but the doctor said there was a risk of another attack...' She swallowed before continuing. 'We took it in turns ter go up an' every time she was sleeping peacefully, or so we thought...' She looked at Mrs Castle. 'We thought that was good didn't we?' Elizabeth nodded sadly. 'I went up just before four o'clock an' she was just the same an' then Elizabeth went up about quarter past I suppose it must 'ave been, an' she was gone...'

Molly faltered and Mrs Castle stepped in. 'It was a second heart attack; in 'er sleep, Doctor Roley told us. ''E's up there now, said 'e'll ring down when 'e's finished.'

The distressed faces of the staff were testimony to the affection in which Lady Constance was held and Max was sad too, humbled by the sense of true loss on their faces. As he looked around, it seemed to him as if the last few years had been dominated by death and sadness; first there was Bert, then his darling Rosie, the untold misery of the war, and now the Countess. But he also felt relief – relief and disappointment. He was pleased that Lady Constance had found the courage to be honest with him and regretful now that they would not have the opportunity to get to know one another, as he had promised. Alone with Eleanor in the peace and splendour of the hills earlier in the day, he had realised that he had a simple choice to make. He could either choose to reject his heritage, or to embrace it, and he had decided upon the latter. But now it was too late and for that he was sorry.

Max was a fair man and whilst he knew he could not make up for the terrible anguish the Countess had suffered in being denied her role as a grandmother, he felt strongly that she deserved the chance to enjoy her great granddaughter in her declining years. In fact, the more he had thought about all she had told him, the more he had begun to appreciate the enormity of the dilemma she and Lord Hugo had faced 30 years ago. In rescuing their son from the consequences of his own selfish act of folly they had cast for themselves a future without the precious gift of grandchildren, and Max could not imagine a more selfless and generous deed than that. However, the Countess's sudden death had consigned all of that to the past and it was the future that mattered now.

'Lady Henrietta must be told, Ma, and the family trustees.'

Molly started, jolted from her reverie by his words. 'Yes, luv, yer right of course but I don't even know where she is. Do yer think she'll still be at that camp where yer were?'

'I expect so, Ma, the best thing would be to contact the trustees and they can take care of that.'

Molly nodded. ''Er Ladyship was talking ter them recently. She asked me ter make the call an' I wrote their telephone number down in that little book Raymond keeps by the receiver outside 'is pantry. It might still be there. What about Lord William? 'E'll 'ave ter be told too.'

Before Max could reply, Mrs Castle snorted angrily. 'What will 'e care? 'E'll dance on 'er grave more like!'

Max made no comment. 'Let the trustees take care of that, Ma. Shall I speak with them for you?'

'Yes please, luv, it'll 'ave ter be in the morning now...'

'Morning room, Mrs Chambers,' said Emily quietly as the sound of a bell interrupted her.

'That'll be Doctor Roley, I'd better go up.'

Molly got up from the table, which was the signal for the others to do the same. As Max watched them it was obvious to him that they did not appreciate how their lives were about to change irrevocably as a result of their employer's death. He knew the only certainty they faced now was that Lord William would neither care about, nor be remotely interested in, their futures.

341

Chapter 58

The invitation from Penrose and Lee, the Gordon family trustees, to attend the reading of the Countess's will at their offices in Lincoln's Inn Fields was waiting for him when he arrived back in London from Lee Moor. As he told Elizabeth that same evening over drinks in the library at Curzon Street, his surprise at receiving the handwritten note on the firm's gold embossed letterhead was unequivocal. The reading was scheduled to take place at the end of the week, the day before he was due to return to the front.

'Why do you think you've been asked to attend?' asked Elizabeth curiously as he handed her a large whisky and soda, 'and who else is going, do you know?'

'It's a mystery to tell you the truth. I telephoned Penrose and Lee to see if I could find out, but they wouldn't tell me anything. The clerk I spoke with was very polite of course but he said he was not at "liberty to divulge anything until the reading itself". All a bit pompous if you ask me.'

'Perhaps you're a beneficiary,' teased Elizabeth mischievously. Then she giggled as a thought struck her. 'That would please the Earl wouldn't it!'

Max looked at her and smiled but made no comment. That prospect had suddenly occurred to him during his telephone call with the young man from the trustees but he had instantly dismissed the notion as ridiculous.

'I'll find out soon enough,' he replied as the butler entered to announce dinner. 'Oh good, I'm starving!' exclaimed Max as he followed Elizabeth out of the room. 'It must be all that Devon air.'

'I want to hear all about your trip, how's Molly taking the news?'

The junior clerk sitting behind a desk in the reception hall of Penrose and Lee's offices looked up as Max entered promptly at ten o'clock on Friday morning. Middle-aged and soberly dressed in a black tailcoat and striped trousers, he looked as if he carried the weight of the world on his shoulders. He smiled briefly as Max approached him.

'Good morning. My name is Chambers. I have an appointment with Sir John Lee.'

'Ah yes, sir, for the reading of the Dowager Countess Gordon's will I believe?' the junior clerk replied. 'Please come this way.' He came round from behind the desk and led Max across the huge panelled entrance hall and showed him into a rather gloomy and uninviting meeting room. 'If you would be kind enough to wait in here, sir, I will take you up when the others have arrived and Sir John is ready for you.'

'Others?' queried Max.

'The other beneficiaries of the will, sir.' He smiled in the same cursory manner as before and then withdrew, leaving Max alone in the room. *So he was mentioned in her will after all!*

He walked over to the tall windows and peered out into the square beyond before turning to gaze around him. There was an unmistakable air of faded grandeur about the room, quite unlike the bright and businesslike feel of his suite of offices above the warehouse in Chelsea. In comparison it felt cheerless and oppressive. A row of portraits hung on the opposite wall and he walked across the dark burgundy rug to take a closer look, squeezing in between the brown leather chesterfields and wing chairs that stood in the middle of the room. The paintings were rather austere and forbidding and did nothing to lighten the atmosphere. There was a small brass plate at the bottom of each frame, which told Max they were all of previous senior partners of the firm. He smiled at the vanity of it and looked at his watch. It was a quarter past ten.

He sat down in one of the winged chairs and ran his hand across the cracked and hardened leather, beginning to grow impatient as his curiosity mounted. Unable to settle, he stared at the rows of books that lined the shelves on the wall to his right and then he spotted a small pile of old dusty journals stacked on a table next to the door. He glanced at his watch again as he stood up and went over to them, picking up the top one entitled 'The New Age, May–October 1914'. He had barely leafed through the first two or three pages and was just thinking it was an incongruously progressive magazine to find in such a staid environment when the door abruptly opened and the junior clerk appeared.

'Sir John will see you now. Would you come with me please?'

'Very well,' replied Max, 'thank you.'

His impatience was turning to irritation and his mood was not helped when he noticed the clerk glance surreptitiously at the single stripe on the sleeve of his uniform. His expression remained impassive, however, as he followed the man up the broad staircase and along a similarly wide corridor to a door marked 'Sir John Lee, Senior Partner.'

'I will announce you, sir,' said the clerk. He knocked respectfully and waited for a reply.

'Come!' boomed a voice from inside.

He opened the door and motioned for Max to follow him. 'Mr Chambers, Sir John,' he said before bowing and retreating.

'Mr Chambers, how do you do? I am Sir John Lee,' he said, holding out his hand. He smiled in a friendly manner. 'I am sorry to have kept you, please do sit down.' He indicated a high-backed chair that was one of three standing in front of his desk. 'As you can see, I am expecting two other people who I am sorry to say have not yet arrived.'

'I am pleased to meet you, Sir John,' he replied as he sat down. The note of disapproval in Sir John's tone was unmistakable. This room was the antithesis of the one downstairs – bright, welcoming and cheerful – and he felt his irritation begin to fade.

'Would you care for some coffee, Mr Chambers, while we are waiting?'

'Thank you, Sir John, that would be very welcome,' replied Max. 'May I ask who else you are expecting?'

At that moment there was another knock on the door and Lady Henrietta swept in with the same clerk who had announced Max trailing in her wake.

'Sir John, how good to see you. I am so sorry to have kept you waiting,' she said apologetically. 'I wasn't sure I was going to make it until last night, the train journey from Dover was interminable and there wasn't a seat to be found.'

Sir John smiled indulgently. He had known Lady Henrietta for most of her adult life and he had represented the family's interests since his father, Sir Geoffrey, the third baronet, had died in 1911. 'I knew you would make it, my dear Lady Henrietta. We were just going to have some coffee...?'

'Thank you, Sir John.' She turned to Max. 'Max, it is good to see you, how is your shoulder?'

Max smiled warmly. It was clear that she was not surprised to see him. 'Fully recovered thank you,' he replied as he rose and kissed her proffered cheek, 'but more importantly, how are you?'

Their eyes met and hers revealed the strain and exhaustion she was feeling. 'I am fine thank you,' she lied.

'I'm not so sure about that,' he said softly, 'and I am so sorry about your mother.'

A look of extreme sadness clouded her face. 'Thank you, Max, it was a shock to receive the news I must say. It hasn't really sunk in yet I suppose, but one just has to knuckle down and get on with things.' She shrugged her shoulders and Max nodded sympathetically.

A secretary had brought in the coffee whilst they were talking, and Sir John handed a cup to Lady Henrietta. 'You take cream but no sugar if I remember correctly, Lady Henrietta?'

She smiled appreciatively. 'You have a very good memory, Sir John.'

'And for you, Mr Chambers?'

'I take mine black thank you, Sir John.'

'Very well then, here we are,' he said, handing a cup to Max. 'May I suggest we commence the reading? I am conscious of time,' he said, sitting back down behind his desk.

Max nodded and looked at Henrietta. 'We are quite ready thank you, Sir John.'

'Let me first of all say how very sorry I was to learn of the Countess's sad passing and also how honoured we are at Penrose and Lee to have been asked to handle her affairs.' He paused and looked up from his papers.

Lady Henrietta nodded briefly, wishing he would get on with it. He cleared his throat and began by explaining how he had received a request from Lady Constance to visit her at Bickleigh Manor in the autumn of 1914 for the express purpose of drafting a new will. The document he had in front of him now was the signed and witnessed result, which, he emphasised, revoked all others. Max glanced at Henrietta who did not seem at all surprised at Sir John's words.

Suddenly there was a loud crash behind him as the door flew open and Earl Gordon appeared.

'I am sorry, Sir John,' stammered the flustered clerk from the doorway, 'His Lordship didn't...'

'That's quite all right, Wilson,' snapped Sir John, unable to hide his annoyance. 'Leave us please.'

He recovered his composure instantly and darted out from behind his desk and held out his hand. 'My lord, how good of you to come. We had only just started.' He smiled but his eyes were like steel.

William nodded peremptorily. 'Sir John. Please continue. I have a luncheon appointment at noon.'

'May I first of all offer you some coffee?'

William shook his head. 'I don't drink the stuff,' he replied rudely. 'I usually have a glass of whisky at this hour of the morning,' he said, looking in the direction of a decanter and glasses that stood on a fine walnut bookcase. He lumbered over to it and poured himself a generous measure without waiting to be asked.

Max watched in amazement as Lord William took a deep draught from the glass before turning round to acknowledge his sister for the first time. She was looking at him with ill-concealed disgust.

'I see the war has not improved your manners, William!'

Lord William opened his mouth to retort but instead spotted Max who had been partially obscured by Sir John up until that moment. 'What the bloody hell are *you* doing here, Chambers?' he roared in disbelief. He swivelled round to stare at Sir John. 'Why is *he* here? Who invited him?' he demanded venomously.

Sir John remained calm. 'I did, my Lord.'

'On whose orders?' Lord William's tone was poisonous.

'On the instructions of your late mother, my Lord.'

'But this is a private family affair!' he exploded with rage. 'He has no right to be here!'

'It is a meeting for all the beneficiaries of your late mother's will, my Lord.'

The significance of his statement slowly dawned on Lord William and he stared open-mouthed at Max, who had remained calmly seated during the bombastic outburst. He returned the Earl's stare impassively and remained silent.

'I suggest you sit down, William and allow Sir John to get on,' said Lady Henrietta. 'That is if you wish to keep your luncheon appointment.' Her voice was heavy with sarcasm.

Lord William glared at her. 'What does he mean 'beneficiaries of the will'? How can Chambers be a beneficiary of our mother's will? *He* isn't family and thanks be to God for that!' He spoke as if Max was not in the room.

'Max *knows*, William. Mama told him everything,' she said steadily, 'so you see, William, he has every right to be here! *Now sit down!*'

Max would have laughed if he had not been so revolted by the figure in front of him. William hesitated, glaring incredulously at them both. Years of over-eating and heavy drinking had finally taken their toll and Max was truly shocked at the obese and raddled man standing defiantly in the middle of Sir John's office. His once thick black hair was now mostly white and thinning and his mannerisms were those of an old man, even though he was not yet fifty.

Sir John, who had moved back behind his desk during their altercation, shuffled his papers rather pointedly and coughed. 'If you would care to sit down, my Lord?' he said, indicating the empty chair beside Henrietta. William did so, slumping so heavily on to the cushions that Max thought the chair would break. The penetrating silence that followed was broken only by the sound of William heaving himself into an upright position, glowering darkly as the effort brought beads of perspiration to his forehead. What had his bitch of a sister said? That Chambers knew everything? It was impossible! There was an agreement! What did this fool of a solicitor mean? Beneficiary! Never! The idea was inconceivable, simply preposterous.

He looked at Henrietta out of the corner of his eye. A faint amused smile was playing on her lips.

Chapter 59

'I, Constance Virginia Mary, Dowager Countess Gordon, of Bickleigh Manor, Devon, being of sound mind and body do hereby declare this to be my last will and testament, hereby revoking all wills and codicils hitherto made by me.'

'Huh!' snorted William sceptically under his breath, 'sound mind and body!'

Sir John glanced up from the page but ignored the interruption. 'I give and bequeath to my beloved daughter...'

'Can we dispense with the legal parlance and just get straight to the point?' demanded William querulously. 'What has she done?'

Sir John stopped and looked directly at Lord William. He really was an insufferable bore. 'There is no legal reason why I cannot do as you ask as long as the other beneficiaries have no objection?' He raised his eyebrows and looked at Max and Lady Henrietta.

'Very well, Sir John, I have no objection,' sighed Henrietta without turning to look at her brother.

Max's expression was inscrutable. 'As you wish, Sir John.'

Sir John leaned back in his chair for a moment and brought his hands to his mouth as if in prayer before continuing. 'It *is* a rather long and cumbersome document, I must agree, and much of it serves to reconfirm the disposition of the family trusts, which were settled by the ninth earl when he died in 1912. They, as you know, my Lord, are automatically inherited by the successor to the title and, as such, are not within the Countess's personal gift. I will therefore ignore these for the purposes of this meeting.' A sly smile of satisfaction spread across Lord William's face. 'However, his late Lordship did insist that two important provisions were inserted into those trust arrangements, which Lady Constance has made full use of, and with great foresight if I may say.' Lord William's eyes narrowed suspiciously at this news, and concern clouded his face. 'Now, moving on to the detail, I shall concentrate on the instructions I received back in...' He referred to the page in front of him. '... September of last year.'

Lord William looked up sharply. 'September of last year, Sir John?' he snapped.

'Yes, my Lord, as I was explaining before you arrived, I visited your mother at her request for the express purpose of drafting a new will. That is the document I have in front of me here.' He held it up for William to see. 'Lady Constance has no living relatives other than yourselves, of course, and a great-granddaughter I believe.' He looked at Max, who nodded with the merest hint of a smile. 'She was, as you know, independently wealthy, having inherited a substantial sum from her late father, but, nevertheless, her bequests are fairly simple and straightforward, as you will see.'

William shifted uncomfortably in his seat at the mention of Eleanor, and an awful premonition struck him. 'You can't describe that child as a relative,' he whined. 'Why, she's ...'

Sir John held up his hand impatiently, not wanting there to be further discord. There was going to be argument aplenty when he had finished. 'Please, my Lord, let me finish what I have to say. Lady Constance expressed to me her desire to provide for her grandson and great-granddaughter in the belief that her late husband had already made ample provision for you, Lord William, and for Lady Henrietta. She has, however, made some additional bequests to Lady Henrietta, and I believe, my Lady, you are already aware of what they are?'

Henrietta ignored William's outraged scowl and smiled calmly. 'Yes, Sir John, Mama and I discussed them at the time and I am perfectly content with the arrangements.'

'W-w-w-what!' exclaimed William in a strained voice. 'Why do I not know about this?' He leaned forward with a sudden jolt as if he was going to snatch the papers from Sir John's hands, his drink-ravaged face turning a deep red. Fresh beads of perspiration trickled down his heavy jowls.

'Mama wished them to remain private until now William,' said Lady Henrietta coolly, enjoying his obvious discomfort with malicious satisfaction.

Sir John resumed his explanation: 'The estate owns seventeen freehold properties in and around London and under the terms of the late Earl's last will and testament, Lady Constance is able to dispose of any two of them as she wishes. This is the first of the two provisions I referred to just now.' He glanced at Lord William who glowered coldy back at him. 'Accordingly Lady Henrietta is to receive the freehold property at Number 3 Belgrave Square, the mews and all its contents, including the paintings, to be used and enjoyed by her during her lifetime. It will pass to her children upon her death but in the event that she dies without issue, it will pass to Mr Chambers. The freehold property known as Arlington Park in Wiltshire, which comprises a ten-bedroom mansion with a full range of outbuildings, stabling for sixteen horses, four hundred acres of land, including two arable farms, and the major proportion of the village of Arlington, with a rent roll of approximately ten thousand pounds per annum, is bequeathed to Mr Chambers.' He paused and took a sip of water from the glass on his desk. 'Lady Constance has also stipulated that Lady Henrietta retains the free and unencumbered tenure of Bickleigh Manor on the Mount Royal estate for her lifetime, with all the furniture and paintings therein, in accordance with the ninth Earl's second provision. Following Lady Henrietta's death, the manor will revert back to its former use as the estate Dower House.'

No one spoke but the tension was almost unbearable, enveloping them all in its mesmerising grip. Lord William was breathing heavily, his hands were shaking and his attention was fixed on Sir John. He remained silent with a supreme effort of will.

'Moving now to the contents of the Countess's personal accounts held at Coutts Bank, of which there are three in total. Lady Henrietta is to receive the interest from the trust account for her lifetime, amounting to twenty thousand pounds per annum at present rates of interest. The capital sum is to be held in trust for Miss Eleanor Chambers and will pass to her upon Lady Henrietta's demise. The balance in account number two, which stands at three hundred and eleven thousand pounds, is bequeathed in its entirety to Mr Chambers with loving good wishes. Finally, the contents of the third account entitled 'Household' is to be split equally between the members of the household staff employed at Bickleigh Manor. By my calculations this will amount to a little over two thousand pounds per person and is bequeathed with sincere gratitude and warmest good wishes. In accordance with the Countess's instructions, a senior clerk from this firm is travelling down to inform them personally and to assist them as necessary.' He paused momentarily before continuing. 'The Countess also had an important personal collection of precious jewellery, which is quite separate from the family heirlooms entailed with the estate. It comprises ... let me see...' He quickly flicked through the papers in front of him. '... ah, yes, here we are, there are two diamond tiaras, a diamond and sapphire suite of necklace, bracelet, drop earrings, brooch and ring, two further diamond necklaces, one of which is set with rubies, a ruby and diamond stomacher, a three strand pearl necklace with diamond clasp, and a quantity of other rings, brooches and earrings. It is the Countess's instruction that Lady Henrietta is to select whatever she wishes from the collection and the remainder is to be held in trust by Mr Chambers for his daughter, Eleanor, until her twenty-first birthday.'

William could bear it no longer and exploded with pent up fury. 'This is an outrage! It is nothing more than the meanderings of a senile old woman! How dare she leave a single penny to this bastard! I will contest!'

His gargantuan body was shaking uncontrollably now and his mouth was contorted by the cold rage that consumed him. The money was rightfully his and he was depending on it to cover his gambling debts. He had promised his creditors and now he was left without the means to pay up.

Max stared dispassionately at him and shuddered with distaste. His mind was still reeling from Sir John's disclosures but his overwhelming feeling was one of shame; how could he possibly be related to this man who so disgusted him with his repugnant behaviour? It took every ounce of his considerable will-power to remain calm, but he was determined to remain in control of both himself and the situation.

Sir John looked from one man to the other and inwardly recoiled at the virulent antipathy so evident between them. They were the very antithesis of one another. Lord William was an arrogant and monstrous bully given to intimidation and offensive behaviour but Max was altogether a more complex and perspicacious individual, just as Lady Constance had told him. Like most bullies, he knew that William was a weak man beneath his aggressive bluster but he had discovered, through his dealings with him as one of his trustees, that he was also an individual of limited intellect. He could tell, however, that Max was a shrewd character who missed little. The hairs on the back of his neck began to rise as he studied them more closely. There was passion in the room, but it was of mutual hatred so potent that it was frightening. However, there was something else as well; the air seemed to resonate with a power and ruthlessness that completely took his breath away. It emanated from just one man – Max.

Sir John swallowed hard and looked directly at Lord William. 'My Lord, I must tell you that Her Ladyship anticipated the possibility of a challenge to her wishes and accordingly she attached a codicil to her will as recently as last month. In it she stipulates that if you should seek to dispute the arrangements she has put in place for the distribution of her assets, the trustees of the Gordon estate are to invoke the default clause contained within the family trusts.' He paused and took another sip of water. 'This clause was added to each trust document by her late

351

husband, and when enacted, all payments from each trust in which you are the sole beneficiary cease immediately. It is quite specific, my Lord.'

Lady Henrietta stared disdainfully at her brother. 'So you see, William, Mama knew exactly what you are like. If you so much as question Mama's will, I shall make sure that Sir John has every help to do as she and Papa wished!'

Max was shocked at the scorn in her voice. William, however, looked at her in stunned surprise.

'But, Henrietta, this is not fair! We are family and he...'

'You are no brother of mine!' she shot back witheringly. 'I stopped regarding you as family after Papa died!'

William's colossal rage and shame at the public slights he had suffered at the hands of his mother and sister forced him out of his chair with uncustomary agility. He raised his hand as if to strike her but Max moved more quickly. He was already on his feet, sensing trouble, and he caught William's arm as it swung round towards Henrietta. He gripped it roughly and forced it behind William's back, making him gasp with pain.

'Sit down, Gordon!' he hissed, 'unless you want to be thrown out on the street.'

William was no match for Max and he knew it. Muttering grossly to himself, he wrenched his arm away from Max and lurched towards the door. 'You haven't heard the last of this!' he shouted before stumbling out into the corridor. He slammed the door violently behind him, which made the windows rattle in their frames.

Chapter 60

The Treaty of Versailles was signed on the day 'Maisonbleu' opened its doors for the very first time. Piccadilly was crowded as London Society turned out for the occasion, with taxi drivers and chauffeurs queuing patiently in the street as they waited for their passengers to alight outside the brightly illuminated entrance canopy. A large crowd had gathered on the opposite pavement to stare at the glamorous scene and the traffic along Piccadilly had nearly come to a standstill as liveried doormen escorted a steady stream of immaculately attired gentlemen and their bejewelled ladies from their motor cars into the most talked about new restaurant in town.

Max and Billy stood at the foot of the grand staircase, which rose up in a graceful arc from the centre of the ground floor, greeting each of their guests as they were announced by Marcel, their new maître d', who was acting as master of ceremonies for the evening. Tailcoated waiters moved calmly amongst the throng with trays of exquisitely presented canapés that Anton had spent many hours preparing earlier that afternoon, and a string quartet played serenely in the background.

'Lady Henrietta has worked wonders hasn't she?' whispered Billy as he watched the last of their invited guests make their entrance. 'I reckon most of *Burke's Peerage* is here.'

'She certainly has, we couldn't have done it without her,' replied Max out of the corner of his mouth. 'Good evening, Your Grace, welcome to Maisonbleu.'

'Would you care for a drink, Your Grace?' asked Billy as he turned with a sweep of his arm towards a waiter standing on his left who was holding a silver tray of crystal flutes filled with deliciously sparkling champagne.

'That's everybody now, sir,' said Marcel, 'I'll let you know when Anton is ready for me to seat them.

'Thank you, Marcel, that was all very well done,' replied Max with a smile as he thought of the fragile state of Anton's Gallic temper as the most nerve-racking moment of the night approached. His wartime comrade had been insistent on serving an asparagus soufflé to begin

353

with, despite the critical timing involved in getting 90 people seated at precisely the right moment. Max had wisely decided to leave all the decisions about the menu to Anton and had concentrated instead on ensuring the evening was well supported by a good cross-section of their future clientele.

The room was crowded with people whom Max either knew slightly or had never met before. Lady Henrietta certainly had been a godsend in advising who should receive the hand-embossed invitations and then personally inviting some of the more illustrious names herself. It had helped that some of the guests were already customers of Chambers & Co with first hand knowledge of the company's reputation for top class merchandise and service, but both Max and Billy knew that it was Lady Henrietta's involvement that had guaranteed such an impressive turnout.

'I'm just going to slip upstairs to the flat to say goodnight to Eleanor whilst I've got the chance,' said Max.

'Right oh,' said Billy, 'give her a kiss for me too will you?'

The two friends smiled at each other. The evening represented the end of six months of particularly hard work since they had arrived home from the war within days of each other in December 1918. Richie and his fellow directors had been working on plans for the Maisonbleu chain since Max had first announced the idea back in 1915. He had found the site in Piccadilly through contacts of Lennie's in the building trade, and as soon as he saw it, he knew it would be perfect. Contracts for the purchase of a 99-year lease had been signed in the autumn of 1917, but work on the interior of the four-storey building had not begun until January 1919.

Situated only a short walk from Fortnum and Mason, it was in an area of London familiar to the fashionable Society clientele Max wished to attract. The kitchens and storerooms had been installed in the basement under Anton's watchful supervision; he had accepted Max's invitation to join them in the venture after his family had been amongst the many civilian casualties of the war. Life in France, and even his own restaurant in Paris, held no appeal for him without them and the opportunity to join Max in England had represented a fresh and exciting new start.

The ground floor was divided into a comfortable bar and reception area with two sumptuously appointed private dining-rooms to the rear. A graceful and imposing staircase rose up to the main dining floor from the middle of this reception area, and at night-time, a magnificent crystal chandelier suspended from the ornately moulded ceiling above cast its flattering glow over the guests as they climbed the richly carpeted stairs to their tables. The top floor contained two offices and a flat, which was occupied by Anton. Max had wanted the ambience to be luxurious but without ostentation and in this he had succeeded brilliantly. Their guests, so used to opulence in their own homes, had marvelled in awe at the quality of the materials Lennie had used in the public areas and at the richness in the fabrics of the soft furnishings and table dressings.

'Daddy, Daddy,' cried Eleanor excitedly as he walked into the flat on the top floor. She scrambled down from Nanny Andrews' lap, her startlingly blue eyes, so reminiscent of Rosie's, shining with delight. A huge smile brightened her face as she ran across the room towards him.

'I've come to say goodnight to my favourite daughter,' said Max, laughing as he picked her up and swung her round. 'It's way past your bedtime, little one.'

Nanny Andrews smiled. The five years she had spent caring for Eleanor had softened the rather dour character Max had encountered when she had first arrived in Gloucester Street to assist with Eleanor's birth, and it warmed her heart to watch Eleanor and her father together. The little girl clearly adored him and Max was such a good father to her; caring, loving and always so patient, although sometimes she did have to step in to stop the little girl twisting him round her little finger, which she was very prone to do.

'But I'm your *only* daughter, Daddy, aren't I?' asked Eleanor with a puzzled expression on her face.

Max laughed again, only this time more loudly. 'You are quite right, darling, how clever of you to notice!' he joked. 'Come on, it's time Nanny took you home to bed. It's been a special treat to stay up tonight but it's getting late.'

'Oh, but...'

'No "buts", young lady, otherwise Mrs Walsh and the others will wonder where you've got to! If you're a good girl we'll go and see the horses at the weekend shall we?'

Eleanor nodded her head enthusiastically. She loved watching the grooms with the horses at Arlington Park.

'Yes, it's well past your bedtime, Eleanor. Let's do as your father says,' said Nanny Andrews. 'Here's your coat now.' She held out a smart red woollen coat as Max lowered Eleanor back down to the floor. 'There's a good girl.'

Max smiled indulgently as Eleanor took her coat and resisted Nanny Andrews' attempts to help her put it on. She was already an independently minded young girl. 'George will be waiting at the back door with the car, Nanny, I must return to my guests now. Thank you,' he said, referring to his new chauffeur who had brought them to the restaurant earlier that evening in the Rolls.

'Very good, sir.'

'Oh, by the way, I nearly forgot,' exclaimed Max suddenly as he bent down and gave Eleanor another kiss. 'That one is from your Uncle Billy.'

The babble of conversation grew louder as he hurried from the flat past the elegantly laid tables on the first floor to the top of the staircase. Quickly descending the stairs, he glanced approvingly at the flower arrangements standing in their display niches in the staircase wall, to his right. They had been sent from the nurseries in Wiltshire and provided just the right splash of colour against the deliberate plainness of the pale cream decor.

'Max, there you are, I've been looking for you,' said Lady Henrietta, coming towards him as he reached the bottom step. 'Everyone's here as far as I can see.'

Max smiled appreciatively as he took her arm. 'Yes, Marcel informs me it's a full house and we couldn't have done it without your help. I didn't realise you knew so many people, you must be very persuasive!'

Henrietta brushed his thanks aside. 'Come on, I'll introduce you round,' and with that she led him into the midst of the spirited laughter and chatter coming from the crowded room.

The evening was a resounding success; Anton and his team excelled in the kitchens and produced some of the most delicious food Max had ever eaten, and Marcel managed the front of house with quiet and efficient authority, delivering a charming and superior service to their discerning and sometimes demanding guests. There were many favourable comments about the striking décor, so refreshing in its elegant simplicity and clever use of colour. This was in marked contrast to most other establishments of the day, and the bookings diary was quickly filled for weeks ahead.

The shop next door to the restaurant was another of Max's ideas. The 'Delicatessen Maisonbleu' was primarily a showcase for the finest of the Chambers & Co product lines, but the first floor overlooking Piccadilly contained a café, which was open all day, from breakfast right through to afternoon tea. Customers had to walk through the shop on the ground floor in order to reach the staircase and here they would stop to browse the many displays of attractively presented merchandise, and smartly uniformed assistants were on hand to help them with their purchases, or to offer advice on which products to buy.

With their shopping completed, the ladies, or gentlemen, could then proceed to the café for a leisurely breakfast, cup of morning coffee, luncheon or afternoon tea. The menu included many of the items on sale in the shop itself and, because of this, the satisfied diners would often make additional purchases on their way out, having just sampled and enjoyed a particular item in the café. Liveried footmen were also on hand to help them with their packages, to open car doors or to hail a passing taxi-cab. The level of service each customer received was unparalleled in London, and both the Maisonbleu establishments quickly became renowned for it.

The success of their first restaurant and delicatessen pleased both Max and Billy and it provided a welcome boost to the company's profits in the immediate post-war period. The businesses had survived the war years remarkably well, thanks in part to their contracts to supply provisions to the forces, and demand for their fine foods and gift lines had already begun to recover to pre-war levels. The recruitment difficulties they had faced from the second half of 1915 onwards were now easing too as men returned home in their droves, desperate to seek work in a 'land fit for heroes'. There were some sad losses to contend with amongst the workforce but on the whole they had been remarkably fortunate.

Richie had fulfilled his temporary role as managing director of Chambers & Co with aplomb, and he and Marjorie were now the parents of two little girls who they had named Josephine and Ella. Lennie was making a name for himself in the building trade, and his skill at fitting out the restaurant and delicatessen for Max had won him lucrative new commissions for his recently formed construction company. Jimmy was at university studying English Literature, paid for by Max, and had aspirations to become a journalist. Billy had settled happily back into civilian life with Elizabeth and Alexander, counting his blessings that he had survived the war unscathed, as they all did, and relishing the challenge of developing the Maisonbleu chain in other parts of the country.

This was just as he and Max had envisaged when they had discussed the idea four years previously, but it was becoming apparent that he could not fulfil his duties as managing director of Chambers & Co in addition to his Maisonbleu responsibilities. Accordingly, Max offered Richie the role on a permanent basis to enable Billy to concentrate solely on establishing Maisonbleu as the leading restaurant group in the country.

One of Billy's first actions was to invite Lady Henrietta to join the Maisonbleu board, much to her delight. He recognised the vital skill she had to offer as one who instinctively understood the wants and needs of their target market because she was from the same social class herself. It was a slightly unorthodox notion because ladies of her background did not usually dabble in commerce, but there was no one better equipped than she.

But then Lady Henrietta had rarely conformed to the socially accepted norms of the day and she accepted with alacrity.

Chapter 61

There was a knock on the study door. Max yawned and looked up from *The Times* newspaper; it had been a busy week and it was going to be an equally busy weekend.

'Sorry to disturb you, sir, the morning post has just arrived.'

'Thank you, Fenton, leave it on the side table over there would you please?'

'Very good, sir.' The butler coughed. 'Excuse me, sir, what time are the guests expected? Mrs Walsh was asking...'

Max looked up from the article he was reading. 'Oh, I'm sorry, Fenton, I should have said.' He smiled apologetically. 'Mr and Mrs Black and the children are due at eleven o'clock and Mr and Mrs Masters and Alexander will arrive in time for luncheon. Oh, and Lady Henrietta is joining us for dinner this evening, did I mention that? She has to leave after breakfast on Sunday so we'll only be five for luncheon tomorrow, plus the children of course.'

Fenton smiled. 'Indeed you did, sir, thank you. I will inform Mrs Walsh accordingly. Shall I bring coffee as soon as the first guests have arrived, sir?'

'Yes please, they'll be ready for that after their drive from London I'm sure, and would you let Nanny know about the children, they'll need nursery tea I suppose? Eleanor and Alexander can join us for dinner in the dining-room.'

He knew Henrietta would like the older children to eat with them as she had become quite the doting aunt to Eleanor and had assumed the mantle of honorary aunt to Alexander. The children adored her; she was always such fun with them.

'Very good, sir.'

Fenton closed the study door behind him with a smile. It was good to see the master entertaining again. He had seemed distracted recently, as though something was on his mind, but he must be feeling in better spirits and Mrs Walsh would be pleased to have people to cook for; especially Richie Black who loved his food.

Max glanced at his watch. It was already half past nine and he had promised to take Eleanor to the stables before the others arrived. She was really old enough to go on her own now but she did enjoy him watching her ride Dusty, the pony he had bought her for Christmas. No doubt she would come rushing in like a whirlwind at any moment, he thought as he picked up the pile of envelopes from the side table on his way to the drawing-room.

He opened the double doors of one of his favourite rooms in the house. The yellow drawing-room held a magical quality for Max, which he had sensed from his very first visit to Arlington Park. The view from the large bow window across the wide rear terrace was spectacular on an early summer's day when the sun streamed in to cast its golden glow on the bright yellow walls, filling the room with a welcoming and cheerful light. When it was reflected in the tall gilt-framed mirror hanging over the fireplace, the effect was captivating. He had furnished the room with beautiful Regency furniture on the knowledgeable advice of Lady Henrietta and acquired, over the past four years, from various country house sales. A fine landscape by Turner hung on the far wall, which marked the beginning of an art collection that now included a Gainsborough, a Reynolds and two Impressionist paintings by Monet and Sisley.

Max was looking through the envelopes in his hand as he walked over to the window and he stopped abruptly as he recognised the familiar handwriting. He was not expecting the next report from the private investigator for another four weeks.

Dear Mr Chambers,
There have been some developments that I think will interest you...

Max quickly scanned the page as he sat down. When he had finished, he folded the letter and put it carefully back in its envelope. His mind was racing but he would deal with it later. He couldn't believe his luck; it had always been just a matter of time before *he* left himself vulnerable, he had always known that, but he had not expected it to happen so soon.

'Daddy!' Eleanor cried as she bounded across the room at the sight of her father. 'Can we go to the stables now please?'

She plumped down next to him in a flash and leaned over to give him a kiss. Her laughing blue eyes looked beseechingly at him. 'Will you watch me ride Dusty please, Daddy, *please?*'

Max tore his mind from the letter and laughed. He knew he would not get any peace until he gave in. 'All right, all right, you little monster, seeing as I promised!' Eleanor smiled with delight. 'Are you ready then, have you brushed your teeth this morning?'

'Yes, Daddy,' she exclaimed in a long-suffering voice, 'I always brush my teeth. Nanny makes me!'

'Good for Nanny,' laughed Max, 'come on then.' He stood up and hurried out of the room after her. 'I could ride with you if you like?'

'Oh yes, Daddy!' said Eleanor excitedly without turning round.

'I'll have to get changed then, darling, I'll catch you up. We'll have to hurry because Josephine and Ella will be here soon.'

Max ran up the sweeping staircase two at a time, his feet sure and firm on the broad red-carpeted treads as he heard the front door slam with a loud crash. He had decided long ago that his daughter was turning out to be a single-minded and determined young lady. This seemed to be increasingly true as the years went by, although at nearly ten years of age, he did sometimes worry that she needed a maternal influence in her life. Whenever he discussed this with Molly or Elizabeth they always told him to stop fussing, which was just as well as there was no one to compare with Rosie. He quickly donned his riding breeches and pulled on his leather riding boots before hurrying after Eleanor.

The breeze against their faces was exhilarating as they cantered across the fields. Eleanor's laughing face was a picture of delight as she gently urged Dusty on across the long green grass. Max sat easily in the saddle of his chestnut mare, keeping pace with her as he admired the confidence with which she handled Dusty's reins. Her love and natural affinity for horses was similar to Bert's, and Max thought how much his father would have delighted in watching his granddaughter now. He could have taught her so much after a lifetime spent with them.

Despite Max's enjoyment of the moment, the content of the private investigator's unexpected letter kept coming to the forefront of his mind. He had engaged the services of the investigator following two incidents that had occurred almost simultaneously two years previously, and since that time he had received regular monthly reports about William's dissolute and aimless life. These were in addition to the details Jim Edwardes continued to feed him about William's business activities, as a result of which he was aware that the family mine and quarries were barely profitable. Agnes, Jim's old and loyal secretary, still worked at the mine in Lee Moor and she was the source of much interesting and valuable information.

It seemed that William's harsh treatment of his men remained intolerable and the enormous potential that existed in both the mine and quarries therefore continued to be squandered. William's finances were under constant pressure for a number of reasons, not least of which was the control over his income exerted by the trustees. Their primary role was to preserve the family fortune for future generations and they were enabled by powers granted to them by Lord Hugo to restrict payments from the family trusts if they had evidence that the money was to be used to cover William's gambling debts. Lady Henrietta ensured that the trustees were kept informed of her brother's ineptitude at the tables.

The first incident took place on the opening day of the third Maisonbleu restaurant in the spring of 1921. The launch party had gone well on the evening before opening day, when most of Plymouth Society had turned out for the occasion; Rebecca had helped compile the guest list and so there was the usual mix of loyal Chambers & Co customers and local gentry. The following day had begun smoothly until a particularly unfortunate scene occurred when a customer complained very publicly about the quality of his food, claiming that his Dover sole was off. He had made such a fuss in front of the entire restaurant, including two journalists from the local newspaper who then printed the story in their following day's edition. It eventually transpired, after much investigation by Max, Billy and Rebecca, that the customer was a paid charlatan and the journalists had been forewarned about the premeditated incident and had therefore booked a table, eager for their headline. A retraction was printed after Max had threatened to sue and the falsehood was duly exposed. The culprit, it seemed, was in the pay of Lord William. It was a tiresome and spiteful episode, deliberately intended to cause Max more harm than it actually did, but it paled into insignificance when compared to the second event.

A week later a letter had landed on the doormat in Gloucester Street from a firm of solicitors in Plymouth. Imagining it to be connected to the Maisonbleu troubles, Max had angrily torn it open, but instead of the anticipated letter, he found a sealed envelope inside addressed to him, the contents of which left him completely stupefied. It was a confession from Makepiece, his hated adversary below stairs at Mount Royal, admitting responsibility for setting the estate dogs loose on Rosie on the day of her accident. In that instant, standing in the hallway at Gloucester Street with the letter in his shaking hands, Max had finally vowed to avenge the deaths of the two people he had loved most in the world, taken from him by the man who, in a cruel twist of fate, had been revealed as his blood father; the man he reviled above all others.

In his letter, Makepiece attempted to atone for his actions by admitting his guilt. He had started out in service with the Gordon family at Mount Royal as a young boy of 16, devoting 50 years of his life to them during which time he rose to the position of steward shortly after his fortieth birthday. He was a faithful and trustworthy servant to the Earl and Countess and privy to the innermost trials and tribulations of their lives, none more so than the scandalous liaison Lord William conducted with Florence Rathbone. Makepiece felt deeply for his employers at the time, genuinely upset at the distress and shame their son's behaviour caused Lady Constance for the remainder of her life. However, this very laudable emotion had unfortunately been translated into an active but irrational resentment, bordering on dislike, of the result of that brief relationship. He claimed that the first thing he had noticed when Rosie arrived at Mount Royal was her startling resemblance to Florence, and to his dying day he was at a loss to understand why Lady Constance had ever employed the girl in the first place. He had eventually concluded that she must have been blind to the similarities, but it was obvious that Lord William was not.

He gradually became convinced that history would repeat itself and, after his interrogation by William in the long gallery on that fateful day, he had resolved to put a stop to what he believed were William's intentions by forcing Rosie to leave Mount Royal. He believed this was necessary to protect the family and so he began by crudely trying to bully Rosie into handing in her notice, but when he realised that she was not going to be cowed into submission he decided instead to frighten her into leaving. Seizing his opportunity when Rosie was on her way to meet Max at The Wheelwrights, he had set the estate dogs on her, intending that they would terrify her into fleeing back to London; he had not meant for her to fall and seriously injure herself in the ensuing chase.

He subsequently realised he had unwittingly been the cause of more misery and pain for the Countess and he had found the burden of guilt almost impossible to bear. He blamed William for everything, despising him for it, and after Lord Hugo's death the frequent humiliations he had suffered at William's hands had turned him into a bitter and vindictive old man. With Lady Constance gone and with Lady Henrietta no longer resident at Mount Royal, and estranged from her brother, he had resolved to tell Max the truth from beyond the grave. It was too late to ask for his forgiveness but he felt that it was his duty to speak the truth; he ended by saying that he hoped his confession might in some way be helpful.

In possession of this shattering knowledge, Max had been faced with an important decision. He acted in characteristic fashion, taking his time to carefully and deliberately consider every aspect of the situation before deciding on his strategy. However, he had been certain of one thing from the very start: William would be made to pay for his sins. The only question was what form the payment would take.

After several weeks of painstaking thought, he had decided to engage a private investigator to unearth as much information about William as possible. He wanted to discover every detail of his activities, his habits, his business dealings, and his private life. Max had always understood that knowledge was power and he knew that possession of it would provide him with the answer. His strategy was simple. He would play a waiting game and allow William to expose his own weakness. Then he would act.

The investigator's reports arrived at the end of every month and he now knew what William did, where he went, and who he saw on a regular basis. Each one made for unedifying reading and the picture that had gradually emerged confirmed beyond doubt that the Earl and Countess had been right to protect themselves and the family fortune from their son.

'Eleanor, it's time we were heading back now,' Max shouted. 'It's half past ten.'

Eleanor turned in her saddle and smiled at him. 'I'll race you, Daddy!' With that she spurred Dusty on and galloped off in the direction of the house.

'Hey, come back here,' cried Max, 'that's cheating! You've got a head start.'

He turned his mare and set off after her, laughing at Eleanor's determination to win. In truth, Dusty was no match for his horse but Max surreptitiously slowed down as he began to draw level with her on the approach to the fence that enclosed the paddock at the back of the stable block.

'I won!' cried Eleanor triumphantly. She leant forwards and patted Dusty's neck. 'Well done, girl, well done,' she said as she dismounted. The horse was panting heavily and tossing its head to and fro. 'Whoa,' she cried, 'easy girl ... easy...' Under her firm but soothing control Dusty soon calmed down and Max watched as Eleanor led her through the gate and into the yard. 'I've got to rub her down before everyone arrives, Daddy and I want to help the grooms with yours too. Is that all right?'

She always considered the horses first and never shirked her responsibilities to them. 'Yes, darling, that's fine but be as quick as you can.'

'All right, Daddy.'

Max smiled. He knew whatever he said would make no difference. She would take as long as was necessary.

Chapter 62

'Richie, Marjorie, how good to see you! And Josephine, and Ella, how are you girls?' He picked each one of them up and gave them a big kiss, which made them go pink with delight.

Fenton was hovering behind them as they stood in the middle of the stone-flagged entrance hall. 'Shall I bring coffee now, sir?'

'Yes please, Fenton.'

'And I believe Mrs Walsh has made some lemonade for Miss Josephine and Miss Ella.'

'Oh, did you hear that, girls?' asked Marjorie, 'isn't that kind. What do you say?'

'Thank you, Mr Fenton,' they chorused in unison.

'It's a pleasure, my dears,' replied the butler with a beaming smile. 'I think Mrs Walsh may have some of your favourite biscuits too.'

They squealed with delight. 'Ooh, thank you, Mrs Walsh,' they said excitedly.

Marjorie laughed. 'She can't hear you from here girls. You do spoil them, Fenton, thank you so much.'

'Not at all, madam.'

'Would you like to go down to the kitchen and thank her yourselves?' asked Max with an enquiring glance at Fenton. Then you can help Mr Fenton bring them up.' The look on their faces gave Max the answer. 'Off you go then.'

'Be good,' called Marjorie as she watched them disappear with Fenton in the direction of the kitchen. 'Do as Mrs Walsh tells you please.'

They both adored Mrs Walsh and her kitchen and she loved their visits.

'How was the journey, not too bad I hope?' asked Max as he led them into the drawing-room.

'We encountered some light traffic as we passed through Kensington but other than that it was fine thanks. We made quite good time actually. It's such a pleasant change to get out of London for the weekend,' said Richie.

'I'll second that!' added Marjorie, sinking down into one of the comfortable settees with relief. 'You know, Max, this is such a beautiful room. I feel relaxed already.' Richie looked at Max and rolled his eyes. 'Where's Eleanor? Josephine and Ella can't wait to see her.'

'Guess,' said Max. 'We went out riding this morning.'

'Ah, the stables then.'

'Where else!' replied Max with a grin, 'but I shouldn't complain. It's good that she doesn't avoid her responsibilities I suppose. They clearly rank above her duties as a hostess don't they? You know, she even wanted to take care of my horse too.'

Marjorie and Richie laughed. 'What time are Billy and Elizabeth due? When I spoke to Billy yesterday he wasn't sure what Elizabeth had arranged.'

'That certainly sounds like Billy,' said Marjorie wryly. 'I sometimes think he'd be lost without her.' They all laughed again.

'Henrietta is joining us for dinner this evening but she has to leave after breakfast in the morning. She's spending next week at Bickleigh Manor I believe.'

'Oh good,' exclaimed Marjorie. 'You know I sometimes feel sorry for her, with that brother of hers.'

Max grimaced. 'Well you certainly don't need to feel sorry for Henrietta you know, she of all people can take care of herself.'

'You can say that again,' Richie chipped in from across the room where he was admiring the view from the bay window. 'She's one of the most capable ladies I know and she's been very good for the business, hasn't she Max?' Marjorie bridled with mock indignation. 'Present company excepted of course, darling.'

'She certainly has,' chuckled Max. 'It never ceases to amaze me how many people she knows and most of them are more than simply casual acquaintances. I always think our launch parties for the Maisonbleu chain would be empty without her!'

Later, once Billy and Elizabeth arrived, and the happy party was assembled, the three men left Marjorie and Elizabeth gossiping merrily and collected Josephine, Ella and Alexander from the kitchen and headed for the stables.

'The lawns are in magnificent condition, Max,' commented Billy as they walked around the side of the house.

It was true. The outdoors staff consisted of four gardeners, overseen by Arthur, the head gardener, who had been at Arlington Park for more than 20 years and knew every inch of the grounds like the back of his hand. He tended to his domain with great care and devotion.

'I always loved the grounds at Mount Royal, you know, and Alf Tomkins, the old Head Gardener there, taught me a lot. He's dead now unfortunately but I think he'd like this,' he replied, with a sweep of his arm.

The children had run on ahead, out of earshot. Max reached into his pocket and took out the letter from the private investigator. 'Actually, whilst the children aren't here, I wanted to show you both this. It arrived this morning.'

He took the letter out of the envelope and handed it to Billy and Richie. They read it in silence and then Richie whistled softly.

'If this is correct, he must be in real trouble this time. *Is it true*, do you think?'

'The reports have never been wrong before so there's no reason to imagine it isn't true,' answered Max with a thoughtful expression.

'What do you intend to do?' asked Billy quietly. 'This might be the opportunity you've been waiting for.'

Max nodded. 'Yes I know but there's no hurry to do anything at the moment because the fool will find it difficult to raise the money it would seem he needs. The mine is barely profitable and the same goes for the quarries so the banks won't accept those as collateral for a loan. He can't touch the Gordon trusts, Lord Hugo saw to that, and the trustees have spent the last eleven years protecting the estate from his profligacy so they are unlikely to change now. He needs a benefactor ... and a rich one at that.'

Billy and Richie looked knowingly at him. 'And that person might be you, is that what you are saying?' asked Billy.

'Maybe,' said Max with a grin, 'I want to discuss it with Henrietta this evening and I'd value your opinions too. Let's talk about it then shall we? Now then, where are these children...?'

Chapter 63

The last of the early evening sunshine poured through the dining-room windows as Fenton and Mary put the finishing touches to the table.

'A little to the left, Mary ... little bit more ... bit more ... that's it! Thank you.'

The flower display had to be positioned exactly in the centre of the long dining table otherwise the whole effect would be ruined, and that would never do. Lady Henrietta was dining this evening and she was a stickler for detail. The master was too; in fact, all the guests would be certain to notice the slightest thing out of place and he was not going to allow that to happen in his house.

'Lady Henrietta is due shortly, is everything ready for her upstairs, Mary?'

'Yes, Mr Fenton, Violet is up there now, makin' sure.' Goodness me, she thought, he does fuss.

The dining-room looked resplendent on occasions like this. The table was laid with the best china and sparkling glassware and gleaming solid silver cutlery was placed with military precision at each place setting. A fire crackled gently in the fireplace to ward off the merest hint of an evening chill and table lamps standing on highly polished cherrywood occasional tables cast their warming glow into the far corners of the room. Individual cruet sets and menu cards stood at the top left hand corner of each setting and candles stood to attention in ornate silver holders on either side of the flower arrangement waiting to be lit just before the guests entered the room. To complete the effect a fine equestrian scene by Munnings hung on the wall at the head of the table. It was rumoured that the artist would soon be elected to the Royal Academy and Max had liked the painting as soon as he had set eyes upon it at auction earlier in the year.

A glorious portrait of Rosie hung above the fireplace in a finely moulded gold frame. Max had commissioned an artist to paint her portrait shortly after moving into Arlington Park in 1918, having decided that the dining-room would be the perfect place to display it. He wanted to be able to sit at the dining table with his guests and see her smiling down upon them. The artist had done a splendid job, working from a photograph that Max had given him. At Max's request he had copied her favourite pearl necklace and earrings, which were the first real pieces of jewellery he had ever given her, and the magnificent Cartier sapphire and diamond ring that she had not lived to see. The painting captured her likeness perfectly.

'I think we're finished here now, don't you. Can you think of anything we've forgotten?'

Mary smiled reassuringly. 'No, Mr Fenton, everything's 'ere.' He always asked her that same question at times like this and she always gave him the same answer.

Fenton grunted. 'Right then, would you let Mrs Walsh know the dining-room is ready and then bring up the canapés and join me in the drawing-room to help with pre-dinner cocktails please? Thank you. I will answer the front door when Her Ladyship arrives if you will remain with the guests. Quickly now, they will be down in a minute.'

'Yes, Mr Fenton.'

She hurried out of the room and clattered down the kitchen stairs in such a rush that she almost lost her footing on the last but one step.

'Careful, Mary! We don't want any broken bones, not tonight!' said Mrs Walsh sharply. 'Less haste, more speed, my girl.' She was busy at the range, vigorously whisking the sauce for the fish course over a large pan of boiling water and did not look round.

But Mary was not listening; she was already halfway up the stairs with the canapés balanced expertly on her left arm so she could negotiate the heavy swing door into the hallway with her right.

'That's a very pretty dress, darling,' exclaimed Elizabeth, seeing Eleanor over by the window as she came into the drawing-room, arm in arm with Billy who looked very distinguished in his evening suit. Alexander followed closely behind with an uncomfortable expression on his face. Dressed in his Sunday best, he was fingering his collar awkwardly.

'My tie is too tight,' he complained.

Eleanor giggled. 'Thank you, Aunt Elizabeth.' She looked pleased. Around her neck she wore a single strand of small and delicate pearls that were similar to ones in her mother's portrait.

'What will you have to drink?' asked Max, 'the usual, Elizabeth?'

'Yes please,' she replied. 'Ooh, these look delicious!' she said as Mary approached her with the canapés. 'Prawns, my favourite! Thank you, Mary.'

Max smiled. 'What will you have, Billy? And lemonade for you is it, Alexander?'

'Champagne too please, Max,' said Billy.

'Yes please, Uncle Max.'

Richie and Marjorie appeared in the doorway and the front door bell rang at the same time. Mary had left the room for a moment and Fenton looked anxiously towards the hall as Richie and Marjorie approached him.

'We'll serve the drinks, Mr Fenton, we know how,' said Eleanor and Alexander quickly, realising the butler's dilemma. 'Then you can let Great-Aunt Henrietta in.'

'Well, I . . .'

Max laughed. 'It's perfectly all right, Fenton. Let Her Ladyship in and these two can hold the fort! I think they really want to, you know.'

'Very good, sir,' said Fenton, unable to keep the relief from his voice.

Drinks served with consummate skill by the stand-in cocktail waiters, they had barely taken their first sips when Fenton's sonorous voice boomed out.

'Lady Henrietta Gordon, sir.'

'Henrietta!' cried Max as they all turned round. He rushed across to greet her, grasping her hand and leaning into her to kiss her on both cheeks. 'You made it then.' The diamond and ruby necklace that had belonged to the Countess sparkled at her throat and matching stones twinkled at her ears and wrists.

'Of course I did,' she laughed gaily, 'the new motor drives like a dream.' She looked across the elegant room and greeted the others with a big smile. 'There's Eleanor and Alexander too, how wonderful,' she added as she watched the two of them coming towards her. Alexander was balancing a glass on a small tray with a look of acute concentration on his face.

'Hello, Great-Aunt Henrietta, look what we've made for you,' said Eleanor proudly.

'Less of the Great-Aunt,' she laughed. 'How lovely to see you both, I'm so glad you're not in bed,' she added, bending down towards them.

'We let them stay up as a special treat,' explained Max as Alexander held up the tray to her.

'Oh, what's this?' asked Henrietta as she took a sip. 'Good Lord! That *is* a nice one,' she said quickly as her eyes began to water, 'thank you very much.'

Mary was busy again handing round the canapés and helping Fenton

371

to replenish the empty glasses, looking for her opportunity to slip away to warn Mrs Walsh that Lady Henrietta had arrived and that he would be announcing dinner in approximately 20 minutes.

'How's the new Bentley?' asked Richie. 'Max tells me you've bought one.'

He admired Lady Henrietta enormously. She was unquestionably her own woman, determined to live life on her terms and unafraid to flout the social conventions of the day; the fact that she drove her own car, and a three-litre Bentley at that, was testimony to her self-assurance so often typical of ladies of her class. But at the same time she was a firm believer in the traditional codes of behaviour and she was quite capable of being authoritarian. In that sense too she was very much a product of her background and upbringing. However, she was kind, considerate and fun to be with and had warmly embraced them all with a generosity of spirit that had not waned.

'It's marvellous!' she replied enthusiastically, 'and very fast. We could go for a drive tomorrow so you can see for yourself, or you could take her out if you like?'

'That's a brave thing to say, Henrietta,' commented Marjorie dryly. 'You know what Richie's driving is like.'

They all laughed.

'Excuse me, sir, dinner is served,' said Fenton, interrupting the gaiety.

The food was superb, and judging by the empty plates Mary loaded into the dumb waiter after each course, everyone had a healthy appetite too. Even Eleanor and Alexander managed to finish most of what was on their plates. Max put down his spoon and fork, leaned back in his chair and looked at his guests around the table. Arlington Park was ideal for entertaining, even on a small scale such as this, and he lifted his glass of champagne that Mary had just refilled and sipped it slowly, savouring the atmosphere in the room. It was at moments like this, when he was sitting at the head of the table and wishing he could raise his glass to her in a gesture of quiet and private celebration, that he still missed Rosie acutely. The sheer savagery of his devastating grief had subsided long ago, only to be replaced by a sad and lonely emptiness that he managed to repress most of the time, but every now and then it would rise to the forefront of his senses and then he would find himself wondering if it would ever leave him, or if he would ever find happiness again.

Fenton's discreet coughing disturbed his reverie. 'Would you like coffee and liqueurs in the library, sir?' he asked.

'Yes please, Fenton, in about five minutes I think. And the cigars please.'

The butler nodded discreetly. 'It's all ready for you, sir.'

Chapter 64

Elizabeth and Marjorie took the children upstairs to Nanny Andrews while the others went through to the library.

'That was a delicious meal, Fenton, would you please thank Mrs Walsh for us?' said Max as they settled in the comfortable leather wing chairs that were arranged around the fireplace. Violet had been in to draw the curtains and light the fire whilst they were eating and a pleasant smell of burning wood filled the room. She had already put out the liqueurs and cigars and now she appeared with a tray of coffee.

'That's splendid, Violet, thank you. We'll serve ourselves now, you may go to bed.'

'If you are sure then, sir, we'll say goodnight,' said Fenton.

'Yes, thank you, Fenton. Goodnight.'

When they had left and closed the door behind them Henrietta stood up and, picking up the coffee pot from the tray, she began to pour the coffee. 'There's something on your mind, Max, isn't there? And you don't want the servants to hear it.' She had learned to recognise the signs; she knew he wanted to talk to them in private.

'Oh dear, was it that obvious?' he replied with a wry smile. 'Yes, there is, but I couldn't discuss it in front of the children.' He reached into the pocket of his evening jacket and took out the letter from the private investigator. He unfolded it and passed it to her. 'This arrived in the post this morning.'

Lady Henrietta handed the coffee pot to Billy and reached into her black velvet evening bag for her reading glasses. She read the letter twice before looking up with a thoughtful expression on her face.

'Well, I might have guessed it had something to do with William,' she said caustically. 'Have Billy and Richie seen this?'

Max nodded. 'Briefly this morning. I had an opportunity to show it to them when we were on our way to the stables with the children, but we haven't discussed it yet. I wanted to wait until you were here as it involves your family.'

Henrietta grimaced. 'I'm ashamed to say it does, but you all know my feelings about my brother so we can speak freely here.'

374

'Has he said anything to you about this?' asked Billy.

Henrietta shook her head. 'We don't talk.'

'There is no reason to doubt what the investigator is saying but I'm surprised the trustees haven't told you he is trying to raise money,' said Max with a perplexed expression on his face. He poured some cream into his coffee and stirred it slowly. 'He must be desperate for the funds if he is putting his mining interests up for sale.'

'The trustees are not obliged to tell me anything and don't forget they are empowered by my late father to withhold payments if they have evidence that the money would be used to cover his gambling debts. The mine and quarries are the only remaining assets he has left that aren't tied up in the trusts.'

Richie had been silent up to this point. 'From what the investigator has said in his letter, William is seeking to raise the money to place on account rather than to actually pay off an existing debt, unless I've misunderstood it? Why is that, do you think?'

'No, Richie, I don't think you have misunderstood the situation, it does seem to be the case, which is one of the things I want to confirm when I telephone him on Monday morning,' said Max. 'I'm not sure why but I will find out.'

'I know why,' interjected Henrietta. 'When the stakes are high in a card game, the players are required to prove their ability to pay in advance and they do this by depositing a surety with the gaming house. It has to be in cash and they can then gamble up to that limit before the house has to authorise further credit.'

'Yes, I've heard that too,' concurred Billy.

Max looked at him and raised his eyebrows. 'Misspent youth no doubt?' he asked with a grin.

Billy laughed. 'Not on your life!'

'So it's the cash he needs then,' mused Richie, 'nothing else will do by the sound of it. He can't collateralise this surety with assets if it has to be in cash. I wonder why he doesn't take out a loan and use the mine or the quarries as collateral, or guarantee it against one of his properties.'

'They aren't profitable enough for the banks to be interested as we said this morning and, anyway, I imagine there would be too many questions to answer if he approached them,' explained Max.

'And I presume any bank would want to know why the trustees were denying him access to the family coffers, and if he told them that, he might as well tell them why he needs such a lot of money in the first place and *that* would be certain to ruin his chances of getting it,' added Henrietta coldly. 'You know, Max, this is your opportunity to teach him a lesson he won't forget in a hurry.'

'We said as much this morning but I think Max is anxious that William is your family, whether you like it or not, and he wouldn't want to do anything...'

Henrietta interrupted Billy. 'Is this true, Max, you're worried about my reaction?' She seemed somewhat taken aback.

'Yes I suppose it is. You know I have never disliked anyone more in my entire life, *hated* anyone more actually, and it would give me the greatest pleasure to avenge all he has done to my family. I used to lie awake at night dreaming of how I would pay him back. Do you remember that morning in my office, Billy?'

Billy nodded. 'When he forced his way into the warehouse and you told him you'd kill him if you ever set eyes on him again? I remember it very clearly indeed.'

'Yes. All that was before I knew he was my blood father.' Max couldn't bring himself to use the words 'real father' because Bert was his real father in every other sense of the word. 'After I discovered the truth, I was even more disgusted and determined to avenge the past, and I have been biding my time until the right moment comes along. And then Makepiece's confession prompted me to engage the investigator. But I didn't bargain on getting to know you, Henrietta, and...' He fell silent for a second or two. '...and that has been one of the joys of the past six years and I have to know how you ... I have to have your blessing.' He stopped rather awkwardly and looked at her.

She had been listening intently and now she sat up straighter in her chair, shaking her head. 'Max, my dear Max,' she began quietly, 'you have absolutely no need to explain your motives. I ceased to have a brother eleven years ago, after Papa died. He behaved so badly then, and for Mama and me, that was the last straw. William has no children ... in the direct line of succession I mean ... and so when he dies, the future of the Gordon title and fortune lies with another branch of the family. I reconciled myself to that long ago and I therefore have no vested interest whatsoever.' She laughed mirthlessly. 'Whatever happens to him is hardly likely to bring any more embarrassment and shame to the family name than he has already caused. He has inflicted so much distress to so many people over the years...' She hesitated and her voice softened. '...as you know only too well ... and I shall never forgive him. I feel guilty about many things, but not about what I am saying to you now. To tell you the truth, it would make me happy to see William punished at last. Mama blamed herself for his behaviour, believing she had indulged him too much as a child. She spent her lifetime making excuses for him and suffering the pain and anguish he heaped upon her. It used to infuriate Papa in his latter years, but even she could not think well of him after she was widowed. I always feared there would be trouble when he succeeded to the title and I vowed that I would do whatever I could to prevent him from hurting anyone.'

She looked down at her hands. 'I think perhaps I failed in that responsibility.' Then she paused and looked at them with pain in her eyes. 'But now there is the best chance there might ever be to even the balance and I urge you to ... no ... *I insist* ... that you take it if by so doing you can prevent him from causing further upset. I will help you in any way I can. Mama began by changing her will, which required little persuasion from me; she was so grateful for the generosity of your response to her that she was determined to do the only thing in her power to try to make amends for what had happened over the years. You allowed her to find peace in her final days and I will always be grateful to you for that. She knew she couldn't change the past but she could influence the future. If you like, it was her way of saying sorry and her attempt at curbing his behaviour after her death, which would have been all too predictably awful if he had inherited her private fortune. Now it is your turn, Max, and you must take it.'

Billy and Richie had barely taken their eyes from Henrietta's face whilst she was speaking and now they both turned to look at Max. The passion and conviction of her words rendered him speechless for a moment, and when he spoke, it was with respect and admiration for her selfless attitude.

'Thank you, Henrietta, I couldn't have proceeded without your blessing,' he said simply.

'But now you must,' she repeated.

'I intend to ruin him, which will put a stop to his behaviour once and for all. I have a plan and I'd like your opinion on it, all of you.'

'Gladly,' said Billy supportively.

Richie nodded. 'So what are you going to do?'

'I'm going to make him an offer for the mine and quarries.'

'But what will you do with them and I don't imagine he would sell them if he knew you were the purchaser?' interrupted Richie quickly.

Max held up his hand and Richie immediately looked a little sheepish. 'I have thought about that.'

'Sorry, Max, of course you have,' he muttered.

Max smiled. 'The Gordon mining interests are barely profitable thanks to bad management and so they could be secured at a bargain price. However, I propose to offer him a sum that he will find impossible to refuse, using some of the money Lady Constance left me. They are actually a sound investment in themselves if managed properly and I'd like to ask Jim Edwardes to return as managing director. He was successful there before and can be again, and he was also well respected by the men.' He raised his eyebrows at Richie. 'We can soon find a replacement for him in Leeds can't we?'

'Yes, it will take a few weeks but we can start looking straight-away.'

'My involvement will remain secret for obvious reasons but I will reveal it when I'm ready. Accordingly, I'd like you to front the transaction, Richie. Will you do that?' Sensing Billy's disappointment he quickly added, 'I can't ask you, Billy, because he might remember your face from that day at the warehouse.'

'You don't even need to ask, Max, consider it done. But how will this ruin him? Won't he just end up with the cash? I know you'll have the business but ... ?'

With an expression of quiet satisfaction, Max explained. 'If I were a betting man, pardon the the pun, I'd say that he'll squander the money at the tables and when the gaming house advances him credit, which they will, he'll end up heavily in debt to them with no means of paying it back. If he's desperate now, he'll be in dire straits then with no way out ... unless I offer him one of course!' He could not prevent a malicious smile from crossing his face.

Henrietta nodded approvingly, at once recognising the poetic justice of his strategy; Max was going to use her mother's money to ruin her son and she would have wholeheartedly approved.

'How *will* you offer him a way out, Max?' asked Billy as he stood up to pour coffee for Elizabeth and Marjorie who had just appeared from upstairs. He saw the brilliance of the plan but recognised that its ultimate success depended on this one final element. 'Would any one else like more coffee?'

Max held out his cup. 'Yes please, Billy.' Richie and Henrietta shook their heads. He thought for a second and then turned to Henrietta. 'What would you say is his most treasured possession? Or, to put it another way, what would cause him the most distress if it was taken away from him?'

'The London house in Chesterfield Square,' she replied quickly. 'He spends all of his time there and much prefers it to Mount Royal.'

'That's the answer to your question then, Billy,' said Max enigmatically and he sat back in his chair with a gratified look on his face.

Chapter 65

Later the following week Max was at his desk in the morning room at Gloucester Street. He looked up from his papers as he heard the sound of a motor car pulling up outside in the street; it was George returning from taking Eleanor to school. The decision to enrol her in day school had been a momentous one that they had taken together and St Paul's Girls' School in Hammersmith was turning out to have been a wise choice. She seemed to be flourishing, eager for knowledge and enjoying the challenge presented by her new environment.

Glancing out of the window, his gaze lingered for a moment on the sleek lines of his new Hispano-Suiza H6. He smiled as he watched George proudly polishing the already gleaming flying stork emblem, which graced the hood, until the ringing of the telephone on his desk interrupted his thoughts.

Reaching for the receiver, he picked it up. 'Yes, Fenton, what is it?'

'I have Mr Black for you, sir.'

'Thank you Fenton, put him through would you?'

'Very good, sir.'

'Hello, Max,' said Richie, 'I've got good news.'

'Oh it's you, Richie, I never know whether it's you, Stan, Lennie or Jimmy when Fenton puts you through! He just says "It's Mr Black"!' He suddenly felt a rush of excitement as Richie chuckled on the other end. 'So tell me what's happened then.' He could barely contain himself.

'It was just as you said, Max. He almost bit my hand off when I mentioned the offer. After my first meeting with him yesterday morning he said he needed a few days to think about it but he called me shortly after two, asking me to meet him at his house in Chesterfield Square at six o'clock. By the sound of his voice on the telephone I'd have said he'd had a very convivial lunch and he certainly hadn't sobered up by the time I met him. Can you believe he started by telling me that he didn't have long because he had a dinner engagement at seven? His arrogance was astounding. Anyway, to cut a long story short, he's agreed to sell the mine and quarries for one hundred and fifty thousand pounds but he's in a hurry. His agreement is conditional on contracts being signed by Friday.'

'Don't forget he has a deadline for the lodging of the funds with the gaming house. I spoke to the investigator just before you rang and he believes that to be by the end of next week, otherwise he will be barred from taking part.'

'I'd have liked to have bargained with him, Max, it would have been like taking money from a blind man. You could easily have got them for a knock-down price given their dismal trading performance.' The disgust in Richie's voice was clear; he thought it took a special kind of incompetence to run a business into the ground in the way William had done.

'It isn't about the money, Richie.' He was careful to hide his exasperation. 'We have to be sure our offer is sufficient for his purposes otherwise the plan will fall at the first hurdle. He has to have enough money to satisfy the rules of engagement otherwise he can't play and then we'll fail.'

'Yes I know you're right,' he sighed, 'but it just seems wrong that he'll get way over their current value, that's all.'

'Worth every penny!' said Max firmly. 'Now, the contracts are already drawn up. In fact, I've got them here on my desk in front of me.'

There was a momentary silence. 'That was a clever move, Max, you must have been very sure he'd bite.'

'I was,' he replied. Richie was correct, Max had been confident that William would accept his offer as it was a generous one considering the state of the company. He had judged the figure perfectly – too low and it would have been insufficient for William's needs, but too high and he might have asked questions, although Max was fairly sure there was little risk of that happening. William was a desperate man with a rapacious appetite for money.

'All I've done is encourage his greed, Richie, played to his greatest weakness you might say, and having the contracts prepared in advance was simply a practical decision. Once I'd ascertained he would have a deadline I wanted to be certain we could meet it. That was critical to success.'

Max had done his homework and paid meticulous attention to detail, as he always did in his business dealings, and in some respects he viewed his plot to ruin William as just another commercial transaction.

'I'll have the documents sent round to you this morning and I suggest you arrange another meeting for Thursday afternoon? As soon as they're signed and witnessed, you can give him the cheque.'

'I'll telephone him as soon as we've finished and offer to meet again in Chesterfield Square. By the way, what a house that is, Max, it's enormous! You could get at least six Wilton Crescents inside it.' He was referring to his own spacious house in Knightsbridge. 'He told me it's got twenty-eight bedrooms when I made some comment or other. He was really boastful actually and I could tell that he loves the place; in fact it was the only point in our conversation when he smiled. For the rest of the time he seemed to be scowling, although it was hard to tell behind all those double chins.'

Max laughed. He won't be smiling when I've finished with him, he thought quietly to himself. 'Didn't he ask any questions about you, or about the company you supposedly represent?'

'Not one, Max, which is incredible when you think about it.'

'So he doesn't suspect anything?'

'No, nothing, I'm sure of it. He was much too interested in getting his hands on the one hundred and fifty thousand pounds.'

'All right then, Richie, thanks for letting me know and well done. I'll get George to bring the contracts over shortly. Now, whilst it's on my mind, have you found a replacement for Jim yet? We'll need him to take over in Lee Moor straightaway, won't we?'

'Yes we will, there'll be a lot to do to get things straight. Our new man can start almost immediately. I've sworn Jim to secrecy about his move but I can tell you he's absolutely champing at the bit.'

'Good and I'd trust Jim with my life. I think he hates the bastard nearly as much as I do. Well, I think that's all we can do for now, so will you ring me on Thursday as soon as the papers are signed?'

'Of course, Max. Until Thursday then. Bye.'

'Bye, Richie.'

Max replaced the receiver and sat back in his chair. The moment he had been relishing for years had almost arrived. As soon as William had signed the contracts and cashed the cheque there could be no turning back. All he had to do then was to wait for him to default on his obligations to the gaming house. A slow smile came to his face. William was going to ruin himself, he thought, and all I need to do is help him along the way.

In truth William was a very willing ally.

'Good afternoon, my Lord, I have the contracts,' said Richie, standing up as William lumbered into his study in Chesterfield Square on Thursday afternoon. It was a large oak-panelled room with a high-flung ceiling and tall windows, which looked out on to a walled garden with a broad expanse of lush green lawn.

'Do you have the cheque?' he demanded without bothering to observe the customary courtesies.

'I do, my Lord,' replied Richie, being careful to maintain a neutral expression on his face. It would have been only too easy to reveal his irritation at William's rudeness.

Amid the opulent luxury of the Louis XVI mahogany furniture, with its gilding and fine inlay, and the dramatic oil paintings, the tenth Earl Gordon looked vaguely unkempt and down-at-heel. His corpulent figure magnified his almost slovenly appearance, which seemed incongruous amidst the elegant surroundings. When he spoke Richie watched as spittle ran down his ample chin.

'Good. Well then, where is it, man?'

'I have it here, my Lord.' He patted his briefcase, which was resting on the floor next to his chair. William held out a pudgy hand as Richie coughed, trying to sound apologetic. 'The contracts, my Lord ... if we may...?'

He reached down into the case and took out the two bound documents George had delivered to him earlier in the week. Then he removed the cheque from the inside pocket of his jacket and placed it clearly on the table in front of him. He saw William's eyes stray towards it and he smiled inwardly. Nearly there, he said to himself, just two little signatures...

'They are exactly as we discussed when we last met if you would care to read them through, or perhaps if your lawyer would like to see them before we proceed?' He felt perfectly safe in suggesting this because he knew William could not seek advice if he was to cash the cheque in time to meet his deadline.

Taking them impatiently from the table, William held out his hand for a pen, which Richie quickly took from the other inside pocket of his jacket and handed to him.

'The final page, my Lord, if you will,' said Richie with admirable sangfroid.

With barely a glance, William signed both copies, squinting hard at the paper as he did so before reaching out to take the cheque without waiting to be asked.

'Thank you, my...'

'They're all yours, Mr Black. I'll leave any arrangements to you,' he interrupted dimissively and held out his hand in a perfunctory manner.

Then without another word, he heaved himself to his feet and shambled out of the room. A few minutes later the butler was showing Richie out of the imposing double front doors and into the square.

Chapter 66

'All we have to do now is wait,' said Max the following day as he sat at the board-room table with Billy and Richie.

There was a knock on the door and Jim Edwardes walked in. Max stood up and moved around the table to greet him. 'Good morning, Jim, I'm so pleased you're here,' he said warmly as they shook hands.

'I'm delighted to be here, Max; it's a grand day for me.' He was grinning broadly.

'It is for me too. I don't think I ever expected to own the mine and the Gordon quarries and I'm grateful that you're going to be running them for me.' It was true. The Gordon mining interests had never featured in his plans, not even in his earliest childhood day-dreams when he used to roam the hills surrounding Lee Moor listening for the piercing sound of the morning whistle before returning to leftovers at the well scrubbed table in Mrs Castle's kitchen.

'Try stopping me, Max!' Jim chuckled easily. 'We can really do something with them. They're in a bad way, I understand, the men are demoralised and production is persistently below target.'

'You're well informed, Jim, Agnes I suppose?'

He nodded. 'Yes, she's still there and I've kept in touch with her over the years. She's only part-time now. She'll have such a surprise when I appear in the yard, that's for sure, and her help is going to be invaluable. Some of the men will be second generation from my previous days but there will be many familiar faces I'm sure.'

'Good. There is one thing though, Jim, that is extremely important,' said Max seriously. Jim looked expectantly at him, immediately detecting his change of tone. 'My involvement must remain absolutely confidential for the time being. I don't want anyone to know I am behind the purchase.' He paused and looked at him for a second. 'I haven't even told Molly and I cannot over emphasise how important this is.'

'Of course, Max, I understand,' replied Jim quickly. 'We can handle that without any problem.'

'Thank you, Jim. I don't like this subterfuge but I'm afraid it's necessary for the moment. Now then, let's get down to business shall we?' He smiled broadly.

Two hours later the four of them emerged from the board-room with an agreed hundred days plan for the new business.

'We'll have to think of a name for the company when we reveal my ownership,' said Max as they stood at the top of the stairs, 'and I'll be down to Lee Moor just as soon as I can, I promise. Good luck then, Jim, and let me know how you get on as we arranged.'

They shook hands. Max could see how happy Jim was to be returning to his roots in Lee Moor and he knew he would transform the profitability and conditions at the pits. This was a part of his phenomenal success that Max enjoyed the most. The material benefits were extremely gratifying of course, now running to many millions of pounds and beyond his wildest dreams. The security and freedom he had craved as a small boy had long since been assured. But it was his capacity to affect, and sometimes dramatically change, people's lives for the better that was particularly satisfying; in fact, he regarded it as a blessing and, walking back into his office, he found himself in a reflective mood. One of the most rewarding privileges of his life, which he valued above all others, was his ability to provide for Eleanor and Molly in a way that would have seemed impossible 25 years ago, when he first worked with Daisy behind the bar at The Wheelwright Arms, and the help he had gladly given to Richie and Lennie, and the rest of the Black family, also gave him the greatest of pleasure.

But if he recognised that his great wealth gave him the power to benefit others as well as himself, he also knew that when vested in the wrong hands and exercised cruelly or irresponsibly, it had the potential to inflict great harm. William Gordon was one such example of that. He had deliberately and persistently wielded the power of his position and family wealth in the pursuit of his own selfish ends, to the frequent and often painful detriment of all others. Well, not for much longer, mused Max, as he picked up the telephone to put a call through to Henrietta.

'Good morning, Henrietta, it's me, Max, how are you?' he asked brightly when he heard her voice on the other end.

'I'm very well indeed thank you, Mr C,' she answered impishly, 'and what can I do for you?'

'I'm just telephoning with the latest,' said Max.

She knew immediately that he was referring to her brother and when she replied, her tone had become serious. 'Thank you, Max. Did he sign as expected?'

'Yes, without so much as a murmur. It was ridiculously simple really. All we have to do now is wait for him to lose the game...'

'That goes without saying...'

'Yes it does, and then we wait for him to realise the seriousness of his situation. He will be vigorously pursued for his debt to the gaming house, without any question, assuming he will have extended his account with them...'

'That's also not in doubt is it?'

'Not for a minute,' exclaimed Max, 'he simply won't have been able to help himself. The only question is how much the debt will be. I have the investigator ready to find out what he can. Then Richie will have to offer him a solution to his problems!'

'What are you going to do with Chesterfield Square when you get it? I've been dying to know.'

'I've been thinking about that of course. I've got one or two ideas but let's not count our chickens, eh?'

'Don't be so mysterious!' exclaimed Henrietta. 'You're well aware I always want to know everything!'

Max laughed. 'Patience, my dear, is a virtue.'

'Wretch!' They both laughed and then were serious again. 'Let me know if I can do anything won't you?'

'Actually *there is* something you could do.'

'Just name it.'

'Could you approach the trustees as soon as he gets into difficulty to find out if he tries to persuade them to clear his debts?'

'Of course I will. Leave them to me! I'll make absolutely certain they stick to the letter of the trust provisions, don't you worry.'

Max smiled. She could be very persuasive when she wanted to be. 'Thank you, dear Aunt Henrietta.'

'Less of the "Aunt" if you don't mind,' she replied tartly. 'Now, I've more important things to do than sit here gossiping to you all day. Was there anything you wanted in particular?'

'Not at all,' chuckled Max, 'I'll telephone when there's any more news. Bye for now.'

'Bye, Max, and thank you.' There was a click as she put the receiver down.

Max walked over to the window and stared out into the warehouse yard below. It was a hive of activity and he watched as warehousemen feverishly loaded goods into the backs of his distinctive burgundy delivery vans that were reversed up along the loading bay. The heavy black gates at the entrance to the yard were constantly opening and closing as full vans left and empty ones returned. He looked at his watch, it was almost midday and he and Billy had an appointment with Anton at the Piccadilly Maisonbleu to discuss the new summer menus. He went back to his desk and quickly shuffled the papers containing the details of Jim's first hundred days plan into a neat pile before placing them securely in his safe. Then he walked through to the outer office to look for Billy.

They did not have long to wait for news. The investigator rang two weeks later to say that William owed his creditors £48,000 and they were already threatening foreclosure.

Chapter 67

It was towards the end of the following month, in July 1925, that Max received the telephone call he had been waiting for.

'Mr Black, for you, sir,' said Fenton from the pantry extension in Gloucester Street.

'Mr Richie?' enquired Max in amusement.

'Yes, sir, Mr Richie.'

'Thank you, Fenton, put him through please.'

'Very good, sir.'

'Hello, Richie, what news?' asked Max quickly.

'Hello, Max, hold on to your seat, we've got him!'

'Really! Are you sure?'

'There's too much to tell you over the telephone. Are you going to be at home for the next hour because I can come straight round if you like?'

'Yes I am, that would be fine, I'll see you shortly then.'

'All right, I'm on my way.' The line went dead and Max replaced the receiver with a brief smile of malicious delight that he could not contain.

'What is it, Max?' demanded Henrietta eagerly, 'tell me, it must be good news by the look on your face.'

'I think it is. Richie is on his way over now, so we'll soon know. I'm glad you're here to receive the news at the same time as me. It seems right somehow.'

Henrietta smiled at him, not knowing whether to feel happy or sad. The only thing she was certain of at that moment was her relief that her Mama and Papa had been spared it all.

'Shall we have some tea when Richie arrives?'

'That would be lovely, Max. More appropriate than champagne wouldn't you say?'

Max nodded and looked compassionately at her. 'Yes,' was all he said, knowing exactly what she meant.

He went over to the drawing-room bell and rang for Fenton. 'Are you all right my dear?' he asked anxiously as he turned round and noticed Henrietta gazing abstractedly out of the window.

'Of course I am! Why ever shouldn't I be?' she replied as her eyes met his.

'I don't feel much like celebrating either,' admitted Max quietly. 'I have waited years for this, for my moment of revenge, and now it appears to have arrived I'm not sure how I feel to tell you the truth.'

The door opened and Fenton appeared. 'You rang, sir?'

'Yes, Fenton, may we have some tea please, for three as Mr Richie is on his way here.'

'Right away, sir.'

Max waited until he had closed the door behind him before continuing. 'I'm not sorry, of course, and with Richie, just now on the telephone, I was delighted, but actually, I'm not so sure. It's odd isn't it...'

'You did what was necessary, Max, and he deserved it. It's as simple as that and I don't regret it at all.' She sighed. 'Now I hope we can put it behind us and forget all about it.'

There was silence as they sat together, lost in their own thoughts until the sound of the doorbell ringing downstairs in the hall disturbed them.

'That'll be Richie, are you quite sure you want to hear the details?' asked Max solicitously.

'Yes,' said Henrietta firmly, 'let's get it over with.'

The door opened and Richie came in, followed by Fenton and Mary with their tea. 'We'll look after ourselves thank you, Fenton, thank you, Mary,' said Max when everything was laid out on the console table over by the window.

'Very good, sir,' replied the ever watchful butler. He sensed they had something important to discuss and so he motioned for Mary to leave the room and he followed discreetly behind her.

Richie began to recount the details of his meeting with William as soon as the door closed. They listened intently, remaining silent until he had finished. The train of events that resulted in Richie's meeting with William earlier that afternoon had begun when William's creditors had finally run out of patience, informing him that unless he settled his debt by five o'clock on 16th July, they were going to issue proceedings against him. William had been beside himself, finally understanding that no amount of delay, obfuscation, bullying or just simple avoidance was going to save him this time. When he made contact with Richie, believing him to represent the wealthy owners of the company behind the purchase of his mining interests, William had no one else to turn to. The trustees would not countenance the release of trust monies to settle the debt and every bank he approached had turned him down flat.

Richie had offered him a 30-day loan of £50,000 on condition that it was guaranteed against the freehold of Chesterfield Square, the favoured jewel in his property crown. The trustees had initially refused to release the deeds of the house in order to have them tied in as collateral, but Henrietta's clandestine entreaties behind the scenes had been successful. She pointed out forcibly to Sir John Lee, the senior trustee, that to do so would not breach her father's stipulation that payments from the family trusts were not to be used to meet William's gambling debts because the deeds to the house were not technically 'funds'.

It had been the only potential problem in Max's entire strategy, which had brilliantly exploited William's weaknesses, and one hour earlier, as Richie explained, he had agreed to the condition in his desperation to repay the debt and satisfy his creditors. In his arrogant stupidity, he simply refused to believe he would ever be called upon to surrender his magnificent London home.

PART FOUR

NEW BEGINNINGS, LONDON

1925

Chapter 68

At 40 years of age, Max was at the height of his powers. He was at the helm of a hugely successful company that he had created with his own hands, tenaciously building it piece by piece with an energy and single-mindedness that remained undimmed. At its centre stood the wholesale food company he had put his heart and soul into, the fishery and meat business originally begun by old Harry Masters, and now the Maisonbleu chain of fashionable restaurants and delicatessens, which continued to expand into all the major cities of the country. Each one was a market leader in its own field and, together, they had brought him riches beyond his wildest imagination.

He stood alongside Billy, Richie and Henrietta, three of his closest and dearest friends and business colleagues, in the grand lobby of 'The Chesterfield'. It was opening day. There was one person missing but how proud his darling Rosie would have been. He watched one of the hall porters adjust the splendidly fragrant flower arrangement, which was displayed on a round walnut table in the centre of the spotless marble floor. The man stood back to review his work as Molly appeared behind him, nodding in approbation. She had insisted on becoming The Chesterfield's first housekeeper at a time when she should have been enjoying a well earned and comfortable retirement. 'The 'ousekeepin' 'as got ter be right, Max, it's what the guests will see,' she had told him and he had known it was pointless to resist. Max smiled to himself, thinking that Lady Constance would have approved; she had always insisted on a beautiful display of fresh flowers in the hallway of every one of her homes. He glanced at Henrietta, wondering if the same thoughts were running through her mind; he started to ask her but then stopped and smiled at her instead, preferring to keep his reflections to himself.

He looked at his watch. There was ten minutes to go before the doors opened for the first time. This was a momentous day and one that he intended to repeat in all of the major capital cities of the Empire. It marked the fulfilment of a promise he had made himself almost 20 years ago to this very day, as he sat in the lobby of The Royal Hotel in

Plymouth, worrying about whether he could afford to pay for the cup of coffee he had inadvertently ordered.

He smiled to himself again. It had been a busy six months since he had appeared on the doorstep of Chesterfield Square with Richie to claim his prize from an unsuspecting William. The memory of that day would remain with him for ever, as would the events that followed it. They had been completely unexpected and, in their own way, shockingly sad. A week after that meeting William had taken his own life, putting a gun to his head in a dingy hotel room on the south coast. He did not leave a note but his final act of folly had closed a chapter in Max's life and now his former London home marked a new beginning.

The hall clock chimed ten o'clock. 'Here we go,' said Max to the others as he and Billy walked forwards to open the front doors. It had been agreed that they should be the ones to do so and the two hall porters, resplendent in their dark blue uniforms and top hats, stood back respectfully whilst the two grand entrance doors were slowly unlocked.

The early spring sunshine streamed in from the square and a young, elegantly dressed lady came up the steps towards them.

'Are you open for business?' she enquired softly and with a pretty smile. 'I have been recommended this hotel by a friend of mine.' She looked directly at Max, holding his eyes in her confident gaze.

'Yes, madam, we are. Welcome to The Chesterfield Hotel,' he said courteously and he stepped aside to allow her to enter. As she passed he caught the trace of a vaguely familiar scent. My God! he thought suddenly, that was one of Rosie's favourites and he turned and watched her walk across the marble floor towards the reception desk as a thoughtful expression appeared on his face.